LET IT SNOW

Sue Moorcroft writes award-winning contemporary fiction of life and love. *The Little Village Christmas* and *A Christmas Gift* were *Sunday Times* bestsellers and *The Christmas Promise* went to #1 in the Kindle chart. She also writes short stories, serials, articles, columns, courses and writing 'how to'.

An army child, Sue was born in Germany then lived in Cyprus, Malta and the UK and still loves to travel. Her other loves include writing (the best job in the world), reading, watching Formula 1 on TV and hanging out with friends, dancing, yoga, wine and chocolate.

If you're interested in being part of #TeamSueMoorcroft you can find more information at www.suemoorcroft.com/street-team. If you prefer to sign up to receive news of Sue and her books, go to www.suemoorcroft.com and click on 'Newsletter'. You can follow @SueMoorcroft on Twitter, @SueMoorcroftAuthor on Instagram, or Facebook.com/sue.moorcroft.3 and Facebook.com/SueMoorcroftAuthor.

Let it Snow

Sue Moorcroft

avon.

Published by AVON
A division of HarperCollins*Publishers* Ltd
1 London Bridge Street,
London SE1 9GF

www.harpercollins.co.uk

A Paperback Original 2019

2

First published in Great Britain by
HarperCollins*Publishers* 2019

A catalogue record for this book is
available from the British Library

ISBN: 978-0-00-832179-6

This novel is entirely a work of fiction.
The names, characters and incidents portrayed in it are
the work of the author's imagination. Any resemblance to
actual persons, living or dead, events or localities is
entirely coincidental.

Typeset in Sabon LT Std by Palimpsest Book Production Ltd, Falkirk, Stirlingshire

Printed and bound in Great Britain by CPI Group (UK) Ltd, Croydon CR0 4YY

MIX
Paper from
responsible sources

FSC
www.fsc.org   FSC™ C007454

This book is produced from independently certified FSC™ paper
to ensure responsible forest management.

For more information visit: www.harpercollins.co.uk/green

Acknowledgements

My thanks to everyone who helped me along the writing journey that became *Let it Snow*.

My brother Trevor Moorcroft offered to undertake a big chunk of my research. The hours I'd usually spend gathering information about artificial insemination, maternity care in Switzerland and the running of licensed premises fell to him. For the latter subject he enlisted the help of Gemma Askew of the Roundabout Hotel, Fareham, England and I'm deeply appreciative of all the hours both Trev and Gemma spent on my behalf.

Rosemary J Kind said, 'If you want to set a book in Switzerland, I'll take you.' And, later, 'Yes, I'm serious!' She drove me to Switzerland and lined up fantastic research trips to Christmas markets, Alpine towns and villages, walks, processions, lakes, cities and restaurants. Both Ros and her husband Chris Platt made me so welcome in their home. Chris also kindly answered questions on snow and cuckoo clocks and Ros introduced me to her Swiss friends: Gina Graber and Erika Kunz. Gina showed me around the beautiful city of

Zürich (where I was thrilled to find copies of my books in German), climbed with me to the top of the Grossmunster and provided comprehensive answers to questions on food. Erika accompanied us to the noisy but enjoyable procession centred around Samichlaus and his entourage.

Wilma the beautiful Entlebucher Mountain Dog shared her favourite Swiss walks. Wilma, I hope you don't mind I gave them to Doggo and that he's a Dalmatian.

Health matters impacted on this story. My (other) brother Kev Moorcroft donated his experience of heart failure to Tubb from the Pub and Alison Turnbull hers of breast cancer to Isaac's ex-girlfriend Hayley. Both Kev and Alison were enormously generous in this. Nurses David Roberts and Julia Roberts answered my many questions on hand injury and helped me find exactly the right one for Lily.

As ever, I owe grateful thanks to Mark West for beta reading the book and for the conversations during its gestation. Sue: 'This book's going remarkably well. Do you think that's a bad sign?' Mark: 'Nah, you'll be fine.' Mark's support is unfailing and I'm glad to be able to beta read his books in return.

Team Sue Moorcroft continues to be a delight. That so many people want to talk to me about my books and help me promote them I view as a privilege. A few even meet me for lunch occasionally.

A huge shout out goes to the teams at Avon Books UK and at Blake Friedmann Literary Agency, who do such a wonderful job of bringing my books to you. Both are a joy to work with and I'm thankful every day to have them at my side. Thank you all.

I love to hear from readers on social media, via my

website or at events, and to read their reviews. From the bottom of my heart, thank *you* for reading my books. Without you, *Let it Snow* and all my other novels would just be files on my computer.

For
Paul Matthews
and
Hollie Clark Matthews
in this special year.
Your happiness brings me joy.

Prologue

'Mum, what's the matter? Why are you crying?' Lily Cortez hurried across the lawn to crouch in front of the slender figure huddled over an iPad in a garden chair. The raw October day had almost ended and the light was steely grey.

'Oh! Lily, we didn't expect you until tomorrow.' Roma swiped at her wet cheeks turning the iPad face down in her lap. Roma Martindale was an all-weather gardener and though the October day was blustery, planters, compost and pots of violets surrounded her.

'I decided to make the journey from Spain over two days rather than three to surprise you.' Lily frowned. The redness of her mum's eyes spoke of a prolonged weep and Roma was no crybaby. Lily felt in the pocket of her fleece for tissues to press into Roma's chilly hands. It was probably ten degrees cooler in Peterborough than it had been in Barcelona when she'd left at the crack of dawn yesterday, driving away from a Spanish husband who was as relieved as her to call it quits. She gave her mum a minute to blow her nose. 'Are you ill? Or is Patsie?' Patricia Jones was

Roma's life partner, a tall and confident lawyer whose dark hair fell smoothly to the shoulders of her dark blue suits.

'We're both fine.' Roma blew her nose again. 'She's doing pro bono work at a women's refuge. And I thought you weren't arriving until tomorrow so . . .' Fresh tears leaked down her cheeks.

'Has someone said something crap about you and Patsie?' Not everyone accepted same-sex couples. Sergio, Lily's soon-to-be-ex-husband, never coped well with Lily having two mothers, for example.

Roma shook her head, searching for a dry area of her tissue. 'No.' She blotted more tears.

Lily had to swallow before she could speak again. 'Please, Mum. I'm imagining all kinds of awful things here.' Then her gaze fell on the iPad. 'Have you received bad news?'

Roma pressed her hands over the iPad and squeezed her eyes shut. 'You've caught me at a weak moment. It's something in the past, really.'

Lily had to blink tears away. 'You're frightening me,' she said in a small voice. What on earth could cause her usually sunny, funny, quirky mum to sob so broken-heartedly?

Still clutching the iPad and levering herself to her feet, Roma took Lily's hand. 'Come indoors.'

The kitchen was warm and welcoming. After hanging her khaki gardening coat by the back door and kicking off her wellies Roma sat down at the table. Lily took the next chair and watched as the iPad's screen sprang to life. Slowly, Roma turned it so Lily could read it: the *Peterborough Telegraph* obituaries.

Lily's eyes scanned the notice on the screen. 'This guy

Marvin's died? He was eighty-seven, so quite a bit older than you, Mum.' Marvin had been a beloved husband of the late Teresa, a loving dad and granddad, a much-missed brother to Bonnie. 'I've never known you cry over a man.' As a gay woman, out and proud all her adult life, Roma's friends were mainly female.

Roma was silent, her face blotched red.

Then realisation caught Lily's breath. 'I can think of *one* man you had a relationship with. But he was some one-night stand whose name you didn't even know . . . you said.' She gazed into her mother's eyes, at the apprehensive, apologetic agony she read there. 'Wasn't he a one-night stand? My father?'

With a noisy swallow Roma shook her head. 'It was a mess. You know most of the story.'

Lily's stomach dropped down a shaft. 'But not all, evidently! Tell me. I want to try to understand.'

Roma covered her eyes. 'Patsie and I wanted a family. She had a settled career with maternity benefits. She became pregnant with your sister Zinnia via the sensible route: anonymous donor. But I got jealous. I wanted a baby too.' She clasped her hand over Lily's as her voice broke. 'Patsie wouldn't agree, particularly before the first baby was even here. I was a freelance photographer scraping a living and there was childcare to be considered. If there *was* to be a second pregnancy then she wanted to have artificial insemination again using the same anonymous donor – possible to arrange even in 1983 – so the babies would be full siblings. I thought she was unbearably pragmatic.' She gave a bitter laugh. 'It wasn't a one-night stand I had, it was an affair. Marvin was an older man, who, in my reckless, heedless naivety I thought wouldn't be hurt by me using him.

He never knew I was only in the relationship to get pregnant.'

The kitchen clock ticked from above the range cooker, loud in the silence. 'Why did you lie when I asked about my father?' Lily demanded, rocked by an unexpectedly keen sense of loss.

Lurching to her feet Roma took down a glass and filled it from the chilled water dispenser in the door of the fridge. Footsteps dragging, she returned to her seat. 'I met Marvin through a photography job – headshots of managerial staff for a company magazine. He developed a thing for me and let it show. He was shocked when I, a woman in her mid-twenties, responded.' Colour flooded her cheeks. 'He was fit and good-looking for early fifties. I thought he'd be kind to me and most of my experience was with women.' She cleared her throat and raised her gaze to Lily's. 'Are you sure you want to hear this?'

Lily's heartbeat seemed to have taken over her whole body, pumping in her stomach, her head, her throat. She nodded.

Roma hooked her hair behind her ears. The wind had tumbled her corn-coloured waves. 'It lasted for five months, the length of time it took me to get pregnant. I was sorrier than I thought I'd be to end things. Poor Marvin was devastated. Said he'd fallen in love with me. Had risked his marriage, the happiness of his kids. He was so hurt. It was awful. I'd been so immature and self-centred that I truly had barely given his marriage a thought. Looking back, I can't believe my own selfish behaviour. And Patsie—' Roma's hands were shaking now. 'I almost destroyed us. She'd been so happy in her planned pregnancy and all the time I'd been betraying her.'

'With a man,' Lily whispered, shocked.

4

A bitter smile twisted Roma's lips. 'Yes. Well. That it was a man didn't help. But I'd betrayed her trust, her plans for our future. It was rocky for a long while.'

Through the enormity of everything she was hearing, Lily craved information on one person. 'Tell me about my father,' she demanded hoarsely.

The semblance of a smile flitted across Roma's face. 'He was a company director. Fair-haired, clean-shaven, looked good in a suit. He liked old-school rock 'n' roll, rugby, tennis, cinema, detective shows on TV, holidays in America.'

Lily felt her insides had been hollowed out with a giant spoon. 'And you didn't think his concern for "his kids" should extend to me?'

Roma rose and quietly poured coffee from the filter jug. Her voice was low and filled with shame. 'I couldn't find a way to make things right. Be fair to everyone. There were two babies on the way; I was desperate for Patsie and I to stay together and be parents to both. The only way to bring that about was for her to know the full story . . . but nobody else. I couldn't risk Marvin knowing about you or you knowing about him because Patsie would have been faced with him in your life.'

Lily gazed at the cup of coffee her mother put before her and felt faintly revolted by it.

Roma sat down and wrapped her arms around her, smelling of fresh air and compost. 'If you only knew the hours we talked about it! Everything, anything I thought of doing just felt as if it would make my wrong wronger, risk my family and risk his family. If we'd told you the truth and you wanted to find him it would change the entire dynamic of our family – you and Zinnia, Patsie and me. Lily, don't hate me! You had two mothers and a sister. I wanted it to be enough.'

'So, on my behalf, you chose to exclude me from his family. One half of my family.' Lily propped her head on her fist. She could actually see how her mother had made the choice she had, though it left her feeling as if she had a black hole where her insides should be. 'I don't hate you, Mum. It's all so . . . you. Chaotic and impetuous. It's just tough to find my father and lose him in the same instant.' Tears prickled her eyes.

Then, slowly, Lily sat straighter, pulling the iPad towards her, rereading the obituary. And in it she saw her consolation prize. In silence, she highlighted the first of two names and tapped it into a search engine. A list of hits filled the screen and it took her seconds to access one. Then it felt as if the words she read reached into her chest and gripped her heart. 'Look. The eldest of my two half-brothers, Harrison Tubb, is the landlord of The Three Fishes pub in a village called Middledip.' She looked up at her mum with a surge of excitement. 'It's here in Cambridgeshire. I could find him.'

Roma sat back with a horrified gasp. 'Oh, Lily . . . no!'

Chapter One

November, two years later

Lily passed a string of coloured Christmas lights through her hands and wondered whether, if she looped it several times, she could use it to gag her sister.

Zinnia, supposedly helping Lily decorate The Three Fishes, had so far done no more than fidget with a fistful of silver tinsel and give Lily earache. 'We're your family!' Zinnia declared, shoving her fingers through her chestnut hair. 'What you're doing could hurt Patsie and Roma.'

Lily climbed on a stool and began to feed the string of lights through hooks above the bar. 'They understand it's my decision. You know this, Zin. Let's not press "repeat" on the conversation.'

Zinnia bulldozed on. 'Aren't we enough for you? You and I grew up sharing a bedroom! We're *sisters*—'

'And you're the loveliest sister in the world.' Lily hoped popping in a positive note would distract Zinnia. She jumped down, scraped her stool towards the next few hooks, gave Zinnia a hug then clambered up again. 'How about twisting that tinsel around the ivy swags along the mantelpiece?'

'Lily!' Zinnia tossed the tinsel onto the polished wooden bar. 'I *know* you! I'm where you come from. I understand how it feels when people think we're weird because we come from a single-sex family.'

'I know,' Lily agreed gently. 'But there's more to my life than that. It's the part you don't share that's the problem, isn't it?' Plus the fact that a couple of years ago Lily had visited the village to find her half-brother and had ended up applying for a job in his pub, finding somewhere to live in Middledip – and here she still was. Zinnia was particularly upset by that.

Zinnia didn't offer a direct reply to the question but her voice softened. 'You've completed your mission and met him. You should either tell him the truth or leave the poor guy in peace.'

By 'he' Zinnia meant Harrison Tubb of course, almost universally known as Tubb from the pub, and her stomach clenched at the idea of him discovering the truth before Lily was ready. If she ever was. She left the Christmas lights dangling and slid off the stool to stroke Zinnia's arm. 'I've completed *half* my mission and I'll complete the other half next month,' she pointed out, with a little leap of excitement that there was a half-brother yet to meet. 'I understand that you're concerned I'm somehow trying to leave our family – which I'm not – but my relationship with our mums isn't affected by where I'm living or who I mix with. If my relationship with you is suffering then it's because you're letting it.'

Zinnia tried another tack. 'You're worth so much more than working in a crappy village pub.'

'It's not crappy.' Lily moved her stool along again.

'In the two years since you came back from Spain you've been wasting your time in this village. You don't seem to want to be near your family—' Zinnia halted, as if realising she might be painting herself into a corner. 'We're your real family, Lily,' she clarified.

'Families have more than one branch.' Lily hooked up the end of the string and got down to judge whether it was hanging evenly.

Zinnia's dark eyes saddened. 'Just get telling him over with so it's not hanging over us all. I feel like telling him myself—'

'That *would* affect our relationship. It's up to me when, and if, I think the time's right for me to spill the beans.' Lily had to fight to keep anxiety from her voice, newly aware that Zinnia, through calling at the pub to see Lily, knew Tubb and could actually have blabbed Lily's secret at any time. 'You don't agree with the way I'm doing things, but this is my business.' *Not yours* hung unspoken in the air.

Before Zinnia could argue further, a calm voice came from behind the bar. 'Sorry to interrupt.'

Both Lily and Zinnia swung around. Lily forced a laugh. 'You made me jump, Isaac. This is my sister, Zinnia. She's helping me with the Christmas decorations. Zin, this is Isaac O'Brien the relief manager Tubb appointed while he was away.'

Isaac, his eyes as brown as apple seeds, hair several shades darker, a single small gold ring in his ear, reached across the wooden countertop to shake Zinnia's hand. His eyes returned to Lily. 'I didn't realise you were coming in this afternoon to do this.'

Lily flushed. She'd learned enough about Isaac in the past fortnight to know he was politely asking why she hadn't cleared it with him. He'd come from a trendy venue where he'd managed dozens of staff and probably brought in an outside company to put up Christmas decorations. 'Janice asked me if I'd do it as she's in Switzerland. They're normally up at the beginning of November and it's the seventh already . . . I assumed she or Tubb had communicated with you.' Janice had a pretty free hand at the village pub and becoming an item with Tubb last Christmas had only elevated her status.

'We open in less than an hour,' he pointed out.

'Right.' Lily covered up a flash of alarm that so much of the interval between closing after lunch and reopening in the evening had been eaten up. 'We only have little trees on the bar rather than a great big thing so the rest won't take long.'

'Thanks.' He gave them a smile then turned and headed in the direction of what was usually referred to as 'the back', the area of the ground floor that encompassed a place to hang coats, the cleaning supplies cupboard and the mixers store, along with doors into the beer cellar, kitchen, car park, upstairs accommodation and staff loos. There was also a desk in an alcove where Isaac's laptop often rested.

'Wow,' Zinnia breathed, eyebrows waggling as the sound of his footsteps died away. 'He's easy on the eye. Tubb will never look quite the same.'

Lily pictured Tubb's wiggle of hair at the front and his smile that turned down instead of up. 'Yes, Isaac's hot,' she agreed in a low voice as she dragged one of the small Christmas trees out of its box. She now had less than sixty minutes to get the bar to a presentable state and if Isaac's appearance had diverted Zinnia from her crusade to reshape Lily's life it might be a good thing. 'His last job was in a hipster lounge in Peterborough. He's reserved, but he has a way of getting people to do things.'

Zinnia gave an exaggerated wink. 'He could get me to do all kinds of things—'

'Shh!' Lily hissed, hoping devoutly that Isaac wouldn't overhear. 'That's my boss! And what about George? Remember him? Your boyfriend?'

Grinning, her earlier mood obviously forgotten, Zinnia shrugged. 'I was just . . . *noticing.*'

Lily grabbed Zinnia's jacket and bundled it into her arms. 'Come on, I'll show you out of the back door. I'm not sure Isaac appreciated you being here out of hours.'

'I haven't done the tinsel,' Zinnia protested as Lily opened the counter flap and waved her through.

'I'll do it.'

Zinnia paused for one last time. 'How's Tubb doing, by the way? Heart failure's no joke.'

Lily softened. 'OK, Janice says, but still a worry. Getting lots of rest, like the doctor ordered, omitting alcohol and fat and stuff from his diet.' Tubb had shocked the village last summer with breathless turns and alarming swelling to his legs and stomach. Janice had got him into hospital and he'd come out with a daily regime of drugs.

For a while they'd managed with him in the background and Janice at the helm but after he'd received a stern warning from the doctor that he needed a complete break from the seventy-hour weeks and heavy lifting involved in running a pub, he'd agreed to take sick leave. The pregnancy of Janice's daughter-in-law in Switzerland had run into trouble about the same time that Isaac was brought in, so the couple flew off to move into Max's spare room, Janice to help look after the other two children in the family and Tubb to rest for a few months. Lily had

had a year and a half to get to know and like Tubb by then, to value the man who grumbled and griped a bit but loved his pub and the village. She'd seen the little acts of kindness behind his gruff exterior and been delighted for him when he'd found love with Janice. She missed him but phones and computers made it easy to keep in touch. She missed cheerful, unflappable Janice too.

Zinnia hugged Lily goodbye and allowed herself to be ushered off the premises, then Lily returned to the decorations. Swiftly, she hung baubles on the mini trees.

Isaac reappeared. 'Vita should have been in by now but she's just rung. Her husband's been held up coming home to take over childcare so I'll bottle up.' Isaac began rearranging mixers as he restocked the shelves. 'Kind of you – and your sister – to take on the decorations. I should have asked what usually happened.'

Lily paused in her clearing up, arms full of boxes and a roll of tape like a bracelet around her wrist. 'Last year I did it with Janice.'

He gave one of his slow nods, dark eyes hard to read. 'Should I pay you additional hours? What would Mr Tubb expect?'

Lily felt laughter bubbling. 'He's not big on paying additional hours,' she admitted frankly. 'A few things happen around here on a voluntary basis over the festive season, like the decorations, Christmas lunch and running the raffle. He pitches in himself so nobody minds.'

He raked his fingers through his hair and it fell back into the same gleaming layers. 'But you have your own business too, don't you?'

'Yes, I'm an exhibition designer. But I like Christmas so putting up the trees and stuff was fun.'

'OK, thanks.' With customers and staff alike Isaac was

warm, articulate and cheerful but his resting expression was often serious with hints of thoughtfulness. It was, as Zinnia had indicated, hot.

'Um,' she said. 'Nobody calls him *Mr* Tubb, by the way. He's just Tubb from the pub. Or you can call him Harrison, like Janice does. A few of the older customers call him Harry.' When he merely produced another nod Lily edged through the counter flap to dump the boxes then wheeled the vacuum cleaner out of its nook ready to slurp up the threads of tinsel from the carpet. Seven minutes to opening time. Just right.

The bar was almost ready for the six o'clock session and Isaac could hear the chefs clattering in the kitchen as Lily returned from stowing the vacuum cleaner. He was still getting to know the staff but already had Lily down as one of the easiest to deal with: punctual, reliable and with a sunny nature, though that hadn't stopped her standing up for herself with her sister, judging from the snatches of spirited discussion he'd overheard.

He made a mental note to find a way of acknowledging her giving up her time unasked. Or unasked by him, he corrected himself. Apparently Janice, who he didn't know well as she'd been preparing to leave for Switzerland when he'd arrived, had felt comfortable casually suggesting Lily give up her time. Almost two weeks he'd been here but he felt like the new boy at school putting on a show of fitting in, covering up how hard he was trying to process the ways his life had changed in a few short months.

He went to the safe to gather up an armload of coin bags as Vita rushed in, apologising breathlessly as she dragged off her coat. He reassured her and made an adjustment to her hours worked, then went into the bar he considered dated with its open fire and dark wheelback chairs, signed into the till and began to count in the float as he had on innumerable other occasions in other jobs, latterly at Juno Lounge.

'The Juno', where he'd been licensee and leaseholder, had been an edge-of-the-city pub in Peterborough that hadn't closed on weekday afternoons as The Three Fishes did. Opening for breakfast, it had gone through until closing time with extensions at weekends for the busy function room. As it had once been a chapel he'd kept some of its original pews, adding sofas, an eclectic collection of dining chairs and oversized glass light fittings hanging from the Victorian cast-iron beams with their ornate tracery. Its style was quirky, semi-industrial chic.

Had been, he reminded himself, feeling the familiar swell of unhappiness that, through pure bad luck, Juno Lounge was no more. The furnishings and equipment had been auctioned off. The red-brick building was ornamented with the brewery's 'lease available' sign and awaiting a new leaseholder when it could be reopened in a few months' time to bring it back to life with chattering diners and laughing drinkers as it had been . . .

. . . before it failed.

It was no comfort that he hadn't been at fault. Once a venue had no customers, it had no value. Juno Lounge had limped then staggered and, as a leaseholder, Isaac's work had been cut out to wind it up fast enough to hang on to some of the money he'd made in the preceding six years.

He hadn't hung on to Hayley but he wasn't sure why he'd expected it. Hayley wasn't into failure. Kindly but unequivocally she'd ended their relationship and he'd made

14

no attempt to change her mind. When you were in trouble you saw people's true colours and he hadn't cared for hers.

She'd actually been the one to hear through the grapevine that a fill-in manager was needed at The Three Fishes and, apart from irritation that it had been her who found the temporary job for him and that it was at such a brass-and-beams pub, Isaac had been filled with relief. It was good to have money coming in and refreshing to be back in the countryside. His dad had been a tenant farmer and Isaac had loved his childhood spent on the fenland farm half an hour north of here between Cambridge and Spalding.

'What do you think?' The voice jolted him from his thoughts and back into the cosily traditional bar of The Three Fishes, where, he realised, Lily Cortez was on the other side of the counter smiling, palms upturned in a gesture that welcomed him to admire the fruits of her labour.

He closed the till and joined her to gaze at the strings of coloured lanterns looped jauntily along the beam above the bar, reflecting in every glass in the rack below. Tinsel spiralled around the thick wooden posts and the bar-top Christmas trees twinkled with a rainbow of baubles and lights. Santa ornaments dragged their toy sacks along wooden beams towards silver stars and golden bells and a thick swag of greenery twisted with tinsel festooned the mantelpiece above the open fire.

'Great,' he said. Last year, Juno Lounge had been artistically decorated with silver twigs and golden wire with red origami stars but that had been his place. This wasn't. When you went in somewhere as relief manager you kept everything as the publican wanted. The homely decorations

15

exactly suited The Three Fishes. He gave her a smile. 'Very jolly and welcoming. Thanks for all your efforts.' Her eyes were a clear blue, he noticed, like the reflection of the sky in a lake he'd once camped beside with Hayley in New Zealand – if you could count living in an upscale motorhome camping. Hayley liked the outdoor life only if she could also look after her nails, skin and hair.

Lily's smile flashed, making those eyes sparkle. 'It was fun.'

'Thank your sister too,' he remembered to tack on, though the sister had done little but give Lily a hard time about something, from what he'd heard. The alarm on his phone pinged to inform him it was six o'clock and he sent one last glance around the bar. 'Perfect timing. I'll open the doors.'

Lily and Vita were on duty with Isaac that evening. They worked together well, chatting to punters, drawing drinks, tapping orders into the now tinsel-bedecked till, smiling, moving around each other easily. Vita, large glasses glinting in the lights and brown hair in a poker-straight ponytail, had a few years on Lily who, he knew from her staff file, was thirty-six.

The bar was doing OK for a Thursday night, partly due to the darts team having a home match. Stools surrounded the dartboard area and the spectators cheered, groaned and exchanged banter. Isaac was returning to the bar after a foray to the beer cellar to check temperatures when he heard a male voice exclaim, 'You gay girls get everywhere!' followed by a cackle of laughter.

Turning, Isaac saw a red-faced late-thirties guy smirking at Lily, his over-bright eyes unfocused. Then, when he copped a freezing glance in return, he laughed. 'C'mon, darlin', it's just a bit of fun.'

Coolly, Lily finished pulling a pint of bitter. 'What's funny? Lesbians in general? Or that I might be one?'

The red-faced man's grin faded. 'Don't hop on your high horse. It's only banter.' He pronounced 'banter' as 'ban-urr'.

Lily added the pint to the three already ranged on the bar before the man. 'That's £15.44, please.' Unsmiling, she took his twenty-pound note.

Isaac watched the man ogling the curves beneath Lily's black polo shirt as she tapped at the till. He could step in and suggest to the punter that he go easy on the bar staff or find somewhere else to drink but his rule was to allow his team to handle irksome customers themselves first. Unpleasant behaviour had occurred frequently at Juno Lounge but it was the first he'd witnessed at The Three Fishes.

The cluster around the dartboard cheered a good score as Lily dropped the change in the man's hand as if reluctant to touch him. She turned to the next customer with a contrastingly warm smile. 'Hiya, Gabe! How's the menagerie?'

Gabe was an older man, easily recognisable by his silver ponytail and the smile that creased his face. Isaac already knew him as a regular with a smallholding that apparently provided a home for old and stray animals. 'Eating me out of house and home,' he complained with a broad grin that hinted he wasn't really complaining. 'Have you heard how Tubb is?' Just about the whole village was worried about Tubb and shook their heads over how odd it was not to see him behind the bar at The Three Fishes.

While Lily chatted to him about Tubb apparently enjoying his sojourn in Switzerland, the red-faced customer gurned in her direction and – clutching the four pints –

stumped back towards the zoo around the dartboard. Isaac watched as he said something to his cronies, leered at Lily and burst into a huge guffaw. His friends joined in the mirth.

Apart from a tinge of extra colour, Lily did nothing to acknowledge the guy acting like a dick.

Isaac decided to cover the dining area himself so neither Lily nor Vita had to run the gauntlet past the increasingly rowdy darts players. The red-faced guy soon became puce, his raucous laughter ringing around the room and grating on other customers, judging by how many were casting the oaf disenchanted looks before finishing up their drinks and pulling on their coats.

The next time the man broached the bar again he was positively weaving and the darts players were almost the only customers. Vita went to serve him but he waved her away. 'I want Little Miss Lezzy to pull it for me.' He burst into lewd, suggestive laughter.

Isaac, who'd been clearing plates, turned and headed for the bar. Lily, however, stepped fearlessly up to the man, only the bar counter between them. 'I'm afraid I can't serve you further alcohol this evening.' She held his gaze for a moment, then turned away.

The man reached between the beer taps and grasped her arm. 'Oy! Don' you friggin' walk away from me—'

Isaac was there in two strides but Lily had already broken the man's grip. 'You need to leave, sir,' she snapped.

The man sneered. 'I'll leave when I'm good an' ready.'

Lily seemed effortlessly composed. 'My option is to call the police, sir. Two seconds to decide. One—'

'Stop bein' so up yourself.' Red-faced man was looking decidedly ugly.

'Two.' Lily reached for the phone on the wall.

Standing behind the drunk and watching Lily handle it, Isaac saw the man's friends pulling on their coats and scowling. 'C'mon,' one of them called. 'Not worth it. Crappy little pub in the arse-end of nowhere. They're welcome to it.'

Lily put the phone to her ear and her finger on the first button.

The red-faced guy shoved abruptly away from the bar. 'Your beer's piss anyway.'

The men clattered chairs over and harrumphed a few more insults but they did blunder out of the front door. In the silence left behind, Lily replaced the phone.

It was ten past ten and the bar was empty. Fantastic. At least the men had put plenty into the till before their behaviour cleared the place. 'Vita, perhaps you could start collecting glasses?' Isaac suggested, to give him a quiet moment with Lily. As Vita moved off, he turned to Lily, intending to check she was OK.

'Sorry,' she jumped in before he could speak. 'I should have handled that without antagonising him. I let him get to me because I hate it when a woman turns down a date and the man says she must therefore be gay, especially when "gay" sounds like an insult.' Her blue eyes were stormy. 'It always touches me on the raw because Zinnia and I are from the kind of family with two mums and no dads. I thought I'd tell you because I've come to the conclusion that it's easiest all round when people know.' She tilted her head and waited for him to react.

Chapter Two

It was obvious Lily was at least half-expecting something negative from him. Isaac wondered how many people had hurt her on this subject over the years. 'The whiff of homophobia is always unacceptable and I can see why the awkward customer wound you up particularly.' He smiled. What she'd outlined wasn't precisely a situation he'd encountered before but he didn't see why he should treat this differently to any other personal topic a member of staff had chosen to bring up. 'Are you OK? I thought you dealt with the offensive customer well.'

She shrugged. 'He was nothing compared to drunken stags in Barcelona. My ex-husband's family ran a bar just off Las Ramblas. Bar Barcelona was a big place, firmly on the map so far as stags and hens were concerned. It got rowdy and I learned to ignore most bad behaviour . . . but tonight I let that guy get to me.'

'He was offensive,' he repeated. 'Your husband was Spanish?' It explained her surname of Cortez.

'Yes. We met when he was in the UK gaining some experience of hotels because his family was thinking about opening one. He tried to live here and pined for Spain, so I tried to live there.' She gave a tiny quirk to her eyebrows. 'I think I could have lived in a different part of Spain, or in a different way. But I never settled into the family business.'

'Because your main job's as a . . .' He paused, groping for the title she'd given him before but unable to get past 'exhibitionist', which was a distracting thought and definitely not what she'd told him.

'An exhibition designer,' she completed for him. 'I design stands for things like trade shows – functionality of the space, branding, display, that kind of stuff. But that wasn't seen as more important than working in Bar Barcelona. Sergio's brother Nando and his wife seemed happy to muck in and my wanting to pursue my own career caused friction.'

Isaac stepped to one side to allow Vita through with a stack of glasses. 'And here you are working in a village pub so I guess you like bar work.'

She hesitated, glancing around at the brass and beams and the winking Christmas decorations. 'It's more that it's where I seem to end up.' As if that reminded her that she was supposed to be working she gave him a brief smile and swung off to the dining area to collect salt and pepper cellars to refill.

Vita bustled past for more glasses and soon as many closing jobs had been accomplished as practicable without them actually closing. Isaac sighed at the sight of the empty bar. 'It's not going to take three of us to finish up. One of you can take an early night.'

'Vita can,' Lily said, looking up from sorting sauce sachets into caddies. 'Her kids get up at the break of dawn.'

Vita couldn't hide a flash of relief though she said fairly, 'Or we could flip a coin.'

Lily waved the idea away. 'We can even things up another time.'

The other woman needed no further cajoling. She vanished into the back and soon came the sound of the outside door closing. Isaac checked the time. Ten thirty. He could easily have sent Lily off as well but this wasn't his pub and he wanted to improve his feel for things. 'Is it often as quiet as this?'

'Never in all the time I've worked here.' Lily rolled her eyes. 'It was that obnoxious guy and his obnoxious mates. We almost never have aggro in The Three Fishes and it sent everyone home.'

He puffed out his cheeks in relief. 'Good. I'd hate Mr Tubb to think I'm running his business into the ground.' Though he wasn't serious, saying the words out loud made his stomach give an unexpected lurch.

She stepped closer, frowning. 'We must have taken enough in the early part of the evening to make up for the last hour being quiet.'

'"Quiet" like the *Marie Celeste*?' But he grinned. 'You're right.' He was just going to make another joke, this time about the novelty of ringing 'last orders' in an empty pub, when the front door opened and a woman strolled in. Wearing her forty-something years easily on her tall and willowy frame, streaked brown hair tossed artfully around her face, she was all but hauled towards the bar by a large Dalmatian dog whose tail became a blur when he spotted Isaac.

'Doggo!' Isaac heard himself say stupidly.

Doggo whined ecstatically, ears back, his doggy grin a mile wide as he bounced and danced, giving a loud bark,

22

obviously frustrated by the restraining lead. Isaac strode around the bar and crouched to fuss the excited canine, choosing to focus on the dog he'd lost along with everything else, rather than on the woman watching with an indulgent smile.

Hayley.

In a long cream woollen coat and high-heeled black boots she looked as polished as fine china. What the hell was his ex doing here? And why did it have to be now, when there wasn't a single customer in the place? Frigging typical, he thought bitterly. In her eyes, it would make him look more of a loser than ever.

'He's pining for you so I thought I'd bring him over as a surprise. See how you were settling in.' Hayley sounded as composed as if they'd last met yesterday rather than two months ago, when he'd moved out of her flat in Peterborough, a forty-minute drive away, and into his sister's spare room in nearby Bettsbrough until taking up residence in one of the seldom-occupied guest rooms upstairs a couple of weeks ago. Hayley glanced around the deserted bar. 'Have you had a bomb alert or something?' First she looked astonished and then, to his disgust, compassionate.

'Aggro,' he said briefly, still stroking Doggo, whose eyes were so much easier to meet. 'Boys who can't hold their beer. Locals cleared out when it kicked off.'

'Ah.' Then she said pleasantly, 'Hello. I'm Hayley.'

Isaac heard Lily's voice reply, 'Hi. I'm Lily.' Her footsteps came around the bar and then her legs, clad in black super skinny jeans, passed Isaac. Doggo gave her a glance and a tail wag. She said, 'Lovely dog,' then moved into the dining area and busied herself replacing the recharged condiment caddies.

Reluctantly, Isaac realised he was going to have to interact with Hayley because she was still standing on the red-patterned carpet of the bar, quite obviously waiting for him to finish his love-in with Doggo. Rising, he brushed off his trousers and gave Hayley a bland smile. 'Drink?' He strode back behind the bar.

'Great.' She slid onto a bar stool. 'What do you have in red?'

'Sangiovese?' he suggested, knowing her predilection for Italian wines, and took down two glasses. Then, on impulse, 'Fancy joining us, Lily?' He was not in the mood for a tête-à-tête in the presence of staff, even if he carried Hayley off to a distant corner.

Lily looked startled. 'Um, oh. Thanks.' Diffidently, she joined them.

Though surprise flickered in Hayley's expression she smiled courteously at Lily, who took the wine glass Isaac pushed across to her.

Isaac cast around for a subject that would involve a conversation long enough for the wine to be drunk and take them up to closing time. He hit on what had been a subject of much chatter on both sides of the bar since he'd arrived. 'Lily's going over to Switzerland in December to do something for Mr Tubb. Aren't you, Lily?'

Lily took another sip from the dark red wine looking slightly ambushed. 'Tubb's brother Garrick and Janice's son Max, really. They work for British Country Foods, which sells traditional British bakery products and conserves. I've designed their stands for the Zürich Food, Lifestyle & Health show and a Christmas fair in Schützenberg. The company's sponsoring a group of us – the Middletones – to go over to sing at the events and lend an air of Britishness to things.' Doggo squeezed round

Hayley's bar stool to approach Lily with his doggie smile and she smoothed his head and scratched him behind his ears.

Hayley was too polished to give any sign whether she found the conversation odd or uninteresting. 'Are you driving or flying to Switzerland? We used to drive all over Europe.'

Lily glanced between Hayley and Isaac but didn't ask who 'we' was made up of. 'We're driving through France. We could've flown to Zürich but there are nine of us and we'll need transport while we're there, especially for the keyboard, guitar and PA system. Our local performing arts college is hiring us its minibus as four of its students are involved. And a road trip will be an adventure. I've been practising driving and parking it in the grounds of the college with the site supervisor.' She'd told Isaac she'd been pleasantly surprised that turning a corner hadn't been like wrestling a bear as she'd suspected it might be.

'It sounds great.' Isaac made sure he was watching Hayley's face when he added, 'I hope to be driving in Europe again soon. When Mr Tubb comes back I'm taking instructor courses in survival training and outdoor education, one of them being in France. I also intend to work abroad when my training's complete.'

Hayley's gaze flew to his. 'A complete career change?'

Isaac felt a sense of satisfaction that she looked a touch thrown. 'One I'm more than ready for,' he replied smoothly.

After more similarly stilted conversation, the last minutes of opening hours ground past and Isaac was able to lock the doors, shooting the brass bolts on the heavy wooden door. He smiled at Lily. 'If you could just set the washer going I'll empty it and clean the filters after I've cashed up. You get off home.'

'If you're sure.' Lily looked relieved. She grabbed their wine glasses, said goodnight and slipped behind the bar. A few moments later Isaac heard her hurrying footsteps and the sound of the back door.

He planted his elbows on the bar and sent Hayley a level look. 'Now, suppose you tell me what you're doing here?'

Her neat eyebrows lifted. 'You don't sound pleased to see me.'

He shrugged, never removing his eyes from hers. 'I didn't think we'd left things in such a way that either of us anticipated seeing the other, so I don't know how to feel.'

She had the grace to look uncomfortable as she fiddled with Doggo's lead. 'I didn't know you intended to leave the country.'

'Why shouldn't I?' he said, straightening, pulling off his tie and unbuttoning his collar. 'Surely, after the last painful months, when you ended things by admitting the failure of the Juno lessened me in your eyes, you're not disappointed I'm going? You know I like the outdoors. I grew up on a farm and living in the city never stopped me loving the country.' He'd been with this woman for several years and sometimes he thought he barely knew her.

Seconds ticked past. Hayley frowned and seemed to struggle with her thoughts. Then she sighed. 'I came to ask if you'd take Doggo.'

He did a double take. 'When we talked about it when we broke up you wouldn't hear of it.'

She shrugged without meeting his eyes. 'The dog walker's moving away and I thought that as you were living in a village he'd be happy here.' She paused. 'If you can't have him, I'll have to rehome him—'

26

'You can't get rid of him like an out-of-season coat!' Isaac interrupted, outraged. How could she stand to think of Doggo's sadness and bewilderment at finding himself in a strange home with strange humans or, worse, in some kind of rescue centre? They'd bought him as a puppy four years ago and he'd never known other owners. He made an instant decision. 'OK, I'll have him. The pub's dog-friendly.' He thought about taking walks every day with Doggo and his heart lifted as if catching a wave. He didn't know how Tubb would feel about a dog living in the pub accommodation but he'd pay for a steam clean or something when he left. The idea of having big, boisterous, joyful, loving Doggo back in his life was such a bonus.

It hadn't been appropriate to fight Hayley for him before because not only had his immediate future been uncertain but he'd been staying with his sister Flora, and Jasmine, Flora's youngest, was allergic to pet fur. When he'd moved to The Three Fishes, Doggo had still been living happily at Hayley's city centre penthouse with a terrace and views of the cathedral.

'What about your new life in Europe?' she asked doubtfully.

'He has a pet passport.' Isaac refused to dwell on the fact that he literally didn't know where his life would take him after the instructor courses.

After a few moments, she nodded. 'OK then. I have his things in the car.'

They went out together to her Audi and Isaac took possession of Doggo's bed, sack of food, bowls, toys, travel crate and spare lead. Helpfully, Doggo tried to grab a tug o'war toy, tail whipping madly, and Isaac almost went headlong over him. 'Idiot,' Isaac said fondly. When the canine possessions had been transported to the area just inside the back door, Isaac took Doggo's lead.

Hayley gave it up without demur but took a moment to gaze up at Isaac. A tiny smile touched the corners of her mouth. 'Lily seems nice.' Her voice lifted at the end of the sentence as if it were a question rather than a statement.

His hand tightened on the loop of the lead, making Doggo fidget and look up as if feeling the tension vibrate all the way to his harness. 'Lily is young and uber-attractive,' he said, equally irritated whether Hayley was fishing for information or giving him a hint as to how to interact with staff. 'But you know I have a perfectly good code of conduct with co-workers. I waited until I'd left the casino to ask you out. I'm not in need of coaching.' In fact, their time at the casino hadn't overlapped by much. He'd been in the throes of buying the lease of the Juno when the chain had brought Hayley in as general manager, a hotshot they'd poached from another group. He'd admired her: so good at her job, so groomed, it had been a no-brainer to ask her out once he could.

Hayley flushed. 'Then I'll butt out,' she said stiffly. She took a step back and he wondered whether it was from his rebuff or from the word 'young', which he was a little ashamed of now he'd said it. At nine years older than him Hayley had always been defensive about her age. She crouched down and slid her arms around Doggo, stroking the top of his head with her cheek. 'Be good for Isaac,' she whispered. Doggo tried to lick her face so she straightened up, said goodnight and stepped smartly towards her car.

Isaac watched her drive away, mentally apologising to Lily for using her to show Hayley that she'd lost the right to comment on his life. Then he looked down at Doggo and murmured, 'But Lily is uber-attractive.'

Doggo wagged his tail as if to agree. Isaac sometimes thought Doggo was an old soul. His eyes were wise even if he still acted like a puppy.

Chapter Three

On Saturday morning Lily stretched and yawned in the compact comfort of the apartment in Carola's basement, peeking through the curtains at frost sparkling on the shrubs and turning every twig to etched glass. The apartment had once been Carola's ex-husband's den and movie room. By the time Lily had come to Middledip assuming she'd stay for a week or so it was an Airbnb. Now she'd lived in it for two years and it was her home.

Carola's house was built on a slope so though the apartment was underground at the front it faced the back garden via French doors that allowed light to flood in. It was smaller than both the Peterborough semi and the Barcelona apartment she'd shared with Sergio, and Carola and her daughters lived above her, but she loved it. It was her space: a bedroom, a lounge/kitchen combo and a shower room. A bijou hallway led to steps up to Carola's kitchen, but though that door was generally unlocked neither of them burst through it unless expected.

A burst of laughter wafted down from Carola's part of the house and Lily grinned to hear Owen Dudley's rich baritone chuckle. He'd only just progressed to staying over when Carola's teenage girls, Charlotte and Emily, were at home. Carola and Owen had met on a dating site last winter and showed every sign of falling hard for each other. Lily was deeply glad. Carola had told her how flattened she'd been by her husband Duncan's defection nearly three years ago.

Lily hopped out of bed and made for the shower, remembering last week when Carola's happiness with Owen had prompted Duncan to ring and check that their daughters weren't being neglected for 'your new man'. Carola had been opening the door to Warwick, Alfie, Eddie and his dad Neil at the time but she hadn't let that prevent her from hissing, 'As you left the family for Sherri I don't think you're in a position to question me!' The others had looked awkward at bearing witness to Carola arguing with her ex.

And on the theme of 'awkward' and exes . . . Lily frowned as she turned on the shower, her thoughts flitting to the tense conclusion to her Thursday evening shift at The Three Fishes when the woman called Hayley had turned up.

Though polite enough to Lily she'd obviously been there to talk to Isaac and the tense way he'd greeted her had made Lily decide on 'ex' as their most likely relationship status.

Throwing off her black PJs covered in pink hearts – a Christmas gift from Zinnia last year – Lily stepped under the hot shower and turned her face to the spray. She liked Isaac and couldn't help being aware of his storybook 'tall, dark and handsome' looks and the tiny gold earring that put an edge on his groomed style. His eyes at once fascinated and unsettled her – dark and thoughtful, even brooding, she thought she read sadness in them. Had Hayley put it there? Immaculately turned out and obviously several years older than Isaac, she'd reminded Lily of a Cruella de Vil who'd finally got her glossy Dalmatian dog.

In contrast, after her shower Lily pulled on jeans and a purple jumper depicting a snowman in a Christmas pudding hat and opened her laptop to work on her designs for the British Country Foods stand at the Food, Lifestyle & Health show. British Country Foods was a Swiss company, despite their name, creating typically British baked goods and conserves. The Swiss loved their food and were international in their tastes.

She hummed 'Let it Snow' as she pulled up the files and let the other Christmas songs the Middletones would perform float through her mind. She'd hit on the idea of a singing group when tossing around ideas for the project. BCF had leapt at the idea and had quickly come up with a sponsorship package. Carola, who'd been in choirs when she was younger and whose daughter Charlotte was at the local music school, had not only involved herself but known exactly who to invite to join the group.

BCF's stand would be in the food section, obviously, and would include product shelving, plinths for display and tables and chairs for meetings. It gave her a buzz to know that the physical versions of these had already been ordered from a provider local to British Country Foods in the Swiss canton of Zug (pronounced Zoog, Janice's son Max Gasly had told her). Presently she was going over the elements designed to provide a British flavour. A loop on a TV screen would show the crosses of St George and St Patrick superimposing themselves on the saltire of St Andrew to form the Union Jack. Others would feature moody fade-ins/fade-outs of Welsh valleys, English farmland, the Giant's Causeway in Northern Ireland and Scottish mountains. BCF's products were ethically produced and mindfully packaged and trade show focus was on growing their presence in perfectly chosen retail outlets and online stores.

On the other side of the coin, at the Schützenberg Christmas market the BCF stall would be aimed at selling products directly to the public – especially the Christmas line at this prime time for consumer spending. Apparently expat Brits would give their eye teeth for mince pies or jars of brandy butter, whilst Swiss people had an appetite for wholesome, ethically produced international foods. 'Britishness' was BCF's USP.

The stall was to be provided by the organisers in the shape of a jolly red chalet and Lily was busy on an interior backdrop. Corporate branding would be low-key to take advantage of the local, crafty feel of the market but it would be there. It wasn't the sort of thing a designer would normally be employed for but Lily was contracted on a whole-project basis. 'Whole-project' had never before included her leading a group of British village singers through Europe to provide cultural authenticity but so what? The company CEO Loris Aebi – known as Los or Los the Boss – was keen on encouraging grassroots arts. She couldn't wait for her first trip to Switzerland. She hugged to herself a vision of sipping spicy glühwein in between crooning 'White Christmas' and 'Mistletoe and Wine', wrapped up in a parka and boots as smiling shoppers paused to listen.

It would be great to see Tubb again too. His spell of ill health had been alarming but she was reassured by his and Janice's regular contact with The Three Fishes.

Would she ever feel the time was right to tell him she was his half-sister . . .?

Shaking off the question that she seemed to spend half her life wrestling with, she turned to perfecting the designs for the trade stand banners and 'clings', the film containing corporate branding that adhered to the stand. She sank into her work, making tiny tweaks to sizes or positions and the rest of the morning flashed by until her phone lit up with a FaceTime call and *Max Gasly calling*. Quickly, she picked up.

'Hey! Just working on your stuff.' She turned the phone to give him a flash of her laptop screen then turned it back towards herself.

Max's image grinned at her, sandy hair sticking up on top of his head. 'Great! Everyone's loving your ideas. Sorry to call you on a Saturday but I just want to check we're on schedule for final files.'

'I'm sending you stuff for approval this morning. When you've okayed them they can go to print,' said Lily.

'Fantastic,' he replied. 'Oh, hang on.' The image on her screen whooshed around for a couple of moments and when it steadied again a small beaming boy had appeared on Max's lap.

Lily, recognising Max's youngest son, also Janice's grandson, beamed back. 'Hello, Keir!'

'Yo!' Three-year-old Keir waved both his hands energetically. 'I wiv Daddy! I got a car on my jumper that Grandma made me.' He pulled at the royal blue jumper depicting a bright red car to make sure she understood.

'It's gorgeous, you lucky boy,' Lily enthused.

Then the head of Keir's five-year-old brother Dugal entered the shot, pushing in front of Keir. 'I've got a dog on mine.' Proudly, he stuck his chest out for Lily to admire.

It took a minute of negotiation before Max had the call to himself again. 'Regarding the Middletones' visit, I've asked my Swiss colleagues for suggestions of what you might like to do in your free time.' Max's image came nearer and then retracted as he picked up a notebook and pushed up his glasses. 'Suggestions are: a visit into Zürich, a procession here in Schützenberg, another Christmas market, watching ice-skaters, a choir . . . Are these along the right lines?'

Lily beamed. 'Oh, yes! Thank you. People can always opt out from things they don't fancy.'

'Great!' Max looked pleased. 'Garrick Tubb will be around too, of course.'

'It will be great to get to know him.' Max didn't know how great, as to him Garrick was just his mum's partner's brother who he'd helped bring on board at British Country Foods last spring. Garrick had decided he wanted to live in Europe after many years in the US and Max had given his boss Garrick's CV. Neither knew that Garrick was the half-brother Lily had yet to meet.

Max glanced behind him. 'Mum and Tubb want to chat to you too, if that's OK?'

Quickly checking the clock in the corner of her laptop screen, Lily agreed. 'I've got a rehearsal after lunch but I'm OK till then. I've been wondering how Tubb is.'

They said their goodbyes and the image swung jerkily, then Lily was looking at her workmate Janice and her boss, Tubb, who had an arm along Janice's shoulders and was looking relaxed and happy, though thinner than before his illness. 'How's everything going at the pub?' he asked at once.

'Did you get the decorations up?' supplemented Janice. The conversation became chaotic as Dugal and Keir appeared once more to claim adult laps and shout their news over Lily reassuring Tubb and Janice that all was well and the decorations were safely in place. She laughed when she realised the boys had begun to call her boss 'Grand-Tubb', which probably seemed logical to them as he was now partnered up with their grandma. It warmed Lily's heart to see him so much part of a family. When she'd first begun work at The Three Fishes he hadn't had much in his life apart from the pub. Now he was letting his body heal with Janice's family and Garrick – his own brother and her half-brother – was living nearby. 'How are you, Tubb?' she asked.

He smiled his turned-down smile. 'Fine, thanks. Taking the pills as prescribed and attending the local heart failure clinic. I fly home for an appointment with my UK consultant in January but hopefully the baby will be here and settled by then.'

'And how is Ona?' Lily enquired.

Janice pulled a worried face at the mention of her heavily pregnant daughter-in-law. 'Getting frustrated by the placenta being badly positioned, so there's a high risk of bleeding. She's doing very little and they're keeping a close eye on her but they've warned her they might have to induce. We'll all be glad when the baby's safely here.'

'We getting a Kissmuss baby,' Keir informed Lily happily. 'A new one.'

Lily smothered a laugh. 'That's something to look forward to. I'm coming to Schützenberg to see you in a few weeks.'

Dugal's little eyes flashed with interest. 'Will you bring us presents?'

'Dugal Gasly!' Janice broke in. 'People are more important

than presents. We're looking forward to seeing Lily and Carola and all of the singing group, aren't we?'

Dugal nodded, but still looked as if he'd like to know about the presents.

After Lily had replied to a few more questions about how things were going at the pub and how she was finding Isaac – 'Efficient and pleasant,' she assured them – the call ended.

Almost immediately, Lily's phone alerted her to a text from Carola that proved she wasn't letting Owen distract her from the schedule. *Fancy coming up for a sarnie before choir practice?*

Very much! Will bring biccies, Lily sent back. After finishing her task and emailing Max as promised, she climbed the stairs to Carola's kitchen where Owen was pulling on his coat and dropping a kiss on Carola's blonde bob. Lily just had time to say, 'Bye!' before he disappeared out of the door.

Carola was a bit pink after the kiss. 'Owen's going to visit his mum. She's not too well and he says she gets crotchety with visitors.'

'Doesn't sound like you're missing much then,' Lily joked, giving the older woman a hug. 'Are you and Owen getting serious? He's not going to stop you coming to Switzerland is he?'

Despite the obvious stars in her eyes Carola made a mock scream face. 'Of course not. He's not going to stop me doing anything – I had enough of that with Duncan.'

Lily dropped down beside Carola at the white glass kitchen table. 'Extremely sensible. Shall we finalise the programme today so we can send it to the Performing Rights Society and fork over the fee for singing other people's songs?'

Over tuna sandwiches and custard creams they ummed and ahhed about the respective merits of Cliff Richard's 'Mistletoe and Wine' versus Paul McCartney's 'Wonderful Christmastime', Slade's 'Merry Xmas Everybody' or Wizzard's 'I Wish it Could be Christmas Everyday'. Carola wrote down 'Walking in the Air' from *The Snowman* and Lily crossed it out again. 'That puts a lot of emphasis on the sopranos – us! You might be strong enough but I'm not sure I am.'

Carola nicked back the pen and wrote it in again. 'Of course you're strong enough! We don't have to sing like choirboys to carry it off and we're spoilt for sopranos anyway because we have Charlotte and Emily. I wish we had another bass to sing along with Neil, personally.' She tapped the pen on her teeth.

Privately, Lily thought that Charlotte and Emily's voices were pretty but not strong. Knowing Carola wouldn't appreciate that view she just said, 'The sponsorship budget was based on how many singers we could get into one minibus so people can't expect the balance of a proper choir. Now, which carols are we going to include? The trouble with carols is that they're so international they won't give the British flavour Max is keen on. On the other hand, if we sing "Silent Night" then people might join in, which is always lovely,' Lily pointed out. 'Also, it's easy so we're good at it. It would have been nice to include that Polish carol Franciszka tried to teach us, as we have so many people of Polish descent in our region, but we had trouble even with the title, "*Anioł Pasterzom Mówił*", let alone the rest of the words.'

Carola laughed. 'Let's stick to easy stuff. Have you heard how Tubb is, by the way?'

Lily was happy to update her and then the rest of the

afternoon passed in a flash. Once the first Middletones arrived – Warwick, Eddie and Alfie – filled with all the noisy ebullience of seventeen- and eighteen-year-olds, Charlotte and Emily emerged from their rooms. The boys were all music student chums of Charlotte from the local performing arts college, Acting Instrumental. Eddie tuned his guitar. Warwick set his keyboard on its stand and plugged it in while Emily, only fourteen so still at school, chattered to him, beaming and giggling.

'I'm going to have to watch Emily,' Carola muttered. 'She's developing a crush on Warwick and a lad of eighteen is much too old for her.'

Neil – Eddie's dad, turning up at the same time as Franciszka, who lived in Drake's Close around the corner from Carola's on the Bankside estate – gave her a re-assuring grin. 'I think Warwick's got a girlfriend at college anyway.'

Soon they were ready to begin. 'Let's crash on with the carols,' Lily suggested. 'They're a good warm-up and have lots of lovely harmonies.' Lily and Carola arranged the songs between them, usually based on what the Middletones could sing best.

Eddie slung his guitar around his neck and Warwick perched on his stool in front of the silver keyboard. Carola took her place facing the group as a sort of unofficial leader. 'We'll begin with "Once in Royal David's City".' She counted Warwick and Eddie in then the voices soared in to join them. Next came 'Hark the Herald Angels Sing' and 'O Little Town of Bethlehem' before they began on the Christmas pop songs.

Later, when they took a break to sip water and refuel on shortbread, they talked over what they'd wear to sing on their Swiss trip and decided on red bobble hats and scarves with black overshirts. Carola noted sizes and agreed to do the ordering, reflecting that it was as well that BCF was covering the expense.

In the second part of the afternoon they worked on 'Walking in the Air' – which even Lily had to agree was coming along nicely – and the flirty, dashing 'Let it Snow' to open a set. By the end of the afternoon they'd also settled most of the programme for the trade fair – a set of ten songs rounded off with a rousing rendition of 'We Wish You a Merry Christmas' – and knew how they'd expand the set for the Christmas market, which would be less formal and possibly lubricated by glühwein and *eierkirsch* – mulled wine or eggnog.

'Right,' Lily said as Franciszka hurried off because she'd promised to give her daughter a lift into Bettsbrough. 'That was brilliant, thank you everyone. Hands up who's looking forward to travelling to Switzerland!' She laughed to see a forest of hands – two from each of the teenagers.

'I still feel bad I can't share the driving as I first promised,' Neil admitted sheepishly. 'My punishment's affecting a lot more than just me.' He hung his head.

Eddie pulled a face as he slid his guitar back into its gig bag. 'Yeah, Dad's Taxi is rubbish since you lost your licence.' But he clapped his father on the shoulder sympathetically. Neil had had a heavy evening at a hotel with fellow sales reps at a 'company jolly' and the police had lain in wait with their breathalysers in the morning. Seven out of ten reps had retained sufficient alcohol in their blood to blow positive and one of them was Neil, who'd avoided unemployment by the skin of his teeth. He'd been offered reassignment in the Bettsbrough office at a lower grade but some of the others had found themselves looking for new companies to join.

Lily knew how terrible Neil felt about his lapse and though she hadn't bargained for driving all the way from Cambridgeshire to central Switzerland gave him a consoling smile. 'I'll manage. We'll make lots of stops so I can stretch my legs.'

Carola smiled apologetically too. 'If only I could drive on the wrong side of the road. I get panic attacks at the thought.'

'I'll manage,' Lily repeated. Once everyone had called goodbye she slipped down to her flat to change into black trousers and a polo top. She redid her hair, plaiting a section to tuck into her ponytail, watched TV while she made and ate an omelette then burrowed her way into the down-filled parka she'd bought ready for Switzerland and hurried through the village towards the pub, her hands tucked in her pockets against a wind that carried the scent of snow on its frozen edge.

Though it was barely the second week of November Christmas lights were appearing on houses and trees twinkling from windows. The outdoor illumination at The Three Fishes had been organised before Tubb left the country and it looked as if someone had cast a giant net of sparkling white lights over it, making the building shimmer.

Lily hurried in through the back door and was hanging up her coat when Isaac appeared and sat down at the desk in the alcove. He was all in black – shirt, tie and trousers – and his dark hair had a lustre like a crow's wing. He gave her a quick smile. 'So you came back despite that guy on Thursday.'

She returned his smile as she smoothed her ponytail, remembering the belligerence she'd encountered at Bar Barcelona without any of Sergio's family showing any sign of noticing. "Course. You must've had plenty at your last place – it was Juno Lounge, wasn't it? Big, busy venue.'

He shrugged. 'There, yes, but it's different in a village pub.'

He turned to his laptop and Lily went through to the bar. Several tables in the dining area were already occupied and the bar was filling nicely considering it was only six o'clock. The Christmas lights reflected in glasses and beer pumps and even the smiling eyes of the customers. Tina was on duty too. She was the staff member who was licensed to deputise when Isaac was off. In her fifties, Tina was soft and round with a frizz of curls on top of her head, unflappable and efficient. She drove in from nearby Bettsbrough where she lived with her husband and two sons, all of whom seemed as affable as she whenever Lily encountered them.

Tina smiled at Lily. 'Got quite a few bookings for the dining area tonight so listen for Chef's bell when he needs service or he'll go off on one.'

'Got it,' Lily said, taking an order for three pints of bitter and a sparkling water from a short man with a beard. The level of noise rose as more punters arrived for a Saturday evening's entertainment. When Isaac re-appeared in the bar Lily checked with him, 'OK if I do a round with the raffle tickets if there's a lull?' The proceeds of the raffle went to the children's party at the village hall.

He glanced up as he waited at the pumps for a stream of near-black Guinness to fill a pint glass. 'Sure. I'll get the stuff out of the safe for you.'

So Lily sold raffle tickets, pulled pints, ferried food, sanitised and relaid tables. Finally it was eleven o'clock, the bar was empty and Isaac was locking the doors behind the last customer. The kitchen staff had clattered out already.

As Isaac took the till reading and released the till drawer ready to cash up, Lily and Tina began to clean tables and rearrange chairs. Then Tina wriggled into a silver-grey puffa coat that made her look a bit like an airship, shouted goodbye and stepped outside. Lily was about to follow when Isaac reappeared, with Doggo bouncing at his heels. When he saw Lily Doggo gave a single bark, trotting over with his tail whipping as if he'd remembered that they'd been introduced on Thursday night.

'Hello, Doggo, I didn't know you were still about.' Lily stroked his smooth head and he put his ears back to enjoy the fuss. She glanced up at Isaac, his tie gone and collar undone, hair beginning to flop into his eyes. It was the first time she'd seen him anything but perfectly groomed but she liked the tousled look. It was as if he'd let his guard down and allowed end-of-a-long-day fatigue to show.

Isaac smiled. 'He's living with me now. I've cleared it with Mr Tubb.'

Lily straightened. 'I assumed he was Hayley's.'

'If he'd been just Hayley's his name would have been Rolex or Gucci,' he said drily, then hesitated. 'I'm sorry if you found the atmosphere strained on Thursday. Hayley and I used to be together. I felt defensive about the pub being deserted when she swanned in. She has a brilliant career as general manager of a casino.' He smiled crookedly.

Lily felt a burst of sympathy. 'I can imagine how I'd have felt if it had been my ex because Bar Barcelona was always jumping.'

Isaac's expression relaxed. 'Galling, isn't it? It's bad enough that she knows Mr Tubb and it was her who suggested me for this job.'

Lily grinned. 'Tubb might have shut when the pub emptied.'

Isaac quirked a brow. 'That would have been worse. I can only imagine how I'd have felt if she'd found this place shut early.' He grimaced. 'Anyway, she brought me Doggo, which is fantastic. I'm off on Monday and Tuesday so I'm looking forward to finding some long walks.'

'Just stick to the footpaths when you're crossing the Carlysle Estate because it's private land.' Lily pulled on her outdoor things and prepared to brave the cold weather. 'See you tomorrow evening if I can move after having Sunday lunch with my parents.'

'Enjoy it.' He began to turn away, Doggo at his heels. 'My dad's not well so I try never to visit my folks at mealtimes because Mum's his carer and has enough to do. Maybe I'll invite them here. They might enjoy it.'

Walking home, snug in her parka despite the icy air, Lily thought that it was nice of Isaac to give his folks a treat if they were in difficult circumstances. She turned her mind to her own parents, Roma and Patsie. After what Zinnia had said on Thursday she definitely needed a word with them.

Chapter Four

Late on Sunday morning, Lily's snazzy purple Peugeot hatchback whizzed her through the country lanes on her way out of the village. Bettsbrough's outer ring road took her past a retail park fronted by an enormous plastic snowman in a tinsel scarf and spat her out on the dual carriageway to Peterborough. The hedgerows were winter-bare and glistening with frost. The sky was blue and she half regretted not getting up in time for a walk this morning.

The journey to Longthorpe, west Peterborough, where Roma and Patsie lived took forty minutes. Their stone house had begun as a small cottage but had been extended when Lily and Zinnia were teenagers into an L-shape with five bedrooms in the roof and a double garage. When Lily pulled onto the gravelled drive she paused a full minute beside the car to admire the garden with its arches and trellis, shapely shrubs and stone-edged paths. She always felt as if she looked into the hearts of her mothers when she looked into their garden. Even now, as winter bit, the hedges were neat and the paths swept. This year the pots had been planted with heathers and what looked like broad blades of pink grass.

She let herself into the house shouting, 'It's me!' In the familiar sitting room, which still boasted its cottage credentials of beams, a stone fireplace and a black wood-burning stove, she found her mums sharing a sofa, Roma reading while Patsie tapped on her laptop to a background of Pink Floyd.

Both rose with welcoming arms. Roma's blonde curls tumbled loose around her shoulders; Patsie's darker locks were swept up behind her head. Both women wore comfy jeans and big smiles. 'Hey, gorgeous!' Roma welcomed Lily with a huge, effusive hug.

Patsie's 'Lily, darling,' was more restrained but just as warm. Lily couldn't remember an occasion when Patsie had treated her any differently to the daughter she actually gave birth to, Zinnia. Nor did Roma ever give a sign of favouring Lily over Zin.

Lily beamed as she returned the hugs. 'Glorious smells coming from the kitchen.' She lifted her nose to sniff.

'We made your favourite chicken and chorizo bake once we knew you were coming.' Roma put on her glasses and regarded her daughter through the turquoise frames. 'Always wonderful to see you but you sounded as if something was bothering you on the phone.'

Patsie's pansy-dark eyes fixed themselves on Lily too.

Lily had been wondering how best to broach what was on her mind so decided to offer a direct answer to their direct questions. She licked her lips. 'I came to make sure you know I love you.'

That caught the attention of both her mothers. 'What?' Roma's grey eyes grew round. 'Yes, we do.'

Patsie's brows lifted. 'What on earth's brought that on?'

46

Lily made herself meet their eyes. 'Zinnia's upset with me. She minds me living in Middledip, or, at least, the reason I'm living there – to get to know Tubb and work for him. She says that's hurting you.' She looked from Roma to Patsie and back again. 'Is she right?'

Patsie and Roma exchanged glances and Roma sighed. 'How can I complain when it was me who precipitated the situation?'

'Let's not rehash the history,' Lily suggested hastily, worry inching its way through her tummy as she noted tension on Patsie's face. 'Is it harming our relationship that I've sought out a member of my natural family? You see,' she went on honestly, 'I think Zinnia feels I should leave Middledip and start again somewhere else and it's affecting things between us. But I like Middledip. I like the community, working part-time at the pub, the friends I've made and singing with the Middletones. And I like my half-brother.'

Roma looked stricken. 'We haven't asked you to give those things up.' Patsie took Roma's hand comfortingly.

'No, nobody's actually asked me to. But is my living there hurting you?' Lily persisted.

Patsie sighed. After a moment, she spoke in what Lily thought of as her 'lawyer's voice', careful and thoughtful. 'You want to know your family. The same could have gone for Zinnia because children of anonymous donors look for ways to find the male too. That Zinnia doesn't feel that need shouldn't be relevant to what you do.'

Lily gave her gaze for gaze. 'But *is it hurting you*?'

Roma's smile was tremulous. 'It's you not telling your half-brother who you are that's tricky to deal with.'

Lily shifted restlessly. 'Zinnia said something similar,' she admitted. 'But you know why I haven't decided whether to tell him.' She'd meant to . . . until the day when she'd been working with Janice getting ready to open for lunch and Tubb had stormed in after a visit to his Aunt Bonnie. Lily shuddered to remember standing there as Tubb opened his heart to Janice, obviously barely registering Lily's presence. His aunt, with the confusion of age, had spilled some family beans, all about how her brother Marvin had had an affair with a woman he'd considered leaving his family for. Tubb had exploded to Janice that he hoped to hell his dad hadn't done anything awful like leaving bastard kids around and Lily had wanted to sink through the floor.

She swallowed, reliving that hideous moment when she'd known what it was like to feel despised for merely being alive. 'I don't want him to hate me.' She heard her voice quaver. 'And, to be honest, I don't really see why it should make any difference to you or Zinnia whether he knows.'

Roma glanced again at Patsie before once more addressing Lily. 'It's dangling over us. What will happen if you finally confess? Will you get hurt? I'm worried what it will do to you if he reacts badly and, being honest, I quail at the idea of ever having to meet him myself. He's not going to have any love for me, is he?' Perhaps realising she was being too frank she added, 'However, you're the one it affects most.'

Then Patsie's phone began to ring and she glanced at the screen and sighed. 'Damn, that's Andrew from work. I'd better take this.' She rose gracefully as she answered the call and Lily listened to her voice moving out into the hallway, growing fainter.

Lily changed sofas so that she was sitting next to Roma and lowered her voice. 'Is it causing trouble between you and Patsie?'

Roma gave a pensive smile, brushing Lily's hair gently back from her face. 'When I was so headstrong and unfair as to have an affair with a man in order to get pregnant it took Patsie a while to forgive me and I suppose we're hearing an echo or two of those horrid days.'

Patsie came back into the room, dropping her phone on the table. Lily's unhappiness was growing but she hated the idea of her actions bringing tension into the relationship between her mums so she asked, 'Do you both agree with Zinnia that after I've been to Switzerland I should leave the village to make things easier on the rest of you?' A lump jumped into her throat even at the thought of leaving Middledip behind.

Roma and Patsie exchanged looks. It was several moments before either answered and then it was Patsie. 'Darling, I don't think anyone can make that decision but you.'

'So,' said Roma with the bright air of one determined to turn the conversation. 'What else is going on with you? You're so pretty, Lily, and it has been over two years since you and Sergio said your goodbyes. You ought to be out having lots of lovely dates.'

Lily submitted to the change of subject, needing time to digest her dismay that neither Roma nor Patsie had dismissed the idea of her leaving Middledip as totally unfair. She managed a smile. 'I haven't had a date for ages – although a man in The Three Fishes asked me on Thursday. He was drunk and horrible.' She decided not to go into the part of the story where she'd politely refused and he'd sneeringly declared she must be a lesbian. Roma and Patsie were capable of groaning loudly and moving on but Lily believed that every cut left a scar and didn't see why she should be the one to add to their number.

Patsie wrinkled her nose. 'You definitely don't want a drunk and horrible man. Zinnia says your new boss is hot. How about him?'

'Wouldn't argue with Zin about his hotness. I'll ask him out and tell him one of my mums said I have to, shall I?' Lily managed to smile again.

Her mothers laughed together as they all moved into the kitchen to dish the pasta, pour wine and talk about the plans Roma and Patsie were making for the garden next year.

On Sunday evening, having driven home and snatched a quick nap in front of the TV, Lily turned up to begin her shift at six at The Three Fishes. A rumble of conversation was already coming from the other side of the bar and a clinking of cutlery from the dining area. Baz, at twenty the youngest staff member, was supposed to be on with her but he raced in five minutes late, his trendy long-at-the-front haircut flying.

She grinned at him as she poured a glass of rosé for Melanie from Booze & News, the village shop. 'Couldn't you get out of bed?'

Baz, or Sebastian, as it said on the payroll, glanced around with a hunted expression. 'Playing Grand Theft Auto and forgot to get ready for work. Is Isaac stressing?'

'Not noticeably.'

'But it never is noticeable,' Baz groaned. 'He just quietly gives the impression you're a world-class tosser.' Baz had dropped out of uni last year and was working longish part-time hours while he decided what to do next. Popular with customers, he had a ready smile and had been brought up in Middledip. As Isaac emerged from the dining area Baz hastily found a customer to serve.

Lily turned the card reader so Melanie could make a contactless card payment. It would be her last shift until the end of next week as she only worked at the pub fifteen to eighteen hours a week: three evening shifts with maybe a lunchtime thrown in, usually over the period Thursday to Sunday, the pub's quietest days being Monday to Wednesday. She liked the pattern. When she'd first returned to the UK it had been with the idea of building up her design business. She'd thought checking out the situation in Middledip would keep her only a few days. But then she'd seen the advert for bar staff and it had seemed meant to be and though when she'd left Bar Barcelona she'd planned never to stand behind a bar again . . . well, she'd applied and here she was. The work wasn't onerous and left time to freelance on exhibition projects, which had a less predictable income stream because business was proving slow to build. Currently, her future work schedule consisted of two stands for the London Book Fair in March and the prospect of more work from British Country Foods, the company Max and Garrick worked for. That wouldn't be exhibition design so much as two-dimensional work such as layouts for brochures but she had the skills and she wasn't precious.

On the plus side, rent at Carola's wasn't high and Sergio had bought Lily out of their apartment, which had given her a modest nest egg and him a bigger mortgage with a Spanish bank.

It was after nine when she turned from ringing up two large glasses of white wine and a Hendrick's gin with elderflower tonic, and a smiling woman ordered half a pint of lager. As Lily passed her the change she asked, 'Is Isaac O'Brien around, please? Will you tell him Flora's here?' Her brown hair was pulled into a knot at the nape of her neck and her expression was open and friendly.

Lily smiled back, thinking '*Another* pretty woman looking for Isaac?' before answering cheerfully, 'He's around somewhere. I'll find him.'

She whizzed out of the bar and discovered Isaac talking to Chef. His eyes lit up when he heard Flora was waiting. 'I'll be right there.'

Lily did as requested, then went out into the dining area to clear plates. From there she was ideally placed to see Isaac arrive behind the bar, open the counter flap, hug the brown-haired woman and usher her through. When Lily took the same route, a pile of plates and cutlery in her arms, she glanced all around the back area on her way to the kitchen but there was no sign of Isaac and his visitor.

Perhaps he'd found a replacement for the glamorous Hayley already? Good-looking men never need be short of company.

Chapter Five

It was meant to be one of Isaac's days off but Monday didn't seem to have got that memo. He'd already taken a call from the wholesaler to order soft drinks and bar snacks, shown his face in the bar at lunchtime to see Tina was OK and to check the beer cellar. He was a better build than Tina for hauling beer kegs and firkins around.

Back upstairs, he went into the kitchen, which was the only part of Tubb and Janice's accommodation he used. His own space was a nice bedroom with en suite, once one of two sets of guest accommodation, but it had nowhere to make meals or do laundry. He made a cup of tea and a chicken sandwich and sat down at the table to phone Tubb, who was unused to leaving his pub in the hands of others for long and got antsy. After reassuring the owner that everything was hunky-dory, Isaac called his parents and invited them to The Three Fishes tomorrow evening. 'Flora's offered to drive you over,' he added. They'd moved into Peterborough when Isaac's dad had had to give up farm work so maybe they'd enjoy a trip to the country, even if just for an evening.

He ate his lunch, Doggo watching fixedly. 'There's time for a good walk today. Really stretch our legs,' Isaac told him, popping the last of his sandwich into his mouth without sharing. 'I've printed a map of the area from footpathmaps.com. I need to think about getting myself ready for the instructor courses I'm taking. A fast eight-mile walk will do today and maybe tomorrow we'll drive off into Derbyshire and find some hills.'

Doggo wagged his tail.

'I've moped around long enough, feeling adrift. I don't have an exact end-date for this job but it's an OK stopgap. I cannot wait to leave the atrocious hours and perilous rewards of the hospitality industry behind forever. Losing the Juno made me want out.' The Three Fishes was informal and laid-back after the Juno but that wasn't necessarily a bad thing. Being with Hayley for so long had made him so bloody aspirational that he'd almost forgotten how it felt to jog along within his comfort zone.

He rose, causing Doggo to bound to his feet too, and went into his own room. It hadn't seen heavy use before he arrived and, decorated in cream, brown and blue was a pleasant enough place to live. It looked over the car park and the playing fields. With not much in the way of household tasks to weigh him down and no girlfriend to worry about he was enjoying an uncluttered style of living. Much of his personal stuff was stored in Flora's loft and he'd worked things out with Hayley financially rather than take any of their furniture. His career-in-waiting as an outdoor pursuits instructor would take him to pastures new and would include staff accommodation.

Beyond work, Isaac was pretty isolated these days. The mates from before he met Hayley had faded away over the years. Although initially intrigued by his glam older girlfriend, his friends had come to think that Hayley was too focused on her career and what it brought her and that Isaac had grown the same, especially once he was running his own business. He'd seen it more as going into a shared future and increasing his capacity to earn . . . but all that had been before he'd failed to meet Hayley's gold standard, of course.

She certainly had exhibited no need of his friends. Her own good friends numbered just Vicky and Nicola, a pair of sisters who were so similar to each other and to Hayley in dress and attitudes that they might as well have been one person. Hayley had been tight with them since uni days when her own parents had died and she'd spent a lot of holidays at their home. Vicky had a husband, Adie, and Nicola a Colombian boyfriend called Javier, but though Isaac had got along OK with all of them, he wasn't in touch post break-up.

It was nice to have an excitedly wagging Doggo around for company. Isaac pulled on boots and a jacket and threaded Doggo into his harness. He slid his map into a plastic sleeve and clipped it to a lightweight backpack containing hat and gloves and added a couple of water bottles, enough for Doggo too, though Doggo generally seemed to prefer puddles. Plugging his earphones into his phone he found his 'walking' playlist, then jogged downstairs and out of the door at the side of the building to the rousing sound of 'Goldfinger', heart lifting to be striding out, first across the playing fields and then over Port Road and onto the first bridleway. He let Doggo's lead reel out and picked up his pace, the chill air nipping at his ears.

As he strode, he mentally planned fitness building. His first course would be Outdoor Instructor's Training in Wales, including navigation, climbing, first aid, water sports, orienteering, cycle training and group communication skills. Next would come Survival Training in the New Forest and then he'd move on to France to develop his climbing skills. After that he'd start looking around for work because he'd need an injection of cash, though he hadn't lost quite all his money over the Juno closing.

Just all of his pride.

He marched faster as if to outdistance the sense of failure, then decided to jog for thirty seconds out of every sixty for the next ten minutes. Interval training would toughen him up and the faster beating of his heart might help him go forward rather than look back. As he increased his pace Doggo looked around, eyes bright and tail whipping as he joined in too. Once he got running Doggo flowed like a black-and-white cheetah but he began with a plunge like a rocking horse. It made Isaac grin.

It was dark and a few minutes after six o'clock opening time when Isaac arrived back at the pub, returning the way he'd come over the playing fields and car park. Pleasantly tired, he'd dropped his pace to a stroll, giving his muscles a chance to cool down. Doggo wasn't even panting as he flattened his ears neatly against the wind.

Isaac's footsteps were muffled by the grass as he approached the tarmac car park. Two women were standing next to one of the cars. The taller one had planted her hands on her hips and the smaller was glaring up at her. Her voice was low as she snapped, 'I thought we were going to have a nice dinner together. I didn't realise it was another opportunity for you to try and run my life.' Isaac's step faltered as he recognised Lily's voice.

'You need to be aware of how Mum and Roma feel about this brother thing—'

He was pretty sure that was the sister again, the one with the odd name. Zinnia? Her hair was being dragged around as the wind rose and she yanked up her hood.

'Back off!' Lily exploded, voice tight and high. 'Shut the front door, Zinnia! If you can't keep your opinions to yourself then I'm going.'

Zinnia sighed and her voice softened. 'It's just that I care about you, Lily.'

'I'm sure you do.' Lily sounded choked now. 'But you might as well go home and have dinner with George. I work at this pub and I'm not up for you embarrassing me in front of my workmates or my new boss by giving me a hard time.'

Her words prompted Isaac to go gently into reverse to spare her exactly that embarrassment, though Doggo, who was no doubt anticipating dinnertime, gave him an aghast stare. They could circumnavigate the pub car park on the playing fields, circle onto Main Road and then come at the side door from there.

But Zinnia's next remark halted Isaac as he took the first stride. Her laugh was low. 'Oh, yes, the hot boss you're going to ask out. How's that going?'

Isaac turned back to stare at the two figures illuminated by the lights from the pub.

'I was joking with the mums about asking him out,' Lily responded despondently. 'Though I did say he was hot. You said so yourself. It's about the only thing we've agreed on lately.' She hugged herself against the bitter wind.

That was the moment Doggo chose to indicate that he'd had enough of lurking in the damp darkness instead of being taken indoors for dinner and a nap. He gave a couple of loud woofs.

Isaac cringed. Both women swung around. Doggo wagged his tail as if pleased to have caught their attention.

Lily, in the car park light, looked horrified. She turned away in slow motion, head tilted and eyes closed in an obvious 'Ooooh noooo'.

Isaac stood rooted to the spot. Realising that Zinnia was still gazing at him with an expression torn between 'Oh, shit!' and laughter he decided to take control of the situation. And by that he meant . . . totally pretend he hadn't heard.

'Evening, ladies,' he said genially, strolling onto the car park on a trajectory aimed at the side door.

'Evening,' Zinnia echoed in a strangled voice. And then as she caught sight of Lily turning and trudging away her voice rose uncertainly. 'Hey, are we really not having dinner, Lily? I honestly didn't mean to . . .' Her voice tailed off as Lily shook her head and kept moving, heading towards the side of the building, probably to walk past it to Main Road.

It would have been less awkward if Isaac could have used the back door but with Doggo in tow that really wasn't possible because it would have taken them across the route where food was carried to the dining area and bar. He could have stopped to check his phone to give her a chance to make her escape, but Doggo was straining on his leash. Isaac tried to keep his steps slow so he wouldn't overtake her as, behind him, he heard Zinnia sigh, 'Oh, Lileeee,' before there came the sound of a car door opening and then slamming shut.

Lily's steps faltered, her head drooping. Isaac thought he heard her sniff. Then she swung around, taking a hasty step as if she meant to stop Zinnia driving off. Shock flashed across her face as she found Isaac immediately behind her.

In the light from the headlights that came on as Zinnia's car started up he could see tears glittering on her cheeks like ice crystals. Isaac stared down at her. The car headlights swept across them and then Zinnia's car drove on.

For several moments the wind buffeted, threading icy air into collars and up sleeves. Isaac's hair blew into his face and he felt the first sting of rain. Then it came faster, heavier, hitting his scalp like pellets. Lily groaned, 'Oh, great!'

Isaac reached into his pocket for his key and heard himself say calmly, 'It's going to pour down. I'm going in for a hot drink. Fancy one?'

He threw open the door on a gust of wind as the sky broke and all the rain it held fell out.

As Isaac moved forward an eager Doggo did the same. Unfortunately, as he was on the other side of Lily, the taut lead caught painfully across the backs of her legs. Wrong-footed – literally – she stumbled over the threshold behind Isaac. Part of her wanted to turn tail for home but the rain and gusting wind tried to get in behind her and, reflexively, she closed the door. 'Um, thanks,' she muttered.

'No prob.' Isaac strode upstairs behind Doggo as if assuming she'd accepted his invitation to join him in a hot drink and would follow. As her other options were to stand alone at the foot of the stairs or brave the monsoon hammering down outside, reluctantly she did so. When she gained the landing Doggo was rolling and wriggling on the carpet to dry himself. 'No, Doggo!' Isaac's voice floated from an open doorway and Lily and Doggo both followed it.

She'd been up to Tubb and Janice's flat and knew the kitchen. A pine table stood in the centre and she hung her coat on the back of one of the chairs, trying not to meet Isaac's gaze as she sat down.

He fed Doggo, then filled the kettle as rain hit the window like handfuls of gravel. 'Sounds like quite a squall,' Isaac commented, glancing at the dark glass and taking down two mugs. One bore the picture of a Dalmatian and the words *Kind, intelligent and batshit crazy*.

Lily cleared her throat. 'The radio said it might turn to hail or sleet. We're heading into a cold snap.'

'Oh?' He fished a carton of milk from the fridge. He seemed no keener to meet her gaze than she was his.

Crap. That almost guaranteed he'd overheard. She sighed and decided to get the embarrassment over with just in case he'd invited her up here on the assumption she'd be an easy conquest – though he hadn't struck her as the sort. 'Sorry you were treated to a sisterly spat. Contrary to what you might have observed so far, Zin and I do love each other. Luckily, she's funny and warm as well as opinionated. Did you hear much of what she said?' She tried to sound nonchalant but her cheeks were burning.

He turned to the kettle as if he needed to check he'd turned it on, although it was already making growling noises. 'Not all of it,' he answered vaguely. 'Maybe I automatically switch off when it comes to sisters. You met mine, yesterday – Flora. Always on my case about something.'

Diverted, she regarded him with interest. 'She's your sister? She seemed nice.'

'As sisters go.' But he smiled as he finished making the coffee and carried the mugs to the table. Lily took hers with thanks. He'd given her the Dalmatian mug.

A *ting!* hit the air and Isaac pulled out his phone. He hesitated and frowned at the screen.

'Do you need to answer?' Lily asked politely. 'Or I can leave if you need to make a call.'

'It's voicemail.' He tapped a couple of times, listened, then slid the handset onto the table. 'The call came in when I was in a no-signal area hiking around the fens. My accountant. It's after office hours now so no point calling till tomorrow.' He rubbed his temples as if the mere idea of it made his head ache. 'Giving up the lease at Juno Lounge and winding up the business produced a lot of paperwork and process.'

'Oh.' She added milk to her coffee. 'I hadn't realised you were a leaseholder. I'd assumed you were just the manager.'

His jaw tightened. 'It was my business so it affected me pretty badly when it went belly-up. It was nothing I did wrong but it hurts.'

'I'm sure.' She wrinkled her forehead, trying to bring to mind what had happened to Juno Lounge, the kind of place that once had been very much part of the scenery. 'I suppose it was affected by the closure to the parkway, was it?'

He nodded. 'A bridge was suddenly found to be failing dangerously and that was it. Road closed. It cut the life-blood to the Juno. There was a back lane access but it was small and out of the way. With the parkway closed large, jolly "Open as usual!" signs had no effect. People found other places to go and in no time I was in the crap.' He paused to sip his coffee.

'Can't you insure against interruption to business?' she asked sympathetically. No wonder he always had shadows in his eyes.

'You can.' He nodded. 'But it only applies to specific circumstances and a bridge that had gradually deteriorated wasn't an "insured peril". Two bridges further up were found to need work too, which proved the death blow. The brewery bought me out of the lease, in the circumstances, but it wasn't a generous offer. They're more able to afford to sit out the months while the bridges are repaired than I am but they must still be losing money, as I closed up in July. They expect to reopen in March but by then I'll be on my way. I'm sick of the hospitality business.'

She gave a quiet snort of laughter. 'I keep saying the same. Then I end up working in a bar.'

'Well, I won't,' he said positively, dark eyes flashing. 'I'm working here because I need to do something while I tie up the loose ends.' Then he became more cheerful as he told her about the outdoorsy instructor courses he was to take, calling up a website on his phone to show her pictures of people in backpacks and helmets. While he waxed enthusiastic, Lily found herself relaxing, listening to him talk about hill walking and kayaking rather than what he might have overheard.

Until he moved the conversation on. 'So you have a brother as well as a sister? Does he live locally?'

Lily half-dropped her mug, splashing the dregs of her coffee down her jeans. 'Sorry!' she gasped. She used her sleeve to mop the splashes from the table. Doggo trotted over and licked up the splashes on the floor. 'What do you mean?'

He was staring at her warily. 'Um . . . I thought I heard your sister mention a brother. Sorry if I got it wrong.'

She polished at the table some more with her now damp sleeve. She'd almost prefer he'd heard the bit about asking out the hot boss rather than this. 'You didn't get it wrong,' she admitted reluctantly. 'I have two half-brothers. Do you—' She regarded him anxiously. 'Do you mind not mentioning them in the village though?' Her tummy turned over at the thought.

'If that's what you want,' he replied uncertainly. Rain or hail flung itself at the window anew, making Doggo growl. Now still didn't seem like a good time for Lily to leave but she began to wish she hadn't allowed herself to be ushered up here for coffee. She should have run into the pub and sheltered for a bit . . . though she wouldn't have wanted Zinnia to follow her in there and run her mouth off.

A sigh rasped through her like physical pain. Now she'd made such a dramatic appeal, she'd have to explain it so that he understood how vitally important silence was. 'Thanks,' she said quietly. 'As the relief manager, I think it's probably best if you have some insight into the story. Zinnia's getting agitated and uncontrolled. She's badgering me here at work, as you've seen. My family's non-conventional, as I told you.'

'Because you have two mums.' He nodded.

'Exactly.' She paused to gather her thoughts, gazing at the table top. This wasn't a subject she discussed much outside of her family. 'The trouble is that Zin was conceived by artificial insemination and the anonymous donor gave—' her cheeks burned '—what he gave knowing what he was doing. But my mum, she had an affair and I was conceived. It was only when she ended the relationship that she understood how badly she'd used him. He'd fallen in love with her – he was older and maybe she'd thought he was past all that – and he was gutted. She never told him about me because she saw how unforgivably she'd messed with his life. He had a wife and two sons who were sixteen and twenty-one at the time.'

Isaac was silent, his gaze sympathetic.

She tried to laugh but it emerged brittle and hard. 'Zin and I are only three months apart. It caused remarks all through school. Though we consider ourselves sisters others considered us stepsisters as we have no blood tie and different surnames. Thing is, there's no manual on how to *be* a child from a same-sex relationship. I feel I've missed out on half of my family but Zinnia's the opposite and says she's got two amazing women as parents and has no need to know her sperm donor.'

. For several moments she fell silent. The rain continued to pound and Doggo yawned and stretched out against the radiator. 'Mum let me think my father was a one-night stand,' she continued eventually. 'Then I caught her crying over his obituary and in the emotion of the moment, she told me.' She shook her head. 'I felt gutted, cheated, and the only way I could think of making it up to myself was to try and find my half-brothers. It was a compulsion.'

Her eyes prickled and she realised it was a relief to be able to talk about it with someone other than her family. 'I found my eldest brother straight away via the internet. I know where the other one is but I haven't met him, his wife or two kids.'

Isaac had apparently become too invested in the story to listen in silence any longer. 'What did the one you've met say to finding out he had a half-sister?'

'Nothing,' she admitted frankly, feeling the familiar snake of worry. She had to pause to swallow. 'Because of something very specific I heard him say I know that if I tell him he could refuse to have anything to do with me. So I'm not brave enough to try.'

She propped her head on her palm. 'It's a mess. My parents are worried. Zinnia's got all pugnacious, scared of having to share me. She can't stand not knowing. She wants me to choose her, I suppose, as if it were a competition. It's like a new, prickly Zin has turned up in my life and I'm feeling pressure to leave the village but not until—' she hesitated '—until I've met the other brother. I'm resentful that Zin's being difficult but also feeling guilty because I'm scaring her. And my mums too,' she added fairly.

'Wow,' he said.

She glanced at him. 'So I hope you see why it's important that you don't mention my brothers to anyone. I think whether they ever learn who I am is up to me.'

To her relief, Isaac nodded understandingly. 'Of course.'

Chapter Six

Tuesday morning. Bleurgh. Isaac was making notes to help his accountant sort out the Juno's VAT and tax situation. When his phone sounded an alert he stopped to read a text from assistant manager Tina.

Vita should be on with Andy and me tonight but she has a tummy bug. Baz has plans and Lorna can't get childcare so have asked Lily to come in and Vita will take Lily's shift on Friday.

Isaac returned, *Thanks for letting me know and for sorting it out.* Andy, in his late fifties, had taken early retirement from whatever his job had been and worked part-time in the pub. Well . . . worked? He certainly enjoyed being behind the bar, but leaning on it, talking to the punters – all while getting paid. When Isaac had gently challenged him on it the first time they were on shift together he just laughed. 'All learned from our glorious leader!'

Prickled, Isaac had raised eyebrows. 'If you're referring to Mr Tubb, he's entitled.' As the subtext was plainly 'And you're not', Andy had taken a huff and had since only accepted shifts on Isaac's days off.

He looked forward to seeing Andy's face when he discovered tonight that Isaac and his family would be eating at the pub. His parents hadn't seen The Three Fishes yet. His mum had never been completely on board with his relationship with Hayley because of the age gap yet had reacted with exasperation rather than sympathy when the end had come. Exasperation was probably his mum's normal state. His dad suffered from ME and Isaac supposed that she hadn't expected to greet her sixtieth birthday having been his carer for a decade and living on benefits.

He hoped Lily wouldn't mind working with lazybones Andy. What a troubled story she'd told him last night. For the weeks he'd known her a sunny smile had been her default expression but last night worry had puckered her forehead and drawn down the corners of her mouth. It had tugged at Isaac's heart.

He turned back to his notes, trying to pull together everything the accountant needed. Apart from the accountant's bill, HMRC was his final creditor. As soon as the 'closed' notices had gone up at the Juno he'd satisfied his payroll and other creditors and sold fixtures and inventory so he had a reasonable idea of what he was worth, which was a whole hell of a lot less than he used to be worth, but he was not sure where he was emotionally. That was harder to determine.

When Flora phoned Isaac at six thirty in the evening his paperwork had prevented him managing the trip into Derbyshire he'd hoped for, but at least he'd managed to walk the circuit of the bridleways around the village twice, which totalled over six miles according to his app.

'Hey!' Flora breezed. 'We're in the pub car park.'

'On my way down,' he responded. 'Has Dad got his chair?'

'No, he's having a good day and says he's OK on his stick.'

Isaac pulled on his jacket and, closing the door to his rooms behind him, ran downstairs and out of the back door. Spotting Flora waiting beside her aged Ford Mondeo in the car park lights, he gave her a quick hug.

She hugged him back. 'If you can help Dad, I'll bring Jeremy and Jasmine.'

'Yep, great,' he agreed.

But his mother, Stef, was first out of the car. 'Evening, Isaac,' she said, pulling her coat close around herself and shivering. 'Blimey, it's parky. Nothing to stop the wind, out here in the sticks.'

'True.' He gave her a hug, glad to see her even if he knew this was probably the first of many complaints he'd hear this evening, then went around to the other side of the car in time to help his dad to his feet. 'Hi, Dad. How are you doing?'

'Much as usual, thanks,' puffed his dad. Unfortunately, 'usual' for Ray O'Brien was weak and exhausted since ME had ravaged his body and made him prone to infections and depression. But he gave Isaac a smile and told him it was good to see him as he leaned on his arm for the short walk to the pub's front door.

Flora's kids, four-year-old Jasmine and six-year-old Jeremy, were leaping from the car, trying to evade Flora's guiding hands, shouting, 'Uncle Isaac, we're going to eat dinner at your pub!' And, 'Have you got burgers?'

Isaac grinned at their excited faces haloed with brown curls. 'We might have burgers for good children. Not sure about you though,' he added.

'We're good!' they chorused. Jeremy usually fitted that description but Jasmine greeted mischief with open arms

68

whenever she met it. Isaac had missed them after he'd left Flora's for The Three Fishes.

He led the party into the warmth, exchanging greetings with regulars such as Lily's friend and landlady Carola with her boyfriend. Lily and Andy were working behind the bar. Lily smiled while Andy pretended he was too busy serving to have noticed Isaac coming in.

Ray looked pinched by the time he released Isaac's arm and dropped down into his seat in the dining area. 'I'll keep my coat on till I just warm up. Lovely in here, boy, isn't it?' He gazed around at the tinsel on the beams and baubles fixed to the old stone walls.

'It's a nice change.' Isaac hooked his own jacket around a chair, making sure he got one that gave him a view of Andy, now leaning on the bar and chatting while Lily pulled pints. Andy realised he was being watched, straightened up and moved slowly in the direction of a waiting customer, still talking.

Isaac's mum took the seat between Isaac and Ray, leaving Flora and the children to sit together on the other side of the table. 'I cannot comprehend why you gave up Juno Lounge for this little place,' she said, proving the visit to rural life hadn't softened her up much. 'Were you just in a mood because of Hayley?'

'The relationship with Hayley ended afterwards,' Isaac pointed out. He'd made it sound like he had a choice about letting the Juno go so as not to worry his parents. Better his mum make a few caustic 'cannot comprehend' remarks than worry about him losing a heap of money.

'Still, it's nice that folk talk to you when you come in,' she said, as if realising she'd been unnecessarily negative.

The children claimed her attention and Isaac noticed Andy nattering again while Lily flew around taking up the slack. Trying not to keep watching Andy as Tina appeared behind the bar to serve too, Isaac transferred his gaze to Lily as she grabbed an order pad and approached their table with a cheery, 'Evening!' to Isaac and a smile for everybody else. 'Hello! I'm Lily. May I give you your menus?' She passed out the folded cards, then said to Flora, 'Would the children like some colouring things?'

'Thank you!' said Flora, smiling, while Jasmine and Jeremy said, 'Yes!' loudly and Stef said, 'I think you mean yes *please*, don't you?' And, 'Thank you, dear,' to Lily.

Menus were perused while Lily fetched small paper carrier bags for Jeremy and Jasmine, who took out small boxes of crayons and colouring booklets and began to discuss the pictures.

The adults tried to converse above their heads but it was stilted. Flora and Dad were complimentary about the menu while Stef kept looking around commenting how small everything was compared to the cavernous Juno Lounge with its mezzanine at one end and giant light fixtures dangling from the beams high above.

'Tell us how you're getting on,' she demanded of Isaac, turning her gaze onto him. 'We've hardly seen you these last few months. You're temporary here, aren't you? Will you be working all over Christmas? Or do you shut Christmas Day? Surely no one needs to be at the pub on Christmas Day – they should all be home with their families.' Her tone suggested that Isaac should be with his family too.

Isaac had avoided his parents during the crisis at the Juno and in its immediate aftermath from a wish not to worry them, so he went straight to the question of Christmas. 'Whether my job lasts as long as Christmas

Day isn't quite decided because the owner's in Switzerland and hasn't been cleared to come back to work. I think I'm likely to stay on into January.' Isaac became aware that Lily, passing out menus at the next table, had stopped to glance at him. 'The pub does open on Christmas Day and lunch is in the diary,' he went on. Lily's eyes widened before she returned her attention to her other customers.

Stef's eyes reddened. 'I'd just hoped that with Hayley out of the picture we'd have a proper Christmas with you this year.'

Isaac chose not to pick up on her slightly barbed comment about Hayley, understanding that his mum must be fed up with the way things were going in her life. Fifteen years ago, before Ray had become ill, they'd had good jobs and a roomy farmhouse to live in. They'd both worked on the farm, Ray working tirelessly in the fields and Stef providing meals for the farm workers and looking after the chickens and their few cows. Now Stef and Ray lived in a small house on an estate on the edge of a city. There was never enough money. No nice things. Stef, though she tried valiantly to hide it from Ray, chafed. She didn't mean to take it out on everyone around her but picking fault was free entertainment.

'Sorry, Mum,' he said, meaning it. 'I'll do my best but there has to be a licensee near enough to call on. It's the law.'

Before Stef could reply, Lily turned to their table. 'Are we ready to order?'

'Burger, chips and a b'nana,' Jasmine requested promptly.

Lily grinned as she wrote it down. 'Shall we save the banana for your dessert? Just have burger and chips for now?'

Jasmine beamed and nodded and Lily noted everybody

else's wants briskly. Her hair today was plaited down the back of her head and looped in a shiny band. 'I'll bring your drinks right over.' And she whisked away, disappearing through the counter flap in the direction of the kitchen.

'Nice girl,' observed Ray. Isaac was glad to hear him volunteering even such a short comment. He spent so much time inside himself, zapped by chronic fatigue. Generally, he reserved what energy he had for fighting his latest health crap.

Isaac turned back to Stef. 'This may be my last Christmas in the licensed trade. I'm looking for a more fun career.' And he told them all about the courses he'd booked to open the door to jobs in the fresh air.

Stef listened with visible interest. 'Will it mean you being home *next* Christmas?'

Isaac laughed. 'I will if I can.'

The drinks arrived, Lily wielding her tray as if it were a part of her. Jasmine and Jeremy dropped the crayons they'd been beginning to bicker over and fell on their Fruit Shoots with cries of, 'Yeah!' and 'Yummmmmmm!'

After a couple of appreciative sips of white wine, Stef turned back to Isaac. 'So all we need is you to settle down and give us more grandkids.'

Isaac refused to be ruffled. He gave Jasmine and Jeremy a pointed look. 'You have the best grandkids in the world already.'

Stef regarded them fondly, gently easing the Fruit Shoot bottle from Jasmine's hand. 'Don't drink it all at once, lovie, or you won't have room for a lovely burger.' She turned back to Isaac. 'But we need some more to carry on the name. Jeremy and Jasmine's surname is Scrivens, like their dad.'

'But there must be plenty of O'Briens in the world,' Isaac objected. As he was neither on duty nor driving tonight he'd ordered a pint of Amstel and he took a long draught of it.

'But not our family,' Stef pointed out. If she'd stopped there then Isaac would happily have let the conversation drift onto other topics and felt that things were going OK. However, Stef obviously couldn't resist harking back to exactly what had caused discord between them for the past several years. 'Trouble was,' she said, 'you spent all that time with Hayley and kids weren't on the cards, with her being a decade older than you.'

Lily had returned to the next table to serve drinks, chatting as she did so.

Perhaps out of embarrassment that she'd probably over-heard, Isaac found himself saying tartly, 'It was nine years and, next time, I promise to find a brood mare.' Then he felt bad for letting his annoyance show and laughed, slinging his arm around his mum to give her a hug. 'Hayley could have been younger than me and we might still not have had kids. People do make that choice. Anyway, as we've split up, it's a good job we didn't have any.'

Then he saw Flora's startled and hurt expression and cursed himself for being a thoughtless prat. He definitely needed to put a brake on his mouth. 'I'm just going to check on something.' He sought sanctuary by going behind the bar and out into the back. He was checking his phone for messages when Lily bustled in behind him carrying a pile of dirty crockery.

'Hello,' she said, sounding surprised to encounter him there. 'Something wrong?'

He looked up from his inbox. 'Me. I'm finding nothing to do for a couple of minutes while I work out how to apologise to my sister for being negative about single parenthood when she's a single mum and I love her kids to bits.'

She took a step towards the kitchen. 'They're lovely children.'

He agreed. 'And Flora's coped brilliantly since she discovered her ex-husband was using scuzzy dating sites while still married to her.' He stopped, wondering what made him tell Lily things.

'That's awful,' Lily exclaimed. Then added, 'Dating sites aren't all scuzzy though.'

He cringed. 'Crap. Have I just insulted you too? If you use dating sites then I'm sorry—'

'Not me,' she reassured him with a grin, moving off towards the clatter of the kitchen. 'But look at Carola and Owen all loved up. They met on a dating site and Carola's one of the least scuzzy people I know.'

He slid his phone back into his pocket, saying drily, 'I'm sure their site was respectable and allowed a lot of people to find love. But the one Billy used wasn't respectable and it allowed him to find extra-marital sex.'

She wrinkled her nose and resumed her course for the kitchen while Isaac, having given himself a timeout and a talking-to, made his way back into the bar. Unfortunately, the first thing his gaze lit on was Andy leaning on the bar and chatting. Beside him Tina served one customer while several others waited their turn.

Isaac's bad mood found an outlet. He came up behind Andy and said in his ear, 'Got a minute, please?' and turned on his heel.

After a few seconds Andy followed him into the back area wearing an expression that was both pugnacious and defensive. Isaac got straight to the point. 'It's great you're on friendly terms with so many villagers and I'm sure that's an asset to a village pub. However, you need to serve as well as talk, I'm afraid. I'm sure you don't mean to leave the work to others, but that's what's happening.'

Andy turned away dismissively. 'Don't worry about it, young man.'

'Andy!' Isaac's voice cracked out so loudly that Andy swung around in surprise. He spoke his next comments softly in contrast. 'Mr Tubb has left me in charge.'

The older man began to bluster. 'Harry Tubb's been my mate just about all my life. *He* trusts me.'

'In that case,' Isaac said deliberately, 'you're letting him down.'

Face turning a dull red, Andy stalked over to where the staff members hung their coats and snatched his down. 'You can take my name off the rota until Tubb gets back.'

'Noted.' Isaac watched while he struggled into his coat, saw him from the premises and strode back into the bar area. Quietly he said to Tina, 'Andy's going home and says he'll be off the rota until Mr Tubb returns. Can you and Lily manage, or shall I give you a hand?' From the corner of his eye he watched Lily race past with a plated meal in each hand.

Tina rolled her eyes. 'We're OK for now. I'll give you a shout if we get desperate.'

'Great.' Isaac had made a mental note to gently challenge Tina tomorrow on why she hadn't had a word with Andy herself but decided to leave it for now. Lily was quick and Tina, although she looked as if she strolled everywhere, got work done. Then, as he turned, he saw, waiting for him at the counter flap, his sister.

Passing through, he hugged her. 'I'm such an idiot. I let Mum wind me up. You're the best mum and your kids are the best kids. I didn't mean to imply that you're letting Jeremy and Jasmine suffer for Billy clearing off.'

Colour touched Flora's cheeks but she waved his apology away. 'I know you said it in a different context. You love the kids.' She hesitated. 'I wanted to talk to you about something else. Have you got any bar work going? I was going to sound you out more subtly but I heard what you just said to that lady—' she glanced at Tina '—and thought I'd better register my interest before you got anyone else.'

Isaac stared at her, drawing her slightly to one side to let Lily bustle through and begin serving the customers waiting at the bar. 'How will that work with the kids? Is Billy having them? Or moving back in?' His heart sank at the idea of the latter. Billy hadn't been a particularly hands-on dad and he'd made a bloody fool of Flora.

She shook her head. 'No, my friend Willow's moving in with me. She's a single mum with a girl and a boy, like me. She's moving into the spare room, her son will move in with Jeremy and her daughter with Jasmine. We're each going to work part-time and share the babysitting. We've got to do something because Billy's got himself sacked from work so he has no real income, so he doesn't have to pay for the kids and Willow's ex has done a runner. It's a nightmare, Isaac. When you were living with us and paying me board that money made all the difference.'

Around them, people laughed and chatted. Isaac stared down in dismay at his sister's embarrassed expression. 'I didn't realise or maybe I could have got a job where I didn't live in.'

She set her mouth obstinately. 'We're not your responsibility. I'm happy to work my way out of trouble.'

Hating Billy with fresh force, Isaac said, 'I'll ask Mr

Tubb as soon as I can get hold of him tomorrow. Do you need money to be going on with?'

She laughed. 'Why? Have you got any?'

'Some,' he replied honestly. He wasn't yet in a position to know what would be left after coming to agreement with HMRC and he'd paid for his courses and his living expenses while undergoing them, but he was pretty confident it would be 'some'. He had regular income while he was working here.

She gave him a hard hug. 'I'll keep you as a last resort.'

When they returned to their table in time for Lily to bring over their delicious-smelling meals he helped Flora break the news of her altered living arrangements to their parents and be very reassuring that *of course* it would work out and it was really quite an exciting and fun solution to Flora's problems.

Stef's sharp gaze saw straight through the good face Flora was putting on things and she saddened. 'Oh, Flora, I'd help you if I possibly could. But with living on benefits and caring for your dad—'

'You've got your hands full already,' Flora agreed reassuringly. 'I'll be fine if Isaac can get me a couple of shifts a week here. Willow will share the rent and utilities so you don't need to worry, Mum.'

Stef nodded but Isaac was uncomfortably aware that if the Juno hadn't fallen on its arse he would have had more in the bank to help his sister if she needed it.

Isaac Skyped Tubb next morning, Wednesday. His absent boss's face loomed on the laptop screen. 'Andy's been texting me,' he began before Isaac could raise the subject.

Not shocked to hear it, because if Andy was a buddy of Tubb's then getting his retaliation in first was an obvious strategy, Isaac told Tubb frankly about his issues with the older man, wondering whether he'd be believed. He was the unknown quantity, after all.

Tubb gave a wintry smile. 'I've already rung Tina and she confirms Andy's been taking the pee.'

Isaac nodded, liking that Tubb had sought other insight on the situation rather than taking just one person's word. 'He says he doesn't want to be on the rota till you return.'

Tubb frowned, looking restless. 'Can you find enough cover for him until the New Year? Lily's trip over here in December means you'll be down another three or four shifts because she's taking ten days. I could have a few words with Andy – but it's you who has to work with him.'

'He's made it plain he doesn't wish to work with me and someone did approach me for a couple of shifts a week,' Isaac said slowly. 'My sister, Flora. Her only relevant experience dates back to the student bar at uni. She's bright and pleasant, though. I know she'll work hard.'

Tubb's gaze sharpened. 'Does she know the pay's modest?'

'I haven't discussed that with her.' He gave the bullet points of the difficult situation in which Flora found herself. 'She just needs enough hours to give her some financial breathing space,' he finished abruptly, feeling angry about Billy all over again.

Tubb sat back. 'OK. Let's offer her 50p over minimum hourly wage. But I can't promise two shifts every week once we've cleared New Year. It goes dead for a bit.'

Isaac murmured his thanks. 'Erm,' he hesitated delicately. 'But when you return, if Andy wants his job back, then what for Flora?'

Tubb gave an even more wintry smile. 'I don't think we'll invite him to our side of the bar again.'

'I'll tell Flora she has a job.' Isaac made a note on his phone then, 'On the subject of New Year, do you know yet how long you'll want me here for?'

'Janice wants to be here in Switzerland for Christmas and Ona could have her baby any time from mid to late December anyway. And my brother Garrick's living here too now and I haven't spent Christmas with him for years.' The look in Tubb's eyes was half hopeful and half challenging.

Isaac considered for a moment, fidgeting with his phone on the desk, remembering his mum's despondence over not seeing him on Christmas Day. He knew she was struggling with the unfairness of life. 'You want me here to keep the place open on Christmas Day?'

There must have been a loud note of uncertainty in his voice because Tubb sighed. 'Put it this way, if you can't then those who've signed up for the usual Christmas lunch will be disappointed. I can't take over the reins again unless the doctors say so. My girlfriend would give me hell.' He said the word 'girlfriend' bashfully. Isaac smothered a smile. He knew from various members of staff that Tubb and Janice had worked together for years and then suddenly fallen for each other last Christmas, surprising the whole village. Tubb, divorced for ages, had fallen like a ton of bricks. Tubb cleared his throat. 'I thought you'd planned for being available into January.'

Isaac nodded. 'I had. It's my parents.' He explained his father's illness and his mother's mood.

'Got it.' Tubb picked up a pen and rolled it between his fingers. 'Your family's invited to Christmas lunch as guests of the pub, if that helps.' He checked his watch.

'Get Lily to tell you about the lunch because she was there last year. You'll see why I don't want to shut – some people don't have other places to go.'

'Leave it with me.' Isaac would at least get paid a solid sum for Christmas Day and if he could invite his parents and Flora and the kids then maybe they'd have a great time. He hoped so, anyway.

Once a few other operational matters had been covered they ended the call and Isaac first rang Flora to tell her she had a job, eliciting a whoop of relief and a profusion of thanks, then went online. Black Friday deals were already making an appearance though it was only mid November so he went onto the Mountain Warehouse website and looked at down-filled coats for his parents. Neither of them had looked warm enough in what they were wearing last night and this was going to be a cold winter, by all accounts.

As if to bear him out, a news alert flashed on his phone screen: *Brrritain brrraces itself for cold snap!*

He pressed 'buy now'. He should be glad of his uncomplicated family. His mum's occasional moroseness was nothing in comparison to the way Lily had to walk the tightrope between her families.

Chapter Seven

'Are you free tonight? Or is there any chance of you swapping shifts so you can be?' Zinnia's voice was cheerful and excited over Lily's phone.

It was just after lunch on Friday and Lily was at her small workstation, pleasurably knee deep in plans for the Switzerland trip, a big mug of coffee at her elbow and Paramore providing a soundtrack to work to.

She hadn't heard from her sister since the argument in the car park of The Three Fishes on Monday. Although Lily hated the way things were over her inconvenient desire to know people with whom she shared DNA she'd made no attempt to communicate. Maybe it was guilt . . . or maybe it was hurt.

She made her tone light and neutral. 'As it happens, I have this evening off.'

'Good!' Zinnia sounded delighted. 'You know that new club in Bettsbrough – the Ballarat? I know someone working in promotions who's offered me tickets to the opening shindig tonight. A crowd on opening night will get pictures on all the online nightlife sites. The club's super-posh and we probably won't be able to afford to get in once it gets underway.'

Lily hesitated. 'Don't you want to take George?'

'No, I want to take you,' Zinnia coaxed. 'Let's have a fab sisterly evening. I'm sorry for how I've been lately. I promise not to go on about family – any family – for the whole evening. As Bettsbrough's so near your place, I thought I could stay over,' she went on. 'We can have a meal at The Three Fishes and then go on to Ballarat for free cocktails. We'll take a taxi.'

'Why's it called the Ballarat?' Lily played for time, wondering whether Zinnia intended to keep to the letter of her declaration about family or would find a way to work on Lily to leave the village anyway.

'It's the place in Australia the woman who owns it comes from,' Zinnia said impatiently. 'Please say yes, Lily. My treat.'

She said the last so plaintively that Lily's heart melted. 'OK,' she agreed, opting to take the handsome offer at face value: a chance for them to get back on better terms. 'It sounds fun.'

Zinnia whooped gleefully. 'We'll get really glammed up. What time shall I get to yours?'

After they'd made arrangements Lily spent the rest of the afternoon working on the Switzerland trip, planning the minibus road route through England and France, researching the best motels for the overnight stop in each direction, formulating an estimate of costs for Eddie, Warwick and Alfie to discuss with their parents. The Middletones needed to support themselves so far as eating and drinking was concerned and Switzerland wasn't cheap, even if travel and accommodation expenses were being picked up by British Country Foods. Because

Acting Instrumental students were making up part of the contingent, the college was hiring the twelve-seater minibus to them at cost – though the insurance doubled that.

In just over two weeks they'd be on their way! Lily felt a ball of excitement spin in her stomach as she happily conjured up visions of Christmas markets and processions and snow. Hopefully snow. She looked at the weather app on her phone. Schützenberg was about a thousand metres above sea level but there was no snow yet. In her imagination Swiss winters always meant glorious landscapes of thick, glistening snow looking so much like scenes from advent calendars that the shutters on chalets would pop open to reveal chocolates inside.

She became so buried in her project that she barely left enough time to shower and had to pause in drying her hair to let Zinnia in when she knocked at the French doors. Wearing a big smile and carrying an overnight bag, Zinnia gave Lily a bear hug. 'This is great! I'm so glad you agreed to come. Do you want me to finish your hair?'

As Zinnia was obviously determined to embrace their sisterly love, Lily relaxed and let her wield the hairdryer, lifting her voice over its drone to update her on the Switzerland plans. Then they put on their make-up, making golf-ball eyes into the mirror while applying eyeliner and mascara. They rarely went clubbing together and it took Lily back to when they were teens living at home with Roma and Patsie. She enjoyed the fuzzy feeling it gave her.

Zinnia unzipped her bag and shook out a fuchsia pink glittery asymmetrical sheath dress, boasting one sleeve and a mid-thigh hemline. 'Ta dah!'

'Wow. You meant it when you said "glammed up".' Lily

caught the sleeve and let the sinuous, slightly scratchy material slither through her fingers.

'So what have you got?' demanded Zinnia, throwing open Lily's wardrobe without ceremony. 'How about this? This would look amazing.'

Seeing that Zinnia was brandishing a short, sequinned topaz-blue number, Lily clutched her heart and laughed. 'I haven't worn it since Bar Barcelona party nights. It's *short*.'

'Perfect for tonight.' Zinnia laid the shimmering garment on the bed. 'It's a par-tay.'

As there was nothing else in her wardrobe anywhere near as glam as Zinnia's slinky pink outfit, Lily thought she may as well give the blue dress a try and let Zinnia zip her into it. It clung to every curve under the heavy, shining sequins. She slipped her feet into black shoes. 'Erm,' she said doubtfully, gazing in the mirror at what seemed to be the entire length of her legs on show. She had to admit, though, that the dress was flattering. 'It feels really, really short.'

Zinnia emerged from wriggling into her own dress. It wasn't as short as Lily's but hugged her like a second skin. 'You look gorgeous,' she breathed. 'You have to wear it. Opening night at a posh club. Get us!' Before Lily could decide to try another outfit, Zinnia snatched up a tiny cross-body evening bag just big enough for a phone and a couple of credit cards and swung Lily around. 'Come on, let's go before they stop serving food at The Three Fishes. Do you think Carola might give us a lift down to the pub to save us staggering about in these heels?'

Carola took the request as an opportunity to visit the pub herself as she wasn't seeing Owen that night, and soon the three of them were standing at the bar with glasses of wine. Carola was drawn off into a conversation with Alexia, a woman Lily knew to be connected to the village coffee shop, the Angel Community Café, where Carola worked. Vita and Isaac were serving behind the bar.

Although she felt pretty conspicuous at being dressed for a club in the work-day surroundings of The Three Fishes, Lily had to take off her coat and sling it over a bar stool or risk cooking in the warm pub interior. Isaac's eyebrows vanished into his hair and he paused in refilling the ice bucket on the bar. 'Glad rags tonight,' he observed.

Flushing, she explained about the tickets to the new, upscale nightclub and wanting a meal first. 'If you have any tables,' she added, glancing into the dining area.

'No prob if you can wait a few minutes. My sister's joining the staff tonight and she's out the back doing the formalities with Tina. I'll get her to clear tables as soon as they come out.'

'Great, thanks.' Lily sipped her wine, deciding not to offer to clear a table herself as bending over in such a short dress might leave her feeling . . . vulnerable.

As Isaac turned away Zinnia edged closer, murmuring, 'Any progress with His Hotness?'

'Ssh!' Lily hissed in alarm. But, judging Isaac to have moved out of earshot, murmured back, 'He's not here for long.'

'Even better.' Zinnia grinned into her wine glass and waggled her brows. 'Little Christmas adventure?'

Lily gave her sister a playful nudge. 'Behave.' She was conscious of her heart giving a flutter but decided it was because she and Zin were having a lovely time together. Joy washed over her. If things improved between them then perhaps she wouldn't feel the only way to preserve their relationship would be to leave the village after Switzerland. Impulsively, she gave Zinnia a hug. 'I do love you, Zin.'

Zinnia returned the hug. 'I know. I love you too.'

Neither of them said, 'I'm sorry,' or 'I forgive you,' but sisters didn't always have to specify that stuff.

Flora appeared from the back, recognising Lily with a quick smile but hurrying in Tina's rolling wake to be shown how to clear a table – not difficult: sanitise, tidy the condiments then reset it with cutlery rolled in black napkins from the dumbwaiter and wine glasses from behind the bar.

Lots of locals were in tonight, a crowd of men frequently referred to as 'the blokey blokes' grouped around the dartboard, pints in one hand while they threw darts with the other, barracking each other and dissolving into gales of laughter. Vita and Isaac were kept busy behind the bar as Tina showed Flora the ropes.

Lily and Zinnia fell to chatting to those around them and, apart from feeling ludicrously overdressed, Lily thought she wouldn't be too unhappy if Zinnia forgot all about going on to the Ballarat. The Christmas lights reflected and refracted from every polished surface and they were surrounded by smiling faces.

A woman, entering via the front door, paused to take in the friendly, crowded, noisy scene. Lily froze, her glass of wine almost to her lips. It was Hayley, elegance personified in a narrow black dress with a stand-up collar beneath her open coat, which Lily felt pretty sure she recognised as Karen Millen, though she never shopped there herself unless in a seventy-per-cent-off sale. Her own shimmering sequins felt as garish as a Christmas tree. She watched Hayley thread her way to the bar.

'Hello, Isaac.' Hayley raised her voice over the hubbub.

Isaac's head lifted, though his hands continued to splash tonic into a tumbler containing ice, lime and gin before grabbing a fresh glass and pulling a bottle of chardonnay from the ice bucket behind him. 'Hello,' he replied neutrally, then, to the customer he placed the two drinks before: 'That'll be £8.90, please.' He took a tenner and turned to the till.

Tina smiled at Hayley. 'Can I help you?'

Hayley smiled back but said, 'I'll wait for Isaac.'

Tina nodded and moved on to serve someone else.

When he turned away from giving his customer change, Isaac's face was impassive as he moved towards Hayley. 'What can I get you?'

'If we could have a word—' she began.

Isaac leaned over the bar so that his head was close to hers but, as she was leaning on the bar herself, Lily was near enough to hear. 'I can serve you with a drink but I'm too busy to chat.'

Hayley's smile didn't waver. 'I understand. I'll have Fever-Tree tonic with ice and lime and wait until you have a moment.'

Isaac nodded but Lily could see from the look in his dark eyes that he wasn't happy. He served Hayley briskly and took her money, handing her her change and moving on to someone else.

Hayley turned away from the bar and her gaze fell on Lily. Not sure whether to feel complimented or insulted at the way Hayley's brows flew up as her gaze fell on the sequinned dress, Lily said hesitantly, 'Hello again.'

'Well, hello. Don't you look glamorous!' Hayley replied.

Lily no longer felt glamorous. She felt conspicuously

shiny. 'It's the opening of the Ballarat in Bettsbrough tonight.'

'And you got tickets? How clever of you.' Hayley smiled a perfectly lipsticked smile.

Lily wasn't sure if it was genuine or condescending but introduced Zinnia as the ticket procurer.

Flora bustled through the counter flap, took down four wine glasses and turned, skidding to a halt as she came face to face with Hayley, gazing at her with frank amazement. 'What on earth are you doing here?'

Hayley smiled. 'I should say the same to you. Are you working here? How nice—'

'Sorry,' said Flora, clicking back into motion. 'Busy night. Lily, your table's ready if you'd like to go over. I'll bring the menus.'

'Thanks.' Lily picked up her coat, glad her conversation with Hayley had been interrupted. The older woman was *so* . . . well, just so. Groomed. Sophisticated. Polished. Assured. Lily didn't feel any of those things.

But then Zinnia's phone began to ring and she fished for it in her evening bag to read the screen. 'It's George.'

As she stayed where she was to take the call from her boyfriend, Lily picked up Zinnia's coat too, intending to take both to the table when Zinnia let out a piercing squawk of dismay. 'Oh, no! How? Are you OK? Oh, *no*, I can't *believe* it.'

Lily halted, alarmed.

Without interrupting her conversation, Zinnia pulled her coat from Lily's arms and began to wriggle into it. 'Of course I'm coming home! I'll be there as soon as I've picked up my car from Lily's.' Ending the call with her eyes full of tears, Zinnia fumbled the rest of the way into her coat. 'That was George. We've had a kitchen fire! The fire brigade's there and everything. It's an absolute mess, apparently.'

'That's awful!' Lily gasped. 'Is George OK?'

'Fine, but, oh, Lily, our lovely new kitchen! We haven't even paid a year off the loan yet. I've got to go. I can't go clubbing and leave him with it.' She sloshed what was left of her wine into Lily's glass.

'Should I come? Can I help?' But Lily was already talking to Zinnia's back as she hurled herself through the crowd, waving distractedly behind her.

With a feeling of anticlimax Lily explained the situation to Flora as she ferried crockery around. 'So I won't take up a dining table. I can have my fish and chips here in the bar.' People were drifting into the dining area now tables were clear and the bar wasn't quite so busy. She told Flora how to put the order through on the till and, giving Hayley a parting smile, slid into one of the vacant seats at a small table in the middle of the bar. She was startled when Hayley slid into the other chair.

'I might as well wait for Isaac in comfort.' Hayley smiled. 'How has he been? I expect he's settled in well here.'

'Fine,' returned Lily, wishing her meal would come.

Hayley hesitated, seemingly choosing her words. 'Is he on a nice even keel? I expect he told you that we quite recently split up.'

Really not wanting to be part of a conversation about her boss, and wondering whether Hayley was hoping to be told Isaac was pining for her, Lily took a swig from her wine. 'Isaac seems absolutely fine whenever we're together. I wouldn't worry.' She realised that made it sound as if she was friendlier with Isaac than was the case but Hayley taking aside a member of Isaac's staff for information made her skin itch.

Then Flora, who'd chosen that moment to arrive with fish and chips, cutlery and condiments on a tray said with a mischievous twinkle, 'Isaac's doing great. He missed Doggo, of course . . . but now he's got him back.'

'Of course.' Hayley gave an uncomfortable smile.

Isaac's first shock of the evening had been the sight of Lily and her sister shucking off their coats to demonstrate that on the scale of dressing up to the nines they'd achieved ten. The dark-haired sister was attractive in shocking pink but Lily was sexy as hell in a dress that looked to be made entirely of ice-blue sequins. Isaac's heart misstepped as he noted what it did for her curves and shapely legs. He was usually drawn to dark-haired women like Hayley but Lily smiled and glowed like the sun glinting off frost. It was the first time he'd seen her blonde hair down and it was just long enough to fall to her breasts, curving around them almost like a pair of hands . . .

Impatiently, he told himself to stop thinking with that part of his body and concentrate on his work. The bar was crowded enough to keep the staff on their toes and it was Flora's first night. He'd purposely left her in Tina's hands to demonstrate to other team members that being sister to the relief manager at The Three Fishes wouldn't get her special treatment.

The second shock of the evening had been when he heard Hayley speak his name. Irritation prickling through him, he'd wanted to say, 'What are you doing here again?' Instead, he'd made her wait until he wasn't as busy which, in his estimation, might be a while.

When he spotted her talking to Lily an hour or so later he felt uncomfortable, though he wasn't sure why. Maybe it was Lily's wary expression and stiffly folded arms.

Tina was serving at the same time as keeping an eye on Flora so once Lily had been served her food Isaac slipped over to their table and touched Hayley's arm. 'Would you like to follow me?' He picked up her drink and led her to a small table in the corner of the dining area. He didn't get a drink for himself or give any indication that this was a social event.

Gracefully, Hayley sank into the chair opposite him and smiled. 'How are you?'

'Busy,' he replied economically. 'What can I do for you?'

Her smile widened. 'I'd hoped to see Doggo.'

Isaac was swamped by a wave of anger. Leaning his arms on the wooden table, he dropped his voice so Hayley had to crane close in order to hear. 'Surely you don't think you can just turn up out of the blue and I'll stop work to take you up to my accommodation to make nice with Doggo?'

The smile became fixed. 'It was . . . an impulse.'

'But uncharacteristic of you to not only spend another of your evenings off to come here but to expect me to stop work. Is something else motivating your actions?'

The smile vanished and her chin lifted. 'Like what?' There was a hint of injury in her tone.

People who didn't know how to read her might let that hint of injury make them doubt their instincts. But not him. 'I think what brings you here is me.' He held up a hand as she tried to interrupt. 'No, I don't mean that I suspect you of wanting to reverse the break-up. I'm sure you're entirely comfortable with your decision to move on with your life. I think it's what I represent – failure.'

Hayley frowned, obviously wrong-footed but, rather than rush into a slew of questions, she propped her chin in her hand and waited.

'That I cut my losses at the Juno was, to you, a failure. But it led you to fail too,' he expanded. Ignoring the shocked widening of her eyes he pressed on in his softly spoken assault. 'You've realised you failed me when I sailed into trouble – the rat to my sinking ship. When you kindly recommended me when Mr Tubb was looking for somebody it was out of a need to reassure yourself that you're a good person. And now you're circling back to see how I'm doing in that job to fulfil a need to square your conscience. You think that you've rehomed me, like Doggo.'

Hayley sat perfectly still, but she'd paled, her lipstick appearing very red.

'If you'd really like to see Doggo,' Isaac continued, still in the same soft voice, 'then contact me ahead so we can agree on a convenient time. A busy Friday evening is not it.'

When she replied, her voice was hoarse. 'You sound bitter. I'd hoped we'd always be friends.'

He considered her words. 'I suppose I am bitter and I expect more of my friends than to let me down. I certainly expected more of my partner and lover than to end things by telling me that my attraction was my success. And my success had gone.' He saw her flinch.

'I'm sorry I made you feel that way,' she whispered. Shakily, she smoothed her hair – unnecessarily. As usual, it was a smooth, shining cap. 'Isaac, you were always so kind.' She halted.

When she didn't say any more he rose, softening his voice. 'I certainly don't want things between us to be sourer than needs be but I need to get back to work now. Ping me a text about Doggo when you want to see him. Maybe take him for a walk.' He didn't want her in his space upstairs. He said goodnight and returned to his post behind the bar, smiling at Carola who was waving a twenty-pound note.

As he moved on to the next customer and then the next, observing everything going on around the bar, he sent Flora off to clear tables and reset them, then to tell a group apologetically that the kitchen would be closing soon so she'd have to take their dessert order now or never. He was aware of Hayley slowly finishing her drink at the table in the corner, shaking her head when Flora asked her something.

Lily had finished her solitary meal and drifted over to talk to a group near the door, her back to him. Despite his good resolutions, his gaze lingered on the perfect round-ness of her behind in the clingy dress. Of course, that was the moment Hayley had to stalk across the room, sliding neatly into her coat ready to greet the winter outside.

Quite obviously catching the direction of his gaze, she drew on her usual poised, protective armour, looking between him and Lily with an expression that said, 'Oh, Isaac. Really? A junior co-worker?' before she turned, her long coat swinging, and flipped her way through the front door.

If she'd given him that look to annoy him then she'd succeeded, making him feel like asking Lily out just to annoy Hayley back.

OK, it wasn't just to annoy Hayley . . .

Mentally, he rolled his eyes at himself and as the bar thinned went about his duties, reminding himself about the disadvantages of hitting on any co-worker. Relationships between team members fostered favouritism, causing resentment amongst the non-favoured. Awkward atmos-pheres resulted.

It had always been against his code. Or, he mentally corrected himself, against the code that had been in place at the casino and he'd taken with him when he set up Juno Lounge. A lot of the female staff at the Juno had been students, much younger than him and more vulnerable, even if they sometimes didn't act it. He still broke into a sweat when he remembered the eighteen-year-old girl who'd offered him what she termed a 'boss with benefits deal'. That definitely came under the heading of 'wrong' in his mind. All in all, it was better to be in the habit of not thinking of co-workers romantically.

But then Lily turned up in a dress that brought her curvaceous body sharply to his attention. Lily was a thirty-something like him and he was pretty sure she knew her own mind, though she was junior to him in the team, if you could call the bar staff at The Three Fishes anything so official-sounding as a team.

They still had to work together.

But not forever. Not for long, in fact.

Lily was leaning on the bar now, chattering with customers and bar staff alike. She'd taken off her high-heeled shoes and hooked them neatly over the brass foot rail. Wine glass in hand she was laughing at something one of the men from the garage had said, hair tumbling down her back. There was something a bit Kate Winslet about the direct way she looked at everyone. As Isaac watched, a couple of the blokey blokes from the darts game came over to join the conversation, then the whole group laughed. She caught Isaac watching and gave him a long look, one he couldn't decipher.

Heaving an inner sigh, he took himself off into the back area and on into the kitchen to see how their clean-down was going and how Chef, a bear-like man with bushy brown hair and a shorn beard and whose real name of Brian no one ever used, had coped tonight. They'd been so busy that Isaac anticipated a request for an extra kitchen porter on Friday and Saturday nights until after Christmas and New Year.

Chef was, as with most chefs Isaac had encountered, king of his domain, always in action and always grumpy. He was stuffing his chef whites into the laundry bag when Isaac found him. The rest of the kitchen staff had already gone home. When Isaac asked how they'd coped with the numbers tonight he looked around his gleaming-clean kingdom and grunted. 'Not bad.' He put on his coat leaving Isaac to surmise, as the outside door swung closed behind him, that if Chef needed another kitchen porter he'd say so.

Isaac checked his watch. Soon it would be time to close and cash up. He looked up and saw Lily hovering, regarding him uncertainly. Her shoes were back on her feet; her hair shone under the lights almost as brightly as the sequins of her dress.

'Going clubbing now?' he asked, as she didn't immediately state the reason for standing alone in the back instead of out in the bar with her friends.

She grimaced. 'It went out the window. Zinnia had to rush home because they had a kitchen fire. She's texted to say the fire's out, no one was hurt but it caused a lot of damage and now the back door won't shut so her boyfriend's trying to find someone to make the house secure. Looks like the blaze began in the extractor.'

Isaac hadn't even noticed Zinnia leaving. 'Horrible mess to clear up, I expect.' He made to skirt around her and return to the bar.

'Um . . .' she began, fidgeting with her fingers. 'I've sort of got to tell you something.'

He paused. 'OK.'

She glanced behind her, as if to check they were alone. Her cheeks were pink, probably from the wine she'd been drinking steadily all evening. 'Hayley, well, she seemed to be making a point of asking about you. I felt uncomfortable so I was a bit cool with her and may have made it sound as if we're cosier than we are. Then I realised that if she was here to try to reignite your relationship then I shouldn't have.'

'Don't worry,' he said, not really comprehending why Lily was feeling the need to confess. Was there some kind of *in vino veritas* thing going on? She'd had a drink and was letting things show that she'd usually hide? Or was that just wishful thinking on his part because he was over-aware of how incredible she looked? 'Hayley was behaving oddly tonight but I don't think it was about reigniting anything. It's not in her character to look back or have regrets. She rarely admits, even to herself, that she's made a mistake.'

Lily's nose wrinkled just at the bridge, where she had a few faint freckles. 'She must have had some reason for the way she was asking about you. Maybe she's missing having someone to confide in.'

'She's incredibly self-reliant,' he replied. 'Her parents died young, she has a couple of good friends but she's not one to need much in the way of emotional support.'

Just then Flora barrelled in from the bar. 'Tina says to tell you she's locking up. Isaac, by the way, I sort of hinted to Hayley you missed Doggo more than you missed her. I think she was embarrassing Lily, fishing for information about you.'

'Right. Thanks for rushing to my rescue,' he said, in such a way that he could have been speaking to either woman. 'Don't worry. I don't miss Hayley.'

And that could have been directed at either woman, too.

It was almost midnight, after he'd closed up and taken Doggo out for a quick last walk, checking everything was OK around the outside of the pub, when Isaac made his way to his room, yawning. He kicked off his shoes and stripped off his shirt, then took his phone out of his pocket and saw a text from Hayley.

I didn't mean to annoy you tonight. You're right, I shouldn't just turn up and expect things but I have a lot on my mind and I suppose I was insensitive. Is it possible for me to pick Doggo up and take him for a walk tomorrow (Saturday)?

Isaac replied: *That would be great as the pub will probably be busy all day. Afternoon?* He hesitated, then added, *I'm sorry if I was abrupt with you.* He threw off the rest of his clothes and brushed his teeth before his phone chirped again.

No problem. OK to pick Doggo up at two?

He said it was, then went to bed reflecting that Hayley having a lot on her mind might be the reason she hadn't snapped back at him when he'd been angry with her. She usually met any challenge to her behaviour with an icy salvo.

Next day, she continued with the uncharacteristic restraint. After arriving punctually at two she waited quietly in the bar while Isaac fetched Doggo. She made no move to interact with his staff apart from to offer courteous smiles to Lorna behind the bar and Baz, waiting tables. Doggo flung himself at her, writhing in delight at her feet. When she turned for the door with his lead in her hand he burst into his rocking-horse gallop on the spot.

She returned him nearly three hours later, and he was still waving his tail. 'Here he is, safe and sound.' She smiled brightly as Isaac came around the bar to take the lead. Then she crouched beside Doggo and gave him a big hug, her eyes becoming suddenly pink.

It made Isaac wonder why on earth she gave Doggo up but she didn't hang around and, after watching her hurry out, Isaac took Doggo upstairs no wiser as to the workings of Hayley's mind.

Chapter Eight

Blackened kitchen units and ceiling, melted appliances and food packets, the warped blind at the window: they were like festering scars on Zinnia and George's sweet little terraced house in Peterborough. The smoke had painted long black-brown shadows in the hall and sitting room too.

George had burns to his hands and wasn't allowed to help with the clear-up when Lily, Roma and Patsie drove over on Saturday afternoon. Zinnia hugged everyone and cried. Even if helping meant she didn't get to singing practice, Lily knew she'd done the right thing as she watched her mum and Patsie bundle back their hair, roll up their sleeves and wage war against the greasy black soot. Later, as sleet whispered at the windows, they all squashed cosily into the sitting room together and ate fish and chips from a nearby takeaway.

The next day, Sunday, Lily wasn't due at the pub till evening so had plenty of time to devote to a planning meeting with Carola. It was only two weeks and one day before they'd be on their way to Switzerland! Owen cooked

Sunday lunch in Carola's large, well-equipped kitchen watching the grand prix on the kitchen TV through his trendy glasses while Lily and Carola sat at the dining room table with lists. They went over the programmes, who'd share rooms, a checklist for instruments and equipment. Lists, more lists, and lists of lists.

Over the following couple of days Lily felt as if she ate and slept the Switzerland trip. After Max's approval she sent the final files to the printer for clings, backdrops and signage – which would be applied by a crew in Schützenberg as she travelled from England and would be in place when she arrived – and reconfirmed details of the rented furniture for the trade fair stand. Then she sent her video loops to Max and copied in Kirstin, another contact on the show team.

On Wednesday evening they rehearsed the songs to be performed at Food, Lifestyle & Health in programme order. At nine they took a break to eat fruit loaf Carola had made, then Lily broke out the black overshirts that had arrived earlier in the week.

'This is a freakin' tent!' Eddie mocked, holding his up.

'Or a bedspread,' Warwick contributed, curling his lip as he inspected his shirt front and back.

Warwick was never shy at voicing his opinion and knowing others often took their lead from him and seeing Charlotte and Emily already rolling girly eyes, Lily hastened to head him off before she got a chorus of, 'Not wearing that!' from the teenagers. 'I don't think they'll be too big, actually. Everybody put your coat on and do it up. Now put the shirts over the top, and add your hat and scarf.'

With a show of reluctance from some, everyone

complied. 'There! We look great,' Carola said, adjusting the angle of her hat.

'Oh, right, yeah, that's better,' Warwick conceded, while Emily threw him a red knitted hat.

Good humour restored with a bit of hat pulling and scarf strangling, Carola got out her selfie stick and they all squashed together for a group photo to put up on the village Facebook page.

'The red and black go well together,' Neil said with satisfaction.

'Not as crap as I expected,' added Alfie, doubling his scarf and pulling the ends through the loop.

Carola glanced at her phone. 'Isaac's commented on the pic I just put up on Facebook. He says come down to have our photo taken in the bar for the pub's social media channels and he'll stand us all a drink.'

'Awesome!' The teens turned as one and headed for the door, Franciszka and Neil in their wake.

Lily rolled her eyes at Carola. 'I'd hoped to get another run-through.'

Carola sighed. 'I shouldn't have just read that out loud, should I? Eddie and Warwick are already eighteen so I definitely read the light of "free beer" in their eyes.' Then she brightened. 'Let's go along though. I have an idea.'

She refused to be drawn while the group hurried through the frosty evening and burst into the bar, cheeks almost as red as their hats. The bar was about half full and the group clustered around the bar while Isaac, as good as his word, gave them all a drink and, Lily noticed, paid for the round himself, using the contactless payment feature on his phone.

'Right,' he said, coming out into the customer area, his phone still in his hand. 'Let's get some photos of you with the bar in the background and all the Christmas lights above your heads. Tall people at the back and shorter in front.'

That effectively meant the four males at the back and five women in the front to say, 'Cheers!' and raise their glasses at Isaac as he snapped shots. A couple of other people in the bar took pictures too and Carola, being very businesslike, called out, 'Use the hashtags "Middletones" and "Middledip" if you're putting us on social media.'

'And "The Three Fishes",' Isaac added, sending Carola an approving look.

But Carola was already organising the next shot. 'How about a vid of us singing? Let's begin with "Let it Snow". We'll have to do it unaccompanied but let me give you an E.' She opened the musical keyboard app on her phone and touched the E key. 'Ready, everyone? Three, two, one . . . *Oh* . . .'

Well-rehearsed, the Middletones took the melody up, Neil filling with low *boom boom booms* between phrases; Franciszka, an alto, closing her eyes to join him in the harmonies.

Isaac began to move slowly across the front of them with his phone on video and more phones appeared amongst the clientele. Carola made the 'sing up!' signal to what had now become their audience and several joined in, swaying as they sang. Melanie from the shop held hands with her boyfriend, sharing a table with Cleo and Justin, Cleo's sister Liza and her blond husband, Dominic, Gabe, and another half-dozen people who Lily knew by sight.

Lily felt the lift in her chest that came with blending her voice with the voices of others. She was boiling hot though and, without pausing in singing about snow not

102

stoppin', pulled off her hat and unwound her scarf, dropping both on the bar. Slowly, she pulled the overshirt over her head and then, after smoothing her hair and flipping it back over her shoulders, unpopped a button on her coat on the first beat of each bar, sliding her arms out of the sleeves just in time to follow the slowing tempo indicated by Carola's conducting hand and to deliciously draw out the final *snooooow*.

The makeshift audience burst into applause and, laughing, Lily glanced over at Isaac.

His phone was still in his hand but his gaze was unwaveringly fixed on her.

She swallowed as she heard an echo of Zinnia referring to him as 'His Hotness'. For several moments everyone else seemed to fade from the room.

Then she became aware that the applause had ended and the others began to take off their overshirts and outdoor things too, heaping them on bar stools as Carola announced 'Hark the Herald Angels Sing' and sounded an F on her phone app before counting them in.

Lily joined in automatically, bringing her mind back to the well-known words, keeping Carola in her peripheral view for cues, letting her throat relax and the melody soar.

Before long the Middletones had performed all of their short programme, which meant Carola and Lily had got the second run-through they'd wanted. The entire bar joined in with 'We Wish You a Merry Christmas' and the Middletones broke formation to join those seated at tables and adding their voices to the general chat.

Isaac returned to his post behind the bar beside Lorna as customers queued to be served. Lorna, probably the quietest of the bar staff, smiled at Lily. 'That was lovely.'

'Thanks.' They chatted about the approach of Christmas

and Lily watched drinks being poured. When the rush was over Isaac disappeared, probably to perform one of the dozens of jobs that fell to him – assessing the diary, making any adjustments to the staff rota, checking temperatures in the beer cellar. Lily carried her wine across the room to grab a place on a bench seat next to Carola, close to the fireplace she'd decorated with greenery.

Isaac reappeared with Doggo wearing his harness and lead and a big canine grin. Isaac blew on his hands. 'I've just taken Doggo for a comfort break. It's Antarctica out there. As there are no other dogs in the bar right now I thought I'd bring him in for a bit of company.'

Gabe, animal lover extraordinaire, beamed. 'Quite right. Dalmatians get destructive if they're left alone too much. It's like putting them in prison.' He gave Doggo a fuss around his ears, which made him shut his eyes in bliss.

Carola moved closer to Gabe, patting the space she'd made between her and Lily. 'Sit down and get the benefit of the fire, Isaac.'

After a hesitation, Isaac smiled. 'Thanks.' He sat down, his wide shoulders filling the space, his arm touching Lily's. She lifted her wine glass to him. 'Thanks for the drink.'

'My pleasure.'

She lowered her voice, which had the effect of making him dip his head close to hers in order to hear. It hadn't been premeditated on her part but she found herself enjoying his proximity and the whiff of shaving gel. 'Was it a smooth move on your part to get the Middletones down here to fill up your bar? Or were you just hit with the urge to buy a large round of drinks?'

He laughed under his breath. 'Neither. I'd talked to Mr Tubb about reinvigorating our social media channels and

I was looking around Facebook when I saw Carola had posted a pic of you guys. I invited you on impulse. But it's true I've noticed people go home early on winter's evenings sometimes and your singing made them stick around.'

'But,' she said, watching Doggo shove his head onto his master's thigh and Isaac lifting his large hand to fondle the dog's ears, 'you've no need to implement initiatives, have you? You're just minding the place for Tubb while he's off sick.'

When he shook his head his hair slipped over his forehead. 'I just like to do the best job I can – within the bounds of this being someone else's pub. It took me a while to appreciate the charm of The Three Fishes but it's growing on me. I like living in the country.' He went on, telling her about his childhood when his dad had worked on a farm and he and Flora had had a lot of freedom.

As she listened, sipping her wine, she envisioned him as a boy, climbing trees and lending a hand on the farm. Doggo moved over to hook a big paw over her knee. As he'd obviously intended, she took over the ear fondling, letting the silky fur pass through her fingers. It was nice to be this side of the bar, relaxing, she thought. Cosy. She could admire her handiwork with the lights around the bar a jumble of glowing colours above the bijou Christmas trees.

'Of course, Dad was well then,' Isaac sighed. 'Before bloody ME got its horrible claws into him.'

'Poor guy,' she sympathised. She thought about the evening his parents had come to The Three Fishes and the gaunt, pale man who'd leaned heavily on a stick. 'By the way, sorry I was eavesdropping but I heard you saying to your family that you might be here for Christmas

Day. Do you realise there's a lunch and that Chef doesn't work on Christmas Day?'

His eyebrows lifted. 'So Nate runs the kitchen?' Nate was the second chef.

She laughed. 'None of the kitchen staff come in. Tubb cooks it all himself. It's his foible. Apparently he knows what it's like to have nowhere to go and no one to be with on Christmas Day so he opens the pub. There's just the one menu for the Christmas Day lunch – two if you count the veggie option. Last year, Janice did desserts but otherwise it's down to him.'

'Fucksake,' he murmured under his breath, frowning blackly. 'I hope everyone wants salad. There are about fourteen people booked.'

A laugh shook through her. 'Oh, dear. But fourteen's not too bad, not when you're serving more or less the same thing to everybody and you have a catering kitchen. My parents have often given dinner parties that size. And besides, the kitchen staff do a lot of prep for the Christmas lunch before they leave on Christmas Eve.'

'So you could do it?' Isaac asked in a hopeful-but-not-optimistic way.

Lily put up her hands to halt him there. 'I'm expected at Mum and Patsie's for Christmas lunch. Otherwise I would at least take Janice's role and do the desserts.'

Further up the table Gabe was trying to get the singing going again, teaching them all his own words, singing, fairly melodiously, 'We wish you a merry Christmas and a sausage on a string. We hope it will choke you for making us sing.' A wave of laughter greeted his ditty and people began to join in, putting great whooshes of emphasis on 'We WISH you a merry CHRIStmas' and trying to come up with silly words to trump Gabe's.

106

Beneath the noise Isaac said with mock solemnity, 'I wonder if I can get your mums to disinvite you? Tell them I want you?'

When he smiled something twirled inside her. Was it because he'd said he wanted her? He'd said it in innocent enough context but his gaze was . . . well, she was pretty sure it was interested. And what Zinnia had said about a little Christmas adventure flashed into her mind. She'd only slept with one man since calling it quits with Sergio and it had been too soon, a brief rebound affair, a rite of passage as a single-again woman. She was thirty-six, for goodness' sake. Forty was only a few years away and wasn't that when everything from skin elasticity to eyesight began to suffer? She shouldn't let life pass her by. And sex was part of life wasn't it? She was acutely aware of the warmth of his arm and his thigh brushing hers.

Playfully, she narrowed her eyes at Isaac. 'Patsie does the most incredible side dishes like sweet potato and cream cheese with cashew nuts. It's a meal not to be missed and don't even think about getting me disinvited . . . no matter how much you want me.' She added the rider experimentally and saw something flare in his eyes, giving her reason to believe he hadn't missed the way she'd batted the 'want' word back at him.

'Shame I can't tempt you.' His eyes smiled and there was an instant of hesitation, of connection, before he rose, returning to his usual, workaday self. 'Then I'll have to get Chef to talk me through how to manage on my own. C'mon, Doggo. The kitchen's shut now so you can come in the back with me until closing.' He said his goodnights and left Lily staring after him, thinking that he definitely could tempt her. In fact, she wished he would.

* * *

The next morning was icy cold when Isaac took Doggo out. Huge purple clouds piled up in the sky and the wind whipped the branches of the trees and made Isaac's face sting. He pulled down his beanie hat and tugged up his coat collar.

Doggo raced around with his ears back as if iron cold was his favourite thing, his breath a small white cloud around his snout. He looked at Isaac, eyes shining and tail beating as if to say, 'Isn't this *great*?' Sometimes he raced back and pranced around Isaac's feet, then arrowed off again to sniff and snort at the scents lurking in the nettles that edged the path.

Isaac soon covered a couple of miles across the playing fields and down the bridleway at the edge of the Carlysle Estate, vaulting a stile and following the path into the woods around a small lake. The path crossed Little Lane then ran by the stream that fed the lake and over a fallen tree used as a bridge. Soon he was heading towards the ford that stood across the road and down the bank from The Three Fishes. His original plan had been to continue on the footpath around the top end of the village, the newer part, and back into the Carlysle Estate via the home farm to emerge again in Port Road near the playing fields. However, he'd kept an eye firmly on the sky, which had become increasingly dark. The ford would allow him to cut short his walk and head back to the pub, avoiding whatever was brewing in those purple clouds.

As he strode, his mind wandered to Lily. He was building up quite a store of mental images of her. Most prominent was how she'd looked in that short, tight, shiny blue dress a few evenings ago, her blonde hair hanging loose, but even in her pub uniform of black polo shirt and trousers, designed to be effacing, he was aware of her. Last night she'd looked different again in blue jeans that clung and a lilac jumper bearing a picture of a white kitten in a snow globe. He found himself smiling as he remembered her teasing him, flirting, daring him to react. *No matter how much you want me.* Lying sleepless in bed a couple of hours later he'd wanted her so much his quilt had been in danger of combusting.

Like a saddo, he'd even viewed the video of the choir he'd taken to watch the way Lily's lips moved.

Then suddenly he had a brand-new image of her because there she was as he rounded a curve in the path, standing by the ford and wearing a navy coat embroidered with flowers and a turquoise scarf that fluttered in the wind. She was watching the thunderclouds boiling across the sky. Her hair was pulled into a ball atop her head and tendrils flew around her face. He wanted to take out his phone and take a picture to capture her intensity. *Girl and sky.*

Before he could do anything so stupid Doggo gave a bark and plunged into a gallop, tail beating as he recognised a chum.

Lily turned. 'Hello, Doggo,' floated back to Isaac on a gust of wind.

Doggo treated her to his happy dance before racing back to Isaac as if to say, 'Look who I found!' Lily watched Isaac approach with a smile.

'It's wild this morning.' He watched the wind trying to blow her hood up onto her head.

She shoved it back, her eyes sparkling. 'It's crazy. I was going to go for a walk but the sky looks ominous.'

'Not working?' Isaac stuffed his hands in his pockets, Doggo's lead jangling from his wrist.

'Day off.' A smile lit her face. 'I've pressed the button

on everything I need to do with my designer's hat on for Switzerland – the Food, Lifestyle & Health show and the Christmas market. I'm thinking about either calling in at the Angel café or calling one of my old friends in Peterborough to make good on one of those vague social media exchanges about meeting up.' She grinned. 'You're looking pretty off duty yourself.'

He rubbed his stubble. 'It's good to have a couple of down hours before I start on my working day.'

A gust of wind pushed her an involuntary step towards him. 'Whoo! I think I'd better go back.' Barely were the words out of her mouth when thunder rumbled overhead. Doggo's tail ceased to wag and he curled it between his legs instead. Lily sent an apprehensive look skywards. 'Make that I definitely need to go back.' Then she jumped as a hailstone bounced from the top of her head. 'Ow!'

She hastily dragged up her hood as, with a great clap of thunder, more hail flew on the wind, plopping in the stream beside where they stood. White balls bounced from the ground and from poor Doggo, who hunched his spine and rolled his eyes, scrabbling at Isaac's legs as if trying to scale them. Isaac gazed around at white missiles bouncing from the ground and from their coats. 'Hailstones? They're huge.' As they came under still heavier bombardment twigs began to snap from trees that bowed before the howling wind, creating an astonishing level of noise.

Isaac grabbed Doggo's harness and clipped on the lead. 'Come on, let's make a run for the pub.'

'You're always sheltering me from inhospitable weather.' But Lily picked her way across the ford and scrambled up through the moving curtain to the road, squeaking and trying to hold her hood to shield her face from the vicious white onslaught. Isaac grabbed her free hand as

110

she slithered on the marble-like chunks of ice that drummed on the road. Ice stung their faces and slid into the collar of Isaac's coat. Doggo whined, too upset and worried to even growl back at the ever-louder thunder, skittering between them as they ran, in danger of sending them flying.

It looked as if someone had covered the tarmac of the car park with white marbles when they rounded the corner and Isaac let go of Lily's hand to fumble with the door key, hampered by Doggo trying to shelter between the door and his master's legs. Turning her back on the driving hail, Lily crouched to pull Doggo into her embrace. Shielded, he immediately calmed, though his tail tip quivered as if to signal 'I don't know what's going on but I don't like it!'

When Isaac flung open the door Doggo launched himself into warmth and safety, almost knocking Lily onto her back. Possessed of slightly better manners, Isaac helped her inside and slammed the door. The hail clattered against the wood as if angry at being cheated but at last they were safe from its spite.

'Phew, that was Siberian.' She wiped her damp pink face with her hands. 'Thanks.'

'My pleasure.' He pulled off his hat and, turning it inside out, used it to dry his face. It was too early for anyone else to be at the pub. Even Franciszka wouldn't be in to vacuum carpets and clean the loos for another hour.

Doggo, restored to his usual ebullient self now the attack of the hailstones had stopped, raced ahead and was already rolling on the landing carpet when Isaac got there. 'Stop it!' he commanded. Then, to Lily: 'Would you like to go into the kitchen? I'll get his towel.' He let himself into his own room while Lily crossed the landing, chatting to the dog. When Isaac caught up with them, she'd hung her coat on the back of a chair. Isaac grabbed Doggo and briskly rubbed his black-and-white coat. Doggo tried to play tug o' war with the towel, growling with a ferocity belied by the furious wagging of his tail.

'Has he settled down in the village?' Lily asked, leaning on the table, laughing when Isaac used the towel to tow Doggo around the kitchen floor.

'Apparently. I sprint up regularly to take him to the dog loo and maybe throw the ball for him. With that and long walks, he's doing OK.'

'And how about you? How do you like living here?' Her blue eyes were watching him now. Tendrils of hair had escaped her bun and frizzed around her head as if she'd received a static shock. She wore no make-up this morning and her skin was pink and fresh.

'I like it but I won't be settling. I came here as a stopgap before I set off on my change-of-career adventure.' He let go of his end of the towel and Doggo pounced on it, shaking it savagely. Then he dragged it into his bed and lay on it as if to show it who was boss.

Lily gave a reminiscent smile. 'I didn't intend to stay here long, either. Then I fell in love with the place.' Her smile became wistful. 'How long I stay is up for debate. Zinnia extended an olive branch by inviting me out on Friday but I know she'd like me to move on after Switzerland.' She sighed.

Isaac moved closer, captured by the regret in her eyes. 'It seems unfair if she expects you to change your whole way of life to accommodate her insecurities.'

She pulled a face. 'Agree. But I can't push her on it now she's up to her ears in the aftermath of the fire. I've made up my mind to forget it for now and just enjoy the run-up to our trip.' Wistfulness gone, she sent him a mischievous glance. 'Like you, I'm ripe for a little adventure.'

All at once the atmosphere was charged. There was something in her gaze, the deliberate way she delivered the words as if he was meant to pick up a cue. It made him imagine what it might be like to share an adventure with Lily, an adventure that might also be called a fling and involve hot kisses and discarded clothes. As if the vision were controlling him he inched closer. 'Intriguing,' he murmured. Her eyebrows rose as if encouraging him to go on and he told himself not to, even while his mouth said, 'You're intriguing. I've been trying hard not to like you.'

Interest sharpened her gaze and she replied seriously, 'How's that going?'

He sighed. 'You're hard to get out of my mind. I like you more all the time. I'd love to . . .' He looked at her mouth. Stopped. Collected himself. 'But I really am not staying long. If Mr Tubb decides to retire then he'll sell. If he comes back then he won't need me. Either way, I'm gone. I think you have a right to expect more than that.' Tentatively, he looped his fingers with hers, not sure if it was wrong to even discuss it or worse to let her pass out of his life without acting on the attraction he felt.

'Expect?' she said softly. 'I expect little from men. Maybe it's because I was brought up in an all-female household but I honestly don't think I've relied on one in my life. Even Sergio. It wasn't that hard to part from him – and we were married.' This time it was she who took a tiny step closer.

Another inch and they'd be touching.

His hand tightened on hers. 'A gorgeous, sunny woman

who doesn't mind men who don't want to be relied upon. My Christmas may have come early.' His heart rate had picked up at her nearness, at the fresh, damp smell of her hair.

Lily laughed. Her low, husky chuckle always caught his attention. When somebody said something witty first her eyes would smile, then dance, before the chuckle escaped onto the air to touch a chord deep inside him. He leaned forward and kissed her.

It wasn't really a decision. It was a compulsion; something to which he could only give in. Her mouth was warm in a cold face, sweet and tender. When he pulled back she looked at him unspeaking, her eyes soft and unfocused. He did it again. And she did it back.

Her arms slid up around his neck, her body slowly settling against his by voluptuous degrees. Pleasure rushed through him, sensitising his skin and heating his blood, sharpening his hunger for more. He ran his palms over the smooth contours of her back, her mouth moving sensuously against his, her tongue stroking and teasing as he returned the caress. He felt, rather than heard, a groan in the back of his throat.

Then his conscience brought him up short. Reluctantly, he paused. 'I know I'm only temporary, but I am your line manager. I've always avoided this situation.' He groaned against her skin.

Slowly, slowly, slowly, her embrace slackened. Then, smoothly, she stepped back with a regretful but understanding smile. 'Of course. I remember how uncomfortable Sergio used to get at being hit on by girls working at Bar Barcelona. He said it was a minefield.' She glanced out of the window. 'Looks as if the hailstorm's over. See you next time I'm on shift.' Pulling her coat from the back of the chair she swung it around her and shoved her arms into the sleeves, stooping to give Doggo a farewell pat in passing.

Isaac watched, struck dumb by her decisive reaction, unable to frame a way of saying, 'Hang on, I was still making up my mind,' or, even, 'I was hoping to be persuaded.'

At the door, she paused. 'It didn't seem to bother Tubb that Janice worked for him.' She grinned and then she was gone, clattering down the stairs, leaving him staring at empty space and hearing the echo of the back door closing.

'I just earned my moron credentials for an entire decade,' he said aloud, hearing his own incredulity on the empty air. Doggo thumped his tail but remained in his cosy bed by the radiator. 'She told me she didn't have to rely on men, she proved it by making a move and I shut her down. And *then* she pointed out the absolutely bleeding obvious, that our boss is in a relationship with a member of his staff so relationships aren't a problem here. This woman really writes her own rule book.'

Doggo regarded him pityingly.

Isaac wanted to race after her but a glance at the clock told him it was nearly eleven already and he needed to have a shower and a shave and put on his shirt and tie. He took out his phone but neither a call nor a text seemed to him the right medium through which to continue their conversation.

As she'd said, they'd see each other next time she was on shift.

Chapter Nine

The last days of November were trudging by as if deliberately holding back the fun and sparkle expected in December. More than a week had passed since Lily suggested an 'adventure' to Isaac.

And had been turned down.

She felt like an idiot, even though she kept telling herself not to, to feel only regretful – though 'regretful' might not be the perfect term. 'Put out' or 'annoyed' might be more apposite. He'd initiated their kiss and seemed pretty damned enthusiastic about it, the heat of his mouth curling her toes, but he'd prioritised his personal relationships-at-work code above sleeping with her . . .

She was a woman who'd told a man what she wanted and been turned down. *Deal with it*, she told herself over a consolatory lemon meringue at the Angel Community Café. Her situation was not the same as Isaac's. She was part-time bar staff, only a step up from a casual, and he was the full-time manager, bearing responsibility for the business, its premises and its staff while the owner was out of the country. Responsibility was something he appeared to take seriously. Also, it was perfectly true what she had told Isaac about Sergio. Female staff at Bar Barcelona had given him the come-on. Apart from making him feel awkward with his wife working alongside him he'd been wary of leaving himself open to trumped-up claims of harassment.

She *hated* to think Isaac might view Lily in the same light. Hated it.

Fortunately, she'd been able to avoid being alone with him on this week's shifts. Tina had been on for much of the time and Lily had stayed in her vicinity as much as possible, brushing past Isaac with a sunny smile and pretending not to hear when he'd twice murmured, 'Lily—'

Last Sunday, having had a conversation with everyone in the Middletones about having proper cold-weather kit because what they wore in a UK winter would probably be insufficient for Switzerland in December, she drove Neil, Eddie and Alfie to Mountain Warehouse because none of them had remembered to buy boots. Carola decided she, Charlotte and Emily needed thermal base layers and came along in another car. Charlotte and Emily bought their base layers in what Carola described as 'screaming pink' while Carola chose what Charlotte decried as 'sensible black'.

Stepping into Costa for a drink before setting off home, Alfie suddenly gave a great squawk. 'Look! It's snowing!' While fellow Costa patrons gazed out of the window at a fine day, puzzled, the Middletones crowded around Alfie's iPhone on which he'd brought up a snow cam at Schützenberg that was showing, from a vantage point on a slope above the town, a white layer on every rooftop.

Lily gazed at the grainy picture with bubbling excitement. 'What excellent timing! Only a week before we get there. I can't wait.'

Carola tapped at her own phone. 'Look,' she squeaked, turning the screen to show Lily a row of clouds and snowflakes. 'The forecast is for snow for when we get there.'

'Yay!' the teenagers all cheered.

Neil was the voice of practicality, eyes smiling through his dark-rimmed glasses. 'Thank goodness the college minibus already has snow tyres or we'd be forking out a fortune.'

Lily stifled a pang of something perilously close to alarm, remembering that she would be the only driver and it would be down to her if the minibus tobogganed off a mountain. 'Max says the Swiss are brilliant at keeping roads clear. It's not like here, where we don't get enough snow to learn to cope with a Pest from the West let alone a Beast from the East.'

On Monday she telephoned Don, the site supervisor at Acting Instrumental, and arranged to visit the college to have another little drive of the smart but serviceable minibus – white with comfy grey seats – and get an idea of how much luggage space they had to play with. She also handed over a copy of her driving licence and completed the insurance paperwork. Don showed her how the rear three seats, a single and a double, could be removed to provide stowage for luggage for nine people for nine days plus the guitar, keyboard, leads, pedals and attendant PA system. She asked each Middletone to restrict her or himself to one suitcase and one backpack.

On Tuesday evening Lily met Roma, Patsie, Zinnia and George in Peterborough for a family dinner. Lily liked George, with his floppy hair and toothy smile. He was quiet and measured, the opposite of Zinnia's assertive and impulsive, which probably explained how they'd made their relationship last for three years now. He was the one who'd taken on the pragmatic task of laundering just about everything in their house while Zinnia chivvied up the insurance company and the organisation replacing their kitchen appliances.

On Wednesday Lily went out with Zinnia to buy replacements for smaller items like utensils and plastics that had melted in the kitchen blaze and Wednesday and Thursday evenings there were rehearsals for the Middletones.

Friday evening rolled around and Lily turned up at The Three Fishes for her shift with a renewed rush of embarrassment at having to face Isaac again, but a fervent hope that he would have realised from the way she'd avoided him last weekend that her suggestion for a Christmas adventure was not to be revisited.

Unfortunately, Tina was off work with a heavy cold so Isaac tended the bar all evening. He tried to talk to her almost as soon as she came on shift but she sidestepped him. 'I don't think I should leave Baz alone in the bar.' A couple of hours later he tried again and she whipped off with, 'Sorry, there are loads of tables to clear and the kitchen needs stuff going through the washer or they'll run out.'

It was as the kitchen staff were beginning to leave that, with misgivings, she heard him say to Baz, 'You can go off at eleven tonight. Lily and I can clear up.'

Lily sent Baz a meaningful look. 'But if you want the extra half-hour's money, Baz, I can be the one to finish early.'

But Baz just beamed. 'Nah, it's epic if I can get off 'cos I'm going clubbing and there's a girl I like.'

119

'And they say youth's wasted on the young,' Isaac murmured. By the time they'd closed up and Baz had shouted 'Bye!' as he scooted out of the back door, half in and half out of his coat, Lily had decided attack was the best form of defence.

She turned to Isaac just as he approached with a purposeful look in his eyes. 'I'm glad to have this opportunity to talk,' she said crisply. 'I shouldn't have said what I did about Tubb having a relationship with Janice because you're entitled to choose whether to get involved with someone and I'm not entitled to try and pressurise you.'

His expression flipped to one of astonishment. 'That's not what I was going to say,' he began.

Face crimson, Lily cut him off. 'But, see how right you were! Even this conversation is making us both uncomfortable – exactly what everyone says is the pitfall of workplace dating. Please can we just pretend the whole scene never happened? I'd really appreciate it. I only have two more shifts after tonight and then I'll be off to Switzerland.'

His dark, unsmiling eyes remained fixed on her face for what seemed like hours. 'You don't seem to be leaving me a choice,' he said eventually.

'That is the general idea,' she answered gently. 'I honestly think it's for the best.'

'I see.' He waited, but when she said no more he nodded once and she cleared the bar while he took a till reading and carried the drawer away to cash up.

Saturday was the final day of November. Lily woke slowly, feeling an unfamiliar weight in her chest. Isaac had barely spoken after she'd pre-empted whatever he'd intended to say last night. She'd said goodbye when the clock had shown eleven thirty and he'd replied politely, 'See you tomorrow night.'

She got up and showered, dressing in a blue jumper depicting a reindeer with a red sequinned nose, and ate brunch. To cheer herself up she did most of her packing for Switzerland before they began rehearsal at two, the last one before they met at Carola's house at eight thirty on Monday morning to pack the minibus. What went into her case was mainly jeans, jumpers and thermal base layers along with her padded waterproof overtrousers. Nightclothes and underwear went around the edges and her Middletones black overshirt and red hat and scarf lay carefully on top. She stuck a nightshirt and underwear in her backpack for the overnight stop in France along with her sponge bag.

Much of the allotted rehearsal time was frittered away with everyone going over and over the arrangements. 'Mum's dropping me off on her way to work.'

'Who am I sharing with in the hotel in France?'

'Do we get breakfast at the hotel?'

'Is it still snowing?'

'Are we taking posh clothes?'

Lily took charge. She perched up on Carola's breakfast bar so everyone could see her. 'Yes, we get breakfast at the hotel in France, which is at Chalons en Champagne. Sharing rooms: Carola, Charlotte and Emily in a family room, Neil with Eddie, Alfie with Warwick, me with Franciszka.'

Franciszka, her hair brushed back into a floppy sort of ponytail, smiled at Lily and wagged her finger. 'No snoring.'

Everyone laughed.

'In Schützenberg,' Lily went on, to cut through a flurry of teenaged jokes about farting being worse than snoring, 'most of you are at the Little Apartments, which are like hotel rooms with a kitchenette in the corner. Franciszka and I are being put up in an annexe in the garden of the CEO of British Country Foods, Loris, who is known as Los.'

'Los the Boss.' Eddie grinned.

'Exactly,' agreed Lily. 'He's Max's boss and also Garrick's boss, and Garrick is Tubb's brother. Los is the one who gave the green light for the whole trip and the sponsorship from BCF, so we all need to be really, really nice to him. OK?'

'OK,' they chorused.

Carola, who'd been frowning, clapped her hands. 'But you know this stuff and we can go over it again in the minibus. Let's sing! That's what we're here for.'

Lily wasn't the only one to blink at the snap in Carola's voice. Warwick and Eddie moved slowly to plug in their instruments while Charlotte muttered, 'Wow, chill, Mum.'

Her good nature did seem to return once they'd begun because there was something about singing that was especially good for the heart, and they finished in time for Lily to get ready to go to work. *Only two more shifts*, she said to herself. The awkwardness between her and Isaac would surely be forgotten by the time she got back.

She turned up on time, as always. Tina still wasn't at work and Lily was on with Vita and Isaac. 'The dining area's booked out tonight,' he greeted her. 'Lorna cleared the tables and replenished the dumbwaiter before she left at lunchtime, but can you check the bookings and put out reserved notices?'

'Will do.' Lily shot off and the first half of the evening hurried by in a whirl of serving drinks and clearing tables. Gabe was perched on a bar stool chatting to everyone he knew – which was most people. The men from the garage and their wives had taken over a corner table. Ratty, the garage owner, sat with his arm around his wife, Tess, playing with a lock of her long strawberry-blonde hair. Jos, the quiet one, held hands with his wife Miranda, who had new glasses in navy blue. Pete and Angel, both fair-haired, cracked jokes and made the others laugh.

The blokey blokes were monopolising the dartboard, as usual, all sporting the shaven-head-and-stubbled-face look. Lily had understood from Janice that the blokey blokes had been a bit of a hazard for female bar staff in the past but of late they'd mellowed and, happily, were nothing like the red-faced abusive darts player of a few weeks ago.

The whole time, Lily was aware of Isaac just along the bar from her.

By nine thirty the rush had slowed and Lily served Carola a glass of white wine. 'You OK?' she asked as she pushed the glass across the bar to her landlady and friend. 'No Owen tonight?'

Carola jutted out her bottom lip. 'Haven't heard from him for a few days.'

'Oh. That's not like him.' Lily took Carola's money and rang it up.

Carola gazed down into her wine. 'He's blanking me.'

Lily stared in surprise. 'But you two are crackers about each other! Maybe there's a reason for him not to be in touch – maybe something's happened to his mum or he's ill?'

'Too ill to answer a text?' Carola looked woebegone.

It was hard to know how to answer that because someone would indeed have to be really ill not to answer a text. Lily was thinking of something comforting to say when the door opened and Zinnia strode in, hair flying. Diverted for a moment, Lily beamed at her sister. 'I didn't expect you tonight.'

Her smile faded as she took note that not only did Zinnia not smile back but that her eyes were emitting furious sparks. 'I hope you're happy now!' she hissed. 'You just had to go ahead, didn't you? And fuck everyone else.'

'Ooh!' said Carola, giving Zinnia an affronted look. Carola disapproved of the F word.

Jaw dropping, Lily gazed at Zinnia in astonishment. 'Pardon?'

Isaac was suddenly at her side. 'Perhaps you should take this conversation somewhere quieter?' he murmured, and swivelled his eyes in the direction of the back area.

'Of course.' Lily lifted the counter flap and motioned her sister through. Feeling oddly shaky, she marched her to the corner near the back door so they wouldn't be on the route between kitchen and bar and folded her arms. 'This better be good for you to come storming in here—'

'Mum and Roma are splitting up.' Zinnia planted her hands on hips, cheeks boiling red. 'I've just come from their place. They're having a trial separation and it's Mum who's packing. You *knew* your friggin' mission to find your precious brothers was putting a strain on them. You *knew* it raked up old grievances but still you had to bulldoze on.' She put on a falsetto voice that, presumably, was meant to be Lily. 'Just let me find my brothers. Ooh, no, I daren't actually tell the one I've found who I am. I'm just going to hang around him and make the family I grew up with feel as if they're not enough for me.' Her voice returned to her own, but hoarse with grief. 'So now look what you've done!'

Nausea swept over Lily in a cold, sweaty wave. 'Splitting

up?' she repeated through cardboard lips. 'Mum and Patsie?' She clapped a hand to her mouth in horror.

'Oh, yes. And it's your fault, you with your blind spot about your brothers, putting them – virtual strangers – ahead of your real family, the people who may not all happen to share your DNA but who have shared your life from the moment you were born, the people who loved you and protected you.' Zinnia's words hit Lily like bullets.

'Zin, wait.' Lily tried to catch her sister's arm but Zinnia, having said her piece, was now heading off like a train back the way she'd come. 'Zinnia!' Lily cried in frustration, forcing her legs, wobbly with shock and grief, to carry her in her sister's wake.

Zinnia, though, fuelled by her righteous anger, steamed through the open counter flap before she turned with a snarl. 'You've smashed the fucking family, Lily.' Then she grabbed the counter flap and crashed it down.

Isaac, who had been crouching to reach for mixers from beneath the bar, was already surging up saying sharply, 'Whoa, whoa, whoa, cool it!' He couldn't see the counter flap descending with strength of Zinnia's rage behind it.

'Stop!' yelled Lily, seeing, as if in slow motion, Isaac's head rising to meet the slamming wooden flap. Blindly, she thrust out her hand . . . then screamed as the flap smashed onto her delicate fingers. It felt as if her hand had burst into flames, the fire shooting up her entire arm.

Dimly, she heard Zinnia shout, 'No! Oh no, Lily!' and a chorus of horrified gasps.

All the background noise in the bar was suspended apart from Isaac hissing through clenched teeth, 'Get out of the way and let me see to her.' Lily's hand was suddenly free but the agony stormed on, pounding and scalding through her. She tried to clutch her hand to her chest but someone had her by the wrist.

'Don't, sweetheart,' said Isaac's voice. 'Vita, get me two clean tea towels and fill one with ice. I'll get her to hospital in Peterborough. She'll need X-rays.'

Then Zinnia's voice, low and shaky. 'I'll take her.'

Isaac snorted, an ugly, jagged sound. 'You've done enough.'

Lily fought for breath to bear the fiery, pulsing thing her hand had become. She was aware of being cradled, drawn into the back area, a chair being found for her, Isaac crouching to gently cocoon her hand in a towel filled with ice that did seem to cool the burn a bit but at the same time increased the throbbing. Vaguely she was aware of the kitchen staff standing in the doorway in their chef whites. Someone brought her coat and he helped her slide her right arm into it and tuck it around her left shoulder. Isaac issued instructions to Vita to stop serving though it was before ten because there would be no licensee on the premises and he wouldn't be able to return if needed. 'As soon as people have drunk up, please can you take Doggo outside and then give him a Bonio to take to bed?'

'I could take him home with me,' Carola volunteered. 'Give him a quick walk round the village first.'

'That would be great.' Isaac sounded properly grateful. Amidst a flurry of murmured good wishes, he helped Lily up and, an arm around her, guided her out of the back door to his car in a corner of the car park.

He shut the door behind her. Lily, shaking, but the pain not as all-consuming as it had been, heard him talking to someone. The driver's door opened as he said to whoever it was, 'If you're going, take your own car.' Then he was in, checking she was coping then driving away with swift, decisive movements.

Lily put back her head and closed her eyes. Her hand pounded. She felt sick but that came from another pain – the knowledge that not only were her beloved parents apparently splitting up but that it was all her fault. They'd loved each other for forty years. They'd pursued their same-sex relationship at a time when it had brought unpleasantness their way, had fought for the right to be left alone to bring up their daughters. *But all the time the pain of Roma's affair with Marvin had bubbled beneath the surface,* Lily reminded herself.

And it was Lily who had invoked that unhappy time again.

Tears seeped from beneath her closed lids.

Isaac put a hand on her knee. 'I don't have any tissues or anything,' he murmured apologetically.

She shook her head. It didn't matter. She was in a world of pain from within and without.

Forty minutes later, when they'd parked, Isaac changed the tea towel as the first one was by now wet. He used that to clean her cheeks.

She gave an almighty sniff. 'Mascara?' she managed.

He nodded, his smile gentle. 'Feel up to walking across the car park to A and E?'

'Of course.'

He got her out of the car and escorted her to the big canopy over the doors. The accident and emergency depart-ment proved to be busy, as always on a Saturday evening, filled with the product of brawls and accidents. Drearily, as they queued at reception and a nurse came out to assess her, Lily realised she'd been involved in a pub brawl herself.

They sat down to wait.

Isaac slid his arm around her. Lily closed her eyes. It was only when she opened them in response to a kerfuffle between drunks near the door that she realised Zinnia was sitting on a chair opposite, regarding Lily with huge, unhappy eyes.

When she saw Lily's eyes open, Zinnia leapt off her chair and landed on her knees before her. 'I'm so sorry. I didn't mean to hurt you. I didn't know you'd put your hand out.' She, too, had been weeping, but Isaac obviously hadn't offered her the benefit of his damp tea towel as lines of mascara inked her cheeks.

Lily shut her eyes again. 'If I hadn't, that heavy flap would have hit Isaac's head.'

'I know now. I've apologised to him. Patsie's not answering her phone but I've called Roma,' Zinnia whispered.

'Don't you think she's got enough to worry about?' Lily replied dully. She was answered by silence.

It was after she'd been to the X-ray department and was waiting in a cubicle for a doctor, Zinnia and Isaac standing beside the bed in silence, that Roma turned up, as pale as snow but for red-rimmed eyes. 'Lily, darling.' Roma took Lily's good hand and gently stroked it. 'What have you been doing to yourself?'

Heart overflowing with sadness and remorse, Lily began to cry. 'I'm sorry, Mum. I'm so sorry. Zinnia told me you and Patsie are splitting up all because of me and I'm so sorry.' She paused to suck in air, feeling as if her lungs wouldn't expand enough.

Roma perched on the side of the bed, squeezing Lily's good hand. 'I don't know what you mean, darling.' Her voice wavered. 'Patsie has found someone else. How can that be your fault?'

Zinnia gave a horrified gasp.

Roma took one of her hands too. 'I'm sorry if I'm the one to tell you that, Zin. There's a woman she met at the music appreciation society. You know how she likes all that classical stuff and I'm more into Meatloaf. Anyway.' She gave a gurgle that could equally have been a laugh or a sob. 'She's moved into a hotel for now. We'll have to see if there's anything to be salvaged.'

'Holy crap,' breathed Zinnia. 'You said it was something that happened over the past few months but had been coming for a long time and I thought you meant Lily's situation.'

Roma laughed bitterly. 'If "Lily's situation" as you call it was going to split us up it would have done it thirty-six years ago, not now.'

A doctor arrived to tell Lily that she had crush injuries to her left hand – she already knew that – tendons were damaged but no bones broken. He talked about soft tissue and contusions. Said the skin had torn but it didn't need stitching. A nurse was going to put her hand in a sling and she should keep it elevated as much as possible.

'Are you left- or right-handed?' asked the nurse as the doctor swished off to her next cubicle of pain.

'Left,' said Lily wearily, gazing down at the red, bloodied, swollen mess of her left hand that the nurse was gently cleaning. Roma and Zinnia had gone into a huddle in the corner and Lily could see Zinnia making explanations and Roma tutting and muttering at her.

'It's often the way. It's the dominant hand that's injured because it's the one people automatically stick out,' said the nurse. 'I'm going to give you some codeine for the next couple of days and after that you'll be able to manage with paracetamol and ibuprofen. What's your job?'

'I did this working part-time in a pub,' Lily sighed. 'My other job only needs a computer.'

The nurse nodded. 'Stay away from bar work for at least a week, then see your GP for a certificate if you're not fit to return by then.'

'I'm going to Switzerland on Monday.' Lily could hear the flatness in her voice. 'I can't miss it,' she said, to forestall any such suggestion.

'Oh-kay,' the nurse said in a voice that suggested Lily was bonkers. 'Well, there will be discomfort involved in travel and the codeine might make you sleepy.' She began to fit the sling. 'Come back or see your GP if the swelling doesn't begin to go down after a week. Anyone at home to look after you? Get your meals? Do up your buttons?' The nurse glanced at Isaac as if to say, 'Wow, him? Lucky you!'

'No. I'll be OK,' said Lily at the same moment as Zinnia and Roma both said, 'You can come home with me.' She shook her head at them. 'I'm going home to Middledip.' Roma and Patsie had enough to deal with and, even putting aside the post-fire condition of Zinnia's house, she did not feel like cosying up with her sister right then.

Zinnia hovered as the nurse went off to get some paperwork and the codeine. 'Lily, I honestly thought . . . I'm just so sorry.' She gulped. 'You must hate me but please believe I'm sorry.'

Wanting to shut out her sister's guilt-ravaged face Lily closed her eyes again. 'I know. We'll talk another time.'

It was more than an hour past midnight when Lily was finally okayed to go home. Drunks and brawlers were still staggering in through the doors of A and E as they left and Isaac kept an arm thrust out to shield her from any of them reeling into her damaged hand which, despite her having taken the first dose of codeine, throbbed sickeningly. Zinnia and Roma hovered like anxious guardians either side, standing, watching, waving as Isaac helped Lily into his car then reversed from the parking space.

They drove home through the night in silence apart from Lily saying to Isaac, 'You've been brilliant. I'm really grateful.'

He replied, 'Glad to be there for you.' For a moment his hand rested on her leg, then he moved it to change gear and didn't put it back. Lily turned her head and watched the passing scenery, the Christmas lights on buildings, the parkways that eventually gave way to the lanes where leafless hedgerows looked petrified by the winter moonlight.

In Middledip, Carola's house was in darkness apart from the illumination down the steps to her flat. Indoors, she slid out of her coat and lowered herself onto the two-seater sofa. She gritted her teeth. 'I feel like shitty death. What's going to happen about Switzerland? I'm the only driver and the trip begins—' she glanced at the clock on the microwave '—tomorrow.'

Chapter Ten

Tears had washed away Lily's make-up and pain had drawn lines on her face. The sight of her injured hand – protruding from the sling, ballooning and purple-red – made Isaac wince. She held it as if she could hardly bear the touch of the air and he tried to imagine what state he would have been in if the heavy counter flap had crashed down on his unprotected head. It might have killed him.

He owed her big time.

He crossed to her kitchen units, filled the kettle and switched it on, working his way through cupboards until he located mugs and coffee. He glanced around himself as he took milk from the fridge. He liked the airy, unclutteredness of the living space they were in, which contained the kitchen area, the small blue sofa Lily was presently collapsed upon, a workstation with a laptop on it and a table shoved against the wall with two chairs. He could see into a little hall that there was a bathroom and assumed it also led to her bedroom.

He wondered whether he'd ever find out. Since he'd made such an arse of things when she'd come on to him she'd been as distant as the moon. It had taken her sister inflicting actual bodily harm on her for her to let him near.

Isaac didn't think he'd ever forget the deafening crash of the counter flap and Lily's agonised scream. He shivered at the remembered rush of horror. It had been automatic to take control of the situation, to establish she didn't need an ambulance and to get her into his car. It wasn't until he'd been sitting with her beneath the unforgiving lights of A and E and he'd watched her quivering with pain that reaction had caught up with him.

Waves of nausea had rolled over him at the sight of her bruised and bloodied hand. Sweat had beaded on his forehead when she'd trembled in pain. He'd wanted to scoop her onto his lap and cradle her, to try and absorb some of her hurt.

He'd actually found it hard to be civil to Zinnia but Lily hadn't tried to send her home so they'd been stuck with her, apologising tearfully until Isaac had to literally bite his lip on, 'A bit late to be sorry now, isn't it?' Tempestuous, flame-tempered Zinnia. He could shake her for barging in to the pub and screaming at Lily. It had been a really shit way for Lily to learn her parents were splitting up.

When he'd made the drinks he took them over, sat down beside her carefully so as not to joggle her injury and took her good hand in his. 'Do you think you should miss the Switzerland trip?'

Her head rolled slightly side to side. 'Can't. I'll have to find another driver, that's all.'

He stroked her hand. 'Carola drives, doesn't she?'

'Not on the "wrong" side of the road. Has panic attacks. And Neil lost his licence a few months ago so he's out too. The teens are too young to meet the conditions of the insurance.'

'So where are you going to find this other driver?' he asked gently.

Her lip quivered, sending pain darting through his chest. 'I don't know, but I'll have to. It's too late to try and fly. Skiable snow has come early so loads of people will have snapped up flights to hit the slopes and we'd still have to get to and from the airports. More importantly, what would we do for transport once we're there? How would we shift the guitar, the keyboard and the PA around? I have to make it work.'

He made his voice gentler than ever. 'Lily, it may not be possible. You're hurt.'

Slowly, her head turned towards him. Her skin was almost luminously pale. 'I'm going,' she said simply. 'It's not just the Middletones and the trade show and the Christmas market. You know the half-brothers I told you about? Well—' she let out a long, slow breath '—they're Tubb and Garrick.'

Surprise washed through Isaac. 'Wow,' he murmured, trying to reorder his thoughts. Being so new to the village it had never occurred to him to even wonder if he knew either of Lily's brothers. 'That makes sense of you working at the pub, working with such a remote client as the company in Switzerland – everything.'

She let her head fall back on the cushions of the sofa. 'Even though Mum insists it isn't my meeting my brothers that has split up Patsie and her, it's obvious my sticking it out in Middledip added fuel to Zinnia's rage.'

She looked so exhausted, so miserable that Isaac's anger glowed. 'Zinnia at least has no right to guilt you, especially after the stunt she pulled today!'

Her fingers tightened around his. 'But it's how she feels. Feelings don't always take account of right or logic or justice. They come from inside and sometimes they're all that matter. She didn't mean to hurt me. But I'm not leaving before I've met Garrick and had the chance to assure myself that Tubb's heart failure's under control. It's so hard to tell from the occasional Skype session because he always just smiles and says he's fine.'

Choosing not to argue the point, though the swollen red claw peeping from Lily's sling didn't make Isaac feel charitable towards Zinnia, Isaac listened while Lily explained her decision not to tell Tubb of their shared DNA, about affairs hurting people even when long in the past. How Tubb's aged aunt, in the forgetfulness of age, had talked to him about his dad Marvin's affair as if he knew about it.

Her face creased in a faint smile. 'He was having a right mantrum about this unknown woman sleeping with a married family man. He'd tried to discover when the affair had taken place and it had been mixed up in his aunt's mind with the invasion of the Falkland Islands so he looked it up and that was 1982, Garrick would have been sixteen and Tubb twenty-one. I was born in 1983,' she added in a small voice. 'Marvin had confided in Tubb's Aunt Bonnie that the "other woman" had been the love of his life, which made Tubb feel hurt and diminished on his mum's behalf. It made him angry and disappointed with his dad at a time when he should have been mourning him. The conflicting feelings really got to Tubb.'

Lily paused and reached for her coffee cup. Isaac passed it to her, making sure it was steady in her hand before he let go. After she'd drunk several mouthfuls, she went on. 'Tubb presumed the woman to have been a similar age to

135

his dad at the time – early fifties. He said he was devoutly thankful that they'd been too old to make babies or he'd have horrible half-siblings crawling out of the woodwork.' Her eyelids fluttered closed. 'There's no real downside to leaving things as they are. I like him and I still want to meet Garrick.'

Heart clenching, Isaac helped her put her cup down and lifted the fingers of her good hand to his lips. 'Hard on you though.'

She nodded fretfully. 'Maybe you can see why I have to find someone to drive. But it's the early hours of Sunday now and we're supposed to leave on Monday at nine a.m.'

Wordlessly, Isaac stroked the side of her face. 'Zinnia owes you,' he said carefully.

Her eyes flashed open. 'Apart from her work and the state of her house after the fire, I don't think now is the time to spend nine days cooped up with her, four of them in a minibus. Mum, apart from being in pieces over Patsie, has to go on a photographic assignment to Scotland and Patsie is scheduled to be in court.' She gave him a rueful smile. 'It's been revolving in my head all the way home from hospital.'

He'd seen her sad, he'd seen her angry and he'd seen her upset, but never before had he seen her so close to being beaten. 'I'll drive,' he said impulsively. 'I've driven a minibus a few times.'

Her eyes grew wide. 'But what about the pub?'

'We'll find a way to make it work. I'll call Mr Tubb first thing tomorrow. And I certainly owe you a huge thank you for stopping that counter flap landing on my head.'

'It was instinctive,' she protested. 'Anyone would have done the same.'

'I doubt it. But I'm not going to let you miss this trip,

miss seeing your brothers, because of it, so I'll drive.' He halted, seeing Lily's blue eyes suddenly brimming with tears. 'Hey,' he chided her jokily. 'That was supposed to cheer you up.'

She gave a half-laugh, half-sob. 'Thank you. Just . . . if you can swing it with Tubb, then thank you. *Thank* you!' She smothered a yawn.

'You need to go to bed. Let those painkillers work.' He glanced at his watch. 'In fact, if I'm to be ready to start out with you at nine on Monday morning then I need to go too.'

Lily yawned again and struggled to her feet, ungainly in exhaustion.

He regarded her thoughtfully, looking at the buttons on her top, the zip of her trousers. 'Are you going to be able to undress yourself?'

'Um,' she quavered, colour edging her white cheeks.

'Don't worry, I don't hit on women who only have one hand to fend me off with,' he told her drily. 'You can't wake Carola up at this hour. Let me help.' Shyly, she led him to her bedroom where gently he unfastened two buttons at the neck of her polo top then removed her sling, treating her as if she were made of rice paper as he threaded her good arm through her sleeve, eased the fabric over her head and down her arm, over her swollen hand. He turned his attention to the button at the waist of her black trousers, heart hammering at the brush of the soft skin of her stomach against the backs of his fingers. Silently, he undid the laces on her Skechers so she could toe them off and shimmy out of her trousers.

Then he paused, meeting her uncertain gaze. 'This is probably the exact wrong time but I want to apologise for the way I handled things when you suggested we should

137

get together.' He watched a new crimson tide flood the face that had been so pale for the last few hours. He pressed on. 'I wasn't making excuses as to why I didn't want to. I did want to! Hugely. It was Good Isaac making a last-ditch attempt to make his voice heard by Bad Isaac and I was going over the edge of control so I said it aloud. You must have thought I was an idiot, kissing you and then saying all that. It *has* been a rule I've followed slavishly but . . . well, I don't want to follow it any more. Not now. Not with you.'

He'd been trying manfully not to let his eyes skim over her body, clad only in skimpy white underwear, but now his gaze sank down over her naked shoulders, the roundness of her breasts in silky white cups, the dip of her waist and curve of her hips. 'This isn't the way I'd fantasised about undressing you but don't think I don't want to, Lily, because I do.'

'Oh!' She blinked, blushing more furiously than ever.

He laughed softly and lifted her good hand to his lips, not moving closer, letting her know that he knew the time wasn't now. 'Let me help you to bed and then I'll go. Where are your night things? You're shivering.'

'Oh, I need . . . I'll put them on in the bathroom.' After pulling something chequered white and blue from the nearby chest of drawers she hurried towards the bathroom.

'Can you manage your—'

'Yes!' she threw back firmly, leaving him reflecting that her back view was every bit as good as the front. Restless and hyper aware of being in her bedroom he paced, trying not to look at the double bed with its fresh-looking white cover, wondering whether he'd gone some way to mending bridges. She hadn't said much in reply to his apology but she hadn't told him to forget it.

138

When she returned the blue and white fabric had resolved itself into pyjamas, which she was wearing, clutching the jacket closed across her chest. 'Luckily my toothbrush is electric so I could manage it with my right hand. But the buttons . . .' She glanced down at herself. 'I can leave them open but they told me to sleep in the sling for now so I kind of need help with that.' Her cheeks were on fire.

He swallowed. 'I can do the buttons. I'm exercising iron control.'

Awkwardly, she kept herself covered by clutching the fabric together while he slid buttons through buttonholes. 'This is killing me,' he murmured, seeing his fingers shake as they worked, which at least made her giggle and, he hoped, would make her forgive his state of arousal if she looked down at the front of his trousers.

He resituated her sling and gingerly she slid her hand back into it. 'Thank you.'

He thought about saying, 'My pleasure,' but decided it might not be the moment, got her a glass of water and her next dose of painkillers to leave by her bed and plugged in her phone to charge where it was within her reach. 'Ring me if you need me. Otherwise, I'll be in touch in the morning.'

He left her to climb into bed on her own. There was a limit to his self-control. And he'd reached it.

Chapter Eleven

The five hours of sleep Isaac grabbed felt far less. When his alarm went off at seven he dragged himself out of bed and into the shower, knowing he had a lot of ground to cover.

When he dressed and took Doggo out, jogging to give the grinning black-and-white animal the most exercise in the shortest time, he found that December had swept into Cambridgeshire, whitening Middledip with frost that glittered like a Christmas card. Ears nipped by the chill, he jogged across the playing fields and over Port Road to the bridleway that brought him out in Little Lane, then joined Main Road at The Cross and hurried back to the pub. Doggo, the most accepting of canines, trotted happily alongside, utilising the flexibility of the long lead to arrange his sniff stops and attend to business.

They breakfasted in the kitchen, Isaac on granola and Doggo on Bakers' Meaty Meals, then Isaac began on the business of the day. He recorded Lily's accident in the accident book and took a long look at the staff rota spreadsheet, frowning over how to cover his absence. He received a text from Lily: *Did you mean it? Got a lot to organise today . . .*

Decoding that by 'it' she meant driving to Switzerland he replied: *Yes, and ditto. Will see you shortly but have to sort stuff with Tina and Mr Tubb.*

He rang Tina first, crossing his fingers that she wouldn't mind being disturbed at nine a.m. on a Sunday when she'd been suffering a heavy cold. Beginning with an apology, he laid out the situation.

Tina sighed when he'd finished. 'Well.' She sighed again. 'We can't let them down, can we? They've worked towards it for months and it's not Lily's fault. I can come back to work today and then cover your absence. I'll sleep over in the other guest room while you're gone.'

'You are a star,' Isaac breathed on a wave of relief. If Tina had said no or been too ill to co-operate he wasn't sure where he'd have gone from there. Tubb was unlikely to be super-keen on an outside relief-relief manager coming in and it would probably have cost Isaac a month's income or more, even if it could have been arranged at ultra-short notice. 'Can you cover this afternoon while I get everything organised? Then I'll come back for the evening to give you a short break before you take over as designated premises supervisor from the 2nd to the 9th. I'll try and get back for the evening shift on the 10th, which is a Tuesday.' They discussed logistics for a while before Isaac rang off.

Over a cup of coffee he came up with a staff rota to support Tina in his absence, emailed it to Tubb then sent him a text. *Can we Skype ASAP? Something's come up.* Within two minutes of opening his Skype app on his computer, *Harrison Tubb calling* flashed up.

Tubb's image was grainy and jerky but Isaac had no

trouble seeing his furrowed frown. 'What's up?' he demanded.

So Isaac explained, keeping his voice even, stressing that the situation was under control but had changed, omitting Zinnia blaming Lily for their parents' split-up for fear that Tubb would want to know why and Isaac wouldn't have a good answer.

Tubb looked angry and upset, smoothing back his thinning hair. 'Why would Lily's sister come in and have a row with her?'

'She seems a bit excitable,' Isaac said diplomatically, then moved swiftly on. 'In the circumstances, I've emailed you a draft rota so you can see what I intend to do. I should have consulted you before committing to take the driving on but I explored other avenues with Lily and she's really struggling to find an alternative driver at the eleventh hour. There seems a real danger of the whole trip having to be cancelled.'

'Shit,' Tubb said succinctly. He looked away from the screen and said, 'Have you been listening to all this, Janice? It's going to leave Max in an awkward position if the trip's cancelled so maybe I should fly back to take over—'

Isaac barely had time to feel a quiver of alarm on Lily's behalf before a calm female voice chimed in from out of shot. 'Strictly against doctor's orders and Isaac's got Tina in place to run the pub.' Janice's face loomed into the on-screen image. 'Hi, Isaac. This is a pain in the bum, isn't it? Have you got the staff to agree to the extra hours?'

'I thought I ought to speak to Mr Tubb first.' Isaac's eyes flicked to the clock in the corner of his computer screen. The morning was draining away.

Though he rubbed his chin worriedly, Tubb did pull the staff rota out of his email and look over it.

Janice gave him a reassuring pat as she read it over his shoulder. 'It's no different to when we went on holiday together, is it? Tina's running the show, which is why you paid for her to get her licence.'

'Suppose.' Tubb looked as if he were allowing himself to be talked round.

On-screen Janice smiled. 'How long's Lily going to be off? According to this rota she's due back on the 13th. Will that be too soon for her injury?'

'It could be.' That had been next on Isaac's list. 'I think we ought to give her that weekend off with pay. She would have been self-certifying this week if she hadn't been down for annual leave.' Quickly they covered Lily seeing her GP for a certificate and Isaac reporting the incident to the Health & Safety Executive.

Tubb nodded. 'It'll be busy by then, mid-December.'

They worked through all the organisational details that would allow Isaac to take an abrupt leave of absence. 'I've just about accrued enough annual leave to cover the trip,' he said finally.

Tubb grinned, his eyes twinkling. 'I won't let you lose by it. I suspect Max and his boss will see you as the hero of the hour.'

When the call was ended, Isaac tried to call Hayley but it went straight to voicemail. He left a message asking her to call back as soon as possible, then, for good measure, texted her too. *Sorry for the short notice but is there any chance of you taking Doggo back from today until the 10th or 11th December? Something urgent's come up.*

The next message went to Lily. *Tina and Tubb on board. Working my way through details but we can go ahead with me as driver.*

He rang Flora next, explaining as briefly as he could.

143

'So, two things. Is it OK for me to call at yours and grab my cold weather gear out of your loft? And can you work an extra evening shift? It'll be Wednesday the 4th.'

Flora sounded pleased. 'A chance to earn more money? Yes, please. Willow doesn't work on Wednesdays so she can have the kids.'

'Great, thanks.' Isaac ended the call and tried Hayley's phone again. If he was to deliver Doggo it would save time if he could do it on the same trip as going to Flora's. Once again the call went to voicemail. Damn. She hadn't asked to come over to see Doggo this weekend. Maybe she was away. He tried the number of the kennels that had looked after Doggo when Isaac and Hayley went away together but found they were booked up. He read reviews on a couple of others but wasn't keen. Shit.

He hurried through handover notes for Tina to cover his absence then grabbed a sandwich and ran downstairs to find Tina had arrived and was preparing to open up with her usual stolid good humour. 'Thanks again,' he called as he cut out through the back door. He kept trying Hayley as he drove to Flora's house, munching the sandwich. Once there, he had to spend ten minutes with Jeremy and Jasmine because it would have taken a harder heart than his not to meet their screaming excitement at seeing him with anything but hugs, tossing them in the air and tickling them while they giggled with delight.

'I wanna go in the loft with you!' Jeremy declared, running to the bottom of the stairs in preparation.

'An' me!' bellowed Jasmine, following her big brother.

'Ask Mummy,' said Isaac. 'But I think she'll say no.'

'No!' gasped Flora.

'Aw, pleeeeeease,' began the children, tears starting in their eyes.

144

A compromise was reached whereby Isaac, holding on firmly, took each of them to the top of the ladder to peep into the roof void, by the light of his torch, at boxes and cobwebs. Then he gave them back into Flora's care while he searched out boots, base layers and padded trousers.

Flora's voice floated up to him through the loft hatch. 'Get the Christmas decorations down for me while you're up there, please.' So he located the tree and its boxes and lowered them down to Flora while Jeremy and Jasmine danced around excitedly. 'Can we put the tree up *now*? Is Uncle Isaac going to help? Aw, pleeeeeease . . .'

After testing the Christmas lights and putting the tree on its stand he handed over to Flora, resisting all childish blandishments to stay longer. He tried Hayley again as he finally drove away but with no more success than before. It was looking increasingly likely that Doggo would have to come to Switzerland. It was a good job he had a valid pet passport.

He headed straight to Lily's place. He received no reply when he knocked at the French doors that provided entrance to her apartment but she must have seen him arrive because his phone rang. 'I'm in Carola's part of the house. Can you come to her front door?'

She was awaiting him there by the time he'd retraced his footsteps up to the front of the house. Her leggings and oversized purple hoodie went quite well with the navy blue of her sling and her cheeks were less wan than when he'd left her last night. 'I was about to ring you,' she said by way of greeting as she ushered him into the house. 'The minibus insurance might delay us tomorrow because I can't phone up with your details until eight a.m. but we can change the tunnel crossing by an hour and still easily make the hotel at Chalons en Champagne for the night.'

She paused to glance back and as if he hadn't been letting his gaze stray to the movement of her behind he blinked his eyes to hers as she went on, 'I've been in touch with Don at Acting Instrumental. He says we'll have to retain one of the seats that were going to come out but we should still be all right for luggage space. He's okayed the change of driver with the head guy. The beauty of the college being a small independent is that they can cut red tape and the head guy would never stop a band hitting the road if it could be avoided.'

They entered a huge dining room with a stack of stuff at one end and a load more on the table. Carola sat amongst it all, blonde hair tucked behind her ears and her gaze on her laptop. 'Glad you're here,' she said briskly. 'I need to book your rooms for the overnight stops in France.'

In between providing the details she needed he broke the news about having to take Doggo. 'I can't get hold of Hayley and Flora can't have him because of her daughter's fur allergies.'

Lily groaned. 'Just when you think you've thought of everything.'

'Luckily, the hotel has pet-friendly rooms,' Carola interrupted, focused on her own task and tapping furiously.

'Doggo's crate takes up room in the luggage compartment,' he warned Lily. 'An alternative is to put him in a doggy seatbelt but that means you'd have to have another seat in and he's more comfortable in the crate. You can stack luggage on top of it,' he added helpfully.

Lily rolled her eyes. 'Then backpacks will have to be stowed under seats. Ten people, ten backpacks, instruments, the PA and now a Dalmatian in a box.' Lily turned to Carola. 'Let's add Isaac and Doggo to the Eurotunnel booking.' Lily turned back to Isaac. 'I've phoned Max about your accommodation in Switzerland and he said leave it with him. He was so mega relieved that you're saving the whole venture – and his face – that he said he'd put you up in a hotel at his own expense if necessary.'

'So long as I don't have to sleep in the minibus,' Isaac said easily.

The two women continued to fire their way through the rejigging of their trip. Carola seemed more brusque than usual and twice hurried upstairs to scold Charlotte and Emily for taking too long over their packing.

'How are you today?' Isaac asked Lily, afforded a minute's privacy by one of these trips.

'Fine,' she said absently, squinting past him at the pile of things by the door.

'"Fine" as in, your hand is a purple, squashed mess and you're having to deal with all this crap instead of resting and getting better? Does it hurt much?'

A smile flickered over her face. 'Fine under exactly those terms,' she admitted. 'It's throbbing like a galloping horse, to be honest. But I'll be able to rest tomorrow once we're on the road and Chauffeur O'Brien does all the driving.' She paused, pushing back her hair with her uninjured hand and her smile grew warmer. 'By the way, I don't think I've thanked you for putting your life on pause to do this. You're being brilliant.'

Her face turned up to his, eyes smiling, and it seemed like the perfect opportunity to kiss her, but then Carola returned, grumbling about teenage girls spending more time arguing and texting than packing, so he just reminded her, 'You stopped me from getting my head caved in. One good turn deserves another.'

When, quarter of an hour later, Carola charged upstairs yet again in response to raised voices from the upper

147

storey, Isaac had no chance to cosy up to Lily as he really, really wanted to because she whispered, 'Carola's upset because her boyfriend, Owen, hasn't contacted her for several days. She's even driven to his house but he didn't seem to be home.'

He frowned. 'This is the guy she met through the dating site? I hope she isn't being ghosted.'

She grimaced. 'Is that the thing where rather than ending the relationship they just go totally silent or block you? I hope not. He seemed like such a nice guy.'

When Carola came back in, scowling, Lily gave her a hug. 'I think we've done everything we need to for now. I packed on Saturday, luckily, but I can't do up my case and my backpack needs some last-minute additions. Isaac, could you pop down with me and manage the zips?'

'Glad to,' he said, meaning 'Glad to be alone with you.'

After making his farewells to Carola, who looked pale and unhappy, he followed Lily into Carola's well-equipped kitchen and through a door that led to a narrow staircase down into the bijou apartment downstairs. Carola certainly had a hell of a place.

Isaac paused at Lily's suitcase lying on the floor. 'Have you packed that blue sequinned dress?' he asked hopefully.

She laughed, flushing prettily. 'Just jumpers and boots. I need chocolate.' She headed for the fridge and extracted two Mars bars. 'And codeine.' With one hand she managed to pop two little white pills out of the blister strip lying on her table and gulped them down with a glass of water before lowering herself carefully onto the sofa and offering him one of the Mars bars.

'Thanks.' He let himself down beside her. 'Have you heard from your sister today?'

She ripped her bar of chocolate open with her teeth.

'She rang this morning and asked to come over but I said I wasn't ready to talk yet. She's very sad and apologetic, full of self-blame, but talking things out with her could take hours I don't have and we both need to cool off. Unfortunately, the basic facts haven't changed. She's being eaten up by what I'm doing.' She bit off the end of the Mars bar. After she'd chewed and swallowed she added, 'Even if she's not being fair, I can't just ignore how she feels. It's always been us, you see. Us against a not-very-understanding world. People gossiping or making fun of our two-mums situation, being quite horrible sometimes. We've always been a unit, even if we don't deal with things in the same way. She feels threatened.'

'By the existence of your brothers?' Isaac thought he could see that, even though Zinnia wasn't high on his list of favourite people right now.

'Exactly.' Lily sighed. 'So when I get back from Switzerland I'm going to have to decide where I go from here.'

He digested this. 'You mean literally? You've definitely decided to leave?'

A tear formed on her cheek and she dashed it away. 'I'll have done what I set out to do, met my brothers.'

They ate their chocolate. Isaac enjoyed the sugar jolt. He'd hit the ground running this morning and his day was going to be long. 'So you've come up against a lot of negativity about your two mums?'

Lily screwed up the chocolate wrapper. 'Ohhhhh . . . loads. I always thought it was better to educate the people who gave us a hard time but Zinnia used to go off like a firework sometimes.'

'Zinnia has a temper?' he asked ironically. 'You amaze me.'

149

She snorted a laugh then said, thoughtfully, 'As you were younger than Hayley I suppose that could be counted as a non-standard relationship so you know how it feels. People comment. I generally preferred to increase their understanding of our situation. As a kid I wasn't aware that the way I'd been conceived had caused issues between my parents. Even if it was unusual, our home life was great, so how could it come from something bad? In the last year of primary school I told this snarky boy that there was no standard human being. We differ in skin tone, hair and eye colour, size and shape. We have various preferences, different physical needs, different medical needs. I told him he had no right to presume he was "normal" and therefore anyone not like him was "weird". It was illogical, arrogant and ignorant.'

'Impressive for a primary school kid,' he commented. Then, wanting her closer, he slipped an arm around her. After a moment she sank against him. 'It was a version of a speech Patsie often gave at home,' she admitted with a twinkle. 'But a passing teacher was so struck he asked me to say it all again at assembly. He asked permission from Roma and Patsie and then worked with me to shape the speech so it was no longer aimed at one individual. Teachers congratulated me afterwards. Some kids went with it and talked to me about it. Some said no, I was wrong, it *was* weird. I raised awareness but with mixed results because some parents, once made aware of the situation, didn't want their kids to come to our house. Zinnia reacted to the increased scrutiny by preaching positive bias and shouting about positive discrimination and how proud she was to be the daughter of two women. I suppose you could argue that my actions impacted on her then, just as they are doing now.'

Isaac eased her closer, careful that he didn't brush her throbbing hand. Lily was pressed all down one side of him now. He brushed a featherlight kiss on her hair. 'Or she thinks there's only one way to do things – her way.'

For several moments she was quiet. Then she said, 'Those things aren't mutually exclusive.' She edged herself around so she was turned more towards him. 'Did you just kiss me?'

'I did,' he admitted, gazing at the different-coloured flecks in her eyes – green, gold and grey amidst the blue.

Her gaze moved across his face as if examining every feature for the truth. 'What do you expect now?'

'I don't have expectations.' He kept his own gaze fastened on hers, showing her he had nothing to hide. 'I have hopes. I hope you're going to let me kiss you again.' He didn't exactly make it a question but then he didn't exactly not make it a question.

She stared at him with level blue gaze. 'And then?'

He felt himself tighten at a vision of exactly how he'd like to progress. 'That's a conversation I would very much like to have.' He glanced at his watch. 'But it's nearly five o'clock and I told Tina I'd be back by five thirty to hand over so she could be gone by six. During my shift, I have to ring round the staff and finalise the rota, make sure the beer cellar's as sorted as possible and make up the wholesaler order for Monday morning. And pack. And I have to get some sleep as I'll be up early and driving a minibus all day tomorrow.'

'We definitely need you awake,' she agreed, but a crease had dug itself above her eyes. 'But,' she said, 'just to be clear on the headlines: you want us to begin something? Going against what you said you've believed in your whole working life?'

151

He took a moment to think about that because he hadn't put it that way to himself but what she said was true. Did that mean he wanted her more than he wanted his job? Wow. He'd never acknowledged such a situation before. 'I am,' he agreed.

Suddenly, her face cleared. 'I suppose we're both in temporary jobs, so we can have temporary rules.'

'Right.' He mulled this over. 'What are the rules of temporariness?'

Her eyes smiled. 'We enjoy each other while we can? And we stay in it as long as it's what we want. Now you need to hurry back to The Three Fishes and race through that long list of jobs so you're fresh as a daisy to drive us into France tomorrow.'

He began, reluctantly, to prepare to withdraw, but her hand landed lightly on his knee. 'After we seal the deal with one of those kisses you promised.'

He barely made it to the pub by five thirty.

Chapter Twelve

Monday the 2nd of December began with the kind of energy that felt like chaos.

Excited and anxious, at six Lily gave up even trying to sleep. Her uber-tender hand was like a big fat claw that had tried to keep her awake all night, even while the painkillers had tried to drag her into sleep. The resultant restless dozing had made the short night seem long.

She showered, discovering how difficult it was to dry herself with one hand, and dressed in ski pants and a purple jumper with a pink unicorn wearing a holly wreath. Ski pants and leggings were easier to manage than jeans, with their zips and buttons, so she coaxed the zip of her suitcase open a few inches and stuffed a couple of pairs inside. Then, hand pounding, swollen and stiff, she managed to thread herself back into her sling.

Awkwardly, with her right hand, she sent a series of *Don't forget . . .!* texts to various members of the Middletones then ran upstairs, where Carola did her hair for her, talking about the day to come as she brushed the long blonde tresses and deftly wove them into a

French plait, all the while shouting up the stairs to Charlotte and Emily that they'd better get up *now* and one of them could use the shower in the en suite to save time. Sitting meekly as her hair was done, Lily felt like Carola's third child.

Granola was all they had time for for breakfast then Lily and Carola hopped into Carola's car and they drove to The Three Fishes where Isaac waited outside, his breath hanging in a white cloud before his face and frost twinkling around him.

'Morning,' he said, sliding into the back seat. 'Yes, Lily, I've got my driving licence and I've also sent a scanned copy to the insurance company email address you gave me, yes, my packing is done, and yes, Doggo will be ready when we come back for him.'

Lily giggled. 'Sorry about all the texts. I just wanted to be sure.'

Carola whizzed the car out of the car park, up Main Road into Great Park Street and a mile up Port Road to Acting Instrumental, nosing the vehicle slowly under the black arch and up the drive because students were arriving already.

Don came out and as Isaac had confirmed he'd driven a comparably sized vehicle before, talked him through the minibus handover and helped scrape the ice from the windscreen while Carola turned her car round and spun off home where the Middletones were to assemble. Lily, pacing up and down by the hulk of the minibus, waited in the insurance company telephone queue. Finally she got to speak to an actual person, the formalities were completed and Isaac held the door while Lily scrambled awkwardly into the front passenger seat.

He ran around the big vehicle and hopped up behind

the wheel. 'Wagons roll!' He lifted a hand to thank Don and grinned at Lily. They swung by The Three Fishes – pausing in the car park long enough for a few kisses while nobody was looking – to pick up a bouncing and excited Doggo and his and Isaac's things. Isaac hefted Doggo's crate into the back of the bus and got Doggo into it and they rumbled up outside Carola's house in the white minibus at eight forty-five.

Carola, Charlotte, Emily, Neil, Eddie, Warwick and Alfie were scuffing about on the drive, shoulders hunched against the cold, suitcases lined up ready. While the excited teens tried to talk over each other, Neil and Isaac began slotting suitcases into the luggage compartment with Carola advising.

Franciszka puffed up, towing a suitcase and beaming. She picked her seat in the minibus, which proved the cue for the teenagers to all clamber in too. From his crate, Doggo woofed as if to tell the luggage handlers to hurry up. Lily stuck her head inside the minibus. 'Everyone got their passports?'

'Mum's already checked like twenty-five times,' Charlotte grumbled.

'Check twenty-six then,' said Lily good-humouredly and grinned as passports were dragged out of pockets and waved.

Another few minutes and the suitcases were stacked on and around Doggo's crate and Isaac fastened the straps that would prevent the luggage mountain shifting.

As Lily was in charge of itinerary and paperwork she got in the front seat beside Isaac with Carola on her other side. Isaac set the sat nav for Folkestone, called, 'OK, everyone?' Receiving loud agreement he shoved the minibus into first gear and drove out of Carola's drive.

Lily breathed a long sigh of relief. 'Phew! More or less on schedule too. Aaaand . . . relax!'

Carola gave a small smile.

'I said "relax",' Lily pointed out. 'That means you can smile properly too.'

With a nod and a barely perceptible widening of her smile, Carola turned to gaze out of the window at the frosty village.

With her left hand in the sling, Lily couldn't reach to pat Carola's arm sympathetically but she knew Owen's puzzling silence was eating her friend. In contrast to Carola's reticence, the babble from the back of the bus provided a wall of sound under cover of which Lily could dip her head closer to Carola's and say, 'Not heard from him?'

Carola shook her head. When she turned back to Carola her pale blue eyes were sad but she'd arranged the corners of her mouth in an approximation of a smile. 'Don't worry. The Middletones are on their way!' But she turned again to gaze out of the window as they drove up the lanes, through Bettsbrough, through the centre so they could pass beneath the Christmas lights: white and ice blue snowflakes this year.

Lily was very conscious of Isaac a few inches away in the driver's seat, his gaze moving between the road ahead and his mirrors as he guided the big vehicle through the traffic. Evidently feeling her gaze he turned and sent her a smile that shot through her like a flame.

'How's the hand?' he asked.

'I'm trying not to think about it too much.' Gingerly, she tried to flex her purple-banana fingers. 'It's not appreciating the jostling but I can put up with it.'

Whatever Isaac had intended to reply was interrupted

when his phone rang. He'd paired it with the Bluetooth system before they set out in case of calls from Tina or Tubb with pub-related queries. After a quick glance down at the screen he pressed the phone answer button. 'Hi, Mum.'

A woman's voice floated from the vehicle's speaker. 'Hello, Isaac. Dad and I just received a parcel and it contained two lovely new coats from you. Thank you so much! You shouldn't have spent so much money on us but they *are* lovely and so warm.'

Isaac flushed. 'You're welcome.' He slowed down for a lumbering lorry that pulled out in front of him. 'They're for Christmas really but it seemed stupid to hang on to them when it's cold now.'

Lily felt a little melty sensation in her chest at Isaac doing something nice for his parents and everyone else seemed to feel the same judging by the chorus of 'Awwwww . . .' from the body of the bus.

With a self-conscious cough, Isaac added, 'Um, Mum, I should mention I'm in a minibus heading for France and Switzerland so you're on speaker. The trip came up so quickly that yesterday was crazy and I didn't have a chance to tell you where I was going.'

'Oh.' Lily heard the disappointment in the single syllable. 'So you're already on your way to your courses, then? Aren't you needed at that little pub any more? Won't we see you for Christmas? Or are you coming back for that?' The hope in the last few words was plain.

Lily was pretty sure Isaac had to swallow before he answered. 'I'm not on my way to my instructor courses.' He quickly explained about the Middletones trip. 'And I'm definitely going to be at the pub for Christmas Day. But the good news is that the owner, Mr Tubb, has asked me to invite you and Dad for Christmas lunch on the house. Will you come? It would make a nice change, wouldn't it?'

'Oh!' This time the syllable rang with pleasure. 'How nice of Mr Tubb. Thank you, Isaac! Let me talk to Dad about it but I'm sure we'll come.'

Lily's eyes actually burned at Isaac's mum's pleasure.

Isaac ended the call looking slightly embarrassed, especially when Charlotte called from the back, 'Who's mummy's good ickle boy then?'

Everyone laughed but one of the lads called, 'Good on you, Isaac,' and Lily knew that nobody could overhear that conversation and not be touched.

The interchange brought her own mum's trials sharply to her mind. Roma had told Lily to 'just let us get on with our own disasters, darling,' but Lily was still having trouble taking in the fact that her parents' relationship, volatile as it had been from time to time, was in tatters. Patsie had feelings for another woman. Lily had to admit to herself that if either of her mothers had strayed she would have put money on it being Roma rather than Patsie . . . She shifted uncomfortably in her seat, hoping this wasn't some long-delayed tit-for-tat over the affair Roma had had with Marvin, stirred up again by Lily wanting to know her half-brothers.

With everything that had happened since Saturday evening she'd hardly had time to absorb the magnitude of the disaster of her parents splitting up, but sitting here as the miles passed beneath their wheels was providing her with plenty of time to think. And it hurt. Were you ever too old not to mind when this happened? she wondered. If you were, she hadn't reached that age yet because despite the happy atmosphere and the bursts of

'Frosty the Snowman' currently emanating from behind her, sadness weighed her down.

She put up her good hand to cradle the injured one, which seemed to be pounding in slow, heavy beats, just like her heart.

'Are you OK?' Isaac asked in a low voice.

Lily blinked. 'I need my painkillers.'

Isaac flicked on the indicator. 'Here are the services so you can get a cuppa to go with them.'

After they'd pulled into the service station and climbed out Lily called, 'Back at the minibus in fifteen minutes, please! Buy your lunch if you haven't brought it with you because we won't necessarily stop again before we get the train.' They'd been on the road about an hour and a half and even if their journey continued to be trouble-free it would be a similar length of time before they reached the Eurotunnel terminal in Folkestone.

Carola checked that her daughters were OK and then fell in behind them as they made for the service station building. Lily hooked her backpack awkwardly over her right shoulder but Isaac promptly took it from her. 'Are you going to manage?' His eyes looked particularly dark in the hard winter sunlight.

She let her good hand brush against his. His skin was warm, despite the temperatures that had her zipping up her coat. 'I'll be fine when I've had my pills.' She found herself flinching as a tide of fellow motorists pushed their way through the doors and Isaac stepped to her left side to make himself into a human shield for her throbbing hand. She used the Ladies, just about able to manage alone because of the ski pants, emerging to find Isaac waiting in the corridor outside. They grabbed coffee and sandwiches and made their way back to the minibus, weaving through the constant coming-and-going traffic in the car park.

Carola was back before them, sitting by the window and sipping tea. She hopped out to let Lily back in between herself and Isaac, then got Lily's codeine out of the pocket of her backpack and popped two pills to take with two paracetamol before relapsing into silence again. Isaac got Doggo out of his crate and escorted him to a nearby patch of grass. The rest of the party returned in twos and threes, chattering and laughing, the teenagers in a group, Neil and Franciszka bringing up the rear. Isaac put Doggo back in his crate. Neil called, 'All present and correct,' and soon they were rolling again.

Once she'd finished her coffee, the combination of a broken night and codeine caused Lily to sleep almost the whole way around the M25 and down the M20 to Folkestone Eurotunnel terminal. She blinked awake as Carola said her name softly. 'We need the paperwork now, Lily.' Then, with a return to something nearer her usual efficient persona, 'Neil, can you collect the passports from everyone in the back and pass them forward, please?'

Passage onto the Eurotunnel le Shuttle was ridiculously easy, Lily thought, fumbling to give Isaac everything to pass to the woman in the border control kiosk. She hadn't used le Shuttle since returning from Barcelona two years before. It felt like a lifetime ago. Isaac was relaxed, handing over ten passports (Doggo's wasn't required at this point) and answering questions about their trip. Despite all the anxieties of Saturday evening and running around like headless chickens on Sunday, and despite leaving home a little late, they'd made the train. They were directed to the single-deck taller-vehicles section and Isaac drove carefully on board. The train differed from passenger versions in that it had fewer windows, more lights and no seats.

They followed a people carrier with skis on top until they were directed to stop.

'Handbrake on, engine off, windows open,' Isaac said, suiting his deeds to his words.

'I'd forgotten about opening the windows because of the pressure.' Lily still felt fuddled by sleep and was glad that driving onto the train was easy compared with the long queues at check-in and security whenever she'd travelled by air.

The excited chatter in the back grew louder because not many of them had travelled through the tunnel before. Doors closed to form their carriage and safety messages were broadcast in English and then French. Neil led an expedition to find the toilets. Isaac gave Doggo a drink of water and a Bonio to gnaw as they were last vehicle in their carriage so he could get to the rear doors of the minibus.

The train was rumbling along and in the tunnel before Lily quite realised. Apart from visiting the facilities – which were tastefully wallpapered with a picture of a lavender field – she sat in her seat and ate her chicken sandwich. It barely seemed as if they were travelling at all, apart from a slight popping of the ears. She spent the rest of the time trying to curl and uncurl her hand to keep it moving and turning in her seat to peep through the headrest and chat to Neil and Franciszka in the seat behind.

Then they were coming into Calais, popping up into the daylight as everyone did up their seatbelts and the minibus rolled off.

'Hooray! We're in France! Isn't it weird to suddenly be in another country?' shouted Emily in her high, excited teen-girl voice. 'Oh. It doesn't look much different to England.'

Lily agreed, except for vehicles driving on the right and the French language on signposts. They were staring out at countryside that looked a lot like what they were used to in Cambridgeshire. Mainly flat. Some industry. Some fields. Lots of roads.

Lily fell asleep again after the next pit stop and more codeine. Whenever she surfaced she blearily hoped she hadn't dribbled or snored, but, though her arm was getting cramped and uncomfortable in the sling, she just couldn't keep her eyelids open.

She finally woke up properly, trying to stretch her legs and her un-slung arm. 'Where are we?'

'Chalons en Champagne,' Isaac said, swinging the big vehicle onto a small road off a larger one. He drove the minibus into a car park and parked, taking up two spaces. He looked at her with laughing eyes. 'We're at the hotel, Sleeping Beauty.'

Then she noticed it was dark outside and looked at her watch. It was after five. 'Oops,' she said sheepishly. 'It's the codeine.'

Everyone laughed, getting out of the minibus stretching and groaning, glancing around at the very ordinary-looking hotel, dragging on their backpacks and regarding Lily expectantly. Oh, yes, she was heading up the trip. 'Let's check in,' she said, trying to wake up sufficiently to get with the programme.

Emily had appeared beside Carola, giving her mum a hug. 'Look at all those bird nests in the trees, Mum. Some of them are enormous.'

Isaac gave her ponytail a tweak. 'It's mistletoe.'

'Really?' Everyone stood and stared at the great clumps

162

of leaves at the forks of trees. They did look like haphazard, messy nests. Mistletoe made Lily think of kisses. Isaac's kisses. As if he read her mind, his fingers tangled with hers for a moment and she blushed.

When the teens had taken loads of photos of the mistletoe phenomenon where the halo from the car park lights made it possible and then put them on Instagram or SnapChat the party traipsed into the hotel and were soon checked in. Arranging to meet for dinner at seven, they dispersed to their various abodes. The teens were noticeably less boisterous than they had been at the beginning of the day, having used all their energy for singing and talking on the bus.

Once in their room, which was decorated in shades of beige, Franciszka flopped on her bed and switched on the TV.

Lily had done little but struggle out of her coat and kick her boots off when she received a text from Isaac. *Taking Doggo for a walk. Fancy coming with? xx*

Her stomach skipped. Maybe they'd get under some of that mistletoe . . . *Yes, sounds great. xx* she typed in briskly.

Meet us in the foyer in five minutes. xx

As Franciszka's eyes had already closed, after quickly cleaning her teeth Lily shoved her feet back into her boots and got one arm into her coat, wrapping the other side of the garment around her. Pocketing her key card, feeling suddenly alive and awake, she quietly let herself out of the room and hurried down the brown-carpeted corridor.

Doggo did a tail-waving happy dance to see her and Isaac planted his foot on the end of the lead so the energetic canine couldn't stray. 'You can't go outside without your coat on properly. The wind's freezing.' Gently, he unthreaded Lily's arm from her sling, manoeuvring her sleeve carefully to inch it up her arm without hurting her.

'Ow, my elbow feels like a creaky gate,' she complained, though it wasn't stopping her from enjoying his gentle but assured touch, his body's proximity. 'I'd never realised that being in a sling makes you feel so cramped.'

Slowly, he zipped up her coat. He didn't touch anything except for the tag on the zip fastener but a slow rush of desire followed his hand as it whispered past her breasts. He met her eyes and smiled as if sharing the moment before helping her back into her sling, then pulling a blue knitted hat out of his pocket and putting it on. It had an odd plastic square on the front. 'Ready?' At her nod, he held the door open, shortening Doggo's lead when the excited dog began plunging on the spot.

'Poor Doggo must be ready to shake the kinks out of his joints too.' She laughed as Isaac was almost pulled off his feet.

'He's a really good boy on long journeys but it's only fair to give him plenty of exercise too,' Isaac said. 'We seem to be in the midst of a lot of fields and a little industry. I've looked on Google Earth and there are tracks between the fields so Doggo can stretch his legs.'

Outside, the air was cold enough to nip at Lily as they crossed the car park and she pulled up her hood. Isaac took her uninjured hand once they were out of sight of the hotel, tucking it in his pocket with his. Doggo's lead made a soft *zzzz* each time it extended or retracted as Doggo investigated whether French dogs left the same scents as their English counterparts. Periodically, he looked back as if to check up on the humans following his lead – literally – and acknowledged their good behaviour with a wave of his tail.

Isaac took a big lungful of the frigid air. 'This is great.'

Lily glanced at him in surprise at his tone of great contentment. 'Really?'

His grin glinted in the small amount of light coming from the moon and stars that was all they had now they'd walked away from the hotel and turned away from the main road that had been running parallel with them. 'I love to travel but I haven't had a holiday this year because of the Juno. Now I'm out of the bar, in the country, sharing the evening with a beautiful woman. And about to embark on an adventure.'

She felt her face heat up, pretty sure she knew what he was referring to but said casually, 'Driving to Switzerland?'

'That,' he agreed. Then he paused to turn to face her, dropping her hand in order to pull her in to him. 'But the beautiful woman once offered to share a Christmas adventure with me and I'm really hoping it's going to be soon.' His voice was low, his arm tightening around her as he brushed his warm lips over her cheek, then her mouth. 'The more I think about this trip, the more I like it. Not just because while you guys are doing your own thing I'm pretty much getting a free holiday and can be walking or snowshoeing but—' he paused to kiss her again, his lips warm despite the crispness of the evening '—because I get to spend a lot of time with you.'

Her heart redoubled its rhythm. 'But we're kind of . . .' She hesitated, trying to envisage beginning something while the others were in such close proximity.

'Our style is being cramped?' he asked, kissing her lightly again. 'I'd noticed. Don't worry. I don't expect to conduct our sex life in the public gaze.'

It wasn't possible for Lily's face to feel any hotter. 'You're a pretty straightforward guy, talking so matter-of-factly about a sex life that hasn't even begun.'

Isaac grinned lazily. 'I'm not shy with a woman I'm involved with, if that's what you mean. If I thought I could take you back to my room and make love to you now without embarrassing you in front of your friends, I'd be desperate to make it happen. I want very much to go to bed with you.'

She giggled at the note of frustration in his voice and Doggo's lead went *zzzz* as he came back to bark at them, obviously not impressed by standing still when there was a perfectly good walk to be had. It was an odd, snuffling bark: 'Hnuh, nhuh, WOAH! Hnuh, nhuh, WOAH!' He pricked his ears and tipped his head on one side. 'Hnuh, nhuh, WOAH!'

Isaac regarded him balefully. 'Trying to train your human, Doggo?' Reluctantly he dropped a last kiss on the end of Lily's nose and they returned to their walk, Isaac showing Lily that the square of plastic she'd noticed on the front of his hat was actually a lamp, which lit their way as the track took them deeper between the fields and away from lamp posts or lighted windows.

Although her injured hand seemed to ache more in the cold Lily enjoyed the icy, starlit walk, the sharp smell of frost on soil, Doggo patrolling in and out of the wavering light from Isaac's hat, happy again now they were keeping moving. When, half an hour later, they felt they'd walked far enough, they retraced their steps.

Before they got within proper range of the car park lights they paused again. They were close to the main road here and aware of a constant whoosh of traffic. Lily snuggled against Isaac – after he'd turned off the headlamp in his hat so as not to blind her – and pressed

166

kisses against his neck, his five-o'clock shadow brushing her cheek.

'Mm,' he breathed, stroking her back through her coat. 'I'll be glad when—'

'Oh! Sorry!' And suddenly Carola was there, a hat with side flaps over her blonde hair, hands dug in her pockets.

Lily sprang away from Isaac as if she'd been caught snogging a boy behind the bike sheds at school and Doggo gave her a puzzled look as if to say, 'Didn't you hear her coming? I did,' then wagged his tail at Carola and flattened his ears.

Carola regarded Lily with a discomfited expression. 'I didn't realise,' she said stiffly. 'Excuse me.' She turned and hurried away.

'Don't worry—!' began Lily, but Carola was already scurrying out of earshot. Lily said sadly, 'That was awkward. I suppose when you're feeling a bit broken-hearted you don't want to see your friends getting together. Poor Carola. I think she really fell for Owen. If he's ghosted her he's a cowardly bastard. How could anyone be so horrible to such a nice person?'

Isaac's jaw had set grimly. 'I wish I knew. Judging from Flora's experience some people seem to feel that as soon as a dating site is involved then the rules of normal life don't apply.'

The moment spoilt, they disengaged and returned to their respective rooms until they met up again at dinner.

When dinnertime rolled around Isaac left Doggo in their room and arrived in the bar in time to grab a beer. The apparently inexhaustible teens were playing an uproarious game of table football. While Isaac drank he texted Hayley to explain about Doggo being on his holidays. She'd never replied to his text yesterday and he didn't want her to find out by turning up at The Three Fishes to walk Doggo on her day off.

Duty done, idly he watched a little table football. Emily, the youngest, seemed to lose every time. Charlotte, Eddie and Alfie were inclined to laugh at her but Warwick was kind enough to give her some tips, reaching around her to show her how to cheat a bit by spinning the controls.

Emily, managing a savage spin, succeeded in scoring a goal against Charlotte. Punching the air victoriously she nearly thumped Warwick in the face and Eddie and Alfie almost cried laughing.

Isaac grinned as he watched Emily giving Warwick an apologetic hug and Charlotte taking the chance to score a retaliatory goal, bringing howls of protest.

His attention was swiftly redirected when Lily walked in laughing at something Franciszka and Neil were saying, her plait looped over her shoulder and her arm cradled by its sling. Many of those in the dining area were men and Lily received several interested glances. Isaac rose to join them as Carola arrived. They sat down, the same man who'd checked them in earlier passing out the menus and saying he'd come back for their order. His English was better than their French.

The teens chattered and laughed and Franciszka talked to Neil about her childhood in Poland, which left Isaac with Lily and Carola. With an obvious effort, Carola smiled. 'Sorry about barging in earlier. I didn't realise anything was . . .'

Lily instantly went the kind of scarlet only very fair people could. 'It's kind of new,' she murmured.

Isaac just smiled and asked about the Middletones' musical programme for the trip, deliberately picking a subject that would include Carola yet gave him plenty of opportunities to listen to Lily, watch Lily and talk to Lily.

At the end of the meal the teens got up. Carola paused in her conversation about what time they might arrive in Schützenberg tomorrow to call out to Charlotte and Emily. 'You won't wander too far, will you? We need to leave at eight tomorrow.'

'Yeah,' they called back over their shoulders.

Franciszka and Neil drifted off too. Carola was saying, 'Probably going for an early night,' when her phone chirped and she all but yanked it from her pocket, only to sigh and stuff it back again.

'Not Owen?' Lily asked sympathetically.

'Nope.' Carola rolled her eyes. 'Just me being pathetic.'

'I don't know if Lily told you,' Isaac ventured, 'but my sister was involved in a problem concerning dating sites. I'm afraid the bad ones draw a certain kind of people. If something's gone wrong then you're not the only one.'

Carola turned a wistful gaze on him. 'Did the guy just stop contacting your sister?'

'No,' he admitted. 'It was her husband who was one of the—' he'd meant to say 'predators' but judged that term wouldn't make Carola feel any better '—people who abuse dating sites for extra-marital affairs.'

'"Online shopping",' Carola grunted. 'Common, I'm afraid. I've researched it all in the past week or so. A profile stating "not looking for anything serious" translates into "I expect sex on the first date" or even "no date, just looking for booty calls". Confusingly, "looking for someone to love and trust" can mean the opposite. Fake profiles are everywhere.' Tears glistened in her eyes. 'But there are happy stories too. Plenty of people meet their life partners via online dating. I thought if I followed

169

the rules and used only a respectable site . . . but from what I've read I should even have been wary of all his lovely messages and presents. I didn't know it had become a red flag for a guy to send flowers to the woman he's sleeping with though.' She snatched up a paper napkin and blew her nose. Lily used her good hand to pat Carola's arm comfortingly.

'It hasn't for decent people,' Isaac said, feeling the mixture of compassion and anger he'd felt when Billy had messed Flora about. '"Love bombing" is only a bad thing if the sender's doing it cynically, to get something out of you. You didn't lend him money, did you?'

Blowing her nose harder, Carola shook her head. 'No. But that love bombing thing's done as a kind of shield too, isn't it? It makes them seem so nice that you don't look closely enough at what lurks behind. He fits the profile: personable, good-looking. Has a good excuse for long absences.'

'Were his kids that excuse?' Isaac asked tentatively.

Carola groaned. 'A mother on her own and suffering from arthritis. He's supposed to be divorced, no kids.' She fidgeted with her napkin. 'I've done pitiful things like sending a message through the dating site app, even though we always communicated via text. I looked for him on social media even though he said he doesn't do it.'

'Not at all?' Lily asked, screwing up her forehead at the idea that someone might completely eschew Facebook, Twitter, Instagram and all the rest.

'He told me he's an intensely private person and just didn't put himself online more than he had to. He didn't like exposing his life to things he couldn't see, administered by people he didn't know.' Carola groaned. 'And I believed it! I've been ghosted, haven't I?'

Isaac passed her a clean napkin from a nearby table because she'd soaked the one she held. 'If that's what's happened, it's nothing you've done. People who ghost are manipulative cowards who use others.'

'And he did seem like a nice guy,' commiserated Lily. 'What do you know about his ex-wife?'

Carola pulled a grumpy face. 'She could be gun-toting, pregnant and pissed off – and not ex! – for all I know.' A tiny sob escaped her. 'It's not just that I feel stupid, although I *do* feel stupid. It's that I really developed feelings for him. I'm hurt.'

'I know.' Lily slid her good arm around Carola's shoulders but whatever else she'd been about to say was interrupted by Warwick hurrying in.

'Um, Carola,' he began, out of breath. 'Emily's like, fallen out of a tree.'

Isaac stared at the younger guy. As interruptions went it was a floorer but Carola just jumped to her feet and said, 'Where is she?' Grabbing up more clean napkins on the way she raced out after Warwick.

'For crying out loud,' Lily muttered. 'Better go and see if we can help.'

They charged outside, finding Emily coming the other way being cuddled by Carola and moaned at by Charlotte. Eddie and Alfie brought up the rear, looking as if the contretemps was nothing to do with them.

'She's scraped her face but she's OK otherwise,' Carola reported, clearly in mum mode, despite her own tears of only seconds ago. 'Why on earth would you climb a big tree in the dark, Emily?'

Emily sniffed.

Charlotte spoke for her. 'She wanted some freaking mistletoe, didn't she? She thought if she had some then—'

171

'Shut *up*!' Emily hissed, turning to glare at her sister.

Charlotte gave her a supercilious smile. 'I was just going to say *perhaps* you wanted *someone* to kiss you.'

Emily began to cry. 'And, Mum, I landed in *cow poo*. I've got *poo* on my *leggings* and *poo* on my *Converse*. And my face really, really stings!'

By then they were back in the foyer of the hotel and Isaac winced when he saw the raw scrape on Emily's cheek with smears of green lichen all around it. 'It needs cleaning up. Let's talk to the guy in the bar and see if there's a First Aid kit.'

But Carola was evidently experienced with similar crises before. 'I've got a mini kit in my backpack. Come on, Emily.' Then, as an afterthought, she turned back to Charlotte. 'You come to the room too, Charlotte. I want a word with you.'

Charlotte flushed in outrage. 'I ent done nothing!'

'I didn't say you had "done nothing",' Carola said. 'Come along, please.'

Isaac was left with Lily in the foyer. He looked back towards the bar, intending to offer Lily a drink. Then his brows shot up. 'Don't look now,' he whispered, 'but Franciszka and Neil are sitting on bar stools at the bar behind a big pillar, very still as if hoping not to be spotted.'

Lily's eyes grew round. 'Wow. Those two . . .?' Then she groaned. 'Damn. Franciszka was supposed to be washing my hair for me tonight. It's going to be really hard, one-handed.'

He slid a hand to her waist, suddenly feeling the evening was looking up. 'Come to my room. I can wash hair. I was a shampoo boy for my Saturday job when I was in sixth form.'

'You were not!' she exclaimed, nevertheless allowing herself to be steered up the stairs towards room 204.

'I was,' he said truthfully. 'When Dad had to give up farm work and we moved into Peterborough I saw this card in a salon window looking for a shampoo girl. I went in and told them they were being sexist and they gave me the job. Washing hair, making coffee and sweeping up in a nice warm salon seemed a doddle after being brought up working holidays and weekends outside in all hours on the farm.' He winked. 'And it gave me lovely soft hands.'

She'd halted to regard him through narrowed eyes. He began to wonder if she was about to blow him off, but then she smiled slowly, thoughtfully. 'I'll fetch my shampoo and conditioner.'

Chapter Thirteen

On Tuesday morning, Lily woke in the French hotel trying to get her bearings, spotting Franciszka's head on the pillow of the other bed unmoving despite the beeping alarm. Lily had slept like a log herself. It might have been the codeine but it could also have been the long, sensuous scalp massage Isaac had given her last night in the guise of washing her hair.

She stretched and shivered at the memory. It had been a bit of a squeeze in his compact wet room with Doggo trying vigorously to join in whatever puzzling game the humans were playing but Isaac had seated Lily on the dressing table stool, her head over the basin and her injured hand nestled safely in her lap while he made jokes about being used to a salon backwash. He hadn't let that hold him back though. She closed her eyes, recalling the slow, slippery motion of his fingers on her scalp. Who knew that a head could be such an erogenous zone?

The mood had been somewhat sabotaged by Doggo trying to get his nose up to Lily's to lick her anxiously as she'd groaned in pleasure at the lazy circling through the roots of her hair. Isaac shutting Doggo out of the bathroom had resulted in a few rounds of 'Hnuh, nhuh, WOAH!' and then a transition into hair-raising howls. 'Wooooooooooooo, woooooooooooo, woooooooooooooo.' When an exasperated Isaac had thrown the door open again before the unearthly racket got them ejected from the hotel Doggo, panting and wagging happily, had forced himself back into the tiny space.

'Note to self,' Isaac had muttered, rinsing Lily's hair before squeezing on conditioner. 'When you set up a seduction scene, don't bring your dog.'

Lily had begun to laugh but then his talented hands had returned to that exquisite head massage and she'd given herself up to the sensations that filtered down to other parts of her body, especially when he'd kissed the damp nape of her neck. Then he'd proved he'd picked up a few tips in a hairdresser's by knowing about drying her hair with his fingers first then directing the air stream down the hair shaft to dry it with a brush so that it shone.

With a regretful sigh, Lily sat up in bed, flexing her hand. The swelling had eased a bit and so she had more movement. Leaving Franciszka still snoozing, Lily slid out of bed to take first turn in the bathroom, showering with her head at an awkward angle to keep her hair dry as it was frankly impossible to put it up with only one hand.

Then she woke Franciszka – who grunted and rubbed her eyes as if it were two a.m. rather than just after seven – struggled into her sling and went for breakfast. Isaac, up already, helped Lily fill and carry her tray and then left to give Doggo a run.

'Thanks. How's Emily?' Lily asked, sitting in the seat he'd vacated at the table Carola already occupied.

Carola rolled her eyes. Lily had noticed before how the

mothers of teenaged girls seemed to do that a lot. 'Sore and sulky. According to Charlotte, Emily wanted the mistletoe so Warwick would have to kiss her. Emily denies any such thing, hotly and with tears, so it's probably true. I've told Charlotte under absolutely no circumstances should she tell Warwick, but Charlotte isn't known for keeping secrets.' She grimaced.

'And how do you feel this morning?' Lily poured milk on her muesli. It was odd doing everyday tasks with the 'wrong' hand. She almost felt as if the milk would go up instead of down.

'I've told myself I need to wise up.' She managed a smile. 'Owen Dudley's a dud. He's in the past and I'm just sorry I've wasted nine months of my life on him.'

Others began arriving and with a lot of encouragement from Carola and Lily ate fast in order not to hold up departure. Overnight, poor Emily's graze beneath her eye had formed a tender-looking pink scab that wept at the edges. Though everyone was sympathetic Emily was forlorn and kept cupping her hand over it as if to hide her embarrassment.

When they convened at the minibus at eight, Emily put in a plea for Doggo to be allowed to be her seat partner. 'It'll be more interesting than being in a crate. I'll cuddle him.' She stroked the big Dalmatian's head and he whipped his tail as if to support her application.

'Sorry. He's safest in the crate,' Isaac said kindly, looking relaxed in a sweater and jeans, his hair damp as if he'd just got out of the shower after his run. 'He likes it in there and feels safe, like a wolf in a cave. And he gets a treat every time he gets in.'

'Also,' Charlotte drawled patronisingly, 'that would leave us without enough seats. Who would you put in the crate?'

Emily shot her sister a look that quite plainly said, 'You.'

They rolled on into the second leg of the journey. Lily had tried to get by without codeine as she wanted to be awake to pass Isaac the right money for the pay booths on the toll roads, but the jolting of the minibus made her hand ache and prickle so she accepted it was a doomed effort and knocked back a couple of pills before checking her email and messages on her phone then updating Max and Kirstin on their progress. *Just left Chalons on the A4 heading towards Strasbourg. All's well. See you this afternoon!*

Beyond the window, winter-bare trees alternated with ploughed red clay soil or lush grassy fields beneath an iron-grey sky. The windswept landscape became gradually more rolling and woodsy as they drove along dual carriage-ways that seemed to go on forever.

The lads began jokily singing 'The Wheels on the Bus' but when that got them catcalls from Charlotte changed to 'All I Want for Christmas Is You'. Eddie's guitar began the accompaniment so he must have picked his way to the luggage bay to grab it.

As song followed song, Isaac shook his head in admir-ation. 'I've never heard you singing any of these before. You guys must have an amazing repertoire.'

Lily grinned. 'These songs aren't in our repertoire. They'll be getting the lyrics and chords from websites on their phones.' The singing acted like a lullaby and next time she woke up they were making a fuel-and-loo stop. She stayed with Isaac to put the diesel on her credit card while Eddie, Alfie and Warwick took Doggo to a nearby patch of grass.

Isaac and Lily watched as many euros' worth of diesel poured into the fuel tank, and laughed at the boys dashing backwards and forwards on a fifty-metre stretch of grass, a joyful Doggo bucketing along beside them wearing a huge doggy grin, admirably suited to the pastime of running for the hell of it.

Soon they were underway again, Neil and Franciszka having done a tea and coffee run. As they neared Strasbourg the buildings became more colourful and Germanic. They passed east of the city but close enough to see the spire of the amazing cathedral lording it above all the other buildings.

The next hour saw them enter a long area of flat farmland, notable only for the fact that ridges edged the flatland on either side – ridges with snow on top, picking up the morning light. 'Wowwwww,' sighed Emily. 'Snow's so beautiful and shimmery, like icing on cakes.'

'And my weather app says it's snowing in Schützenberg!' Charlotte burst out. 'Can't wait to see real, proper, thick snow.'

They paused at Haut-Koenigsberg for lunch. They'd made such steady progress south and east through France that Lily relaxed. Emily had asked the lady behind the counter for one of the freshly baked *Muffin Mars* and pouted when she discovered a *Muffin Nutella* in her bag instead, but Warwick, who'd done well in his French GCSE, returned to the counter and gallantly got the error rectified.

When Emily gave him a glowing look of thanks Charlotte meanly chimed in, 'Hey, Warwick, what's your girlfriend like? Not a childish blonde airhead with no boobs?'

Warwick looked confused. 'She's dark and, um, good thanks. Same age as me.' Emily looked mortified, evidently all too aware of Charlotte's unkind subtext even if it had whooshed over Warwick's head.

Lily, prickled, made sure she walked back to the minibus with Charlotte, trying to keep warm with her coat pulled sketchily around her because it hadn't seemed worth wriggling in and out of her sling to thread her arm through her sleeve. 'Did you know it was my sister who did this to me?'

Charlotte's eyes widened. 'But it was an accident, wasn't it?'

'Well . . .' Lily mused. 'Technically. But she got in a roaring temper and slammed the counter hatch on my hand. Everyone saw it. It's not like you can hide that kind of thing.' And then, when Charlotte looked uncertain, added meaningfully, 'People do notice when one sister is unkind to another.'

Charlotte suddenly seemed to find the ground fascinating. Lily gave her a quick one-armed hug and climbed into the minibus, content that her final comment had been taken on board.

It was half an hour later when, as if Lily's conversation with Charlotte had invoked her, Zinnia called Lily's phone. Lily decided to take the call. She'd had time to calm down and was less shocked and rocky than on Sunday.

'Oh!' Zinnia sounded half-surprised Lily had picked up. 'I rang to see how you are.'

'Improving,' Lily said fairly, as Isaac drove the minibus closer and closer to the Basel border-crossing into Switzerland, rumbling along, the road an undulating ribbon before them. 'Not so swollen now.'

'Thank goodness! Did you go on your trip?' Zinnia went on.

'Of course. Oh.' Lily paused for thought. 'You hadn't hoped my injury would stop me travelling?' She didn't want to add 'to meet my other brother'. Carola would hear and Lily was confident that Zinnia would follow Lily's thoughts anyway.

'No!' Zinnia denied strenuously. 'I'm really, really sorry. Honestly. If you hadn't been able to go I was going to ask to come over and see you, that's all. I've been thinking about my behaviour and I'm ashamed. I was just so knocked sideways when Mum and Roma said they were splitting up, finding them both crying, Mum packing . . . I jumped to the wrong conclusion. I hate the way things are between us, Lily, and I want to be friends again. I'm trying to understand about your brothers and I promise to stop being an arse.'

Lily felt herself thawing. 'We're both shocked about our mums. My stomach goes into spasms whenever I think about it.'

'Yeah. It's really horrible. I can't imagine how things are going to be in the future.' But then instead of sounding upset Zinnia made a self-conscious sound that was close to a giggle. 'Actually, when I freaked I think I was hormonal.'

Lily was taken aback. Was Zinnia excusing her dangerous actions as being a result of PMT? Her left hand pulsed as if in protest. 'I see,' she said stiffly. 'I'm afraid we're nearly at the crossing to Switzerland so I need to go now. Thanks for wanting to mend fences but it's probably better if we have the rest of this conversation face to face when I get back.'

'Oh. Right. If you think so.' Zinnia sounded uncertain.

Lily said bye and ended the call just as Isaac nodded at the windscreen and said, 'Look!' The teens began to cheer and Lily realised that the sky had lightened from dark grey to nearly white and what was hitting the windscreen now was snow – flakes that spread into crystals before the wipers thrust them away. Flakes were floating down, making trees and bushes look as if they'd been dredged with icing sugar.

'Snow!' the kids shouted, as if Lily couldn't see it for herself. 'Awesome! Snow already!'

Even Carola grinned. 'Only the Brits can get so excited about snow.'

Isaac changed down the gears. 'Luckily, most of Europe is better than us at keeping the roads clear so it shouldn't hold us up, especially with the snow tyres.'

His words proved true. Trundling through a whitening landscape the minibus coped without missing a beat and the singing began again, this time their favourite: 'Let it Snow'. Lily joined in. It was good to open up her throat with a jolly winter song and wash away any lingering bad feelings from talking to Zinnia. The white flakes danced and tumbled around them, magically creating fluffy blankets on fields and roofs.

When they approached border control Isaac followed wheel tracks that were black and wet in the thickening white powder into the tall-vehicle lane under a big curved canopy. Blue signs and cones directed them past manned booths but nobody stopped them and, along with all the other vehicles crossing, they accelerated away.

'Is that it?' called Alfie from the back. 'Are we in Switzerland?'

'That's it,' Lily confirmed on a surge of excitement. 'Schützenberg here we come!' Everybody cheered, even Carola, who had been so down, and Isaac, who was busy picking up the main road again, following signs for Zürich.

Though she'd taken more painkillers with lunch, Lily no longer felt drowsy. This was what she'd been planning, working and rehearsing towards for months. She was going to see this wonderful country for the first time, see her designs translated into physical stands, sing, have fun.

Meet Garrick.

Her heart leapt into her mouth with the familiar mixture of apprehension and curiosity. She'd not only meet her other half-brother soon but his family, her sister-in-law and niece and nephew too. She'd waited so long for this that it was almost hard to believe it was finally happening. She'd seen pictures of Garrick, who looked a lot like a slightly younger version of Tubb. She knew that in contrast to Tubb putting down strong roots in Middledip, Garrick had spent much of his working life in marketing and PR in the States where Tubb had visited him for holidays.

And, of course, Garrick had no idea who Lily really was . . .

The landscape began to ripple into higher and snowier hills, the road passing through them in a series of tube-like tunnels with bright lights down the centre. In the urban areas Carola gazed at the landscape with an expression of surprise. 'There's such a lot of graffiti!'

'Aw, don't pick fault,' pleaded Lily, reaching around to pat Carola's arm with her good hand. 'We're going to have a wonderful time.'

Carola turned to regard her with a fixed smile. 'Of course we are. Fabulous.'

The noise from the teenagers grew and grew as they gazed yearningly at the snow, a good three inches thick where it lay undisturbed now. Lily glanced at Isaac's profile. 'Maybe we ought to stop at a service station and let them have a play in the snow? They've been cooped up for a long time.'

Isaac nodded. 'Fine by me. I'm just the chauffeur, ma'am.'

In twenty minutes they were pulling into a car park at

the Würenlos service station, which spanned the road, traffic swishing along the wet tarmac beneath. As soon as they drew up Eddie and Alfie made a dive for the door and slid it open.

'Brr.' Carola shivered, pulling up her hood and squinting as snow tried to blow into her face.

'Snowball fiiiiiight!' Warwick yelled, belting off towards the margin of undisturbed snow at the edge of the car park. Alfie, Eddie, Charlotte and Emily raced after him, cheeks glowing as they shouted to each other, voices loud in the arctic air.

'Frozen-stiff hands coming up,' Isaac observed, zipping up his parka, pulling up the hood and gloves out of his pockets.

Soon snowballs were whizzing through the air between the teenagers and even Neil and Franciszka joined in though they, like Isaac, wore gloves. Isaac freed Doggo from his crate and took him over to what was presumably a patch of grass when not covered with snow. The instant Doggo had finished what he'd gone there to do he launched himself joyfully into the fray and Isaac let his lead extend so he could dance about in the middle barking madly, trying to catch snowballs in his snapping teeth.

Lily, with only one functioning hand, didn't see herself as particularly suited to snowballing. After a few minutes of watching the others laughing and squealing over freezing snow slithering down necks, she called out that she was going into the services and suggested they meet back at the minibus in half an hour. That ought to give everyone time to get over the snow excitement. Carola went with her.

Once indoors, coats unzipped, they looked about themselves at the large expanses of glass, almost blinded by

183

the profusion of dangling white Christmas lights. 'Wow. These are posh services,' Lily observed, following the signs to the loos but glancing into shops selling organic food and expensive clothing along the way. It wasn't until they'd visited the Ladies at a cost of two Swiss francs, to Carola's indignation, that they paused to properly browse shop windows.

Lily stared at a window display of flimsy lingerie. And was that really a . . .? 'Carola,' she hissed. 'This is a sex shop.'

Carola turned to stare too. 'Oh my gosh. Vibrators!' she said loudly.

And that was when a laughing voice behind them said, 'See anything you like, ladies?' Isaac passed them and headed for the Gents, grinning broadly.

'Oh, great,' groaned Lily, mortification sweeping over her. 'We would be looking in *here* when he came by.'

It was the first time she'd heard Carola laugh for more than a week. She linked with Lily's good arm. 'How's it going between you and him?'

'Well . . .' Lily began. Then, not seeing any reason to dissemble, said, 'We're planning a temporary thing until he leaves Middledip.'

Carola's smile faded. 'It would be convenient if we could decide in advance that feelings are going to be temporary. In my experience, your feelings are in charge of you, not the other way around.'

'Sage words.' Lily knew she ought to listen to them . . . but butterflies were having a rave in her stomach whenever she thought about having a temporary thing with Isaac. It was even outweighing her nerves at the prospect of meeting Garrick for the first time.

Carola led the way to the coffee shop to try a Swiss

184

pastry with coffee while they watched traffic stream beneath them along a road cutting between snowy hills. Isaac joined them. Although he grinned, he didn't mention the sex shop.

Next Neil and Franciszka turned up, having tired of the snowball fight. 'Those kids, they will be turned to ice,' Franciszka observed in her swirling Polish accent, blowing across the surface of her cup of hot mocha chocolate.

Sure enough, five shivering teens soon arrived, still laughing but wringing pink, pinched hands. They too warmed up with mocha chocolate but there were a few raised eyebrows at a price tag of nearly six Swiss francs.

Isaac shrugged. 'It's always been expensive here. Ideally, you need a Swiss salary to go with the Swiss cost of living. Or live in France, Germany or Italy and work in Switzerland.' He began to talk enthusiastically about his plans to change careers and his hopes that it would involve travel.

Lily reminded her butterflies that Isaac had plans but, watching him chat and laugh with the others, hair gleaming, eyes smiling, the butterflies didn't seem inclined to listen.

Chapter Fourteen

They drove towards black-and-white peaks that wore clouds around their heads like scarves. Steep fields and tall pines interspersed modern buildings and traditional Swiss chalets. Lily lost count of the tunnels they whizzed through but for the last fifteen minutes their route had taken them east of a lake called Ägerisee, climbing steadily up, up and up, through a village called Alosen, the snow cleared tidily to the sides of the roads.

Then, finally, they passed a sign saying *Schützenberg* and Emily shouted, 'We're here!' They all craned to drink in the rows of houses perched as if on ledges and shuttered and painted gasthauses, one flying the Swiss flag. Shops clustered together near a church with such a tall, pointed spire that the snow had failed to cling except in a band around the base like an Elizabethan ruff. Cheery Christmas trees or star-shaped lights decorated balconies. Snow lay on every roof like cotton wool and, for some reason, a big orange model of a cow stood on a porch wearing a string of Christmas lights. Its enormous eyes made it look shocked to see the minibus emerging through the snowflakes.

'Max says his house in Terrassenweg is quite high up,' Lily breathed as Isaac changed down the gears when the sat nav pointed them firmly uphill. She could hardly sit still for excitement.

Isaac grinned. 'Thank goodness for snow tyres.'

Evidently they'd been through the middle of town and were now heading into a residential district where drives were flanked by heaps of snow and children were slithering home from school in snowboots, wearing colourful reflective yokes over their coats. Even children who looked to be as young as eight walked without adult supervision.

'Switzerland seems a well-behaved place, doesn't it?' observed Carola.

Finally, Isaac made a right and the sat nav lady pronounced, 'You have reached your destination.' They drew up outside a tall grey building wearing a pretty white hat, fairy lights frothing along its balconies. Isaac turned and gave Lily an expectant look.

'Oh, yes, I have to ring Max,' she said, waking up from gazing at what seemed to her a magical snow scene outside.

But she never made the phone call because suddenly three figures wrapped up in ski jackets and boots were hurrying down the driveway towards them. 'Tubb!' Carola cried, fumbling with the door handle. 'Janice!'

Lily felt an enormous smile stretch across her face, jolted by an unexpectedly deep pleasure at seeing these familiar faces in unfamiliar surroundings. 'And Max too.' Janice's son, Max, had left the village before Lily ever moved there but he was a regular at The Three Fishes when he and the family came home for holidays.

Then doors were opening all over the minibus. People leapt out, gasping at the temperature that had plummeted in the over five hundred metres altitude they'd gained since leaving Würenlos. Hoods went up and coats were hastily zipped.

Isaac put his hand on Lily's knee. 'OK?'

She nodded, aware that he alone knew her dual purpose in being here and suddenly finding it hard to speak.

His hand tightened. 'Just enjoy yourself. You'll make the right choices when the time comes. Exciting, eh?' Then they clambered out to meet the others, Isaac crunching around to the rear of the bus to liberate Doggo, who proved just as delighted to have this cold white stuff to snuffle in as he had been an hour ago.

Lily greeted Tubb, who wore a navy woollen hat pulled down low on his ears. 'Hey! How are you feeling?'

He grinned, cheeks red in the cold. 'I'm fine.'

Janice gave Lily a big hug. 'He's "fine" as long as he gets lots of rest. Otherwise he's fatigued. Don't believe his macho-pride talk.'

Tubb made to put his hand over Janice's mouth. 'Don't take any notice of the bossy-barmaid talk.'

Janice pretended to punch him, making Lily laugh at their happy horsing around, delighted to see her brother looking so much fitter. He'd definitely lost weight but the doctors had exhorted him to improve his eating habits and he'd clearly been exercising restraint when it came to Swiss cheese and chocolate.

With a grin over Lily's shoulder, Tubb extended his hand. 'Isaac. Very good of you to leap into the breach and save this expedition.'

'Not kidding!' agreed Max, seizing Isaac's hand after Tubb and pumping it energetically. He pretended to wipe sweat from his brow. 'You've saved my British bacon with Los the Boss by getting the Middletones out here.' He gave Lily a hug. 'We're eating at Los's house tonight, by the way. He and his lovely wife Tanja are putting on a buffet of traditional Swiss foods for us. Let's go indoors for drinks and cake, then we can get everybody sorted out with their accommodation.'

'Cake? Awesome!' said Warwick and Alfie simultaneously, making everyone laugh.

Inside Max's home, which was the first two floors plus the garden of what looked like a massive house but was actually a small set of apartments, they found Max's sons, Dugal and Keir, five and three, almost bouncing from the walls in excitement at having so many people to chatter to and Max's wife, Ona, looking incredibly pregnant, smiling from the sofa. They'd all been warned that she was on restricted physical activity owing to problems with her placenta.

'Welcome, welcome!' she cried in her soft Edinburgh accent. 'Come away in. Dugal, Keir, let them get through the door.'

'Can we have cake now?' demanded Dugal, bouncing on his tiptoes and eyes and mouth wide with excitement.

'Cake!' shouted Keir.

The clamour in the room was amazing as everyone exchanged news at the tops of their voices or gazed out of the window at the sloping back garden filled with snow and small-boy-sized boot prints. The decor was contemporary, white and black but hung liberally with Christmas decorations of every colour and edged with children's toys. Everyone had met through living in Middledip at one time or another, though Neil, Warwick, Eddie and Alfie didn't know Tubb, Janice and family very well. Cake proved a perfect ice-breaker and soon they were chatting as if they'd been close friends for years.

When they'd filled their stomachs, the visitors piled back

into the minibus and Isaac followed Max in his blue Audi across town to the Little Apartments, a modern building of studio apartments. The luggage belonging to Neil, Eddie, Alfie, Warwick, Carola, Emily and Charlotte was unloaded and then Lily, Isaac and Franciszka were left in sole possession of the minibus, gazing out at snow-covered chalets rising up the hillsides like rows of cuckoo clocks. Mountain peaks towered in the distance, turning to gold where sunbeams slanted through the clouds.

Franciszka gazed through the minibus windows at the mountain village. 'It's good to see the snow. It reminds me of Poland.'

'Are you far from home from here?' Lily screwed up her eyes, trying to envisage the map of Europe.

'I come from east of Warsaw. It would take another two days in the bus.' Franciszka laughed. 'I left when I was a young woman and I'm in my late forties now. I have aunts and cousins in Poland still but England is home.'

Max reappeared, calling, 'I'll take you to where you're staying now,' as he stamped snow from his boots and jumped back into his car. They set off again back to Max's side of town to reach a Christmas-light-bedecked white house in a road called Toblerstrasse. 'This is where Los and Tanja live.' Max gazed up at the traditional chalet with a roof of many shapes and pitches. 'It's a family house but it has an annexe. There's a no pets rule at the Little Apartments so we thought that if you ladies wouldn't mind sharing a bedroom then Isaac could have the other.' From this vantage point they could see most of Schützenberg laid out below them like a model Alpine village, roads zigzagging between roofs and gardens, a stream tumbling through banks of snow, bigger buildings with yards, car parks or pitches – it was hard to tell in the snow. Lights sparkled from balconies and the sound of children laughing and shouting drifted on the breeze along with the peaceful chime of a church bell. The mountain air tasted pure and delicious.

When Max pointed across to the opposite slope to a contemporary building that looked like an enormous sugar cube saying, 'There are the Little Apartments, look,' Lily found herself glad to be staying in a proper Swiss chalet.

They unloaded their cases and Doggo greeted the snow once again with a happy woof. Max carried Lily's luggage because of her hand, leading them around the side of the house and down several steps to a single-storey building that was stuck on the side of the main one. Its door had its own canopy porch edged with white fairy lights. 'Los has given me the key because he and Tanja are both at work.' He turned the handle and they all stepped into a hall with white walls and caramel-coloured floor tiles.

Max showed them two bedrooms, one with twin beds and the other with a double, a bathroom between the two rooms and a compact living area with sofas, a table and a kitchen corner. Doggo snuffled around excitedly, though Isaac was careful not to let him investigate the twin room, which would belong to Lily and Franciszka.

'Wow.' Lily gazed around the elegant little apartment decorated in blues and yellows. For an instant she let herself think about how it would have been to share it with Isaac alone, the squashy blue sofas and the big double bed, then she gave Max a big smile. 'It's fabulous.'

Max said he'd see them later and departed.

Before they went to their rooms to unpack Isaac asked, 'Do either of you mind if Doggo's bed goes in the lounge? I don't want him to start thinking he's got the entrée to my bedroom all the time. It was unavoidable in the hotel but it's an inconvenient habit to foster.'

Lily avoided his gaze. 'Fine with me.' Doggo sharing Isaac's hotel room had definitely been inconvenient. Entering the room she was to share with Franciszka she was acutely aware of Isaac so close, picturing him hanging up his clothes, maybe flopping down to try the bed for size. Maybe thinking of her . . .

Then she heard him call, 'Taking Doggo out for a run!' and the sound of the door closing behind him so she decided to lie on her bed for a few minutes so she could take her arm out of its sling.

'Lily! Lily!'

'Wha'?' Lily awoke to find a grinning Franciszka shaking her gently.

'It is past seven o'clock and we are invited to the meal at seven thirty.' Franciszka was already dressed in a green sweater shift dress that skimmed her slightly apple-shaped figure.

It took Lily several moments to focus on the clock. 'Urgh, I've been asleep for over two hours,' she groaned, rolling onto her side and staggering to her feet. She forced herself awake to grab her robe and sponge bag and make for the bathroom which, luckily, was empty. A quick, refreshing shower and she wriggled – careful of her hand – into a black, grey and red jersey dress that swirled around her as she walked. Back in their room, Franciszka kindly put up her hair for her, then did her mascara as Lily discovered it to be impossible with the 'wrong' hand. They finished just as they heard the sound of a knock at the door and Max's voice greeting Isaac.

'We're ready!' Lily said breathlessly, grabbing her coat

and bag. She'd decided to leave off her sling. The hand wasn't quite so swollen and it was nice to have her arm in a more natural position.

Max smiled a smile made more boyish by his freckles, his sandy hair smartly cut and combed. 'You two ladies look lovely. The others are already in the house. I walked them up here to save Isaac clearing the minibus and fetching them.'

'Clearing the minibus?' Lily queried. Then Max opened the door and she saw fresh snow shifting and swirling thickly in the wind, its chill reaching in to her through the open door. Only Max's footprints were now visible and the rest of the garden was carpeted in unbroken white, a drift forming against a garden table like a whorl of ice cream. 'Ohhhh! That's beautiful.' Lily breathed the sharp tang deep into her lungs.

Max led them around to the front door. As soon as they were indoors a man and woman in their fifties bore down on them. The woman had stylishly short brown hair, the man a grey moustache and glasses. 'Welcome,' boomed the man. 'I am Los, and this is my wife Tanja.'

'It's a pleasure to meet you. Thank you so much for sponsoring the Middletones' visit to Switzerland,' said Lily formally. She hadn't communicated directly with Los as all her dealings with British Country Foods had been via Max, Garrick and Kirstin.

Los beamed. 'Please come into our home and join your friends and some of our colleagues from British Country Foods.'

Lily felt a frisson of nerves she hadn't had time to think about in the rush of getting ready as Los ushered them down three steps into a large elegant lounge filled with people, laughing, chattering, sipping glasses of wine or soft drinks.

She could feel her mouth stretched in a big smile as the words *colleagues from British Country Foods* reverberated around her head and took her breath. And then—

'Hey, Lily, this is my brother, Garrick,' said Tubb.

He was there.

A large, cushiony man, greeting her with a similar smile to his brother's, though, in his early fifties, younger, and with a little more hair. She met his eyes and felt overwhelmed by the same astonishment she'd experienced the first time she'd met Tubb. She and this man shared a father. They were blood. Yet he didn't know.

She had to clear her throat before she could speak and even then her voice squeaked. 'It's a pleasure to meet you at long last.'

Garrick's eyes twinkled. 'Great to meet you other than via email, Lily! I know you've been working for my brother for a while but because we moved from the States to Switzerland in the spring we didn't make it to the UK this summer.' He turned and held out an arm to a woman with coifed silver hair. 'This is my wife, Eleanor. And our kids Myla and Xander are over there somewhere.' He waved a hand in the direction of a corner full of teenagers.

Amongst those she already knew Lily picked out a tall lad who'd probably be pleased when his skin improved and a girl whose hair was shaved at one side. Lily stared, trying to drink them in. *Family. You're my family.*

Then she realised Isaac was pressing a glass of juice into her hand and chatting easily to Garrick and Eleanor, asking how they liked living in continental Europe compared to the States. Lily half-listened to Eleanor replying, 'We loved the standard of living in Connecticut but the canton of Zug is well-off too. Corporate head offices are attracted by low taxes.'

'We're definitely attracted by the idea of earning a lot and spending a lot,' Garrick put in.

Lily managed to unfreeze and join in the laughter. Garrick was friendly! Not just business-friendly as you might be with anyone working on the same project, someone you'd been copied into emails with, but warm and twinkly, as if he already considered her a friend. She'd experienced the same instant ease when she'd first gone to Middledip and met Tubb but hadn't dared hope it might happen again. She listened raptly as Garrick talked about the family travels and how they were looking forward to snowshoeing and skiing now the snow was coming down.

He smiled at Lily. 'Let me introduce you to Kirstin, Stephen and Felix. You've been working with Kirstin on the project and Stephen and Felix will be with her on the stand at the Food, Lifestyle & Health show.' Garrick, as a key account manager, worked more on the meetings that would take place at the show than the mechanics of organising the stand.

Lily nodded and smiled, steadying herself with a good slug of wine while Garrick ushered her through the groups of people, his hand on her elbow. A lump rose to her throat. *Her brother had just touched her*. She gathered herself sufficiently to smile and chat with Kirstin, who was thin, dark and intense. Her Asian grandparents had been the first of her family to come to Switzerland and she spoke Bengali as well as Swiss-Deutsche, English and French. Stephen and Felix could have been brothers with fair skin and mousy hair. All of them seemed excited and even slightly overawed to be invited to the home of the big boss.

'We're all excited by your project,' Kirstin murmured to Lily, eyes dancing. 'Despite being Swiss, British Country

195

Foods is getting more British by the day. Everyone has been talking about "the British visit".'

'It's a fantastic opportunity for us. Are there many British people working at the company?' Lily asked, settling down now Garrick had moved off to talk to Carola and Neil.

Stephen nodded. 'There are lots of British in Zug but French, Dutch, Italian and German too. Los is a good businessman. He headhunts the right people of any nationality.'

'That's brilliant,' said Lily, thinking of Max and Garrick moving their households to Switzerland as a result of getting opportunities with British Country Foods. They moved on to talking about Lily's accident and Lily introduced Isaac so Kirstin, like Max, could thank him for saving the project.

As the evening progressed and conversation eddied Lily edged her way to the teen corner where Emily was animated and smiling despite the crusty graze beneath her eye, possibly because she was sharing a little sofa with Warwick.

Heart lurching, Lily introduced herself to Myla and Xander. Xander grinned and bobbed his head shyly and turned straight back to talking to Charlotte but Myla was chattier. She sounded completely American and was full of when she would begin her university education. 'It's just so cool being here in Europe,' she kept saying. 'There's like so much choice if you enjoy working with languages. I'm so going to do that, when I've travelled.'

'I lived in Spain for a couple of years.' Lily explained about Sergio and his family.

Myla's eyes lit up. 'Maybe you could get me a job there? It would be cool.'

Instantly, Lily found herself feeling protective of this

girl who didn't know she was Lily's niece and maybe never would. 'Not at Bar Barcelona,' she said firmly. 'It's a zoo.'

'Sounds like my kind of bar.' Myla laughed, then turned to talk to Eddie and Alfie, both of whom were drinking beer, getting pink in the face and gazing at Myla.

Tanja and a young woman began setting out a buffet on a large table against the far wall. Bread and bagels, quiche-like tarts called Käseküchlein, small glasses of cold carrot and coriander soup, cheeses set out on cutting boards, sausages in coils of pastry, thinly sliced beef rolled up around cream cheese, salmon rolled with radish, chicken wings, slaw, houmous, slices of pizza, mango rolled in sesame seeds, little cups made of pastry or tortilla with their fillings spilling out, breadsticks and things on skewers . . . it was a colourful feast.

Beside her, Isaac said, 'I didn't realise how hungry I was until I saw that lot.'

Lily agreed. 'It smells gorgeous too.'

'Come on,' he said. 'I'll hold both plates then you can use your good hand to fill them.'

The teenagers had already fallen on the food. Carola went a bit pink and suggested that they might like to let their hosts go first but Los laughed good-naturedly. 'The guests must enjoy themselves! Let the young people eat.'

Tanja laughed too. 'We have a little more in the kitchen.'

When Lily had filled plates for herself and Isaac they found a place to sit down to eat. The teens had claimed bar stools at the bar between kitchen and lounge, which left plenty of chairs and sofas for everyone else.

Lily's hand was beginning to throb and she laid it in her lap, grimacing. 'What I hadn't really appreciated is that when you wear a sling people tend to give you a wide berth. You don't realise how many brush against you usually until it hurts every time they do.'

Isaac put down his plate. 'I'll fetch it.'

Though touched, Lily shook her head. 'I'm not going to stay late anyway. I have a busy day tomorrow. I need to go to Zürich first thing to see the stand and check everything's working, then join you guys for lunch and a trip around the locality before we go to the Christmas market in the evening – our first singing event!'

He nodded. 'Max has been chatting to me about what I'm going to do.'

Alarm wriggled through her. 'Are we imposing too much? I suppose the schedule was set when I was the driver so naturally I'd be available all the time.'

He looked surprised. 'And so will I be, but I told Max about my instructor plans and he says he'll ask one of his neighbours to tell me about the outdoorsy mountain stuff in summer. Lots of hiking, clambering about in canyons, rope parks and water sports apparently.' A light of excitement glowed in his eyes.

'Great,' she said enthusiastically, through a sinking realisation that the clock was ticking on their affair before it had properly begun.

Around them cutlery clinked and voices chattered. Isaac dipped his head close to hers. 'How did you get on with Garrick?'

'He seems just as lovely as I'd dared hope,' Lily murmured back. 'I sound like a love-sick teenager talking about her latest crush but it's an astonishing, amazing thing to meet him. If we'd all been brought up together it would be different but . . .' She had to blink back a tear. 'Eleanor seems very nice too. I wasn't able to exchange more than a couple of words with my nephew, Xander, but Myla's great. Meeting them all was awesome,' she ended inadequately.

The warmth of Isaac's smile suggested he was enjoying her magical moments. 'I'm glad.' His breath was warm on her neck. 'All we need is a little alone time for you and me and then everything will be perfect.'

Heat swept up Lily's body. She began to say, 'I'm not sure how we're going to find alone time—' when she was interrupted by clinking of forks on glasses and a portly man in his forties clearing his throat portentously.

'Excuse me interrupting your meal, but I have discovered that one of our new friends, though she lives in England now, is from my own country of Poland!' He paused while people exclaimed. 'She has kindly agreed to sing a Polish carol for me, *Anioł Pasterzom Mówił*, which means "The Angel Told the Shepherds".'

A smattering of applause greeted Franciszka as she stepped forward, blushing. 'We have no instruments this evening but perhaps the rest of the Middletones can help a little?' She looked at Lily.

Under cover of putting down her plate, Lily muttered under her breath, 'Great. We were all crap at this when we tried it before,' but pasted on a smile and threaded her way towards Franciszka. Wearing apprehensive expressions the other Middletones grouped behind them.

Carola took charge. 'We'll just back you with oohs and ahs and leave the Polish to you.'

Nodding agreement, Franciszka started them off by ascending the scale. 'Ah-ah, ah-ah, ah-haha.'

The tune coming back to them, the others drew breath and followed her lead. 'Ah-ah, ah-ah, ah-haha . . .' Franciszka began to sing, her eyes half-closing as her voice rose, simple and sweet, though the words, apart from obvious ones such as 'Bethlehem', were a mystery to Lily.

Humming and ahh-ing, the Middletones backed Franciszka quietly. They very much winged it but the effect was charming and was met with smiles around the room. Lily relaxed and let her voice soar. To sing, as they were in the country to do, was strangely reassuring.

Carola must have felt the same as when Franciszka had gravely accepted a round of applause she said, 'Shall we do another?' and counted them in for 'Let it Snow', which, it seemed, Swiss people were au fait with, joining in the chorus until the room was filled with the sound of friendship and joy. Lily was sure that her heart had never felt quite so swollen. It felt like a reward for all the work she'd put into this trip during the year, a trip that so nearly didn't happen, and an echo of her joy in meeting more members of her family.

And liking them.

That was a special, warm, private joy.

Chapter Fifteen

Though she'd all but collapsed into bed the evening before, Lily was up bright and early on Wednesday. It gave her first turn in the bathroom and also time to phone her parents. That she'd heard nothing from Roma or Patsie since Saturday had begun to bother her. She carried her phone out to the living area so as not to wake the others. Both her parents were early birds so she didn't think calling them now would be an issue.

She tried Roma first.

'Hello, gorgeous,' said her mother's well-loved voice. 'Have you arrived? Do you have snow?'

'Yes, and yes.' Lily chatted about the journey and the welcome they'd received last night.

Roma hesitated. 'Did you meet . . .?'

'Yes.' Lily wished she didn't have to feel awkward about it. It wasn't as if she was in a relationship and confessing to an affair. 'We got on well. How are you doing?'

Roma accepted the change of subject. 'Patsie's still doing her own thing,' she said drearily. 'We're thinking about things and I suppose she's seeing her new lady.'

Lily's heart ached. 'I just don't know what to say.'

'Nothing to say.' Roma's breath caught. 'I'm going to Scotland today so I'll at least have work to take my mind off things. Look, darling, don't worry about us. We're big enough girls to sort out our own mess. You enjoy your trip and tell us – me – about it when you get home.'

Not feeling any better at the dismal way Roma had corrected 'us' to 'me', after Lily had ended the call she dialled Patsie.

Patsie answered almost straight away. She sounded cautious. 'Lily, this is a nice surprise.'

'I just wanted to touch base,' Lily explained, taken by surprise by Patsie's tentative tone. Surely there wasn't going to be a divide between them because other things had changed? 'I'm sorry I haven't been in touch since I got the news,' she went on, though feeling Patsie could just as easily have contacted Lily, 'but you probably know I had a mishap on Saturday and had to rearrange a lot of stuff so the trip to Switzerland could go ahead—'

'Mishap? No, I didn't know.' Patsie sounded puzzled.

Lily halted. She'd assumed either Zinnia or Roma would have filled Patsie in . . . but maybe that was how things used to be. 'Just a bruised hand,' she said lightly. 'Anyway, are you OK? I couldn't believe it when Zinnia told me about you and Mum.'

Patsie sounded awkward. 'I'm sorry, darling, I can't really chat right now. I have to be in court this morning so I need to get myself in gear. Have a wonderful time and we'll talk when you get home. Bye!' Then she was gone.

Lily put her phone down, thinking how distant Patsie had been, flustered even. It was uncomfortable to realise that Patsie's 'new lady' might have been listening. Even worse if she wasn't, because Patsie *really* hadn't seemed to want to talk to Lily.

For the first time Lily was aware of one of her parents not being related to her by blood. It wasn't a nice feeling.

Max was to pick Lily up at eight fifteen. She threaded herself into her coat and sling, Doggo trailing behind her with a slowly waving tail. 'Sorry,' she whispered to the big Dalmatian. 'I can't take you with me.' She went to wait outside the front of the house.

People were out along the street with snow blowers and snow scoops, heaping up last night's snowfall to access drives and garages. The icy air pinched Lily's cheeks and earlobes and she was thankful for her thermal base layer and boots. The sky was achingly blue, making her glad of her sunglasses in the glare of sun on snow.

Max arrived promptly, cheeks pink. 'Los is going to meet us there. He's taking a great personal interest in your project.'

'How far is it?' Lily struggled to manage her seatbelt one-handed.

'About an hour. The exhibition hall's out towards the airport.' He helped her with the belt and twinkled engagingly. 'Can't wait to see our stand. It's going to be head and shoulders above the rest.'

'Of course,' Lily said hollowly, realising that her butterflies hadn't all been used up on Isaac or Garrick because a whole squadron seemed to have taken off in her belly. It was ages since she'd been involved with a project as intimately as this one.

The amount of snow on the ground decreased as they travelled, Zürich lying six hundred metres lower than Schützenberg. Max had passes to get them through the exhibitors' entrance and Lily found herself crossing the acres of cheap but new carpet peculiar to trade shows with rising excitement. The set-up crew had been and gone and she could pick out the British Country Foods stand – stand E11-07 – from thirty yards away. 'Looking OK,' she said, breathing a sigh of relief. 'The colours on the clings have come out pretty true.' Then she was stepping up onto the stand decorated red, white and blue and gazing around at the physical manifestation of her hard work.

Kirstin, Felix and Stephen, smart in their business suits, were preparing for the start of the show the next day, lining up brochures, stowing cool boxes ready for product samples and making up displays of non-perishables according to the schematics Lily had designed in faraway Middledip.

As she usually worked remotely Lily rarely experienced the buzz of seeing her ideas come to life and the morning passed in a blur as she checked displays and video loops. As the stand stood on a corner she'd designed a fold-out backdrop against which the Middletones would sing.

Los showed up for half an hour, studying the stand from all angles with a nod and a smile. 'This is very good, Lily. Very striking,' before he vanished off back to his office in Schützenberg.

Finally, Max put his hand on Lily's shoulder, interrupting her conversation with Felix about social media. 'Let's take your photo with the stand and then I have to deliver you for lunch. Your friends will be wondering what's happened to you.'

Lily left almost reluctantly after the photo, walking backwards up the aisle to take her last look at the stand. 'It's surpassed my expectations. And Los seemed to like it. Did you think he did?'

Max patted her shoulder. 'We'd have heard all about it if he didn't.' He listened good-naturedly as she chattered about the show opening tomorrow and the Middletones singing while he drove her to Restaurant Raten, its car park cleared of snow, the surrounding slopes blinding white with snow and edged with stands of pines. The majestic mountain-scape of Central Switzerland rose up in the distance, the snow-capped peaks of the St Gallen Alps under a silver swathe of cloud.

As she got out of the car Lily gazed at wooden poles with cables between. 'What's all this?'

'The drag lift. Skiing season is just beginning.' Max zipped his coat then pointed at a big geometric dome. 'That's the ski bar, where you can get refreshment without taking off your ski boots. If this weather keeps up the slopes will open at the weekend. Oh look, the minibus is here already.'

They found the others gathered around a long table inside, frowning over menus written in Swiss-Deutsche. Christmas decorations in turquoise and white glittered from every wall and Christmas trees were positively weighed down by baubles and lace. Isaac looked up and smiled as she and Max approached. 'How'd it go?'

Lily pulled out her phone and her pictures were passed around amidst a hail of exclamations.

'It's going to be great to be singing there tomorrow,' she bubbled. 'We're on late morning and mid-afternoon, and someone's going to take us for lunch in between.'

With Max's assistance they ordered bowls of thick broth with crusty bread and a round of drinks. Lily looked around. 'So what did you guys do this morning?'

Warwick gave a 'what else?' shrug. 'Snowball fight.' Emily, Charlotte, Eddie and Alfie all beamed and nodded.

'I got so soaked I had to change my jeans,' Emily chimed in.

'We walked in the snow, no changes of jeans required,' Neil said, with a gesture in the direction of Franciszka and Carola.

Isaac grinned. 'Max's neighbour talked to me about outdoor pursuits. I think I need to learn to climb in snow.'

Max smiled as the waitress approached with the first steaming bowls of broth. 'I thought we'd go for a hike up the nature trail after lunch. It'll be beautiful.'

So after the delicious concoction of barley, vegetables and bacon they bundled up in coats, hats and gloves and released Doggo from his cave in the back of the minibus. He bounced out stiff-legged, tail thrashing with the joy of being with his pack again. 'Hnuh, hnuh, WOAH!' he barked, nudging Isaac's legs as if to say, 'Let's GO!'

'Oh,' Lily said, looking down at her injured hand in dismay. 'My left glove won't fit. I didn't think of that.'

Isaac passed Doggo's lead to Alfie. 'I've got a spare pair of ski mittens.' He pulled his backpack from the minibus and produced what looked like mini boxing gloves. He examined Lily's hand. 'Going impressively purple.'

'Not as stiff and swollen now though.' She eased her sore fingers in through the opening of the mitten he held out, elastic stretched, and flexed experimentally. 'Thanks, that's brilliant. I won't get frostbite now.'

They set off up a steep snowy path towards a wooded area in Max's wake, the snow crunching and squeaking beneath their feet, Doggo taking advantage of his extending lead to trip up as many people as possible as he trotted back and forth, nose down. The path rose and rose and they were soon all puffing, even Isaac.

'It's the altitude. We're just about an entire atmosphere

higher here than in Middledip,' he observed, pausing to catch his breath, shading his eyes to look back over the snow plain punctuated with lines of dark jagged conifers, snowy peaks rising up behind. They were so clear that Lily felt as if she could reach out and touch them. Apart from the restaurant, there wasn't a building to be seen.

'Look at the lovely woodcarvings.' Carola pointed up the path to where a snail and a bear were carved from tree stumps still rooted in the ground. The trunks of the pine trees edging their way looked almost yellow in the daylight. As they climbed on, slipping and sliding as the trail grew steeper but no less snowy, they came across boards giving nature information and even cow bells that could be played with a stick. Finally the trees thinned and they came to St Jost, a clearing containing a tiny café, presently closed, and a church. The café's pitched roof was thick with snow and the white-walled church had an unusual, bell-shaped tower and narrow gothic arched windows. The clearing was edged with more conifers in deepest green and the Eiger and Jungfrau mountains ranged the horizon like giants who'd paused to rest.

Isaac set Doggo free to dash in circles, spraying snow in his wake, ears flying and tongue lolling.

'He's a wag with a black-and-white dog attached.' Lily laughed, watching Doggo roll exuberantly, pedalling his paws.

Isaac slowed his steps, which made Lily automatically do the same. He dropped his voice. 'What are the plans after the singing gig at the Christmas market this evening?'

She shrugged. 'Kirstin's provided me a list of eating places but apparently it's much cheaper to buy bratwurst and other goodies at the market.'

'And then?' Isaac asked patiently, his eyes fixed on her

as they walked. 'I'm hoping to separate you from the rest of the party and maybe doing something vaguely date-like.'

'Oh!' She flushed, feeling suddenly shy. 'That would be lovely.' Ahead, the others had strung out around the tiny white church and the tall wooden cross beside it. The teenagers were apparently not yet tired of throwing snowballs or finding untouched snow in which to leave a boot print and Neil, Franciszka and Carola strolled in their wake, chatting to Max who was pointing to the various peaks. 'But what do we say to the others?'

'How about you say, "I'm going out with Isaac" and I say "I'm going out with Lily"?' He tried to take her uninjured hand but with his ski mittens and her insulated gloves, their hands slithered apart.

Lily's butterflies dive-bombed back into her tummy. 'It seems kind of . . . particular.'

He slowed to a stop. His voice was soft and low. 'If looking "particular" makes you uncomfortable we can take Doggo and walk somewhere, but I'd like to spend time with you. Not the you looking after the Middletones, not the you doing business with British Country Foods, not the you anxious about the various parts of your family, not the you serving at The Three Fishes. I want a couple of hours of just Lily.' His earring peeped out from his woollen hat beside the ends of his dark hair.

'Sounds lovely,' she murmured.

Doggo raced back in a shower of snow to see what was keeping them and they went to join the others to hear Max telling them that the two-metre-tall sticks along the trail showed how deep the snow would get in the depths of winter. Emily looked at him with frank disbelief. 'They're taller than me. You can't get that much snow.'

Max grinned. 'Believe me — you can! In January and February you'd sink without trace.'

The temperature was beginning to fall as the shadows lengthened so they headed back, slithering down the steep trail through the spiky green pines to Schützenberg to get ready for the Christmas market.

As they reached the car park fresh flakes of snow began to fall, stinging skin like love bites from the Snow Queen.

Isaac was still enjoying the 'king of the road' feeling he got behind the wheel of the minibus, as the snow drifted down like feathers in the darkness. Boys and their toys, he thought, steering the large vehicle out of Toblerstrasse to pick up the others. Everyone was thanking him and praising him for dropping everything to come on this trip but he was having a great time, especially with Lily jiggling with excitement in the seat beside him.

When they reached the Little Apartments the others bounced into the minibus in various stages of anticipation and nervousness to join Franciszka in the back.

'Everyone got their overshirts, hats and scarves?' Lily demanded, craning between the headrests. Amidst assurances that they had Isaac set off downhill to the car park near the central square.

His role was over once he'd parked and Lily had bought the parking ticket until the group needed to be conveyed home but he strolled along with them beneath the Christmas illuminations anyway, pulling up his hood as snow tried to find exposed flesh on which to bestow its nippy kisses. The increasingly nervous-looking singers pulled black smocks over their coats and put on red woolly hats and scarves. Eddie swung his guitar onto his back in its gig bag and Warwick carried his keyboard in a case,

Alfie taking charge of the stand and Neil the PA. All at once, they looked like a group.

They followed Lily's phone map app through the swirling snow, along a couple of small streets until they reached the gently sloping town square surrounded by tall buildings painted in pinks, greys and blues, snow outlining the sills and shutters. On some, the rendering was beautifully painted with curlicues or geometric designs. 'Pretty,' Lily breathed, eyes reflecting the thousand lights suspended like stars in the night sky above rows of stalls like little red chalets with snow on the roofs. Each stall glittered with stars and lanterns so the entire market seemed luminous.

The jaunty red stalls sold everything from food to decorations to jewellery to glühwein. The aisles were thronged with shoppers, colourful ski jackets much in evidence along with sturdy boots and hats of every description. Delicious smells of hot bratwurst and waffles rose on the air, causing Warwick, Eddie and Alfie to take deep, appreciative sniffs.

'Apparently the British Country Foods market stall is near the carousel.' Lily pointed with a gloved hand up the slope to where painted horses on barley-twist poles were performing their up-and-down waltz, gleeful children clinging to their backs.

Isaac could see over the bobbing heads of most shoppers. 'Kirstin's there already.'

'Good.' Lily's led the way towards the stall. Not being a Middletone Isaac was happy to step aside and watch as Lily and Kirstin kissed cheeks. Then Lily inspected the stall, something she described as 'checking the merchandising' while two smiling ladies served a crowd of customers with marmalade and chutney, pork pies, Cornish pasties, Scotch eggs and crumpets. Lily shook hands with the ladies and Isaac heard her repeat their names: Melina and Sarah.

Lily had pushed back her hood under the shelter of the stall and her blonde hair glowed beneath the lights. Her smile flashed as she consulted Carola, checking her watch, her head tipping back as she laughed. The Middletones clustered around, listening, smiling.

She was like a beacon to the others, he thought. It only took a courteous request from her and Kirstin brought out an electrical lead. The teen boys and Neil set up the PA and instruments under a canopy beside the stall, presumably there to prevent anyone getting fried if snow made contact with an electrical instrument. Eddie and Warwick played a few chords then Lily lifted her eyebrows at Carola, who nodded. The group formed up beside Warwick and Eddie.

All eyes were on Carola as she made a 'Ready?' face at everyone then counted Warwick and Eddie in. Their heads nodded as they burst into the introduction to 'I Wish it Could be Christmas Everyday'. Around them, people paused, turned, came closer, some buying glühwein or hot chocolate at nearby stalls as they prepared to enjoy the free entertainment.

The song was greeted with applause when they finished and Kirstin stepped forward, speaking in her own language and then switching to English to say, 'And so our British friends, the Middletones, have driven all the way from England to be the guests of British Country Foods and to sing for us.'

She stepped aside and Carola brought them in for several traditional carols like 'Once in Royal David's City', ending with 'Silent Night'. A number of people joined in, Isaac noticed, some singing the German words and applauding enthusiastically at the end.

The audience swelled and Isaac saw Tubb, Janice, Garrick and Eleanor join the fringes of the crowd.

Lily's face shone. She looked so happy at their reception that he knew she must have been hiding a few doubts behind her apparent confidence in the project she'd put together. They began 'Let it Snow' and, obligingly, the snow began to fall more heavily, as if it, too, wanted Lily and the Middletones to look good. Melina emerged from the British Country Foods stall to offer bite-sized samples of food, savoury on one platter and sweet on the other. Isaac swiped a piece of tea bread as she passed and popped it in his mouth, savouring the sweet, light bread studded with raisins and sultanas. Kirstin glided around with her iPhone, taking photos and videos for social media.

In another ten minutes the Middletones had completed the set, ending with a rousing rendition of 'We Wish You a Merry Christmas', greeted with applause and even a whistle or two. Carola beamed, her pale hair escaping from beneath her red hat. 'Thank you for making us welcome. The Middletones will be singing here again on Saturday afternoon and evening.'

Kirstin moved forward to add, 'And our stall will be here to bring you delicious British food until the market ends on Sunday.'

It was over. The crowd began to disperse, some to browse the wares on the BCF stall and chat to Sarah or Melina. Garrick, Eleanor, Tubb and Janice smiled and said their hellos. 'I hope you don't mind us just dropping by for such a short time,' Isaac heard Garrick say, a knitted hat low on his forehead. 'We're on our way out for a meal.'

Isaac saw a shadow pass over Lily's face as she watched

her brothers leave to spend the evening together. Warwick and Eddie stowed their instruments and the PA in the back of the stall and the Middletones divested themselves of their black overshirts.

Kirstin took Lily aside. 'You are invited to the village's advent brunch on Saturday, I think? Would you think about singing there too? It would just be a couple of carols. It's not a commercial opportunity for us but Los is keen on community events.'

'I'm sure we would,' Lily agreed. 'It'll be an experience.'

The others were evidently focused on more immediate experiences. Warwick gazed lustfully at the nearby bratwurst stall. 'I'm freakin' starving. I'm going to get me one of those awesome big sausages.' Eddie, Alfie, Emily and Charlotte fell in with the awesome big sausage idea and Franciszka and Neil drifted off in another direction. Isaac hung on, beginning to feel the bite of snow in the air despite his heavily insulated outdoors clothes and, finally, Lily and Carola ended their conversation with Kirstin and joined him.

Lily's face was wreathed in smiles and even Carola seemed to have put her misery about Owen aside to beam right along with her. 'That went well,' Carola said.

Lily put her good arm around the older woman's shoulders. 'Well? It went brilliantly! We were the dog's bollocks!' She turned to Isaac. 'Did we sound OK?'

'Fantastic.' He didn't have to augment reality at all. 'Everyone loved it, tapping toes and nodding their heads. One elderly couple even smooched.'

They spent the next hour sampling the delights of the market, buying thick, delicious-looking chocolate, admiring glass ornaments and wooden carvings, consuming bratwurst and beer at wooden tables and benches where they found the teenagers already eating. Waffles smothered in black cherries followed. 'That was gorgeous,' Carola said, smacking her lips. 'But I'd love a cup of tea.'

Although they laughed at her Englishness Isaac fetched three cups from a kiosk that was smothered in gold tinsel, silver baubles and white fir cones. The snow had slowed to the occasional flake but the air was so cold it squeezed their lungs.

Sorting out his Swiss francs ready to pay, Isaac looked back at where Lily was leaning over the table talking earnestly to Carola and thought what a great time he was having with the Middletones in Switzerland.

But man how he was *itching* to get Lily on her own.

In the event, it proved easy. The market closed at eight. They collected their things from the BCF stall and found their way back to the car park. Isaac drove them up the hill, first to the Little Apartments, where most alighted. Eddie took his guitar but the rest of the equipment was left in the bus ready for the trip to the trade show tomorrow. Back at Los and Tanja's home, Isaac parked the minibus and they followed the path, considerately already cleared, to the annexe.

'Anyone mind if I flop down and watch DVDs? There's season 7 of *The Walking Dead* here,' Franciszka said as soon as she got inside, throwing off her coat, pulling the box set out from under the TV and grabbing the remote all in one movement.

Wondering whether she'd noticed the sparks between him and Lily and was helpfully keeping out of their way, Isaac said, 'That's fine, we'll take Doggo for a walk and maybe get a drink.' He had to raise his voice over Doggo's excited basso profundo bark as he flew about like a spotted rocket, bouncing off Isaac's stomach and whizzing around Lily.

214

Upon seeing Isaac grab the lead he performed a last pirouette before standing stock still to have his harness fitted.

Lily's eyes shone as she laughed. 'What a head case you are, Doggo.'

They stepped back outside into the cold and dark, following the path back to the street and turning right down Toblerstrasse. Making sure he was on Lily's right side, Isaac took her hand though it wasn't satisfactory through two pairs of gloves. After an initial caper at the joy of being in the snow again, Doggo settled down to sniffing everything in his path.

'I like the Switzerland Lily, always smiling,' Isaac said, grinning down at her as they walked.

Her brows quirked. 'Don't I smile in England?'

'Of course, but here it seems to be almost constant, as if you're just having an amazing time.' They passed beneath street lights and turned left down the hill into the town. Lights glittered like fireflies on every balcony, making the snow-coated roofs glow in the darkness. The headlights of vehicles glided up and down the hill and passing people were all garbed in the uniform of boots, coats, hats, scarves and gloves.

'I am having an amazing time,' she admitted. 'It seems hard to believe it's actually happening.'

'I suppose it's the "getting away from it all" thing as well.' He clicked to Doggo to wait at the road before they crossed and continued downhill, the snow crunching at the edges of the path.

Her smile dimmed. 'Getting away from the trouble in Family Number One, do you mean? That doesn't stop me worrying about them.' She sighed. 'And I'm only pressing my nose against the glass of Family Number Two to watch them living their lives.'

He slid his arm around her, enjoying the closeness even through their down-filled coats. 'Is that how it feels?' It caused a tug in his heart.

She slid her arm around him too. 'That's how it is.' They tramped in silence for a minute, boots clomping on the pavement before she added, 'It's good to see them contented. I'm more and more inclined to leave things as they are. There are worse things to be than friends with your brothers.'

He thought about it as they bore left again, still going downhill, towards a place he'd researched online this morning when she'd been off doing her stuff at the Food, Lifestyle & Health show. 'Is this because of Zinnia?'

'Not because she's gone into a giant sulk about Tubb and Garrick. It's more that my transparency with her caused trouble. At the moment, I have a good relationship with my brothers but if I tell them who I am, I have no idea how they'll react. Also—' Lily gave a little skip '—I'm leaning more towards staying in Middledip. Zinnia's backed off and is feeling remorseful for hurting me. Mum and Patsie are having problems but it doesn't seem to be my fault. I don't even know if Tubb will come back to live in the village.' She sighed, then she managed another smile. 'My quest's over. The ending isn't quite what I once hoped for but that doesn't make it a bad result.' She transferred her gaze to a structure dripping in Christmas lights and with an outdoor area where the illumination was ultra blue. 'Is that where we're heading?'

'It's a skating rink next to the lake. I know you're not up to skating with your injured hand but there's a bar and Doggo can go in. I found it online this morning.' They paused at the lake for Doggo to drink the ice-cold water noisily then crossed the final road and joined a path across a footbridge edged in yellow lanterns.

'Stunning,' Lily breathed, the lanterns reflecting like floating gold in her eyes.

The blue lights illuminated an ice-skating rink currently populated by a gaggle of children bundled up in coats and hats and two teenagers flicking around a puck with hockey sticks. Lily's smile returned to full power as she watched. 'Look at the little ones pushing plastic penguins along to help them balance!'

'Fantastic,' he replied, looking at her instead.

After watching the children for a few minutes they went indoors to a busy bar. They hung up their coats and Isaac got the drinks while Lily found a small table. The bar was alive with customers of every age from eighteen to eighty and Isaac had to fight his way back.

Isaac picked up her left hand from the table. 'Still multi-coloured.' He turned it gently. The Steri-Strip had come off and the tear in her skin was healing cleanly.

'The swelling's going down.' Her head was close to his as she inspected the maltreated member. 'It's just sore now instead of going *durr-dum, durr-dum* all the time.'

He touched the pad of his thumb to the purple and blue bruise on the palm as he asked her about all the things he'd never had a chance to discuss with her: where she'd gone to uni, whether she'd been brought up in Peterborough, whether she'd ever been to Juno Lounge – he was surprised to realise he felt a distance of more than miles from the Juno now – and where she liked to go on holiday. What kinds of films did she like? What music did she play while she worked and how was her design business going?

Her mouth drooped glumly. 'I've put so much into this

project that once it's over I don't have much on the boil, to be honest. I'm going to have to either find some more project work, though it isn't thick on the ground, or admit defeat and try and get a full-time job.'

He hadn't realised this last was a possibility. 'What will happen about The Three Fishes?'

She shrugged. 'I suppose I'll leave. It's great to work a part-time job around a business but I can't see how it would work with a full-time job. I like the community aspect of working at the pub but I only took that job to get to know Tubb.' She arched a brow. 'By that time you'll probably be a qualified instructor in all that yomping and climbing stuff and be working in another country.'

He shrugged. 'That's the plan.' It didn't seem as important as usual because it wasn't his most immediate objective. He lifted her injured hand and pressed a soft kiss on its back, where the counter flap had slammed into it. 'Let's not think about that now.'

After another drink Doggo emerged from under the table to nudge Isaac as if encouraging him to do something more interesting, so they pulled on their coats and hats and set off around the lake on the path lit by lanterns.

'This is beautiful. Cold but beautiful.' Lily sighed contentedly as she gazed at the pools of light each lantern made, shading the areas in between.

As they left the ice rink behind and were alone Isaac let Doggo's lead out and the big dog vanished to snoop around the shadows. Isaac chose a dim area between lanterns to stop and pull Lily against him, to find her soft lips with his and explore her mouth, to nibble along her jaw to her earlobe.

'Mmm,' Lily said far back in her throat as she tilted her head. The thickness of her coat didn't seem to

218

prevent her from feeling the thickness of him because she circled her hips against his erection. Heat speared through him.

He liked her hair loose and spilling over her shoulders. He threaded his fingers through it, cupping the back of her head. 'How do you feel about getting a hotel room?' Then he answered himself immediately. 'Damn, I can't abandon Doggo in the apartment. Franciszka might not think to let him out if we're not back in the morning.'

She murmured against his jaw, 'Maybe Franciszka has gone to bed already. She seemed pretty shattered.'

He throbbed against her, hardly able to think of anything but getting some – all – of those clothes off her and feeling her beautiful skin against his. 'Let's check it out,' he muttered. 'Doggo wouldn't mind being left in possession of the sofa in the sitting room.' But it was actually several more minutes before they retraced their steps because he found it impossible to stop kissing her, to stop sliding his hands under her coat to cup her titillating behind.

Finally, Doggo obviously having exhausted the interesting smells in the immediate vicinity returned to nudge Isaac's legs and they climbed back up the hill out of town.

They paused when they reached the annexe door. 'Let's be really quiet so we don't wake her if she's out for the count,' he murmured, nuzzling Lily's hair.

But they stepped into the warmth to see Franciszka parading around the annexe looking very much awake, speaking Polish and swooping her phone around to give her family a guided tour on Skype.

'And here are Lily and Isaac,' Franciszka said in English, pointing the phone their way.

They smiled weakly at whoever was on the other end and drifted gently apart.

Chapter Sixteen

The Middletones were in the minibus and on their way to the Food, Lifestyle & Health show by nine thirty on Thursday morning. Lily felt a churning mixture of pleasure and nervousness because she'd received a message from Kirstin that it would be Garrick Tubb taking them to lunch between morning and afternoon performances.

Behind the wheel, Isaac frowned in concentration as a fine veil of snow fell on the busy roads around Zürich. Lily and Carola cast an eye over their programme, as if they didn't know it off by heart.

'How are you doing?' Lily asked Carola under cover of the road noise and the chatter from the seats behind them. 'Still no news from Owen?'

'Owen "The Dud" Dudley?' Carola smiled but it was obviously a mask for pain. 'Total silence. He's moved on to the next mug. After Duncan walking out on me for a younger woman and now The Dud ghosting me I think I've worked out that men are shits.'

'Polite cough,' said Isaac mildly, slowing the minibus as traffic backed up in front of them.

'Present company excepted,' Carola answered, but absently, as if unconvinced.

'You can't judge all men by Duncan and Owen.' Lily patted Carola's hand. 'You don't deserve the problems you've had. Maybe Mr Perfect is in your near future—'

Carola snorted. 'He needn't bother. I was perfectly fine on my own after Duncan left and I'll be perfectly fine again. I don't need a man.'

'Of course you don't,' Lily agreed, but last night Isaac had definitely made her need him, kissing in the frigid air beside the lake, pressing his body to hers as if trying to force himself through their thick clothing. In bed she'd fantasised about what might have happened if their trip had taken place in a Swiss summer rather than icy winter. A quiet place in a wildflower meadow perhaps . . . In her fantasy, Doggo had obligingly closed his eyes and slept through the whole heated encounter.

Beside her, as if picking up her thoughts of his canine companion Isaac clicked his fingers. 'I have to find a vet to get Doggo wormed on Friday or he won't be allowed back into the UK.'

It was a rude hijacking of her fantasy but Lily took out her phone and researched vets in Schützenberg. Isaac had dropped everything to drive the Middletones halfway across Europe so she was happy to help. 'There are two possibilities here. I'll text you the links.'

'Great, thanks.' He shot her a smile as he indicated to take the motorway exit. Soon the great exhibition halls loomed before them and they joined a long snake of traffic waiting to be marshalled into the massive car parks. Once inside the building they had the tedious business of passing security, the instruments being taken to a special table to be scanned and then inspected by a sniffer dog. Next they pinned on their passes and queued to check in their coats. Finally they were free to get into the cavernous hall with its crowded aisles and bright lights, orientate themselves with a bit of help from a young lady handing out floor plans then head for stand E11-07.

The phrase 'as difficult as herding cats' should be replaced by 'as difficult as herding teenagers' Lily thought, bringing up the rear in an attempt to dissuade Warwick from stopping to inspect a stand of travel cups, Eddie and Alfie asking for sample cereal bars and Charlotte from veering off towards a display of cake decorations. Carola was navigating at the head of the group, Neil and Franciszka chatting as they followed her.

Isaac dropped back. 'Lily, according to the floor plan there's a whole section of outdoor stuff. Text me when you know details of where we're meeting for lunch.' Checking no one was looking their way, he dropped a kiss on her hair and headed off, leaving Lily to carry on with the teenager wrangling.

At least when they reached E11-07 it was to find everything ready. Kirstin and Garrick were waiting, an electrical outlet had been reserved for the PA and all they had to do was organise themselves. 'It's too hot for hats and scarves, we'll just wear the overshirts,' Lily decided, shaking hers out. They were over-oversized without outdoor clothes underneath but she was sure no one would mind. Los arrived as they were about to begin so Kirstin became very animated and took lots of pictures of him with the Middletones, then added Garrick to the mix, then Felix, who'd just finished a meeting with a woman in a navy suit, moving a #BritishCountryFoods flag closer and swinging a Union Jack artfully into shot. Lily, deciding she couldn't wear her exhibition designer hat and her Middletones hat simultaneously, didn't protest.

Some of the hurrying foot traffic slowed to watch the photoshoot. Felix encouraged lingering by taking round a bowl of chocolates decorated with Union Jack ribbons. Los and Garrick stepped aside and Carola moved to the front to count them in to 'White Christmas' and soon a little crowd had gathered. Lily felt so buoyed by excitement as song followed song that she didn't even worry about the high notes in 'Walking in the Air' and just let her voice soar up to the industrial rafters of the great hall while Kirstin took yet more photos for social media. On the last notes of 'We Wish You a Merry Christmas' a couple of people asked to have their photos taken with the Middletones and Los watched with an expression of approval that had Kirstin beaming.

Having arranged to meet the others in half an hour, Lily hung back to return the stand to its former configuration and talk to Kirstin about hashtags while Los disappeared and Stephen and Felix began new meetings at the stand. Then Garrick closed the conversation he was having with a woman in a neat red dress and held out his arm to Lily in an old-fashioned gesture. 'May I take you up to lunch now?'

Her heart gave an extra beat as she laid her hand on his sleeve and said shyly, 'That would be lovely.'

As they made their way through the crowds, Lily holding her injured hand to her chest to prevent people from bashing it, Garrick kept up a commentary. 'Los is very happy. It would have been easy for him to look at this project and say there were no direct rewards for BCF but he listened to what we wanted to do and gave us the go-ahead.'

'The sponsorship made it all possible,' said Lily. They were singing for their supper, literally, but having lots of lovely time off to enjoy Switzerland. 'We do realise that it was philanthropic.' She made a mental note to buy a big posh thank you card for Los and each of the team they'd worked with and get every Middletone to sign them.

The others were all already waiting at the foot of the stairs to a dining area where a section had been put aside for them and two smiling young men in black trousers and white shirts quickly laid a parade of dishes down the centre of the table then went round with fizzy water and fruit juice. 'Awesome,' said Eddie, sitting down promptly. 'Pass us some of them pizza slices, Warwick.'

During lunch, Lily warmed even further to Garrick. Much as she'd learned to love Tubb, she wasn't blind to his dour moments and his occasional inability to spend money. Garrick was more relaxed and expansive. He was a great host, keeping the conversation flowing, ensuring plates were passed and drinks refilled. He even got Carola smiling with a gentle joke or two. That feat alone endeared him to Lily.

Then his phone rang and he excused himself to answer. 'Hi, Eleanor. No, it's fine, I'm at lunch with Lily and co. Harry's asked me to invite them . . .' Then his smile faded. 'Sorry? Hang on.' He rose and, excusing himself to the company, hurried out of the room, phone clamped to his ear.

Just when Lily was enjoying her bro's company, she thought, wondering what they were going to be invited to. Garrick always called Tubb 'Harry'. She knew some people had called them Harry and Garry when they were kids, instead of Harrison and Garrick. Then her own phone buzzed like an insect in her pocket. She took it out to see a text from Zinnia.

Are you speaking to me properly yet? and an emoji shedding a tear.

Lily's heart melted a couple of degrees and she almost felt guilty that she hadn't thought much about Zinnia, particularly not in the last few minutes while she'd been with Garrick. She returned, *Yes. Let's talk when I get back. At the trade show right now and have to sing again soon.* And she added a couple of kisses.

Yes, great! xx Zinnia texted back. The emoji this time had hearts for eyes.

When Garrick returned he was back in convivial host mode. 'I'm to invite you to see the Samichlaus parade this evening. I can't tell you much about it because it will be my first too, but would you all like to come to Max's for something to eat first? My brother and Janice are hosting.' He turned to Isaac. 'You don't have to take the minibus if you fancy a beer or two. It's only a twenty-minute walk to the crossroads where we'll watch the parades converging.'

Everyone around the table was up for it. Garrick fell to discussing something with Neil and Lily turned to Isaac in the seat across from hers. 'Had a good morning?'

He nodded eagerly, dark hair falling into his eyes. 'The outdoor living segment of this show's brilliant. And everyone speaks such fantastic English. I've been chatting about boots, tents and all that fascinating stuff.' His eyes laughed at himself but his enthusiasm was obvious.

'That does sound fascinating.' She grinned back but had to force it over a sudden sinking of her heart. It was a reminder that once the fate of The Three Fishes was sealed in a month or two Isaac would be getting the hell out of town. Pastures new. Fresh challenges. Career change. It made her both sad to know their 'thing' couldn't last and more focused on enjoying it while she could. She spoke her next thought aloud. 'Time's a funny thing, isn't it? The good parts go by so fast.'

Isaac's eyes narrowed. 'What brought that on?'

She flushed, not wanting to share her thought process, especially at a table full of Middletones. She shrugged. 'Just thinking about the whole trip. How so much of my time's been taken up with plans and logistics and how I want to savour every moment. I'm glad that you're enjoying it too.'

His smile held a suggestion of heat. 'It's getting better and better.'

Later, in the early evening, she, Isaac and Franciszka crunched through fresh snow to Max's house in Terrassenweg. As well as the Middletones, Garrick, Eleanor, Myla and Xander joined Max's family for supper. Tubb and Janice hosted while Max tried to calm Dugal and Keir who were excited by so many people and so much nice food. Ona looked wan and fed up, rubbing her large round abdomen and grumbling that she'd be glad when the baby was safely born. She'd had to visit the hospital with bleeding but they'd let her out again for now.

'Samichlaus came to our door!' Dugal kept bellowing. 'Mummy gave him money and he gave us nuts and satsumas.'

Max tried to calm the boys down and explain over their heads. 'It's all something to do with St Nicholas. Samichlaus looks quite a bit like our Santa Claus, though with a bishop's hat and crook. He and his sidekicks collect money for children's charities.'

The noise grew as everyone tucked into cooked meats,

cheeses, beer or lemonade followed by chocolate cake decorated with walnut halves. Lily found herself sharing a corner of the dining table with Garrick and took the opportunity to ask about where he and Eleanor lived, lower down in the town. She tried to bring Eleanor into the conversation but came to the conclusion that her half-brother's wife was almost as wintry as the weather outside. She seemed on a mission to reply in as few words as possible, especially compared to warm and chatty Garrick.

Eventually she left Garrick and Eleanor to chat with Ona and instead Lily listened in to Isaac talking to Tubb about making more money at The Three Fishes without losing the good things about it. He talked knowledgeably about how much more Juno Lounge used to pay to the brewery for supplies in wet rent and that it didn't offset the discount he got on dry rent – whatever that meant. They discussed the influence of sports TV on filling a pub and how during the World Cup pubs reported increases in sales of up to two hundred per cent.

'If The Three Fishes was mine I'd probably enlarge the area with the dartboard and TV and partition it off. Make it a sports bar so the regulars who hate the TV and the noise of twenty people shouting at it when footy's on aren't driven away,' Isaac said as Tubb nodded interestedly. Lily began to think it a shame Isaac was leaving the hospitality trade because he obviously understood so much.

Presently, they all climbed into their outdoor clothes and boots and tramped down into the centre of Schützenberg – except Ona, for whom such exertion was banned and who settled down with a sigh and the TV remote. Doggo yawned and got up on the sofa to keep her company.

Plenty of other people bundled in coats and hats were

headed in the same direction as them, chattering and laughing as they tramped down the hill towards the streets strung with lights. Much of the centre had been closed to traffic and the snow cleared. The evening breeze carried a muffled, rhythmic noise and they glimpsed moving lights higher up the slope.

'It's one of the processions.' Max held Keir on his shoulders. 'Apparently there are six and they all meet where the roads converge.'

'And they have donkeys, don't they, Daddy?' demanded Dugal, who Janice held tightly by the hand.

'That's right.' Max looked apologetic. 'I've honestly tried to discover from Swiss people at work what the story is behind the procession but haven't gathered coherent information. Some say it's St Nicholas's birthday, some his death day, but why lanterns and donkeys I don't know. St Nicholas the bishop – or Samichlaus – gave money to the poor so have your change ready so you can contribute to the money raised.'

Once they'd found a handy spectating spot alongside others whose breath hung in white clouds on the night air, they waited.

'Hope this is worth it,' Carola muttered, hunching her neck into her scarf like a chilly tortoise.

Then the background rhythmic buzz they'd been able to hear on the way down grew in volume, punctuated by sharp cracks like pistol shots, and people edged closer to the road, craning their necks.

The noise grew louder, louder, and suddenly men in white smocks appeared from each of the converging roads, cracking large whips. The effort required was obvious as they used both hands on the stock to pull the whip from the air and slash it in front of themselves, then pause and drag it back, causing the shot-like *CRACK!* 'Wow,' said Lily, taking an involuntary step back. It felt as if one of those whips could come loose and hurt someone.

More and more whipsters arrived, stationing themselves carefully out of range of each other. Into this racket processed other white-smocked figures waving long, thin lanterns, rhythmically shaking cowbells that hung from great yokes across their necks. Lily felt as if the bells said *ruddle ruddle ruddle ruddle*. The horn blowers followed, *rouuuuhhh, rouuuuhhh*. Over it all the whips kept up a constant *CRACK! CRACK!*

In each of the six processions walked Samichlaus with his entourage and a pony or a donkey, apparently unbothered by the cacophony of whip, bell and horn reverberating around the crossroads. The processions followed and circled one another. Silken bags were held out to the crowd to throw in their change.

Lily's head clanged almost as much as the bells. She turned to Franciszka, raising her voice. 'I've never heard such a row!'

Franciszka nodded. 'In Poland we celebrate St Nicholas Day, Mikołajki, which is tomorrow, with presents for the children.' She fell silent to watch the procession and Lily did the same, reflecting on all the folklore and traditions of Christmas and how different they were around the world. The UK's Santa Claus was a lot cuddlier than Samichlaus.

Finally, the processions turned back towards the different roads from which they'd appeared, still shaking their cowbells and blowing horns, leaving ringing ears behind them. The men with whips were last, still snapping and cracking the whips in the middle of the road. After several minutes they followed their respective processions with a fading *CRACK! CRACK!*

Lily was about to remind everyone that they had a day off tomorrow and were to visit Zürich when Franciszka turned to her. 'I won't be back to the annexe tonight.' She winked. 'I hinted to Eddie it was a shame he wasn't sharing the room of Alfie and Warwick, so he asked his father if he could.' A sly smile spread across her face. 'Who wants to share with their father while their friends laugh and joke in another room?'

A mini shockwave tingled through Lily. 'So you'll be . . . ?'

'Sharing with Neil.' Franciszka's eyes reflected the myriad Christmas lights suspended over the crossroads. 'A little happiness for us both.' She winked again and turned to join Neil, waiting a few yards away.

Wow. Lily stared after her, impressed at Franciszka's pragmatism. *A little happiness for us both.* She thought about Tubb and Janice living separate, slightly lonely lives until they found each other last Christmas. And her mothers, together for nearly forty years yet now apart. Carola, miserable now her new love had foundered. Her own marriage, which had begun promisingly but fizzled out.

Happiness didn't always come along at a convenient time and it wasn't always permanent.

The group split up and Isaac and Lily set off in the same direction as Tubb, Janice, and the two suddenly sleepy boys, Max with Keir again on his shoulders and Isaac taking Dugal piggyback.

The night was icy now and they had to watch their footing, even in boots. At Max's house Lily and Isaac reclaimed Doggo and said goodnight. As they tramped further up the hill Lily took Isaac's hand and he smiled down at her, Christmas lights from the houses around flickering behind his head. His hat was pulled down over his ears and he had a decided five-o'clock shadow. His gloved hand squeezed hers and his voice was low and rough. 'Did I see Franciszka heading for the Little Apartments? How long do you think we have?'

She sent him a sidelong glance. 'All night.' When his eyebrows shot up she repeated what Franciszka had told her. 'I like the idea of a little happiness,' she added.

Isaac stopped and kissed her slowly and thoroughly, his mouth warm and tender. 'So do I,' he whispered. 'Let's grab it.'

Chapter Seventeen

Unspeaking, breathing fast, they hurried up to Los's gracious white house, windows lit behind the blinds, a Christmas tree twinkling from the upper balcony, and took the path where the snow lay like a carpet on either side. Isaac unlocked the door and let Doggo off the lead. Doggo shook, trotted to his bowls to see if any food had appeared in his absence, slurped up a little water and looked at Isaac.

Isaac pointed at Doggo's bed. ''Night, Doggo.' Doggo waved goodnight with his tail and flopped down with a yawn.

In seconds Lily found herself in Isaac's bedroom watching him pull off gloves, hat, coat and boots as if it was a speed test.

Then everything seemed to slow down.

Gently, he drew her close. His mouth fastened over hers in a deep, drugging kiss as she felt him sliding her hat from her head, her gloves from her hands, slow and gentle with the damaged one. Her hands floated up to stroke his face as he found the zip on her coat and eased it down. The coat slid to the floor.

It was warm in the room, warmer by the moment. His skin was fragrant with the scent of outdoors. She melted against him as his mouth caressed her cheeks, her eyelids and he fumbled with her fleece. 'Stop me if I'm taking too much for granted,' he breathed, sliding his hands under her top and grazing her back with his palms, prickling her skin as every hair stood on end.

'Don't stop,' she gasped as he inched her top up and over her head, her hair tumbling softly back onto her shoulders and upper arms.

'Beautiful,' he breathed, his gaze on her breasts, cupped by her lacy, lavender-coloured bra, stroking her skin above the lace. A delicious tide of goose bumps followed his fingertips and her breasts tightened as he flicked open the bra and slid it from her, lowering his head to bring his mouth to her, licking, nipping, nibbling, sucking until she wasn't sure her legs would keep her up.

Anchoring herself to him, she slid her hands up under his top, sighing at the feel of his skin, his body hair coarse yet silky. A couple of economic movements from him and the top was gone and she dropped her fingers to the fastening of his jeans.

'Damned hand,' she groaned after a moment. 'I can't undress you.'

His rumble of laughter was low in his throat. 'Leave it to me.' His jeans were gone in a moment.

Hers too.

Then he was easing her down onto the bed, the cotton softness of the duvet at her back as she found the satin-covered hardness of him, trickling her fingertips over his flesh, his breath hissing between his teeth as she meandered a pathway of kisses across his body. Struggling with keeping her injured hand out of the way and using the

233

'wrong' hand to touch him she kind of lost her place when he began exploring her, making her clench and push against him, wrap him in her arms and legs. His skin smelled deliciously of outdoors and the fine hair of his body slid over her skin until she felt as if she were encapsulated in a halo of sensitivity and sensation.

Soon she wasn't really thinking. She was just doing.

One of them retained the presence of mind to use a condom – though it wasn't her. His breath rushed against her shoulder as he entered her. Hard flesh stroked soft flesh and she felt him in every part of herself, opening and closing, pushing and pulling, felt the way he moved, caressing her with every part of himself, stroking her inside and out.

And there was nothing in the world for her but that man and this moment.

They definitely didn't get enough sleep. 'But we have to make the most of our time together,' she murmured to him as she was dragged from her slumbers by the intriguing sensation of a hot male body and caressing hands. Whether she woke him or he woke her the tingling sex was unhurried and tender. Isaac made love with intensity and curiosity, enclosing them in a private bubble of pleasure.

Friday morning finally arrived with Isaac's phone alarm going off. He stretched, then caught Lily up against him. 'I have to take Doggo to visit the vet or he won't be allowed to set paw back on British soil. Ona says he can stay with her today while we're out.'

'Awwwww.' She nuzzled the side of his neck. 'I want to stay in bed.'

His laugh was rueful as his hand slid down to stroke her bottom. 'If you want to let the others go to Zürich on their own then let's do it.'

'They can't get to Biberbrugg station without you to drive them there. Hope Franciszka meant she'll be staying with Neil tonight as well,' she groaned, reluctantly letting him slide out from under her hands, out of bed. Then she eased herself from the warm cocoon of Isaac's quilt and began to gather up her clothes.

'The Christmasness of this place is awesome!' Alfie announced. They were exploring the market currently occupying most of Zürich Main Station, passing under the banner reading, *Christkindlimarkt – ENCHANTINGLY WELCOME!* to slaver over chocolate cakes and wince at a price tag of fifty Swiss francs for a single – though beautiful – glass decoration.

The Swarovski Christmas tree, encrusted top to bottom with glittering crystals, was so ostentatiously beautiful it was hard to absorb. Almost more crystal than tree, soaring thirty feet into the rafters of the great building, it was surrounded by display cases of jewellery and even a crystal-encrusted bowler hat.

Charlotte and Emily pressed their faces against the security glass and groaned. 'Mum . . .?'

Carola laughed incredulously. 'Darlings, if you think I have enough money to buy you something amazing from Swarovski then I'm afraid you've got me mixed up with some other mother.'

They left the station below a thousand tiny lights, like fairyland, glittery without being glitzy. Isaac drew level with Lily, swapping sides to take her good hand as an old-fashioned red tram covered in lights and stars and full of children rattled past. Although Lily caught a couple of interested looks directed their way, the hand-holding seemed quickly accepted, especially when Franciszka and

235

Neil followed their lead. Carola cast both couples wistful looks.

It was close to a perfect day. They went uphill in a little old funicular called the Polybahn, also red, which left from a tiny station decorated with stained glass, and they gazed out over Zürich from the front of the university, admiring slender pointed spires and the mountain backdrop. Emily was particularly entranced by golden lamp posts in front of which she took so many selfies the boys photobombed her, making her dissolve into giggles.

They rode the trams past massive adverts for Lindt chocolate and painted buildings and found a fantastic tea room, decorated with curly gilt plaster and red velvet furniture, drenched with Christmas decorations, and ordered hot chocolate and selected their ravishing cakes, enjoying every crumb and sip, despite the bill at the end.

They worked the calories off by climbing the tower of the sixteenth-century Grossmünster Church to look out over the city and Lake Zürich, Lily marvelling that a graffiti artist had been allowed to paint what looked like stickmen in one of the chambers halfway up.

Another Christmas market, this time outside the opera house, more bratwurst and waffles. They bought glühwein too but only Carola, Franciszka and Isaac really seemed to enjoy it. Lily thought it tasted like cough medicine. Warwick drank his and Eddie's, feeling that, at eighteen, he ought to drink alcohol when it was offered, but he felt sick afterwards.

It was while they were enjoying the repast at rustic wooden tables that Lily's phone rang. She read the caller ID in surprise. 'It's Tina,' she told Isaac. 'Maybe she needs to know when I'll be able to work again.' But when Lily answered, she discovered Lily wasn't who Tina wanted at all. 'Is Carola with you?' Tina asked in her usual unflappable way.

'I'll pass you over.' Wondering, Lily said to Carola, 'Tina at the pub wants you.'

Carola looked surprised as she took the handset and said hello. She listened, frowning. Then shock rippled across her features. 'Really?' Tears sprang to her eyes. 'Oh!'

'What's up?' Charlotte was jolted out of her conversation with Eddie and Alfie.

Carola gave her daughter a watery smile. 'Nothing to worry about. I just have to take this call.' She unwound her legs from the wooden bench, stumbling in her haste to rise, and turned her back, phone clamped to her ear.

Charlotte and Emily looked at each other, faces slack with apprehension.

Lily distracted them by asking for help working a map app, letting them explain with teenage loftiness even though she knew perfectly well how to work it. Anxiously, she watched Carola wipe her eyes on her coat cuff.

Her apprehension almost matched Charlotte and Emily's by the time Carola came back to the table wearing a wobbly smile. 'Well,' she said, flopping back to the bench and giving Lily back her phone.

'What's up?' Charlotte demanded again.

'What?' Emily echoed, looking suddenly young and unsure and fidgeting with her mittens.

Carola's laugh shook. 'Tina had Owen in the pub. Owen! He's been mugged.' She wiped her eyes. 'He lost his phone and laptop and was kept in hospital for a couple of days. Then he had several days of creasing headaches and couldn't drive. He didn't have his contact list backed up anywhere. He's still off work so didn't get hands on another computer to send me a message. Once he was well enough to get a mate to drive him to our house on Monday, we'd already gone on this trip. He thought he'd have to wait until we got back but then it occurred to him to go into the pub, thinking someone there would have a way of getting a message to me.' Suddenly she was beaming and laughing. 'I haven't been ghosted!'

'Oh, has he been out of touch?' asked Charlotte, proving how little teenagers needed to know about their parents' lives.

Maybe only Lily got how euphoric Carola was feeling. 'That's brilliant!' she said, giving Carola a hug. 'So you're still a thing?'

Carola nodded, happiness bursting from her. 'Very much so, apparently. I'm going to call him later so we can talk properly. I feel awful for thinking so many bad things about him now and I can hardly wait to get home now to check he's really OK. Such severe concussion's worrying.'

Lily talked to Isaac out of the corner of her mouth like a comedy gangster. 'Don't take a bribe from her to leave early. It's only Friday and we're singing at the Christmas market again on Saturday and the advent brunch. That minibus doesn't leave till Monday, got it?'

Isaac mimicked her delivery. 'You gotta make it worth my while, honey.'

She grinned, signalling with her gaze that she had plenty of ideas in that direction. Judging from the glow in his eyes and the way his hand came to rest on her thigh beneath the table, he received her message.

When the last crumb of the last waffle had been eaten Lily checked the time. 'Stephen told me about this shop that sells cuckoo clocks and people go on the hour to hear all the cuckoos going off.'

'Awesome,' breathed Emily. 'Mum, can I have a cuckoo clock for my room as an extra Chrissy prezzy?'

Carola, whose face had been wreathed in smiles ever since she got the phone call from Owen, gave Emily a big hug. 'I should imagine they'd be a little expensive but we can look.'

'I'd love one too,' Lily said, falling into step beside Emily. 'I don't think I've ever seen one in real life but I'm afraid your mum's right to suspect they'll be expensive. It's a famous brand of clock, I think.'

The shop, when they reached it, was elegant. Warwick commented loudly, 'Swanky or what?' Tourists were gathering on the marble tiles in front of the wall of cuckoo clocks, each one like a little chalet frozen within a scene. At five minutes to the hour a dapper man in a dark suit stepped up to give a quick talk in English, having established that everybody waiting spoke that language, about Lötscher cuckoo clocks.

He smiled around. 'Lötscher has been crafting these wonderful clocks since 1920 and is now the only Swiss manufacturer to create the clocks by hand. Every one, with its attention to detail and use of local material such as linden wood, is a work of art.' He paused for them to assimilate these impressive facts. As he went on to eulogise about clockwork, music boxes and gears, Lily gazed at the beautifully carved clocks in wonder. The figures of people and animals seemed almost real, living daily lives around tiny chalets with shuttered windows.

Emily whispered to her. 'Which one do you like? I like Santa Claus's Chalet.'

'That's one of the most expensive at over two thousand Swiss francs!' Lily whispered back. 'I'd settle for the Brienz Chalet but I can't spend four hundred on it.' The little chalet had flowers at every window and balcony. A stack of logs waited as if for someone to take them indoors for the fire. Above the clock face was the cuckoo's little door. The weights of the winding mechanism were brass fir cones on chains, a pendulum swinging behind.

The man patted the clock that had caught Lily's eye. 'This is our classic, based on the very first Lötscher workshop. Some people say it's the only genuine cuckoo clock.' He twinkled at Emily. 'Miss, you have more expensive tastes but Santa Claus's Chalet features moving platforms for the gifts and the baby deer.'

Then four o'clock arrived and all over the shop little doors popped open and cuckoos bobbed, their 'Cuck-oo, cuck-oo!' mixing on the air with clock chimes. The most elaborate clocks continued with moving figures and pretty music-box tunes.

Carola gave Emily a hug. 'Sorry, sweetie. You'll either have to find a cheaper mass-produced version or to save up your pocket money for a few years.'

After thanking the genial man, the group stepped out of the shop into a darkening afternoon. The temperature had plunged and the Christmas lights like bunting overhead burned brighter as they set off for the last treat on their schedule, something called a singing Christmas tree. Max had exhorted them not to miss it and they arrived at the appropriate square with a hazy idea of an animatronic tree. What they found was by far more charming. The 'tree' was actually a pyramid-shape of balconies one atop the other, trimmed with fir tree branches spangled with lights and a huge star on top. The members of a local choir filled the balconies, looking like Christmas decorations in their gaily coloured hats and scarves. A band played at the foot of the tree and the choir sang 'Joy to the World' and 'Feliz Navidad'. A nearby stall provided beer and hot chocolate and, dancing and singing, the Middletones joined in. Lily, laughing, took a video on her phone and thought she had rarely been so happy.

It felt like one of those special moments when family problems and time running out faded into the background in the face of a special joy.

But as the closing notes of 'White Christmas' faded away she heard Isaac's voice speaking rapidly, angrily, and turned to find him with his phone clamped to his ear. 'Just hold your friggin' horses. I'm in another country. I can't just drop everything,' he snapped. Then, in an altered tone, 'What do you mean? What's happened to Hayley?'

Chapter Eighteen

'Hang on, Nicola. I need to move somewhere quieter.' Isaac turned his back on the singing and dancing that had been engrossing him before his phone rang and strode out of the pool of light and away from the crowd.

When he reached a bench he dropped down on it. 'What's happened?' he demanded.

Nicola's voice was tight and anxious. 'Don't think I wanted to make this call. I'm not doing it to piss you off. I'm doing it because we haven't got a choice.'

'*Tell me*,' he said with quiet emphasis.

So Nicola did, in short, brutal sentences. 'Hayley was diagnosed with breast cancer a few weeks ago. She had a mastectomy and reconstruction on Monday. The op is the reason she asked you to take Doggo. She knew she wouldn't be able to look after him because she can't currently look after herself. My sister Vicky and I agreed to take turns staying with her to cook, help her wash and dress, run her to and from appointments and be with her when she got the histology results. She can't lift anything heavier than half a kettle of water and she's in pain from the wound and the drains.'

Isaac's heart began to beat like a train. 'Why didn't she tell me?' Even as he asked the question he knew the answer. He'd been defensive and suspicious when Hayley began turning up at The Three Fishes. He hadn't invited confidences. With horror, he realised that when he'd thought she'd been checking up on him or hoping to rekindle their relationship she'd probably been trying to tell him what was going on.

'I have my own ideas but you'll have to ask her,' Nicola said crisply. 'The thing is that I'm asking you to help her. She's only four days post-op and our dad's been knocked down by a car in Cornwall and is unconscious. Vicky and I need to rush down there.' Her voice shook. 'It's proved impossible to get Hayley nursing care at no notice on a Friday and you know the only family she has are cousins she never sees. If we could have found someone other than you we would have. But you were in a relationship with her . . .'

'Right,' Isaac said numbly. His heartbeat had slowed until he felt almost lightheaded. Half his brain was trying to work out how soon he could get back to the UK and the other trying to come to terms with words like cancer and mastectomy. As Nicola kept talking, persuading, cajoling, guilting, he imagined Hayley trying to come to terms with losing a breast. He wasn't sure of the details of breast reconstruction but it sounded frightening and horrifying.

'Sorry,' he said into the phone suddenly, cutting across Nicola's verbal torrent. 'Of course I'll come, but you're going to have to give me space to look up flights and stuff.'

'But you'll come tonight,' Nicola pressed. 'I've got to get to my mum and dad—'

'The sooner you leave me alone to sort things out, the sooner I'll know,' he snapped.

Nicola ended the call without saying goodbye.

Isaac rose feeling as if he'd stepped through a portal into a different world. The singing Christmas tree was still singing, lights still blazing, the music still ringing out, yet everything had changed. He realised a figure was coming towards him and it was Lily.

Lily.

His heart twisted. This was going to screw up everything.

'All OK?' she asked breathlessly, concern in her eyes.

He shook his head. 'No.' He recounted the situation as economically as he could, watching shock, horror and sympathy flit across her face as she listened. He wound up with, 'So I feel I have no alternative but to try and get back.' He stopped, realising he was telling the woman he'd slept with last night that he was abandoning her, letting the whole group down, to fly off and look after the woman he used to be in love with.

Lily gazed at him. She looked as if she were absorbing the same truth.

'I'm sorry,' he said awkwardly. 'But she seems literally to have no options. Vicky and Nicola are her best friends. They were going to look after her post-op. It would never have occurred to her that, as they're sisters, if one had a family emergency it would mean both of them did.'

She frowned.

'It's not that we're together any more,' he began again.

'Of course you must go,' she said simply. 'I'll tell the others then you and I can run to the station. We can use our phones to search for flights from the train.' It seemed

244

that while she'd been staring and frowning at him she hadn't been getting angry. She'd been deciding how to help.

They hurried back in the direction of the singing Christmas tree. Lily grabbed Carola and gabbled into her ear. Carola looked shocked and then nodded, raising her voice over 'We Wish You a Merry Christmas'. 'We'll make our own way back when we're ready. Don't worry.'

Then Lily grabbed Isaac's hand and they began to jog to the station, jumping on and off the pavement to brush past people, the Christmas lights reflecting in wetness on the pavements that he suddenly realised came from light snow that was stinging their faces as they ran.

Lily had appointed herself leader of the expedition. On the station concourse she studied the departure boards, dark blue with white writing, and found their train. 'Platform five for the 18.43 to Biberbrugg. We've only got two minutes – run!' Then she stopped so abruptly that he cannoned into her. 'Wait.' She frowned, panting for breath, her gaze fixed to the departure boards again. 'I don't suppose you have your passport with you now?'

He patted the zipped pocket of his coat. 'Yes. I'm one of those tourists who keeps it on them.'

She lifted her gaze to his. 'Unless there are really late flights it's never going to work going to Biberbrugg and then driving to Schützenberg for your things. You'll have clothes and stuff at home so let's get the train straight to the airport. There's an airport shuttle in a few minutes. I can pack up your stuff to bring it home and look after Doggo for you.'

'Doggo! I hadn't even thought . . .' He tried to fold his foggy mind around this new idea. 'You're right. I'll do that.' So they ran to the ticket office. Isaac knew he ought to almost literally be able to run rings around Lily but his legs seemed made from water and it was all he could do to keep going as she urged him through the barrier and onto the train.

Three words boomed through his brain. Cancer. Mastectomy. Hayley.

Oh, shit.

It was a big deal for Hayley to accept help, let alone ask for it. He could only imagine how she was feeling. The resentment and antipathy he'd felt for her over the past few months faded to nothing.

As the shuttle left the station Lily was already on Skyscanner. 'There's a plane to Luton at 20.50, which is doable. It's not seven p.m. yet.' She studied the screen. 'That's about the only option this evening. I'll buy a ticket.'

Numbly, he passed her his credit card and watched her tap in the payment, then his passport details.

She worked rapidly, swaying in her seat with the train's motion. 'You land at 21.40, UK time. Trains from Luton would get you to Peterborough station at either just after midnight or just after one, and then you'd still have to get to Hayley's place. I think it'll be better if we book you a car.'

He nodded, watching her use his credit card again as if trapped in a dream. Then reality made itself felt. 'You're on the train to the airport with me,' he said stupidly. 'You're going to have to get it all the way back again on your own.'

Her eyes twinkled. 'Ten minutes to Zürich Main and then from Zürich to Biberbrugg, for which I already hold a ticket? And then I'll get the minibus—' She broke off. 'Minibus! Give me the keys! I'm not sure how the others will be getting back from Biberbrugg to Schützenberg but Carola has numbers for Max, Tubb and Garrick. I'm sure they'll work it out.'

He swore beneath his breath, earning himself a reproving look from an elderly lady nearby. Now the first shock was over his mind was moving into gear. 'Your hand – you can't drive, Lily.'

'I can if I have to,' she contradicted him flatly. 'My hand's much better and I'll take paracetamol. The only thing that's really worrying me is getting Doggo back to the UK, to be honest. You'll have to ring me when you're home and talk me through where his documents are and what to do.'

He slid his arms around her and rested his cheek on the top of her head. 'You are a diamond. You're coping with this as if it's a walk in the park instead of a tricky situation you could easily have distanced yourself from.' He tilted her face to his and kissed her lips gently. 'Thank you.'

When he looked up, the elderly lady was looking upon him with a little more warmth.

Lily gave him a hug as they whooshed to a halt in the Zürich Flughafen station. 'My role in this is comparatively easy. Much worse to be Hayley.'

Lily rode the train home later having seen Isaac as far as she could through the airport.

It had been odd to see him in the grip of shock, the usually incisive Isaac disorientated, repeating how hard Hayley's situation was to take in. He'd given her a hard hug and a hot kiss goodbye and headed for airport security with just one look back, hesitating as if considering returning. But then, with an air of resignation he'd turned and joined the flood of humanity funnelling in between the barriers. Gone.

Waiting would have been pointless so, the adrenalin of the mad dash to the airport draining away and leaving her feeling surprisingly alone, she'd trailed back down to Airport Level 2 and the shuttle. Isaac had thanked her and thanked her for hustling him onto a flight and it had made her feel ashamed because under the veneer she'd known herself to be resenting a woman with breast cancer for spoiling her good time.

Last night, his bed had felt like their own special world. She'd been prepared for their time together to be short – but not just one night.

As the train rumbled away her hand ached from being jostled as they'd run. She bought a bottle of water when she changed at Zürich and took paracetamol. At Wädenswil she changed for Biberbrugg.

Carola texted: *Are you OK? We're back. Max and Garrick picked us up from Biberbrugg station.*

Lily replied. *All OK. Isaac got flight. I'll be back at Biberbrugg station in twenty minutes. Will phone you tomorrow.* She couldn't face a Carola inquisition tonight.

It was nearly nine thirty when she was finally reunited with the minibus, which was covered in snow. She sighed and dug out the squeegee thing from the driver's door and, standing on tiptoes to reach the high bits, cleared all the windows. It was trickier to get out of the parking space because selecting reverse meant pressing the gear stick down with the middle of her palm where the bruising was worst.

With a loud and violent four-lettered outburst she managed it, then followed the sat nav back to Schützenberg and Toblerstrasse, where she parked, her hand throbbing and burning. She let herself into the annexe and it was so silent that she walked down to Max's house and collected Doggo.

She didn't want to be alone tonight. Her spirits felt like weights slung round her ankles.

Isaac reached Hayley's at ten minutes to midnight. He'd called Nicola from the taxi and arranged to do a handover before Nicola headed south for Cornwall, Vicky having set out already. He'd sat through the short flight in a state of unreality but now he had to get himself together.

It felt odd for Nicola to let him into the flat that had been his home for years. She and Vicky were more thickset than Hayley but equally permanently groomed. Nicola's corn-coloured hair was cut in stylish layers and she wore neat make-up. 'Sorry for screwing things up for you but thanks for coming,' she whispered shortly. 'Hayley's asleep. Come into the kitchen. I've printed you some notes.' She tapped the top of the page. 'Here's the officialese: she had a grade one, stage one invasive ductile non-specific tumour so they gave her a skin-sparing mastectomy with lymph node biopsy and stage one reconstruction.'

His thoughts swam. 'What does it actually mean?'

She sighed. 'Breast cancer, caught early, hopefully not aggressive. They've taken all the insides out of her breast along with the nipple and put in a temporary implant. When they have the results of the biopsy and have decided on further treatment they'll plan the rest of the reconstruction.'

Sweat burst out on his forehead. *Poor Hayley.* Body maintenance was a way of life to her and then this foul thing had come along and savaged her.

Nicola moved on. 'She mustn't lift her arm above her head. She has two drains in and has to carry the bottles the fluid passes into around with her in a bag. Washing and dressing herself, cooking, they're all impossible right now. Can't be left alone. Can't drive. Can't stretch. Can't lift.'

Responsibility settled on Isaac's shoulders. 'I can see why you got in touch with me.'

Nicola pulled a selection of packets and boxes towards her. 'If she could have come up with someone else she would have, I think. Here are her meds. Antibiotics, paracetamol, ibuprofen and Tramadol. Here's the number for the breast cancer nurse. She's brilliant so if you're worried, call her.' She slid the notes onto the counter and headed for the hallway where her bag was already packed and waiting. 'Do you still have my phone number? Sorry I have to dump this on you – but I do have to.'

'I realise.' Isaac tried to make himself function. 'How's your dad?'

A tear formed at the corner of her eye. 'In a bad way. Deeply unconscious, pelvic injury and internal injury. He's out of surgery now. Vicky's there already and Mum's in pieces. She saw him step off the pavement in front of the car that hit him.' She wiped the tear away.

Whispering the usual platitudes that were all you could offer when a loved one had sustained life-changing injuries or worse, he saw her out then walked slowly into the lounge. It looked the same as last time he'd seen it: cream sofas, green curtains, the streamlined chrome lamps Hayley favoured with white glass shades. It was he who had changed.

What should he do? He had no clothes here now. Maybe Flora could bring some stuff from The Three Fishes tomorrow. He peeped into the spare room and saw the bed tumbled, presumably after Nicola had slept in it. Unable to face changing the sheets tonight he returned to the sofa and put the TV on low, preparing to spend the night there.

Then Hayley drifted in like a ghost in a white robe. Tubes emerged from beneath the fabric and looped into the floral bag hung over her shoulder as if she was just off shopping. Her pallor was startling, lines graven on her face. For once, she looked her age – and more. Her voice was a thread. 'You can't imagine how hard I tried not to ask this of you.'

He rose slowly, shocked by her appearance. 'I'm sorry you didn't feel you could tell me what you were going through.'

She drifted to the armchair and lowered herself gingerly into it, disposing of the inappropriately cheery bag at her feet. She sounded irritable. 'It's me who owes you the apology. I ended the relationship and it's outrageous that I should now presume upon your good nature to turn yourself into my carer just as if we were still together. Outrageous. I talked to Bev, my cancer nurse, about it for quite a while but she's adamant that I can't manage alone yet.'

'You don't look as if you ought to be out of bed, let alone managing by yourself,' he said honestly. 'When you handed Doggo over I should have realised there was something wrong.'

'I was feeling alone,' she sighed.

'I'm sorry,' he said, meaning it. 'I leapt to conclusions and was prickly and defensive.'

She sat back, closing her eyes. 'I understand. From your point of view I turned up out of the blue acting oddly. This is going to be awful. I thought that getting a nurse would be easy enough. I have the money to pay privately.'

He sat down again. 'I know from Mum that if she needs respite care for Dad it has to be booked well ahead.'

She nodded. 'I can't work for a while. I might have to have radiotherapy or chemo. I might lose my hair.' Her eyelids flicked open with a glint of grim humour. 'I always said I'd never have an implant or a tattoo and now I'm going to end up with both.'

His brain worked on that. 'The implant I understand but . . . a tattoo?'

She began to ease herself up again. 'They tattoo on a nipple. Non-functioning, of course.'

'Oh,' he said blankly.

She shifted her weight forward and managed to get to her feet. 'Thanks for coming, Isaac. I'm afraid things are going to be incredibly awkward.'

'Then let's not highlight it by continually apologising,' he suggested gently. 'We're both managers. Let's deal with what we have, pragmatically and with as much good humour as we can.'

She managed a wavering smile. 'You're a wonderful man. See you in the morning.' And, as silently as she'd arrived, she glided from the room.

Isaac spent the next couple of hours searching the internet for information on breast cancer and breast reconstruction. Holy shit. And people went through this all the time.

Chapter Nineteen

The fun seemed to have drained from the Swiss trip. After taking Doggo on a morning walk through the fresh, crisp fall of snow covering the grass of the local park Lily met Carola at Max's to reorganise things in the light of Isaac's absence. At least concentrating on the logistics stopped her thinking about Isaac and wondering what was happening back at Hayley's place.

Max offered to drive the equipment to the advent brunch this morning and on to the Christmas market so Lily could put off driving the minibus until she absolutely had to. Lily thanked him and said, 'Lucky this is our last day of singing. We can all relax on Sunday, apart from packing to leave on Monday.' She'd slept badly last night but she would have had a chance to get back on an even keel by then.

Tubb rubbed his hand over his thinning hair. 'Driving back to the UK is going to be a terrific burden for you. Maybe I ought to do it. I can fly back here.'

'I can't let you do that,' she protested, thinking about his dodgy heart. 'My hand's much better now. I'll rest it as much as I can today and Sunday. The rate it's been healing, I'll be good to drive back, especially as so much of the first day is motorway where there will be hardly any gear changes. I'll be fine just to steer.'

'Let's see how you are on Monday morning. We can sort out insurance for me then, if necessary,' he prevaricated, still looking dubious.

Lily wondered how the insurance company would react to a driver in his current state of health but suppressed the urge to mention it. She had no intention of letting Tubb drive.

Normally, she would have loved the advent musical brunch in a pretty shuttered hotel in town. Children played before an impressive Christmas tree festooned with silver ornaments, families listening and applauding, and the Middletones were introduced by the bearded master of ceremonies as 'visitors to our small town and friends of our British friend, Max Gasly, who have kindly brought their little choir to Switzerland'.

They sang. The audience joined in with 'Silent Night'. They chatted with the friendly local people and ate the gorgeous four-course meal.

Two girls of about eight played a wavering clarinet duo and one said something to the other in a strangled whisper as she exited that made everyone within earshot laugh. Max, grinning, translated for the Middletones. 'She said, "Shit! I got it wrong!"'

Lily laughed along with everyone else but she'd noticed with a lurch that she'd missed a call from Isaac while they'd been singing and sidled out to the corridor to call him back. Annoyingly, he didn't pick up. She left him voicemail to ask how things were going.

They arrived at the Christmas market in the afternoon

to the news that this was to be their final performance as Sarah and Melina informed them that a snowstorm was forecast and the organisers were closing the market at five instead of eight. 'No one will come to shop in such weather.'

Lily spent the hour before they were due to sing doing Christmas shopping, knowing that her loved ones would adore presents from a proper Swiss Christmas market.

When it was time to sing they received a better reception than ever but Lily felt flat, very much aware of Isaac's absence. Carola, though on the phone to Owen every hour to check he really was OK after his mugging, was high on the knowledge that he was neither a dud nor a ghoster and made up for it, singing lustily enough for all nine of them.

Lily was so fatigued that Christmas lights were turning from twinkles to blurs in her vision. She was touched, though, that so many from British Country Foods turned up, giving up part of their Saturday to listen to them sing: Los and Tanja, Garrick and Eleanor, Stephen and Kirstin – each with a young man in tow – and Felix with his two little sisters, who'd brought Swiss chocolate bars for each of the Middletones. Tubb was there but Janice had stayed home to take care of Dugal and Keir. The one thing that did lift Lily's spirits a notch was Tubb and Garrick giving her big hugs and telling her what a great job she'd done. For a split second she wanted to spill her heart, to tell them who she was. If only she knew they'd be as overjoyed to have her as she was to have them . . .

Then Los was speaking, presenting the Middletones with a huge hamper of delicious-looking cakes, gingerbread and 'hanselmanne' – little men made of sweet bread. Then he singled Lily out and gave her a case that held a dark wood watch, its hands of gold and the strap of leather.

'Wow!' she said, staring at the handsome timepiece.

Los beamed. 'We appreciate the seamless way you brought together the various elements of this project. We have received many column inches in publications covering the trade fair as well as much notice on social media about your singing group. The design of the stands and the stall were perfect. Thank you.'

'Yeah, thanks, Lily, you made the whole thing happen,' Warwick agreed loudly, and everyone clapped so vociferously that Lily's eyes burned, especially when Garrick gave her another hug and said everyone concerned with the stand at the show had said nice things.

Max chimed in. 'How about you all go back to our place? Ona and Janice won't be left out and Dugal and Keir will be excited to see you all. Tubb can go with you now while I help dismantle the stall and I'll get there later.'

A round of goodbyes began, people hugging those they probably wouldn't see again. But then Emily got carried away and not only hugged Warwick – who she would definitely see again – but gave him a big kiss on the lips.

Warwick stepped smartly back, blurting, 'Whoa, Em. I've got a girlfriend and you're not even legal.'

Emily stared at him, stark horror on her face. She stammered something, clearly mortified. 'Sorry!' she ended on a miserable squeak.

After an embarrassed silence Warwick said gruffly, 'Don't matter.' But he walked ahead with Eddie and Alfie, looking embarrassed. Emily fell in beside Carola, chin tucked down in an effort to pretend she wasn't crying. Carola hugged her and whispered she was sure that Warwick knew she'd just got confused really and not to worry.

Even Charlotte was nice to her, saying, 'Boys are so clumsy, Emily. He just said the first thing that came into his head.'

Emily, though, was not to be consoled. 'Mum, can I go back to our room?' she beseeched between sobs. Carola sighed and agreed. 'We'll both go. Perhaps later, when you're feeling better, you and I can go down to the skating rink and have something to eat there.' Charlotte decided to join them, then Lily caught up with the others in time to hear Neil and Franciszka gracefully declining Max's kind invitation in order to take the equipment back then walk on up the mountain.

Warwick stared after Emily, brick red, and mumbled something about wanting to stay in town. Eddie and Alfie decided to do the same, Eddie hoisting his guitar on his back.

So Lily was left to walk up to Max and Ona's house with Garrick, Eleanor and Tubb, who huffed and puffed up the slope. It was a strange feeling to think that all the singing was over.

Janice and Ona were glad to see other adult faces and Dugal and Keir instantly demanded to know where Doggo was so Lily put her boots back on to fetch him. He'd be glad to be let out anyway. When she returned, Doggo settled happily to the agreeable task of playing chase round the dining table with Dugal and Keir.

Feeling vaguely depressed because she'd missed yet another call from Isaac and again he hadn't picked up when she tried to get him back she drifted into Max and Ona's kitchen to make herself a cup of tea. There, she found Garrick pouring water into the coffee machine. If she stuck to her decision not to confess their shared genes, Lily realised she didn't know when she'd see him after this. When she'd made her cuppa she sat down at the table.

Garrick took the seat beside her while he waited for the coffee to brew. 'Have you enjoyed the trip?'

'So much!' Lily beamed. Leaving out her disappointment over Isaac dashing back to the UK she launched into a description of everything she loved about being in the mountains and how welcome the Middletones had been made to feel.

Garrick looked pleased. 'It's been great for us. We'll miss you when you've gone.'

It seemed completely unexceptional to Lily, even when Garrick bestowed a friendly pat on her shoulder, so she was utterly shocked to hear Eleanor snap from the doorway, 'Very cosy.'

Garrick got to his feet, face reddening. 'I'm just waiting for the coffee,' he said stiffly.

Lily stared at Eleanor in astonishment. 'What's up?' she asked, bewildered.

The question, rather than soothing Eleanor, seemed to irritate her. 'What's up,' she enunciated clearly, 'is that you seem to enjoy the company of my husband a touch too much for my taste. You were lunching together when I rang him the other day.'

'What?' Lily laughed. 'We were *all* at lunch together. It wasn't just Garrick and me.' But then she looked from Garrick to Eleanor and saw they both looked deadly serious. Irritation swept over her. Was Eleanor really that immature and insecure? 'My relationship with Garrick couldn't be more platonic,' she said tightly.

Eleanor just sneered. 'That's what the last one said.'

'Lily doesn't need to know about that,' Garrick muttered, face darkening.

'Oh,' said Lily, getting the significance of 'the last one'. Garrick must have cheated on Eleanor in the past. The thought made her unexpectedly sad. She'd assumed he was happy with Eleanor, like Tubb was with Janice.

Eleanor was glaring at Garrick. 'Maybe she does need to know. After all, your last little affair led to you having to change your job and us all uprooting and coming out here.' She sniffed mightily, gazing at Lily. 'I've seen you hug him.'

Lily couldn't believe Eleanor was making such a mountain out of a molehill. 'I haven't hugged him any more than I've hugged Max or Tubb.'

Garrick implored, 'Honestly, Eleanor—'

'Honestly?' repeated Eleanor bitterly. 'I can see the whole horrible cycle happening all over again. You promised that it would never happen again. You *promised*,' she repeated piteously.

Slowly, Lily got to her feet, finally getting why Eleanor had always seemed so wintry and distant with her. She'd picked up on feelings Lily had for Garrick . . . but oh, were they the wrong ones! Everything that had happened in the past few months crowded in on her. Her parents' relationship sailing into troubled waters, the friction with Zinnia, the 'thing' with Isaac that might be so brief she could have blinked and missed it. And now she'd somehow brought this sordid little scene down on Garrick. 'Of course there's nothing between us,' she blurted out. 'At least not what you think.'

Eleanor stopped. 'Not what I think? That implies there's *something*.'

Garrick looked astonished. 'But there's not,' he objected, furrowing a confused brow at Lily.

A silence grew. Lily tried to think what to do, what to

259

say. She felt cornered by her own words, by the situation, by her unhappiness, by holding on to secrets about things that affected her so fundamentally but weren't her fault. She out let her breath and turned to Garrick. 'I've wondered whether to tell you. I haven't known what to do. But . . . well . . . if I had, this wouldn't be happening.'

Eleanor and Garrick looked at each other then back at Lily. 'What?' Their faces bore matching expressions of frustrated unhappiness.

Lily gazed at Garrick, beginning to tremble. She felt as if she were being sucked towards a vortex and there was only one way out. 'I'm sorry it's such a shock. But apparently my mum and, and . . .' She floundered, not knowing whether to say 'your dad' or 'our dad'. '. . . Marvin Tubb had an affair. And I'm the result. I'm your half-sister.'

Garrick gaped. His eyes were a similar blue to hers but held only outrage.

Then Lily heard a strangled sound. Turning, over Eleanor's shoulder she saw Tubb. His face was ashen, his mouth agape.

'Sorry,' she blurted, feeling as if the vortex was spinning closer, closer. Of all the ways she'd envisaged breaking the news to her brothers, this wasn't it: so clumsy, so out of control. She began to babble in horror. 'Sorry, Tubb. Sorry! I know you didn't want to know if Marvin had fathered more children but I haven't known what to do. Whether to tell you. I wanted to . . . but also, I didn't.'

Her voice dried. Tubb's eyes were suddenly blazing with fury. 'Why did you decide to bring it out now? Garrick didn't know about Dad having an affair!'

Lily swallowed her shock. It had never occurred to her that Tubb would keep that knowledge to himself.

'I'd decided not to tell him,' Tubb went on bitterly,

brushing past Eleanor to come further into the room. 'I didn't want to besmirch our father's memory for him, as it had been for me. Garrick's the youngest. He worshipped Dad.'

Garrick was frozen.

Lily watched, mortified as Eleanor, her jealousy apparently forgotten, crossed the room and took his hand.

'He's not the youngest,' Lily whispered. 'I am.'

Tubb stared at Lily as if she'd said something to deliberately hurt him.

The next minutes were like a nightmare. Lily was rooted to the spot with overwhelming shame she didn't think she should have been made to feel. She had to gulp back tears as Garrick and Eleanor got their coats and left. 'I have to process this,' Garrick mumbled, not looking at anybody. Tubb clapped him on the shoulder as he passed.

Then turned and glared at Lily with such scorching contempt she physically stepped back.

She suddenly had every sympathy for the little girl at the advent brunch because, *shit*, she'd really got it wrong. 'I'm sorry,' she tried to say again. Then, because that sounded as if she were apologising for existing, licked her lips and began again. 'I'm sorry I told him but Eleanor thought he and I were having a thing and I had to make her understand—'

Then Janice burst into the room, eyes wide and panicked. 'Harrison, Ona's having a big bleed. One of us will have to take her to hospital and the other stay with the boys.'

'I could stay with the boys,' Lily began.

Tubb shook his head saying shortly, 'Better for them to be with their grandmother. I'll drive Ona.' Then he turned and hurried out with Janice.

Lily stood rooted to the spot, listening to their voices,

261

suppressed urgency, phone calls being made, the decision being taken to get Ona to emergency care at the hospital in Cham. Lily didn't know Cham but heard Tubb reassuring Janice that it was less than twenty minutes in the car and it was better not to wait for the ambulance.

Except for Doggo coming into the kitchen to look for her, she knew herself to be forgotten or disregarded. She hooked her fingers into Doggo's harness to keep him with her, out of the way of a family drama more important than her grief and hurt. She listened to Ona calling falsely bright goodbyes to her sons as Tubb gave her his arm to help her out to his car, to the front door closing behind and Janice trying to sound breezy as she told Dugal and Keir they'd go up and play in the bath. Later, she'd make them burgers for dinner.

Once their voices had vanished up the stairs, moving as stealthily as a robber caught where she ought not to be, Lily left.

Outside, the promised snowstorm had arrived. The flakes poured from the sky in diagonal lines then backed up on the wind and swirled in the halos from the street lamps. Doggo woofed and snorted, bucking about excitedly and kicking up snow, glancing at Lily as if inviting her to play.

'Not in the mood,' she said to him quietly. She pulled up her hood and trudged the couple of minutes back to the annexe, the snow blowing into her eyes and making them burn.

Isaac had been playing telephone tag with Lily all day. It had been amazingly hard to find a time when he could conduct a call in private. Hayley was drowsy but rarely seemed to fall into proper sleep. She sat propped up in

262

the armchair, a book in her lap or the TV on. She was what she described as 'sore', carrying the area under her arm where the drains emerged as if it were a nest of boils. When he'd helped her wash this morning he hadn't been able to avoid seeing the bloody fluid in the drain bottles and had felt briefly lightheaded as he did what he had to do to help her wash. She couldn't take a bath because of the drains and couldn't shower because of the dressings.

The last time he'd been in proximity to Hayley in any state of undress they'd been in a relationship. He'd known her body then, the body she'd worked hard to keep smooth and desirable.

Now . . . now it was wounded. Altered. Thoroughly unnerved and miserable by having to accept his help, Hayley didn't know whether to be grateful or hateful, so alternated between the two, leaving him edgy and biting his tongue. He never remembered being in such an uncomfortable situation in his life.

For Isaac's part, he felt cornered. If Hayley was the kind of woman who had twenty friends to call on or close family both he and Hayley would have avoided this situation like the plague. She hadn't even told him about her mastectomy until she was forced into it.

He made her meals. They talked stiltedly. He made tea and coffee, watched her take her meds. Hung around for when he was needed. Time dragged. Hayley was emotional and cried twice. He didn't remember ever seeing her cry. The high spot of her day seemed to be when Vicky rang from Cornwall to ask how she was, though Hayley bravely brushed aside her own situation and asked after Vicky and Nicola's dad. 'Not good,' had been Vicky's answer, apparently.

Flora had been unable to fetch Isaac's things from The Three Fishes because Willow was at work and Flora had all four of the children to look after but only two child seats for her car. 'Sorry,' she said, obviously shaken to hear of Hayley's plight and Isaac's part in it. 'I can do it late tonight when Willow gets back but it would be about midnight.'

'Better not,' he murmured, resigning himself to another day in the same clothes. 'It's not fair to disturb Hayley then.'

It was a surprise when the front bell rang at six in the evening and Isaac's mum appeared at the door. 'Your stuff's in the car if you want to run down for it,' she said calmly, stepping indoors and handing him her car keys. 'Sorry to invite myself, Hayley,' she said, sailing into the sitting room. 'You poor thing.'

'Um. That's OK,' Hayley said, looking dazed.

Stef talked to Hayley while Isaac ran down the stairs and hauled two fat holdalls out of the back of her car.

Considering the two women hadn't really seemed to like one another while Hayley and Isaac had been together, they found a lot to talk about. Maybe with Hayley now being incapacitated and Stef having been a carer for so long, they'd found an area of understanding. Whatever it was, Isaac was able to shower and change while his mum kept up a steady flow of sympathetic conversation.

After half an hour Stef rose and hugged Isaac. 'I've got to get back to your dad.'

Isaac found himself unexpectedly glad of a cuddle from his mum. 'Thanks for bringing my stuff. Give Dad my love.'

By the time he'd seen her back to her car Hayley was

asleep in the chair so he crept off into the spare room and closed the door to ring Lily.

And, finally, finally, she answered. 'Hello, Isaac.' Her voice sounded small and far away.

'Hey,' he said, rolling down on the bed, warmth flooding through him for the first time in the past twenty-four hours. 'How are you?'

'Fine,' she said lifelessly. 'How are things there?'

A prickle worked its way up his neck. 'You don't sound fine. You sound as if you've been crying.'

'Crying?' She laughed but it lacked her usual warmth and musicality. 'I've been singing so much my voice has gone. I'm kind of glad to get to the end of it. We've ended early because there's a snowstorm and Ona's been rushed into hospital.'

'Is she OK?' he asked, concerned about the quiet, gentle woman who'd been trying her hardest to get to the end of her pregnancy successfully.

A pause. 'Nobody's told me yet. Fingers crossed.' Then she asked again about Hayley and he told her the facts, being circumspect about making it clear how hard he was finding things just in case Hayley happened to shuffle past the door and hear.

Lily sighed. 'What a difficult time for you both. I'd better let you get back to her.' Then she hesitated and added in a quiet, flat voice, 'Bye, Isaac. Look after yourself as well as Hayley.'

He stared at the dead phone in his hand with absolutely no idea of what to make of the Lily he'd just spoken to. Gone had been every vestige of her usual vivacity and drive. She'd sounded dreary. Deeply unhappy.

Could she be furious with him for abandoning her in favour of Hayley? If so, why had she been his travel agent, minder and cheerleader in getting him on a flight last night when he'd gone into a flat spin?

It didn't make sense.

He wasn't going to be fobbed off like that.

He called her back.

But she didn't pick up.

Chapter Twenty

Maybe Zinnia had been right. Lily should have told Tubb who she was as soon as she'd located him.

But . . . if she had, he would have never let her work with him and get to know him. Love him like a brother. At least the way she'd done things she had the couple of years they'd worked together, built a relationship. It was something.

Up early, Lily found it incredibly lonely to be alone with Doggo in the annexe, Franciszka presumably staying with Neil. She took her canine companion for a tramp up out of town where traffic had kept the road clear and she could walk at the edge. The morning light cast lilac shadows on the six-inch blanket of blinding white lying over the hills and gullies. Doggo plunged around as if starring in his own snow globe. No snow was falling but the sky was heavy with more and the tops of the surrounding peaks had vanished into the clouds.

She gazed around her, at the beauty that was Switzerland, the place she'd worked so hard to see. The majestic, beautiful peaks, the acres of snow glistening in the morning light. Drearily, she replayed the events of Friday and Saturday evenings. Isaac leaving. Garrick greeting her real identity with horror. Tubb furious and betrayed.

Neither of her brothers had contacted her.

Today had been designed as a relaxation day at the end of the trip but now it yawned ahead of her and all she wanted to do was go home. Problems awaited her there too, with her parents' relationship struggling and her own relationship with Zinnia to be restored, but despite that she felt a massive pull towards them, to their hugs, their warmth.

Not caring that it wasn't yet eight a.m. she called Carola and told her what had happened with Ona last night.

'Oh, no!' Carola gasped. 'I hope everything's OK with the baby.'

'So do I,' agreed Lily. 'Max is the link that brought us all to Switzerland so I hate to think of anything bad happening to his family.' She paused before adding tentatively, 'Thing is, I don't want to be in their way and now it's down to me to drive I'm looking at the weather forecast and it's due to begin snowing again at lunchtime. Heavily.'

Carola made a considering noise. 'I can imagine that's a worry. I'm really sorry all the driving has fallen on you.' After a hesitation, she sighed. 'Actually, we had a drama of our own yesterday evening. Duncan, my ex, has been calling the girls so much recently that they've remarked on it. We got a call last night to say he and his girlfriend are splitting up.'

Lily thought how that would seem to two teenaged girls. 'So they feel as if he chucked everything away for no good reason?'

Carola gave a short laugh. 'They haven't said that

but . . . He says he's really, really missing them and the girlfriend was always difficult about it or he would have seen them more . . .' Carola's voice shook. 'He destroyed our family for a woman who doesn't like him seeing his own children. He was always aloof, always working too much, but now he's feeling sorry for himself and says he wants to move back to live nearer the girls.'

'That's certainly a change of heart.' Lily hadn't met Duncan very often as the girls usually visited him in London but she'd heard plenty from Carola over the past couple of years. Duncan had been pretty callous in the way he'd left his family when he'd fallen for somebody else three years ago.

'There's more to it,' sniffed Carola. 'Apparently his contract in London isn't being renewed, which is a huge shock. Most of his money went into joint accounts with his girlfriend and "until we're sorted out" she's whisked it away into accounts in her name alone.'

'Can she even do that?' demanded Lily, scandalised.

'Well, she's done it, apparently. Act first, argue through solicitors later seems to be her strategy. Duncan had already moved out to stay with some colleague in Havering when she did it so he's in a bit of a spot.'

As Carola paused, Lily asked cautiously, 'You're not going to let him move back in?'

'No I'm bloody not!' Carola all but yelped. 'The girls would begin to hope it was permanent – which it would *not* be – and it would make things very difficult with Owen. The situation's made the girls very restless though. Despite the fact he didn't exactly put their happiness first, Duncan's their dad and now that he's upset they want to see him.'

It was the perfect opportunity for Lily to say what had

been spinning dismally in her head. 'How do you think the others would take to us starting home today? Bearing the heavy snow in mind too?' she queried experimentally.

'My vote would be yes,' Carola said promptly. 'And Emily's still moping about Warwick so I think she wants the trip to be over. Let me ring round and ask everyone. I'll come back to you as soon as, OK?' And Carola was gone.

Lily turned Doggo round and strode back down the hill towards Schützenberg, feeling more settled. She'd start to pack. She'd have to pack Isaac's stuff too. Presumably Doggo's documents would be there somewhere. She hadn't given Isaac a chance to coach her through the doggy passport control process last night because a storm of tears had been building in her chest as she talked to him, not wanting to tell him about what had happened with her brothers when he had so much to deal with already. But, oh, she felt so bruised and so sad that she'd barely been able to keep it together to say goodbye.

After ending the call she'd cried and cried, venting her pain at being so thoroughly rejected by Tubb and Garrick and the disappointment of Isaac's absence. Listening to him outline the situation he'd found himself in, the severity of Hayley's incapacity and the fragility of her emotions, she'd realised with a slowly sinking heart that he was in it for more than a couple of days with Hayley.

She didn't know what else she'd expected but somehow the reality that he was living with his ex-girlfriend in their own home had hit her like a freezing cold wave.

Would he ever return to The Three Fishes? He'd talked about Hayley needing somebody with her 'for the next few weeks' so he wouldn't be able to abandon her while he worked. Tubb might replace him or limp along with Tina at the helm until the pub was sold.

Her stomach turned on a fresh thought. Even if Isaac found a way to return, would Tubb want Lily working at The Three Fishes now? She was living proof of his dad's mistakes and, judging by his reaction when she'd finally fronted up to him, not a welcome addition to his family.

Events were conspiring to keep her and Isaac apart. The precious slice of time they'd awarded themselves to be together before he went on to a new life was being used up.

He'd tried to ring her back several times but she hadn't answered. She'd been crying too hard, hurting too much.

It was a less buoyant minibus load of Middletones that set off home a couple of hours later, Carola having been online to change their bookings at the hotel and on le Shuttle. Neil and Franciszka took the front seat so Neil could work the gear stick for Lily if her hand hurt too much.

'Are you absolutely sure you're OK to drive like this?' he demanded, his kind eyes concerned behind the lenses of his glasses.

Lily gave him a beaming and totally contrived smile. 'I wouldn't do it, otherwise.' She was in no doubt that the traffic police would be completely unimpressed with the system but how would they ever know? She was desperate to get away. Nobody seemed to mind leaving early and, as if to back up their decision, the snow came two hours before forecast, tumbling into the windscreen as Lily drove.

They stopped less often than on the outward leg as Lily wanted to make the hotel by evening despite their late start. Her hand began thumping almost as soon as she began driving but she gritted her teeth, took paracetamol and ibuprofen – codeine not being an option if she wanted to stay awake – and accepted Neil's help with the gear lever when she needed it. She breathed a sigh of relief when she was on a motorway and had only to steer.

Isaac phoned. As Lily hadn't thought to pair her phone with the Bluetooth system Neil answered for her, beginning with, 'Lily's driving,' and gathering the information in return that things had not changed at Isaac's end.

When they stopped for lunch, just over the Swiss-French border, the snow had stopped falling and there was little on the ground. Neil put the minibus into reverse gear for Lily, and Franciszka hopped out of the minibus to guide her as she parked.

As they crossed the car park towards the service station Carola asked, 'Has anyone had news about Ona and the baby?'

Lily had been wondering about them but she hadn't contacted Tubb, Garrick or any members of their family since the horrible scene yesterday, not knowing if they'd want to hear from her. The same went for Janice's family. She tucked her throbbing hand into the pocket of her parka as she saw a neat way out. 'I've texted official thanks to Los from the Middletones to BCF but maybe you could thank Max for everything he's done, ask about Ona and the baby and explain that we decided to leave early.'

'Good idea.' Carola took out her phone.

They were lumbering back out onto the motorway half an hour later, having filled up themselves with brioches and cakes and the minibus with diesel, when Carola received a reply. 'Whoopee! Ona had another little boy by C-section late last night. They've called him Ainsley. He's gone into neonatal care because he was three weeks early but he and Ona will both be fine.'

Unexpectedly, although little Ainsley was not a blood relation, Lily felt her eyes fill with tears and had to dash them away to see the traffic. 'Give them my love and best wishes,' she called to Carola when she could speak. Then she settled down to covering the next couple of hundred miles.

By the time they reached the hotel, the same they'd used before, her hand was slightly swollen. She bumbled her way through check-in and joined the others for a meal, eating a big plate of chips, not because she needed them but because it seemed as if she deserved a treat. Then she pleaded tiredness, which wasn't dishonest because she'd slept badly last night and driven for much of the day, and took dear Doggo out for a long walk to make it up to him that he'd been shut in his cave again.

They walked on the verge next to a main road because Lily didn't fancy the dark areas she'd walked along before, when Isaac had been with her. Doggo seemed quite at ease, his thin tail waving in time with his stride, his nose to the ground.

Back in her room she showered, then soaked her hand in freezing cold water for fifteen minutes in an effort to stop it ballooning. She'd put the TV on a music channel and her heart clenched when Jennifer Paige's 'Just a Little Crush' came on, her eyes filling with tears that seemed all too near the surface at the moment. When she sniffed, Doggo came to lay his chin comfortingly on her thigh, gazing at her with melting dark eyes.

'I'll see him again,' she told Doggo dolefully. 'I've got you.'

Doggo's tail thumped.

'It's all right for you to look so pleased,' she told him drearily. 'But I have no idea how you deal with a guy you had one fantastic night with before he took on looking after his seriously ill ex. Do you know your two humans are together at the moment?'

Doggo's ears pricked sharply, as if this were unexpected but welcome news.

'This could be nice for you. Your family's a family again.' Lily stroked his silken head. 'Whereas my families . . . well, my very existence seems to cause problems.'

From where she'd left it charging on the bedside, her phone began to ring and on the screen she read *Isaac*.

Isaac paced around what he still thought of as the spare room, listening to the international ringing tone. It rang six times and then Lily picked up. Relief flooded through him. 'Lily! Are you OK?'

'Yes, thank you,' she said composedly. 'Well . . .' Then she gave him a long story about her confessing to Tubb and Garrick after all and it not going well.

Isaac listened between making sympathetic comments, his heart going out to her as the story unravelled but feeling as if there was a lot more going on behind her carefully toneless delivery than she was giving away.

'So I'm feeling a bit sad but I'll get over it,' she ended. Without giving him a chance to speak she rushed on. 'I was just wondering when you'll want Doggo back.'

Evidently she was intending to control the conversation but Isaac was intent on bringing out what he wanted to. 'You know I had no alternative but to run off the way I did, don't you?'

'Oh, yes,' she replied lightly. 'But now we need to think about what happens once I get home. Do you want Doggo in Peterborough with you? I expect you do. Hayley will want to see him again too.'

Her tone was chatty, as if they were back to being just work colleagues. He felt anger flick at him. Their incredible night together was less than forty-eight hours ago and she was talking to him as if it hadn't happened. 'I know I'm hardly in a position to advance our relationship right now—'

'I understand,' she said quickly.

In his other ear he heard Hayley's phone ring and her voice answering. In his throat the words 'but things *will* change' dried. He wasn't sleeping with Hayley but, unavoidably, he had to be in the bathroom holding her drain bag – the 'bag of goo' as she called it – while she washed. She'd turn her back to him but she was naked and he was right there. It brought her close to tears but she'd had to accept his help. It was an intimacy that made it feel odd to make plans with Lily.

'We could arrange to pass him over on Tuesday,' Lily said now in his ear.

'Doggo?' he replied. 'I have to take Hayley for her drain and dressing check but—'

She broke in, still in that light, bright tone. 'I expect you're working things out as you go along. I'm happy to keep him for a few days. Why don't you get in touch with me when you can have him back?' The tiniest of pauses and then she rushed on, 'Sorry, I've got a call waiting. Give Hayley my best wishes.' Then she was gone.

Isaac was pretty sure there had been no call waiting. Putting down his phone he went into the kitchen and made coffee. Hayley had finished her conversation and accepted the cup with a wan smile. 'Thanks.'

'OK if I go make another phone call?' he asked. 'Need anything first?'

Hayley let her head rest on her fist. 'I'm OK, thank you. I know I'm not at my lovely best because I really didn't want or expect to rely on *you*, of all people. I'm sorry when I'm grouchy because I'm in pain or I'm embarrassed. I do appreciate what you're doing.'

He shrugged. 'You couldn't foresee what happened to Nicola and Vicky's dad.'

She went on, frowning, as if he hadn't spoken. 'Hopefully the drain under my arm comes out on Tuesday then the other one a week later. I should begin to pick up after that. Unfortunately, the consultant's on holiday so I don't get my results till the 23rd.' The life went out of her eyes again, perhaps as she realised today was only the 8th. 'I need a lot of help until after Christmas I'm afraid. But maybe Nicola and Vicky will come back.'

The wave of compassion that swept through Isaac at seeing this bright, self-sufficient woman having to cast around for help in her hour of need took him by surprise. 'I'm here as long as you need me,' he said, because he knew he wouldn't be able to abandon her until she could manage alone. He cast around for something positive to say. 'Do you think you'll be OK to have Doggo around?'

Her eyes lit up. 'Oh, yes! He'll have to learn not to stick his head in the bag of goo though.'

Glad he'd put a smile back on her face Isaac continued. 'Maybe, once you're better, we could dog share? I'm more than happy to keep him but if you only gave him up because of the cancer—'

'But aren't you going abroad?' she broke in, a puzzled frown puckering the bridge of her nose.

For a moment, Isaac froze. He'd got so caught up with

the Middletones trip – and, especially, with Lily – that his plans to work abroad had sunk to the bottom of his mental fish tank. 'I suppose my plans are still fluid,' he said. Then his phone began to ring and he saw *Harrison Tubb* on the screen. 'Sorry, I need to take this.'

'Sure.' Hayley reached for the TV remote.

In his room, Isaac closed his door as he said hello to his employer. 'Glad to hear the baby arrived safely.'

'Yes, he's in an incubator for a day or two but he should be all right,' Tubb replied. 'Sorry to call on you when I know from the others why you left Switzerland early but I need to know whether you're able to return to work on schedule.'

Isaac blew out his cheeks. 'Sorry. I should have been in touch with you already but I'm trying to see my way forward. I do have a lot to work around and I might not be able to do all my hours, but I've got half an idea. I need to talk to Hayley first, and probably her breast cancer nurse so can I call you back tomorrow? I'm not due back at work until the day after anyway.'

'OK. Ring me tomorrow.' Tubb hesitated. 'Have you heard anything from Lily? She and the others have set off a day early.' He sounded guarded, as if he wanted more information without giving his feelings away.

Slowly, Isaac sank down on the bed, thinking back to his earlier conversation with Lily. He'd assumed she'd been in Schützenberg. 'I didn't know that. Is she driving?'

'I assume so as she'd certainly intended to drive on Monday but things got a bit . . . it was down to me to get Ona to the hospital. We didn't want to wait for Max to get there.' He paused but Isaac didn't fill in any blanks. He was pretty sure he wasn't meant to disclose that he'd known for a while about Lily being Tubb's sister or about

Tubb's furious reaction to Lily telling Garrick the truth. If there were sides to be taken here, he was on Lily's. 'Lily's not answering her phone,' Tubb added.

Isaac made a non-committal noise. 'It's nearly ten in your time zone, isn't it? Maybe she's asleep.' He said goodbye, upset and worried at the memory of how empty Lily had sounded. He tried to call her back, ostensibly about Tubb's call but actually to be there for her. Or just to hear her voice.

There was no reply.

He wondered if the Middletones had stopped at the same hotel in Chalons en Champagne as on the way there. He envisaged his room there and Lily in it, the feel of her wet soapy hair slipping through his fingers and her sensitive scalp beneath his fingertips.

He was suddenly swamped with worry for her. Was she able to wash her own hair now?

How was her hand?

Had she coped with the driving on the way home?

Lily had helped him get back to England, which suggested that she thought him helping a post-operative woman was more important than helping one with a badly bruised hand . . . but now, reflecting on her battling valiantly across the continent, possibly in pain, he felt as if he'd let her down.

Chapter Twenty-One

The sight of Middledip had never been so welcome. Lily drove the minibus into Main Road in the middle of Monday afternoon. The village lacked the snow that had made Schützenberg look like a fairy tale but it looked pretty under the bright winter sun and Lily could have cried with relief to be home. It must have been because she was exhausted after the marathon drive.

The journey had been uneventful, lacking the excitement that had bubbled within them all on the outward leg. No problems had cropped up taking Doggo through pet passport control even though Lily had never received the email from Isaac to show the officials she had permission to re-enter him into the UK. Isaac had been too busy nursing Hayley, obviously.

It took another half an hour to drop everyone off at their own homes, pasting on a smile as she jumped out to hug each one as their destination was reached. 'Thanks for being part of our big Swiss adventure! See you soon! Thanks again!'

Franciszka was the last, and then, finally, Lily could drive to Carola's house to empty the minibus of everything that was left, including wrestling out Doggo's crate, which took Lily, Carola, Charlotte and Emily all heaving at once, even without Doggo in it.

Carola said, 'Do you need any help with anything, Lily?' But she already had her phone in her hand and Lily knew she was bursting to be reunited with Owen.

'I'm fine,' Lily assured her, preparing to wheel her case round to her apartment, Doggo's lead clutched in the same hand. 'It's been wonderful, hasn't it? Thank you for taking part!' Lily hugged each of them in turn.

Her smile fell away once she was out of sight. Safely in her little apartment she abandoned her case and backpack and placed Doggo's bed in a corner of the hall next to the radiator.

She worked out how to use the harness that made it safe for him to travel like a human then drove him in the minibus, looking very regal in the front seat, back to Acting Instrumental before it shut for the day. Feeling as if she never wanted to drive again, she and Doggo strolled the mile and a bit back into Middledip, looping around the village to visit Booze & News where she bought dog food and, in a rush of affection for the companionable canine, Bonios and Dentastix.

'Didn't know you had a pooch,' observed Melanie behind the counter, ringing up the purchases.

'Looking after one for a couple of days,' Lily said briefly. She trailed home. Doggo paused at The Three Fishes, its strings of lights burning brightly in the darkness, his ears pricked and one paw raised, gazing at Lily with a 'WTF?' expression.

'Soon,' she murmured. 'You can go back to him.' Then

she went home and locked her and Doggo into her apartment. And the rest of the world out.

Tuesday was spent with the washing machine whirring and, with Carola, tying up the last few trip-related loose ends.

Lily tried not to outstay her welcome in Carola's kitchen, tastefully decorated with holly and red baubles, because Owen was there, on sick leave with bruising on his temple and two black eyes. A stitched cut at the corner of his mouth made him look a bit *Nightmare Before Christmas*. Lily hugged him as if he were made of eggshell. 'You poor thing! I hope the police have the bastards who did this.'

Owen talked cautiously out of the unstitched side of his mouth. 'They have CCTV footage of three people in black hoodies and scarves. Not much to go on.' He and Carola kept holding hands or giving each long looks, Carola bestowing tiny caresses to his poor bruised face and asking if he was quite sure he was all right.

The only thing marring Carola's happiness, it seemed, was the issue of her ex. 'It's bothersome,' she confided under her breath as Lily prepared to depart through the kitchen door to her own quarters. 'It's my turn to have the girls for Christmas but because Duncan's no longer comfortably loved up with Sherri he's gone all hangdog about it. He moved up to Bettsbrough yesterday, sleeping on his brother's sofa as they don't actually have room for him, he told Charlotte. He's constantly on the phone to his solicitor to try and get his dosh out of Sherri. The girls have gone all soppy about him. Emily's even asked whether we can invite him on Christmas Day.' Carola pulled a face. 'It's my first Christmas with Owen but . . .'

Lily pulled a sympathetic face as Carola went back to Owen and Lily opened the door, a dancing dog greeting her on the staircase as if she'd been gone for a month, half a Dentastick in his mouth. 'Go on down.' She laughed, and he ran down looking at her over his shoulder, which seemed tricky but he accomplished it with ease.

Once the washing machine was emptied and the clothes were dancing on the line outside, Lily checked her email inbox in case of enquiries from anyone wanting her exhibition design skills.

Nothing.

She emailed the two clients she expected to work with on their stands for the London Book Fair in March and tried to pin them down to meetings or telephone conversations, Doggo lying comfortingly on her feet as she worked.

She opened her calendar and saw she was supposed to be working at The Three Fishes on Friday, noon till three and six till closing. Friday the 13th. It seemed like a bad omen. Was she even still employed at the pub? Tubb hadn't been in touch. She took her phone out. Nope, still nothing.

After considering her injured hand for a minute and flexing it she rang Tina. It was eleven forty-five so she'd be about to open.

'Hey, stranger!' Tina said warmly. 'How's everything?'

They chatted for several minutes before Lily, concentrating on sounding normal, whatever normal was, said, 'My hand's good enough for me to come back to work on Friday if it can be lightish duties.'

Tina breathed an audible sigh of relief. 'Excellent. I want all hands on deck – even rather bashed-up hands, ha-ha – so I can take time off in lieu of the extra shifts I've worked. My family has forgotten what I look like while you guys have been away.'

'Great, thank you,' Lily said gratefully. She wanted to ask about Isaac but forced herself not to. 'I'll be there on Friday,' she assured Tina, crossing her fingers and mentally adding, 'if no one rings and tells me otherwise'. Unless she had some exhibition work to begin on soon, she'd need her income from The Three Fishes. It paid her modest rent. She had money to fall back on but only as long as she didn't fall too heavily or for too long.

Feeling increasingly loose-endy she took Doggo out, joining the footpaths that looped around the village at the top end so as not to pass near the pub, despite assuming Isaac to be at Hayley's place in Peterborough, when he wasn't driving her to appointments.

As she strode through a landscape peeled bare by winter she reflected on Carola and Owen's happiness and wondered also whether Neil and Franciszka would carry on their relationship now they were back in the village. As they had never discussed what would happen to the Middletones once the Swiss trip was over, Lily didn't know when she'd see Neil, Eddie, Alfie and Warwick.

Lily had spent so much time with them since early summer that she missed them. Felt isolated and left out. And, for that matter, as she halted on a windswept, muddy footpath where brambles shook spiky arms at her, shut out . . . by her brothers.

She took out her phone, standing there with it in her hand so long with the wind whipping across the Fens and into her face that Doggo halted and looked back, his tail stuck out straight behind and a paw raised as if not sure how to go forward.

Then Lily did what she'd so often done when she was

troubled. She texted her sister. *I'm back in England. Want to meet up?*

It was later on Tuesday afternoon when Isaac parked his car behind The Three Fishes. He glanced at Hayley in the passenger seat, her floral bag at her feet, tubes passing to it from beneath her shirt and coat. 'Sure you're going to be OK with this?'

Though pallid, she managed a smile. 'I'm just grateful your boss is letting you move me in. I'd hate you to have risked your job—' Her sentence stalled, a flush fanning her cheeks.

It took Isaac a moment to realise she must have remembered that his job at The Three Fishes and the events leading up to it had been a tricky subject. It all seemed so far in the past now. 'It seems a reasonable solution,' he said, removing his keys from the ignition. 'I've never looked in the guest accommodation you're going to have but I think it'll be OK. Tina said she'd leave it clean and tidy for you.'

Upstairs, they found Tina had left the keys to the second guest room in the door. The room was done out in shades of lavender; there was a rip in the wallpaper near the bed but otherwise it was OK. The bathroom held a shower cubicle, which would give Hayley somewhere to stand and wash, her drain bag hanging beside her while he held a bowl of soapy water and looked the other way.

'You sit yourself down and I'll bring your stuff up.' Isaac watched as Hayley sat down in the grey wing-backed chair near the window then began ferrying her stuff upstairs.

'How are you doing?' he asked half an hour later, when her clothes were put away and the TV was working.

'Knackered,' she said frankly, giving him a wan smile. 'Thank you, Isaac. Thanks a lot. I think I'm going to lie down and try and nap. I'm a lot more comfortable with the first drain out.'

'I'm going into my room next door to check I have clean work clothes, then I'm going down to touch base with Tina when she's opened for the evening session. If you want anything, ring me. I'll only be twenty seconds away.'

Hayley levered herself gingerly from the chair and headed for the bed while he took one of the room keys before heading for his own space. He did have to do the things he'd outlined to Hayley but he had something else to do too.

Letting himself into his room, which felt like a sanctuary after the past four days, he rang Lily.

She didn't pick up but her voicemail invited him to leave a message after the beep.

'Hi, it's me,' he said. 'When you pick up this message, can you please get in contact? I'm back at the pub.' Then, feeling some explanation was needed: 'Tubb said I could bring Hayley back here so she's got someone nearby to help when she needs it.' Hell, that wasn't the right explanation. 'She's in the other guest accommodation,' he added quickly, wishing he hadn't mentioned Hayley at all because some subjects were definitely best dealt with face to face. He looked for a way to start recording the message again but Lily's network evidently didn't support it. Before he could add, 'Are you OK? I miss you,' the end-of-message beep sounded.

Crap. If he rang back to leave another message thinking of her would sound like such an afterthought.

Mood low, he ironed a couple of shirts and a pair of

trousers then went down to go through things with Tina. It was hard to keep his mind on the staff rota, beer temperatures and line flushing when he just wanted to talk to Lily.

When he got back upstairs, feeling a certain relief in having attained an hour's normality before cooking something for his and Hayley's dinner – a sentence he hadn't known he'd ever think again – he realised he'd left his phone in his room.

Lily had rung. He listened to the message. Her voice was quiet and neutral. 'I hope Hayley's progressing well. Do give her my best wishes. I hope you don't mind not getting Doggo back today because I'm out this evening and he's with me. He's being a good boy. I didn't think his enormous dog cave would fit in my little hatchback so I used his seatbelt harness.' Then, after a pause, 'Bye!' The message ended.

For several seconds he stood in the centre of the room that had been home for the past few months, weighing the phone in his hand, wishing that Hayley hadn't needed his help. For her own sake, of course, he wished devoutly that she'd never developed cancer and needed a mastectomy, the effects of which he could only try his best to understand.

But he was selfish enough to wish she'd never needed his help. That very real need was tricky to balance with what he'd begun in Switzerland with Lily.

The fact that Lily seemed to have withdrawn from him wasn't helping one bit.

He thought about calling her back. Maybe now would be a good time to mention that when the Hayley crisis was over he was reconsidering his decision to leave the village. What had begun with Lily in Schützenberg was too good to just throw away and he was sure he could arrange—

His phone rang and *Hayley* appeared on the screen. He glanced at his bedside clock as he answered. 'Hi, Hayley. It's nearly time for you to have more pills, isn't it? I'll get something out of the freezer for dinner.'

Even to his ears that sounded like the old days.

Chapter Twenty-Two

We've still only got half a kitchen but the new cooker is in. Come for dinner at seven.

It was typical of Zinnia that an invitation was phrased as an instruction but Lily decided to accept the olive branch. *Thank you. I'm dog-sitting for a couple of days though. OK to bring him? He's at least as well behaved as me.*

No prob, bring him, Zinnia replied.

A light-up reindeer pranced on the porch of the neat, ex-council semi-detached house Zinnia lived in with her boyfriend George. The narrow street was crowded with cars but Lily found a place to park. As it was still only five to seven she used the time to listen to a voicemail that had come in while she'd been driving from Middledip to Huntingdon. Her heart put in an extra beat when she heard Isaac's voice. 'Hi, it's me. When you pick up this message, can you please get in contact? I'm back at the pub.' Her heart skipped again. Had Hayley's friends returned to look after her?

Isaac's warm, even voice went on. 'Tubb said I could

288

bring Hayley back here so she's got someone nearby to help when she needs it.' Oh.

A hesitation, then he said, 'She's in the other guest accommodation.' The last few words were rushed, uncertain.

He'd installed Hayley at The Three Fishes and he sounded weird about it. Defensive. Lily's heart slowed to a dragging, sinking rhythm, a heart she'd apparently opened up to him in one night of sex, fast and hard or slow and languorous, waking each other for more. Pathways of kisses, stroking fingers, hard flesh in soft.

There would be no more now. It would feel as if she was doing something wrong because he was, on some basis, involved with Hayley again. She sighed.

They had to make contact because of Doggo and the stuff he'd left behind in Switzerland but it was a relief when he didn't answer his phone. She left a message, carefully pragmatic and bland.

From the back seat, Doggo whined as if to say that the car had stopped and so it was now Lily's duty to take him somewhere fun. Smiling at his quivering tail and flattened ears Lily got him out, waited while he cocked his leg on Zinnia's gate post then said, 'C'mon then. Let's see what kind of mood she's in. I hope it's not a difficult one because I could actually do with a hug.'

Zinnia and George did welcome Lily with literally open arms, taking it in turns to pull her in for the hugs she'd wished for. George was the strong, silent type, both good qualities for Zinnia's boyfriend, but he opened up enough to say, 'I'm really glad you've shown up because your sister's moping for you.'

'I am,' Zinnia confirmed, making a faux sad face with big eyes and a quivering lip. Then she hugged Lily again, causing Doggo to try and shove in for his share of fuss.

They went into the kitchen to gaze at the half-stripped, half-burnt surroundings, the new range cooker representing progress. Zinnia went into great detail about how the finished result would look while George nodded along, simultaneously checking on the lasagne in the oven and ripping open bags of salad from the fridge, which had survived the fire. Smoke had damaged other parts of the house but those walls had already been painted.

It was an atmosphere so much like the one Lily was used to with her sister, before the existence of her half-brothers intervened, that her heart blossomed. She felt . . . she felt *safe* again with Zinnia. It was such a relief that her knees actually wobbled.

A dodgy moment arose when Zinnia caught sight of Lily's left hand, currently turning brown. 'Oh, *Lileeee*,' she keened, eyes horrified. 'Just look at that! Poor you. I'm so sorry; you know I'm sorry, don't you? I absolutely didn't mean to hurt you like that. I can't blame you for not wanting to talk to me for a while. You must hate me.' And she burst into tears.

Lily got emotional too, hugging Zinnia anew. 'I knew it was an accident but I needed time to get over things. I'm sorry I went silent on you.' George and Doggo both hovered wearing matching anxious expressions.

Finally, Zinnia blew her nose and recovered herself in time to lay the table. 'I want to hear all about your Swiss trip. How did you get on with Garrick?' She said his name with an air of determination, as if she'd made up her mind to accept his place in Lily's world.

Lily pulled out a chair and sat down with a sigh. 'Disaster,' she admitted.

Dipping garlic bread dispiritedly into the lasagne she recounted the calamitous evening and her stupidity in never considering that Tubb might not have told Garrick about their father's affair. 'So that's that,' she ended bleakly. 'I'm going to stay at The Three Fishes in the short term unless someone says I can't. But I'm obviously not welcome in the family.'

Zinnia looked poised to cry again. 'I'm so sorry it went so crap. Those idiots! They need to get over their own shallow egos and be thankful they have such a wonderful person as a sister.'

That made Lily laugh. 'Zin! It's not long since you were hating them from a distance and setting me ultimatums.'

Zinnia looked abashed. 'Yes, but I'm viewing things differently.' She glanced at George. Colour flooded her face. 'I've been wanting to tell you something but I didn't want to do it over the phone when you were angry with me.' She sucked in a breath. 'We're having a baby.'

Lily dropped her fork, splashing the tablecloth with red dots of tomato herb sauce. 'That's fantastic! *Huge* congratulations!' She jumped from her seat, almost tripping in her haste to dish out hugs, laughing at Doggo dancing around and trying to join in their excitement with his big, deep, 'WOAH! WOAH!' Zinnia hugged Lily back, gladly and hard. 'I never want to be not-friends with you again. I'm probably looking at things with baby-goggles on but I think I have a bit more insight into what a blood tie means now. I'm sad and upset that your brothers acted like arses.'

'Me, too.' Lead settled in Lily's stomach. 'Have you seen much of the mums? What do they think about the baby?'

Zinnia looked even sadder. 'They're happy, I think, but focused on their own crap. I've more or less been told to leave them to sort themselves out.'

'Same here but it seems all wrong for them to be apart.

I know their relationship has had its volatile moments but I thought they'd always stick it out.' Lily heaved a sigh. Life seemed tough at the moment.

Despite what she'd been told, when Wednesday passed with no word from her mum, on Thursday morning Lily decided to drive to Peterborough and call in on Roma in an 'I was passing and it seemed wrong not to' way. They could enjoy the news about the baby together. 'And,' she told Doggo, who was riding like royalty in the front of her car again, 'I can tell her what happened with Tubb and Garrick and be a bit pathetic. You're allowed to do that with your mum.'

She pulled up in the drive, got Doggo out and let him sniff, then went in through the back door as usual. 'Hello, Mum?' she shouted as she kicked off her boots. To her surprise, it was Patsie's voice that answered, 'In the living room, darling.'

Patsie? Lily felt a stirring of hope as she walked up the quarry-stone passage, Doggo's nails clicking. She found her mothers seated on the sofa but not close to one another. It was as if they'd left room for another person between them, symbolically enough. Doggo, after a quick sniff of hands, took possession of the rug in front of the wood-burning stove with a contented sigh.

Roma hugged Lily. 'Hello, gorgeous.' She sounded tired but otherwise composed.

Patsie hugged Lily too, just as always. 'Glad you're here. We were talking about you . . .' She glanced at Roma.

Knees suddenly weak, Lily sat down on the armchair. 'What?'

Patsie looked as if she were about to address a client, clasping her hands in her lap on her smart smoke-grey dress. Roma looked as if she was about to go out for coffee with boho friends, her stripy blue jeans tight and her flowery pink shirt loose. Roma cleared her throat. 'Have you heard Zinnia's news?'

Lily smiled properly for the first time since walking into the house. 'Yes! Isn't it fantastic? Are you guys pleased?'

'We're thrilled,' Patsie said, a smile breaking over her face. She paused, looking at Roma again.

Roma fidgeted. 'Now we know we're going to be grandmothers it's given us a new sense of what's important.' She carefully didn't look at Patsie. 'Lily, would you be OK if we weren't around for Christmas? Someone at Patsie's work has a cottage we can use. We thought it might be a good time to see if there's anything to be rescued. Zinnia's going to George's parents' for Christmas though, so we're a bit worried it will leave you high and dry.' Her eyes were apprehensive.

'You go if you want to,' Lily said immediately, finding herself beaming that her parents might not be splitting up after all. Thinking of them apart, of Roma being sad and left behind, made her feel as if she'd eaten a bowl of cold jelly in one gulp. 'I'll help at the pub with Christmas lunch anyway. It'll be nice to spend Christmas in the village.'

Both Roma and Patsie looked relieved and almost immediately Patsie rose. 'I've got a client meeting at four so I'll leave you to chat. Maybe we can all go out for a pre-Christmas dinner? I'll ask Zinnia and George.' She blew kisses, which Lily supposed obviated the necessity of kissing her kind-of estranged/kind-of thinking of getting back together lover – or not – in front of Lily, before hurrying out.

Roma sighed as soon as they heard the door close behind Patsie. 'Thank you for understanding. It's been—' she scrabbled for a tissue '—really tough. I thought she'd gone for good but then we went out for a glass of wine and she said she'd broken things off with "the other woman".' She made air quotes with her fingers before blowing her nose. 'I demanded to know why she'd felt the need for her, what she had that I didn't, why it had somehow been important enough to split us up but now apparently wasn't important enough to pursue. We had a blazing row in the middle of a pub, swearing at each other like sailors. I thought that was it forever.' She gulped, pressing a finger and thumb against each eyelid.

'Then she rang and said she was missing me and could we talk. So we're talking, but real life's getting in the way. I've got two assignments before Christmas and she's got court dates and stuff. And I don't know if I can get over that other woman. She has pointed out the irony, as I expected her to get over my fling with Marvin.'

Lily shifted to the sofa to thread her arms around her mother. 'I'm sorry it's so painful, Mum, but I think talking is the right thing.' Hot tears welled in her eyes. She wouldn't burden Roma with what had happened with her brothers after all and she didn't want her sussing out that if Lily's job at The Three Fishes evaporated she'd have nowhere to go on Christmas Day.

'It's stopped raining. Fancy a walk?' she suggested instead. 'We could go to Ferry Meadows and have a late lunch at the garden centre.'

Roma sniffed. 'That would be perfect!' and when Lily picked up the dog lead Doggo switched from profoundly asleep to on his feet with a shake and a wag, and they got their coats and set out.

When Lily eventually got home in the late afternoon, the apartment felt quiet and it was dark and gloomy outside. She checked her email but neither of her London

Book Fair clients had got back to her. She'd just risen from the table when Doggo suddenly flung himself at the French doors with a wildly beating tail, 'WOAH, WOAH, WOAH, hnuh hnuh WOAH,' almost giving Lily a heart attack.

Then she saw Isaac standing on the other side of the glass smiling uncertainly and her heart began beating again with a thump.

Slowly, she clicked the unlock mechanism. Isaac slid the pane of glass aside and stepped inside. 'I came to see you this morning but you weren't here.' He crouched to fuss Doggo, who was whirling on the spot with joy, butting Isaac's hands as if frightened he'd forget how to use them to stroke dogs. Isaac's brown eyes never left Lily's.

It felt to Lily as if she were falling, falling, falling, leaving her stomach behind. Isaac was obviously unsure of his welcome. It made two of them. Lily wanted to throw herself on him with every bit as much enthusiasm as Doggo had. But she couldn't.

Roma's broken-hearted sobbing about 'the other woman' jumped into her mind. She sort of felt like the other woman herself. 'So, Hayley's moved in with you at the pub,' she said, as Isaac ended his Doggo love-fest and rose to face her. 'That sounds sensible. You'll be on the premises to satisfy the licence and can work in between seeing to her needs. You'll only ever be a stair-case away.'

He took a step towards her. 'She hasn't moved in with me.' Another step, until he could take her hands.

Lily stepped back, pulling her fingers away and putting them over her mouth. 'Don't kiss me while you're living with Hayley. It feels wrong.'

His dark brows snapped down above his nose. 'She's

in the other guest accommodation; we're not living together. She's in trouble; she's got no one. I've been put on the spot.'

'That she's in a room next to yours is too fine a distinction for me to be good with. She can't live alone, I take it?' She was pretty sure she knew that but wanted to hear it from him.

He made an impatient movement. 'She's only eight days post-op. She can't move her arm above her head, can't pull herself up or push herself up, can't just hop into the shower—' He stopped, as if seeing the misstep he was about to make.

Remembering the feel of his fingers in her wet hair, Lily had to suppress a shiver of longing. 'So you're helping her with her personal needs,' she finished for him. 'You're being intimate with her. I know you feel you've got to. In fact, I even admire you for it because it can't be an easy situation. But for anything to be going on between us at the same time—' she made a to-and-fro motion between them '—is too weird. Wrong. Awkward.' She met his frustrated gaze for a long moment.

Then, in case her own eyes betrayed her sorrow and longing, she turned away. 'I've got your case and backpack here. Let me just get Doggo's stuff together. I'll bet Hayley's longing to see him again.'

After a long, silent moment, he said, 'I'd like to lie about that so you'd keep him a bit longer and I'd have excuses to see you, but you're right. A Doggo hug is just what Hayley needs.'

Her heart clenched like a fist with long, scratchy fingernails.

'Lily—' he hesitated '—you and I, we haven't done anything wrong. I'm not "with" Hayley any more than I

296

was before. She just needs help. If she wasn't my ex or if she was a bloke you'd have no trouble with this.'

'But she is your ex and she isn't a bloke,' she pointed out.

Silently, she helped him cart Doggo's dog cave into his car, which, unlike hers, was big enough to take it, and shove his luggage onto the back seat. Lastly, she gave Doggo's lead back to Isaac, careful not to touch him. Then she squatted down to give Doggo a big hug. 'Thank you for your company,' she said formally, half-blinded with tears. 'See you Friday at work, Isaac. I'm sorry our time was cut short.' And she jumped up and ran down the path at the side of Carola's house.

Soon she was safely shut in her apartment. She closed the blinds over the French doors and switched the TV on, turning the volume up loud.

Chapter Twenty-Three

Snow. Not the lovely Swiss kind like drifting feathers but tiny, twirling flakes that couldn't seem to make up their minds whether to fall down or fly up. Lily drank her morning coffee on Friday, watching through the French doors as the tiny flakes postured and flirted but hardly covered the ground. The lawn looked as if someone had thrown a net curtain over it.

She thought of the snow in Switzerland on the day they'd left, filling the air as if it couldn't wait to erase all the colour in the world. That joyous trek through the snow to St Jost, Doggo bounding, the teenagers laughing and snowballing. Isaac smiling, his eyes alight at being in the great outdoors, the place he loved to be.

The part of his plans where he retrained as an outdoor pursuits instructor would still fit his schedule, she realised. Hayley only needed his help for a few weeks. That those few weeks could have been Lily's made her feel as if she'd been eating the holly leaves from the bush in Carola's garden – prickly and sick.

She cleaned her little flat, changed the bed and did her

ironing, trying not to think about Isaac almost-living with Hayley, helping her with intimate things like washing . . . Finding herself actually envying a woman who had just lost a breast, which was seriously messed up, she forced herself to wrap the Christmas presents she'd bought from the Christmas market in Schützenberg as a penance: Swiss chocolate, delicate glass, gingerbread, wooden figures and beautiful scarves. She'd give her gifts to her family at the early Christmas dinner Patsie was arranging.

Refusing to let her mood sink any lower, she put on her coat, hat and boots and set off for the Angel Community Café. There she found Carola looking harassed. Jodi, who also worked there, grinned cheerily at Lily and said, 'Carola, why don't you take your break with a big cream cake? You can tell Lily all about it.'

'All about what?' Lily ordered a cream horn and a cup of peppermint tea as if a healthy drink would balance out an unhealthy snack.

Carola rolled her eyes, grabbed the biggest coffee éclair from the display and an enormous cappuccino with sprinkles before ushering Lily to a corner table at the back of the room. Several other tables were occupied, people looking up from their coffee and panini and saying hello as Lily and Carola wove through the eclectic collection of chairs. Lily liked the Angel, its floor tiles of cream, brown and the same blue-green as the paint on the tables and chairs; the black-and-white photos hanging on the walls.

Also, the cakes were awesome.

Flopping into a chair, Carola clutched her forehead, shoving her hair up at the front. 'Duncan has asked to move back in!' she hissed dramatically.

'Wow.' Lily took a moment to process that because she

knew it had taken Carola ages to heal after Duncan's defection. She nibbled her cream horn, enjoying the sweet flaky pastry.

'I took him to task.' Carola took a bite of coffee éclair and licked cream from above her lip. 'I told him he had no chance, that I was settled in a new relationship. But Emily's been in floods of tears, pleading with me not to let him be homeless. I don't know how long it's practical for him to sofa surf at his brother's. His brother's daughter and boyfriend live there too and they're expecting a baby.' She bit the éclair savagely, as if eating it as fast as she could would somehow put the situation aright. 'My guess is Sherri's holding their joint savings to ransom so he'll sign away any claim on her house, which isn't unreasonable as she owned it before moving him in, but it's rather taking the law into her own hands.'

'Effective though,' Lily mused. 'I remember how antsy Sergio was because he'd come into the marriage with family money behind him and I hadn't. He at least played everything right down the line though.'

'I'm conflicted,' Carola confessed, mopping up the cream and crumbs from her plate with her fingertip. 'If the situation drags on he could end up living in a skanky bedsit. He's desperately looking for a new job, even if it's just a temporary contract, but you know how much is outsourced these days, or companies have moved to other countries to stay within the EEC.'

'Yes, I'm suffering in the same way,' Lily said with feeling. 'Have you discussed it with Owen?'

Carola groaned. 'Owen's supportive but says he realises Duncan's the girls' dad and I have to consider their feelings.' She began to spoon up cappuccino froth with a teaspoon. 'He's right but I wish he wasn't. The only real solution I've come up with so far is to lend Duncan some of the money that was my part of *our* divorce settlement while he waits to get his share of whatever he's accumulated with Sherri. That doesn't seem right, does it?'

'No,' Lily agreed. Realisation settled on her along with a fresh unhappiness. 'If I wasn't living there, would you move him into my apartment?'

'But you are living there!' Carola declared. But she didn't look at Lily as she said it. 'I just wish Emily wouldn't cry.' She dredged up a smile. 'Anyway, how about you?'

Lily hated the idea of Emily crying too. She also realised Carola was another one who wouldn't have a sympathetic view of anything other-womanish, even allowing for Lily not really being 'the other woman'. So she picked on something other than her and Isaac to grouse about. 'I'm feeling the fall-out from the tricky economic situation, just like Duncan. Clients I'd thought I was working for going quiet – that kind of thing.' In fact, she was just as conflicted as Carola, but about her own situation.

They finished their drinks with some companionable complaining before Carola went back to work.

When Lily stepped back outside, feeling fatter, if not better, the snow had increased sufficiently for her to pull up her hood. It looked so pretty as it coated the hedges like lace that she decided to cross over Port Road and join the footpath back through the Carlysle Estate before going home in an effort to work off a few calories.

Just before she was going to leave the footpath and cross back to Bankside to work her way through the streets of nice big houses like Carola's, their roofs painted white with snow now, she heard a familiar, 'WOAH, WOAH!' and saw Doggo galloping towards her like a small horse, ears back and tail flying. Baz, probably well suited to exercising the big dog as the youngest of the bar staff, was being towed breathlessly behind.

She crouched to fuss Doggo delightedly, greeting Baz with a grin. 'You've got dog-walking duties?'

'Yeah,' Baz agreed, getting his breath back. 'It seemed a good way of earning a fiver.' He dropped his voice. 'Isaac's moved some woman in upstairs. She's ill or something.'

Smile pinned on, Lily tugged her hood up more securely and made to move around Baz, though Doggo seemed to think he might be going with her and stood in her way. 'She's had an op so needs someone to look after her for a bit.'

Baz screwed up his forehead. 'Is that even a thing? Shouldn't you be in hospital if you can't look after yourself?'

Lily actually found herself laughing. 'On the NHS? What planet do you live on?'

When they'd said their farewells, Lily turned in the direction of home. Once there she awarded herself an hour lying on the sofa with a family bag of Quavers and the TV remote. Channel-hopping, she found a new series called *You're Just a Mess* where a combined life coach and house doctor called Ms Might descended on people and threw out all their crap, mental and actual, counselled them, shouted at them, and sent them on their way with a new life. 'Pah!' Lily snorted at the screen. 'What makes you the world authority on everything, Ms Might? How is it helpful to make someone throw out their doll collection if it makes them cry?'

She was just thinking reluctantly about getting ready for work when her phone sang out her FaceTime tune. Turning her phone over she read *Tubb* on the screen and sighed as she muted the TV. She had to speak to him some time. 'Hi,' she said flatly, after tenting her legs to prop up the phone. She counted up in her head. Was it really only six days since that awful scene when Tubb and Garrick had exploded her life?

'Hi.' Tubb cleared his throat. 'Sorry I couldn't be there when you left. Rushing Ona to hospital took precedence but I certainly didn't mean you to leave the country without . . . Well, I never meant to let you leave like that.'

'Right.' She waited. Uttering more words would give her voice the opportunity to shake, betraying the way her heart was beating with a mixture of dread and hope. He'd initiated the call so he presumably had something to say.

Tubb rubbed his hand over his head. His hair had thinned a lot more recently. 'I apologise for the way I spoke to you. Maybe intolerance is a symptom of heart failure.' He didn't smile so Lily didn't either. 'Sorry also that this call has been so long in coming.' It was as if he was reading from a list he'd prepared. 'The new baby, Ainsley, has been causing a bit of concern. Ona's still in hospital with him and Max and Janice have been taken up with hospital visiting while I've tried to fill in the childcare gaps.'

'How are Ona and Ainslcy now?' Lily asked.

'Improving and hoping to be home in the next couple of days.' Tubb's expression lightened.

Now she was over the momentary shock – and flare of hope – stemming from his call, Lily felt she could take the initiative. 'I'm sorry about the way I told Garrick. I feel stupid that it had never occurred to me that you hadn't told your brother about your dad's affair.' And then, deliberately, because anger had decided to join the gang of emotions roiling around her belly: 'Our dad, I mean.'

On-screen Tubb nodded slowly. 'It seems as if not telling your brothers something is a family trait.'

Lily's cheeks scalded.

Tubb went on before she could think of a reply. 'You probably realised from Eleanor's reaction to stumbling over a completely innocent scene between you and Garrick that he had a thing with a younger woman that almost ended his marriage. It was more than a year ago but her reaction showed she's by no means worked through her feelings.'

Lily just nodded. Garrick cheating on his wife wasn't her fault and she hadn't known it had happened.

'So,' Tubb went on, picking up a pencil to twiddle between his fingers. 'I've talked things over with Garrick – the awful balls we made of things with you. I apologise that my anger with Marvin—' he got around the 'Dad' thing neatly '—was misdirected at you. My concern was for Garrick's feelings.'

A spark of hope ignited in Lily's heart. But Tubb's next words made it clear that he was apologising for the way he delivered the message rather than for the message itself. 'I haven't yet got past the fact that you've been deceiving me for the last couple of years,' he went on. 'And that I could have easily met your mother without being aware that she was the woman who recklessly put at risk my family's happiness.'

Again, Lily said nothing. He hadn't met Roma because Lily and Roma had been keen he shouldn't.

'I admit I don't really know what to think,' Tubb went on. 'I've barely got my head around my new state of health and now I'm hit with the knowledge that someone I liked and trusted has been keeping something crucially important from me.'

He gave a dry cough. 'Garrick feels he wants to talk to you, though. Can he ring you?'

'Of course,' she murmured through numb lips. This lukewarm conversation wasn't what she'd hoped for but it was what she'd feared. 'I might as well know the worst. Do you want me to stop working at The Three Fishes?' She needed the dosh but she was pretty sure she could find work at another pub somewhere just before Christmas.

Tubb hesitated. 'No need to rush into anything.'

'No point leaving The Three Fishes shorthanded either,' she agreed. 'I'll go and start my shift then.' Although she was continuing to speak in stiff little sentences she was aware of a growing urge to burst into tears because Tubb, who she'd become so fond of over the past couple of years, was being a toughie.

'Not quite.' He looked down at the pencil he was twiddling. 'News has come to me on the breeze that you and Isaac were close during the Switzerland trip.'

For a moment she thought he was taking a personal interest but then he added, 'You probably know he's got his ex there at the moment. I've just talked to him. I just want to be sure the situation's not going to cause any problems.'

Was Tubb just worried about his beloved pub and whether the lucrative Christmas business would be affected by staff shenanigans? 'Don't worry. It's over,' she said, trying to be as cool about it as he was but hearing her voice crack. Then, because she couldn't maintain a brave face for even five seconds more, she said goodbye and disconnected.

Her eyes felt sore when Lily turned up for work at eleven forty-five. She'd squirted Optrex into them and added

305

eyeliner and mascara so she was pretty sure no one would notice.

Isaac wasn't downstairs when she arrived, although he was on the rota. Flora rushed in a couple of minutes late, throwing her coat at the hooks. 'Hello! Did you have a brilliant time? I couldn't get much out of my dear brother about it but your pics on Facebook looked amazing. All those lights and mountains! Is he upstairs? I'll just pop up.'

'Lovely,' said Lily, pretending to be absorbed in checking mixers as Flora headed for the stairs.

Neither Flora nor Isaac made an immediate appearance but the till was set up so Lily unlocked. The blokey blokes were first through the door. Lily had no idea whether any of them had a job or a partner nor where they'd find time for them either.

'You're back,' said the man Lily knew was called Bell. 'Pint of IPA.'

Lily found the action of pulling a pint hurt her hand because she had to grip as well as pull. Awkwardly she swapped to her right hand and took Bell's money.

After ten minutes a middle-aged lady came in wearing a thick down jacket. 'Is Isaac here?' She smiled at Lily who, after a second, realised it was Isaac's mum, who she'd met a few weeks ago.

'Hello, Mrs O'Brien, he's upstairs—'

'Come through, Mum,' came Flora's voice from behind Lily.

'Call me Stef,' Isaac's mum said to Lily with a smile. 'Hello, love!' to Flora. 'How's Hayley today?'

'Disappointed at not getting her drain out.' Flora's voice diminished as she took her mother through the back area towards the stairs. Lily felt as if she were the newcomer to the pub, not Flora. As a few Friday lunch regulars came in and chose tables she whizzed out with menus and big smiles, reflecting that although Stef had had her problems with Hayley according to Isaac, now Hayley was in trouble, Stef was calling to see her. Was it because Stef had a caring nature? Or evidence that Hayley was re-entering Isaac's circle?

She took drinks orders for two tables and when she turned back saw Isaac behind the bar, his hair shining and earring glinting beneath the twinkling Christmas lights. Her heart flew up into her throat.

She crossed to the till and rang through two pints of lager and two glasses of white wine for the couples at table ten and a shandy, a tonic water and a double gin for the ladies at table five. Isaac watched while she made up the orders and delivered them.

'OK?' he asked, when she returned.

'Yes, thanks.' She made herself sound carelessly composed, as if she wasn't breathlessly aware of him, of his body beneath the pressed-crisp white shirt.

'How's your hand?' He stepped in closer.

'Fine, thanks. I told Tina I'd be OK for light duties. I might have to use my right hand to pull the pints a bit, that's all.'

'Sure?'

She allowed her gaze to meet his properly. His brown eyes were sombre. There was something reproachful in the set of his mouth, like someone who was being punished for something he hadn't done. She said steadily, 'Perfectly sure. Thank you.' With what she hoped was a composed smile she stepped around him to serve a customer.

Lily worked on Friday, Saturday and Sunday with a tight, miserable feeling in her chest. Isaac's manner towards her was professional, with no hint of what had gone on between them.

During the week that followed she tried hard to drum up business for her supposed day job as a designer, making new connections on LinkedIn and joining groups with *show* or *expo* in the title, sending personal approaches to companies found in directories of shows on at Olympia, ExCeL, the East of England Showground and anywhere else that might bear fruit. Phoning follow-ups when she could. 'It's a dead time, less than two weeks before Christmas,' a guy in a Huntingdon beauty and hairdressing wholesalers said. 'Everyone's focused on finishing things up before Christmas holidays or end-of-year deadlines.' Another said she didn't even know their show budget for next year. 'Then they'll say, "How are things looking for the Motor & Tech Show?" and expect answers!'

Lily commiserated, sent a 'Great to talk to you today – get in touch if you think we can work together' email and flopped back in her chair. If things didn't brighten up she'd be reduced to networking breakfasts. Or . . .

In the New Year she could look for a job when the un/happiness of Christmas was behind everyone.

She went out with Zinnia one evening. Roma was away on a photographic assignment. Lily decided not to try and see Patsie in case she thought Lily was checking up on her while Roma was away . . . which Lily could easily feel the need to do if she let herself.

On Wednesday evening Carola got all the Middletones together for a reunion Christmas drink at The Three Fishes. Lily went along, her smiles at the ready, knowing it was pointless to suggest another venue. It was the village pub and they were a village singing group!

It was really great to see the others anyway, exchanging

hugs and jokes. Emily blushed when Warwick arrived but later Lily saw him sitting next to her and talking, making the young teen first smile and then laugh, so she felt Warwick must have apologised for being clumsy when Emily kissed him.

Eddie had brought his guitar so they sang, and none of the non-Middletone customers seemed to mind. A few joined in with the stuff everyone knew like 'White Christmas' and 'Let it Snow'.

Isaac watched from behind the bar but didn't sit with them or join in this time, not even when there was no one waiting to be served. Probably best, Lily thought, especially when Hayley appeared, a floral bag over her shoulder.

Lily's heart jumped.

Hayley looked pale and wobbly, drawn and thin and, without make-up, nobody could mistake the age difference between her and Isaac. 'I heard the music,' Lily was able to catch her saying, then watched from the corner of her eye as Isaac brought a tonic water to where she seated herself in a tub chair in the corner.

By the time he was behind the bar again Lily was up and heading Hayley's way. After asking after her health, Lily offered, 'Come and join in, if you want to.'

Hayley hesitated. 'I feel rather a pariah because I've still got my drain. It's horrible to have to carry around a bag of goo.'

'Bag of goo?' Uncomprehending, Lily glanced into the bag Hayley had been wearing over her shoulder and got a shock to see a tall, thin bottle of pink liquid, its tubing vanishing under Hayley's shirt. 'Oh.'

Hayley grimaced. 'I was scheduled to have the drain out yesterday but I was told there was too much blood and stuff still coming out. I nearly cried with disappointment.

The tube under here—' she lifted her right arm slightly and gesticulated at an area beneath it '—is driving me mad. Honestly, there is no comfortable position. I swear it's rubbing directly on my ribs.'

Sympathy flooded through Lily. She sat down in the chair across from Hayley. 'You've really been through the mill.'

With a brittle laugh, Hayley nodded. 'It's been a nightmare since I found the lump. I should have had the histology results on Monday to find out if there was more bad news but my consultant's on holiday so I have to wait until the 23rd.' She blinked several times and laughed again. 'I feel a little bit as if she shouldn't go on holiday when I'm waiting for something so important!'

Then Carola arrived to join the conversation. She'd had friends who had mastectomies and so was able to chat to Hayley about radiotherapy, chemotherapy and implants. It all sounded so grim that Lily even found it within herself to feel glad that Isaac had agreed to help Hayley.

Even if it had got in the way of Lily having a Christmas adventure with him.

She glanced up the bar and saw he was watching her. His eyes seemed to see right through to her heart before he turned away.

When Lily's phone rang on Thursday afternoon she'd been scrolling through jobs on the internet. No longer did she have the Switzerland trip to look forward to. The thing with Isaac wasn't going to happen. Her brothers hadn't greeted her with open arms. She felt rootless, more so than when she'd come back from Spain because then her parents had been there to give her a home.

She'd found nothing in Cambridgeshire but several

interesting opportunities in London. One brought in a salary of sixty thousand as a Brand Design Lead for a South East Asian hotel chain. She'd have to be pretty audacious to carry that off but except for working with actual hotels she did have all the qualifications, experience and 'required skills' they'd tagged – *design, print, exhibition, space, objects, interior*. She clicked the heart to shortlist the job and then her phone rang. She picked it up.

Garrick. Lily halted, hand hovering. Then she sipped the glass of water she'd had at her elbow as she worked and answered.

'Lily.' Garrick hesitated, as if unsure of his reception.

'Garrick,' she responded, holding her breath and not knowing what to expect. Tubb had said that Garrick wanted to talk to her but not why.

'I want to apologise,' he said. 'You took me by surprise but I acted like an arse, walking out like that. It wasn't a mature reaction and I hear Harry lost his temper. I'm sorry.'

A wash of relief uncurled Lily's shoulders. 'I understand it must have been a shock. I've already apologised to Tubb for never even wondering whether he'd told you about Marvin and my mother, so I need to say sorry to you too.' She'd learned enough from her conversation with Tubb that referring to him as 'our dad' could provoke an emotional reaction.

Garrick's voice held none of the guardedness that Tubb's had. 'I have to confess to being intrigued. Can you tell me the whole story?'

So Lily did, explaining about having two mothers, Patsie approaching desired motherhood pragmatically and Roma going at it completely half-arsed. 'Mum's quirky,' she admitted. As she unfurled the story she paced about the room, pouring herself a cup of coffee from the jug she'd made at lunchtime, finding Garrick's interest much easier to deal with than Tubb's wariness. 'When I read that obituary and Mum explained who Marvin was it triggered something,' she admitted. 'I think it was the finality of learning I'd never meet my father that made me determined to meet my brothers.'

As they talked, the afternoon light dimmed and, through the French doors, Lily saw frost begin to sparkle on the bare rose bushes outside. Something close to happiness grew inside her as the conversation went on, natural and warm. Garrick had reached out to her after all. Her brother, Garrick.

Finally, he turned the subject. 'I was going to telephone you anyway but this morning I had a long meeting with Los Aebi. He was very impressed with your work on the trade stand, the Christmas market and on the cultural exchange aspect of the project.'

'That's good. I certainly enjoyed it.' The project hadn't ended well but that wasn't Los's fault.

'I don't want you to think that this is why I phoned,' Garrick went on earnestly, 'but Los wants me to sound you out about taking a full-time job with us.'

It felt as if the room swirled around her. 'In Switzerland?'

'That's right. You'd report to me but work with Kirstin, Felix and Stephen. We haven't had an in-house designer before but the role would make a valuable addition to our promotions side. It will be more general design than exhibition work but it would be varied and would include a bit of travel.'

'Seriously?' Lily was literally stuck for words. She was being headhunted!

'I know you have your own business,' Garrick went on

quickly, perhaps misreading her reaction. 'But Los really likes motivated self-starters with a can-do attitude. When you backed that up with designs he liked and being so easy to work with, you caught his attention.' Lily listened with a sense of being in a dream as on and on he went, talking about a package of salary and benefits with a relocation grant. The wonderful standard of living in Switzerland. 'Why not come out and meet with Los?' he ended persuasively.

Lily struggled to put together a reply. 'You've taken me by surprise,' she admitted. 'I just . . . well, I'm interested but . . .' She licked her lips. 'I'll have to think hard about it in the current circumstances. I'm not going to waste your company's money by coming out to talk to Los unless I can see a prospect of me being able to seriously consider it.'

Garrick instantly read between her lines. 'Ah. You mean you'll be interested if Harry gets over his snit?' He sounded rueful. 'He doesn't get angry easily but when he does it takes a while for him to calm down. He's only visiting Switzerland, so far as we know,' Garrick added. 'You're more likely to trip over him in Middledip than in Schützenberg but I do think it's a good idea to take your time thinking about it. Moving to another country and giving up your business are things you shouldn't undertake lightly. Give me a call after Christmas.'

Garrick rang off, leaving Lily to stare out into the dark winter garden. At least being given a couple of weeks to consider Garrick's shock, dream-job offer meant she didn't have to completely call time on her and Isaac. Yet.

Chapter Twenty-Four

Although Isaac continued to serve drinks and food, make orders, check rotas and ensure the pub ran smoothly he felt so tired by the strain of acting as his ex-girlfriend's carer that exhaustion would be an improvement.

Last night, unable to sleep, he'd lain in bed listening to the old building's bones creaking as the wind tried to find a way under the roof tiles and he tried to make sense of his life. Though valiantly trying not to show her fear and to come to terms with the big change in her own life, Hayley had ended up between him and Lily as surely as if she'd spent months planning it.

She couldn't know what she was doing. He'd said nothing and Lily certainly wasn't acting as if two weeks ago they'd rolled around on each other as if hot, naked, sweaty sex was never going to be available to them again . . . as was proving to be the case.

When he'd tried to reconnect with Lily she'd reacted as if he was trying to cheat on Hayley. He'd scarcely made an attempt to persuade her otherwise because her wide, horrified gaze had warned him that doing so would have diminished him in her estimation.

Then she'd come into the pub a couple of evenings ago with Carola and the Middletones. They'd all seemed pleased to see him but despite spending most of every day together in Switzerland he'd felt distanced from them by more than the width of the bar. They were having fun; he was at work. It had felt almost inevitable when Hayley had wafted downstairs, drawn by their singing, to make what felt like another barrier between him and them. He hadn't blamed her. Upstairs must feel like a prison. He'd rarely known her cry but now it was a daily purging judging by the number of times he saw red-rimmed eyes, weeping when he was elsewhere, as if to spare him having to react.

Almost as inevitable had been her seating herself quietly to listen and Lily and Carola joining her, drawing her into conversation. He remembered their sympathetic faces as Hayley gestured to her bag of goo, lifting her arm slightly to demonstrate her limited movement. And he couldn't even feel resentful of her because in a lull in the bar's hubbub he'd overheard Hayley tell Lily and Carola that Isaac and his family had been amazing and she was ultra-aware that she was incredibly lucky in the circumstances.

That was the only time Lily's polite smile had not reached her eyes.

Hayley was being brave, even when, today, Vicky had rung to say their dad was still in a bad way and now their mum was going downhill as if unable to bear the shock and had to have someone with her all the time. They couldn't come back and take care of Hayley.

Isaac had been the one who'd wanted to tut and swear and slam things about. If upstairs felt like a prison to Hayley, it did to him too, even if now she was over two weeks post-op he could grab an hour or so to run along the footpaths to try and expend some of his pent-up energy, Doggo loping merrily at his side.

This morning he'd made curry in the slow cooker in the kitchen. At seven he'd take a break to eat it with Hayley. Feel sorry for her. Run back downstairs to work. Be treated with conspicuously distant courtesy by Lily, who he actually wanted to take upstairs and slowly undress – or rapidly undress. Either would calm his restless, edgy frustration.

When Lily arrived ten minutes before her shift began at six, he gave her his best smile but the one she sent him in reply was, as usual, polite. He watched her take off her coat and hang it up. A silver and turquoise charm on a black cord glistened in the opening of her regulation black polo shirt. It made the blue of her eyes so compelling he couldn't look away.

'OK?' she asked him, pausing warily.

He knew she meant 'What's up with you, staring like that?' but deliberately pretended that she was enquiring after his wellbeing. 'Reasonably OK, in trying circumstances. You?'

Her gaze dropped. 'Fine, thanks.' She began to turn away but then swung back. 'I can do the desserts for Christmas lunch now, if you want?'

He barely had time to say, 'Thanks! That's great—' before she nodded and hurried off without giving him an opportunity to ask how or why her plans had changed. As it meant he could spend part of Christmas Day with her he was just pleased. He watched her behind as she swung off in the direction of the bar because there was no one to see him enjoy a lecherous moment and for two seconds it made him feel better.

It didn't last.

A group of two women and three men came into the bar just after Isaac's meal break and found a table near the door. He didn't know them and none of the regulars said hello so he assumed they weren't villagers. One of the men, tall and blond, took one look at Lily and assumed an expression of naked lust. He smoothed his hair as he approached the bar, gave her a smouldering smile and kept his voice low so she had to pay close attention to him in order to catch his words. In his thirties, he was good-looking and not wearing a ring. There was no reason he shouldn't stare at Lily with open admiration, nor to pull up a bar stool and try and engage her in conversation but Isaac had to stop himself from marching over and telling him to piss off. He wanted to remove Lily, find her a job in the back so she wasn't exposed to the customer's smile, his admiring eyes, but he could only continue to do his job.

Lily treated the guy with the same pleasant but cool manner she was using on Isaac these days, which was some comfort.

At nine, Hayley wandered down into the bar. Isaac couldn't blame her for getting thoroughly sick of her own company upstairs. Isaac hoped Hayley would at least sit near good-looking-and-ringless guy and distract him but she tucked herself at one end of the bar against the wall, talking to Lily when she came within range, sipping mango juice. Gabe was nearby too and nobody could resist his good nature and total lack of guile if he decided to talk to you. Then one of the guys from the garage, the quiet one, Jos, joined them, and Hayley seemed to relax in their company.

Isaac could hear her talking about her schedule, about the dreaded results she was due on Monday. How they would seal her fate regarding further treatment. Lily was listening, Isaac was pretty sure. He watched the slight turns of her head as she glanced Hayley's way and then back at whatever drink she was getting.

'Getting results on the 23rd of December might at least mean a happy Christmas,' Gabe observed, pushing back his long silver ponytail. 'Fingers crossed for you.' Nobody mentioned that bad results on the 23rd would mean a very unhappy Christmas indeed.

Lily finished up with her customer and went out to the dining area to clear tables.

The good-looking guy turned to watch her move across the room. Isaac crossed to his area of the bar. 'Are you waiting to be served?'

The guy hardly spared Isaac a glance. 'No thanks, mate.'

Isaac noticed the man's four companions grinning. They didn't seem to mind him sitting alone at the bar. Maybe it was all a bit of a game for them to watch him make his move.

Sure enough, as Lily threaded her way through the customers with a stack of plates on one hand and three pint pots in the other the man slid from his stool and stepped into her path.

She paused with a look of polite enquiry.

He said something in a low voice, smiling in a way Isaac found nauseating.

Lily smiled back neutrally. 'Thank you, but I can't.'

Sidestepping him, she whizzed around the bar and vanished in the direction of the kitchen. When she made the return trip the smile the man turned on her was more knowing. 'Can't? Or won't?'

'Won't,' Lily said briefly and headed for a table waiting to be cleared.

The man's companions' grins widened. Obviously they enjoyed watching him strike out. He turned back to the bar and waggled his empty glass at Isaac. 'Is she involved with someone?' he asked at Isaac's approach, indicating Lily with his head.

Isaac, feeling immeasurably cheered by Lily's chilly reaction, took the glass and placed it beneath the lager pump. 'Got some idiot mooning after her,' he said, which he knew to be the utter truth, and let the guy take that as he would.

Later – it felt like much later – Isaac sent Lily home and mechanically performed his final duties: locking up, cashing out, checking the CCTV was on. Wearily, he climbed the stairs. On the landing he hesitated, seeing a light in the kitchen and wondering if Hayley needed anything from him before he crashed down onto his bed and tried to sleep. Two weeks and four days post-op she was managing dressing better but still needed someone to hold things and steady her when she washed. Her dressing was off her reconstructed breast now and she tried to keep it with its thin, red, diagonal scar and missing nipple, out of his line of sight. If she could only get that last drain out then she wouldn't need him in the bathroom at all.

Then she was there in the kitchen doorway wearing black pyjamas, a steaming mug in her hand. She'd bought the PJs especially for her post-op period, button fronts to make it easy to thread herself in and out of along with elasticated front-opening bras she called 'over the shoulder boulder holders'.

'Need anything?' he asked.

'I'm good, thanks.' She hesitated. 'Isaac . . . tell me to butt out if I'm overstepping but I'm getting that feeling again about you and Lily. If you're not watching her when her back's turned then she's watching you. She enters the room and I can hear your heart beat.'

His heart lifted a notch to hear Lily was watching him but how was he going to handle this? Hayley was so vulnerable now.

Perhaps reading something of his thoughts in his hesitation, she flushed. 'I'm not asking out of some misplaced feeling of ownership of you. I was just thinking . . . I must be in the way?'

Her voice held a forlorn note that touched his heart. Bad enough she had cancer that required invasive surgery, worse the only person able to look after her was her ex-boyfriend, now she was feeling in the way as well. With a smile he took her hands and tried to frame the truth in a palatable way. 'The most important thing here is that you get well. This situation won't continue and I think we're both doing an OK job of making the best of it. Lily and I, yeah, we did start something in Switzerland but we've hit pause. Don't worry about it.'

Hayley blinked hard. 'But I am spoiling whatever you started.'

He tried hard with the diplomacy. 'If it doesn't survive then it wasn't meant to.'

She frowned. 'You could go to her house for a couple of hours here and there. Or tell me when she's coming here and I'll make sure to give you space.'

Gently, Isaac shook his head. 'This isn't something you can control, Hayley. Lily, she has her own rule book and it's not up to you to rewrite it.'

Miserably, she flushed. 'I don't know what to do.'

'Just concentrate on getting well.'

Nodding, she freed her hands. As she turned to head back to the kitchen she murmured bleakly, 'I'm sorry.' Tears were thick in her voice.

Reluctantly, Isaac went after her, searching for something to say that might soothe her feelings. 'I wouldn't normally discuss this with you before I have the vital conversation with her but I have plans, and those plans include Lily. I'm not giving up on my career change but I'm going to rejig things – do my training in this country and have Middledip as my base, at least until I see where it's going with Lily. I have plans to talk to her on Christmas Day, after lunch – only four days away. I have a special present for her. It arrived today.' The moment he'd chosen to execute the plan was about wanting to know Hayley's results and how much support she'd need rather than about the special present, but Hayley didn't have to know that.

She managed a smile. 'Really?' She stared at him through her tears as if deciding whether he was telling her the whole truth before adding, 'Go home with Lily after Christmas lunch. I'll be fine for the rest of the day.' Her smile slipped a notch. 'Hopefully by then we'll know my results are OK. If my treatment means more surgery or something then I'll have time to regroup before it actually happens, to make proper plans for my own care. Nic and Vicky will be back or I'll have enough notice to be able to book nursing care.' She put up a hand to stem his reply. 'Isaac, I'm not having any more negative effects on your life.' With a nod, she slipped inside her room and closed the door.

Right. That felt almost like light at the end of the tunnel, Isaac thought as he let himself into his room, loosening his tie and kicking off his shoes. He turned his attention to the parcel waiting for him on his bed. He'd taken it from a delivery lady this afternoon and popped it up here, knowing what it was. Lily's Christmas present.

Carefully, he slit the tape on the box and checked the contents.

He fully intended to use every trick he had to bring him and Lily together again.

Chapter Twenty-Five

Working alongside Isaac left Lily feeling stretched and thin. So near. So far. So touchable. So not.

If she'd been thinking of weakening over the memory of Isaac's kisses, Hayley's cautious movements and anxious expression on Friday evening had strengthened her resolve. Imagine if they were together and Hayley shouted for Isaac? Or rang him? Lily's tummy curled at the thought.

At least the Sunday lunch planned as 'early Christmas' with Roma, Patsie, Zinnia and George gave Lily something to focus on, even if it was also a reminder that none of her family members would be around on Christmas Day. In addition to the chocolate, glass, scarves and wooden ornaments she'd purchased in Schützenberg Christmas market, for Zinnia and George she'd bought a voucher for a nice restaurant in Peterborough – reasoning that they'd already be saving up for baby stuff – and a squashy rabbit in a Santa hat for the baby. Wrapping that up seemed unreal. Zinnia a mother? Wow.

For Roma she'd selected a book of Escher's drawings

and a garden centre voucher. For Patsie, tickets to a symphony orchestra concert, hoping it would be Roma she'd take with her.

She slipped into a favourite skater dress in amethyst purple, plaited the top of her hair and left the rest loose, slipped into sassy ankle boots and drove to the appointed pub between Bettsbrough and Peterborough.

Roma and Patsie were there already, sitting across from one another at a table by the fire. Roma's curly mop was wilder than usual; Patsie's dark chignon was sensible. Roma's maroon tunic over leggings was made of satin and lace in crazy panels; Patsie looked as if she were going into court and had picked the plainest dark dress John Lewis had ever sold. Lily felt like demanding, 'How many navy dresses do you need? Red looks really great with dark hair, you know! Or treat yourself to stripes or checks.' But didn't. If Roma had dressed as if to make people think she was *ab*solutely *fine* and Patsie had chosen something that made her invisible, there was no upside to Lily commenting.

Once Zinnia and George arrived swinging a black bin bag of presents the atmosphere lifted a notch. Everybody chatted and joked as they read the menu and decided on wine.

Lily enjoyed being with her family but felt ultra-aware of Roma and Patsie not touching and Zinnia and George constantly mentioning the baby. It was such a contrast: one negative and one positive. Maybe others felt the same because they all focused like mad on Zinnia's pregnancy, evincing interest in every detail of morning sickness, maternity leave, medical appointments and scan dates.

Roma and Patsie gave the baby an envelope filled with cash for the furnishing of the nursery – what used to be the spare room/gym/study/dumping ground – and a Christmas card that promised the baby 'all the love we can give you', which brought tears to Zinnia's eyes.

'Lucky baby, if he or she gets the amount of love we were showered with,' Lily said huskily, which made everyone else tear up too.

'We've been very lazy,' Roma smiled when she'd wiped her eyes, passing envelopes to Zinnia, George and Lily too. 'You've all got cash.'

'Always welcome,' said Lily, thinking of her dwindling bank account.

Zinnia and George, having had to pay their excess on the fire insurance, had bought all their gifts from charity shops. Roma's was a rainbow velvet jacket, Patsie's an eclectic collection of decades-old books of poetry by people like Charles Hamilton Sorley and Laurence Binyon, and Lily's a ski jacket the colour of lapis lazuli which still had its tags. 'That's gorgeous!' breathed Lily, putting it on immediately.

'I knew it would bring out the blue of your eyes,' Zinnia said with great satisfaction.

The lunch, as really lovely family lunches seemed to, lasted so long that it slid well into the afternoon. Finally, Lily checked the time and announced, 'I need to get home and changed for work. Have a wonderful Christmas, everyone.' Emotion squeezed her throat shut at the thought of Roma and Patsie going off on their own and she gave them each a big, silent hug.

It was much easier to beam at Zinnia and George. 'Have a fantastic Christmas and look after that baby. Next Christmas will be so different, won't it?'

Finally, the emotional stuff was over and she hurried out to her car. Then suddenly Zinnia was beside her,

325

hugging herself against the December wind because she'd come out without her coat. 'Are you OK, Lily?'

'Of course!' Lily made wide eyes of surprise and an even wider smile of absolute-fineness.

Zinnia hopped from foot to foot to keep warm. 'What about your brothers?'

Lily fished her keys from her bag. 'I've spoken to them both. We're being civilised.'

Doubtfully, Zinnia replied, 'Oh. And I kept meaning to ask you – did anything ever happen with your hot boss?'

Wanting suddenly to cry, Lily unlocked her car. 'Should it have?' Then she winked and hopped in, starting the car and driving away while Zinnia stared after her. She was too fragile for that conversation. After Christmas, after New Year, when Lily had decided what to do next, she might confide in Zinnia about what happened in Switzerland.

Sunday evening was pretty busy in the pub. Lots of villagers had booked in for dinner and the Christmas lights twinkled above full tables and a busy bar. Isaac asked her into the kitchen with him and Chef to run over the final plans for Christmas Day lunch.

Lily confirmed her dessert plans. 'Christmas pud, chocolate mousse and gingerbread people.'

'Everything's on the order to arrive tomorrow morning,' Chef said, fixing Lily with a mock ferocious glare. 'And you clean up my kitchen when you've finished, right?'

Lily rolled her eyes. 'I notice you didn't say that to Isaac. He's going to be cooking the mains.'

'I hoped you'd be helping,' interrupted Isaac in an apprehensive voice. 'My cooking's OK but I've never catered for this many in one go.'

'If you're lucky,' she joked. It relaxed her for them to have a normal conversation, even if it was work-related.

326

The Christmas Day schedule in hand, she went back to serve at the bar with Flora. It might be a different kind of Christmas Day but it wouldn't be too bad. She could spend the morning in the kitchen with Isaac. Good? Or bad? There would be several people she knew at the lunch, including Gabe, Don from Acting Instrumental and his wife, Melanie from the shop and a few other locals, and Isaac's family were coming too. And Hayley, of course, as her Christmas plans had been with the same friends who were away on a family emergency. Later, Lily could veg in front of Christmas TV eating marzipan fruits and drinking fizz.

What happened a couple of hours later wasn't eaves-dropping because Lily was in the back taking cutlery out of the washer and rolling it into napkins when Isaac came to sit in the alcove, opening his laptop. He didn't ask her to give him a minute so she continued, aware of him but keeping her attention on her work.

Then there was a *be boop* from the computer and Isaac said, 'Hi, Tubb.'

Surprised, Lily glanced up and caught a glimpse of her brother, looking round-faced as people tended to on-screen.

Without preamble, Tubb asked Isaac if he'd take the pub on permanently. 'The freehold's available if you want it,' he sighed wistfully. 'Or you could manage it for me on a profit-share basis. I'll be in the UK for my appointment with my consultant in January, maybe even back for good, but I don't think my health's ever going to allow me to return to The Three Fishes full-time.'

Lily found she was holding her breath. A part of her was registering with dismay that Tubb having to admit his heart condition wasn't going to go away but the largest part wanted to know . . .

Would Isaac say yes?

But Isaac, without even a tiny pause to consider, replied, 'I'm really grateful for the opportunity but I'm definitely getting out of the hospitality business. You shouldn't have any trouble selling. It's a great pub with a guaranteed clientele as the only one in the village. I can stick around for a bit while you get someone else or put it on the market but my decision's made regarding my career change.'

OK. Lily knew that. She'd always known. There was no reason for her fingers to shake while she rolled a knife, fork and spoon into a paper napkin and stacked it with the others. No reason for a slow, leaching disappointment that turned her evening grey.

Then Flora called through, 'Lily, are you free to serve?'

Lily called back, 'Coming,' and strode perfectly normally to where Flora was grappling with a rush of thirsty people. Lily smiled and took orders and gave no indication of inner emptiness.

Monday morning and Lily felt distinctly Monday morningish. 'Crap,' she said dismally at the contents of her inbox.

One of the two exhibitors she thought she'd be working with for the London Book Fair had decided they now couldn't attend owing to the fabled unforeseen circumstances. They understood if she felt herself unable to return the retainer already paid. Sparks of anger whirling inside her she typed, *RETAINer means I get to keep it if you welch!* Then, feeling slightly better after she'd added a few swearwords she deleted everything and replied courteously that she understood the situation and did intend to keep the retainer as originally agreed.

With a sinking sensation her eye fell on an email from the other company she was supposed to be working with. Opening it, she discovered a belated attempt to beat her down on the price already negotiated. After staring at phrases such as *uncomfortable task* and *no choice but* and *as no agreement has actually been signed* she politely reversed out of the relationship and wished them well.

Her order book was now officially empty.

Her stab at running her own business had failed.

Not a single one of her recent pitches had borne fruit, and she was realising too late that she hadn't put enough effort into pitching for work in the months preceding the trip to Switzerland.

Failure was her pay-off.

At least she could go all out to find safe employment, maybe apply for that job with the awesome Asian chain of hotels and enjoy the travel. She drummed her fingers. Or, after Christmas, she could ring Garrick and arrange to go to Switzerland to meet Los. It still seemed unreal but Garrick had sounded as if it were a virtually nailed-on offer until she'd hesitated because of Tubb's chilliness towards her.

Her mind strayed to her eldest half-brother. What if Tubb came back? Just because he was giving up the pub didn't mean he and Janice wouldn't live in Middledip. Janice had a house on this very estate. It was rented out right now because last year she'd moved into the pub with Tubb but they could make it their home. His return could be uncomfortable for Lily.

Part of her reason to stay here had been him. Now it was him making her wonder whether she should leave. Yet, unthinkable as Middledip was without Tubb, if he stayed in Switzerland near his brother and Janice's son . . . *that* could be the uncomfortable place to be.

The obvious thing would be to start again somewhere that was neither Middledip nor Schützenberg. Isaac was leaving the village but it kept crossing her mind that if there was still something between them when Hayley didn't need him any more they might be able to arrange their lives in such a way that they could carry on a relationship. In the right circumstances, she could live anywhere.

Ever more confused and undecided, she'd just found and reread the job description for the hotel chain and opened up the application form when Carola called in wearing a hunted expression. 'Bloody Duncan!' she complained. 'I'm sure he's getting the girls to work on me to invite him for Christmas Day. Bastard,' she groaned. 'He didn't give a hoot about me being on my own last year when he was all loved up with Sherri and had the girls for Christmas but now they're making me feel like a monster.'

'Isn't he spending Christmas with his brother?' Lily got up to fetch biscuits because it seemed like their restorative powers might be needed.

'They're going away to her family, apparently.' Carola sighed. 'Maybe I'll invite him in the evening when Owen goes off to spend a couple of hours with his mum.' She brightened. 'Are you sure you won't come too?'

'It's really sweet of you but I'd rather just veg out after the Christmas lunch,' Lily said quickly. She'd told Carola her plans had fallen through but had already decided that if she couldn't be with her family she'd be happier alone, even before she knew about the addition of Duncan to the festivities.

Carola glanced around the room as if for the first time,

as she selected a bourbon biscuit. 'Why don't you have any Christmas decorations?'

'When you work with the lights and tinsel at the pub all the time it's quite restful not to have them,' Lily invented glibly. In fact she simply hadn't felt like getting her box of decorations out of the cupboard.

They chatted, Lily making coffee to go with the biscuits. Carola had just left, fortified by half a packet of bourbons, when Lily's FaceTime alert sounded and she saw *Garrick calling* on her laptop screen and connected the call. Shock shivered through her as she saw not only Garrick waiting to talk to her but Tubb. Frowning.

'Hi,' she said steadily, frowning back.

Garrick greeted her genially enough but Tubb's frown just grew blacker and he wasted no time in stating the source of his annoyance. 'Garrick says you're dubious about taking a role at British Country Foods because of me. I can't have you missing the chance of a good job if you want it. I don't even know whether I'm going to stay in Switzerland. At least come and talk to Los.'

She hesitated. This should solve everything. If she wanted the job . . . Did she? She *ought* to want it. She'd loved Switzerland, BCF was a great company and she felt as if she'd like the work. Until recently staying in the village had been a prime aim but the roots she'd thought she was putting down in Middledip were shrivelling. It was just . . .

Just Isaac.

Garrick, looking more relaxed than Tubb, eased into the conversation. 'What our dear brother means is he'd like to see you again and mend bridges and if you won't come about the job he might actually have to take the initiative.'

Lily was dumbfounded at this unexpected turn of events. 'Mend bridges?'

Tubb scowled at Garrick. 'I would like to mend bridges,' he admitted gruffly. 'I'm sorry, Lily. I've been judgemental. Worse, I've judged you for things that aren't even your fault. I don't want to leave things badly between us. Los says you can stay in the annexe again. Will you come to Switzerland and talk to him? We've got feet of snow now so it would be fun.'

Garrick chimed in about how great it was to live and work in Switzerland ending with, 'I won't hound you for an answer until after Christmas, as we agreed, but I do hope you'll give the idea proper consideration.'

Lily ended the call feeling dazed and having agreed to think about going out to Schützenberg again. She needed a job and this one was falling in her lap so it would be stupid to reject it out of hand. More than that, Tubb was extending the olive branch and had seemed his usual quirky but easy-going self.

Her heart twisted at the idea of staying in Los's annexe without Isaac though.

Moving to another country without Isaac. Living without Isaac.

Almost before she knew what she was doing, acting on blind impulse, she dialled his number.

Heart galloping around her chest, she listened to the ringing tone. She'd ask to meet him away from the pub. Talk about his plans. Get an update on the Hayley situation.

The call connected but instead of Isaac's deep, measured tones she heard female, breathless, wobbly ones. 'Lily? This is Hayley. I'm sorry. Isaac's left his phone with me because I've dropped mine and it's stopped working. I'm waiting for an important call from the hospital.'

All the awkwardness she'd felt about Hayley flooded back over Lily. 'Don't worry, I'll—'

Hayley ploughed on. 'I'm really, really sorry,' she sniffed. 'I know I'm getting in your way but everything's gone wrong today. The histology . . .' Her words strangled and she began to cry.

Helpless, horrified, Lily listened to 'not what we were expecting . . . can't bear it to go on . . . hospital again' garbled by sobs. Then Isaac came on the line.

'Hi,' he said, also sounding out of breath. 'Sorry, I was in the kitchen. I'm afraid Hayley's emotional.'

Lily swallowed hard and mumbled over her thumping heart, 'If you need this line clear for the hospital to ring, I'll go.' How had she forgotten about Hayley getting her results today? And her tears . . . the news must have been bad.

'Sorry,' Isaac said ruefully. 'I've got to take her back to the hospital tomorrow afternoon but— Oh, shit! I've got the call-waiting beep.'

'I'll go,' she gabbled. 'Hope everything goes as well as it can.' Feeling sick she ended the call and wiped her sweaty hands down her jeans. *Back* to the hospital? After the results? Immediately before Christmas? That could *not* be good.

What must it be like to be Hayley right now? And just when nearly everyone else was jumping into the two or three days of almost mandatory fun of the festive season.

Lily paced up to the French doors and stared out into the wintry garden where the grass was flattened by rain and the sky looked like lead, almost exactly matching her feelings. She could hardly believe that a few minutes ago she'd been so self-centred as to think even for an instant that it was OK to check, for her own ends, what Isaac's chances were of finally disentangling himself from his ex-girlfriend.

I've got to take Hayley back to the hospital. Hayley wasn't at the end of her nightmare but in the middle of it. Isaac wasn't the kind of man to abandon her when she had no one else and, more importantly, Lily wouldn't want him to.

Hand shaking, she drank a glass of water to ease the tightness in her throat while she reviewed her life. She'd had three internships after uni and then a couple of jobs before she left to go to Spain with Sergio. There, she'd tried not to be funnelled into his family business but her design work had inevitably become part-time. When she returned to the UK she'd been sidetracked by coming to Middledip in search of Tubb and had failed to give what she grandly called 'her business' the attention it needed.

Her heart might be in pieces but it was time for her to grow. Grow up. Stop waiting around for something good to happen. To take control. And right in the palm of her hand was a chance to take a giant career stride at the same time as forging some kind of relationship with her brothers.

She rang Garrick and as soon as he picked up the phone blurted, 'I don't need to wait until after Christmas to decide. I'd like to meet with Los.'

'Excellent!' he boomed. 'When?'

Her thought processes hadn't taken her that far. 'Erm . . . When would be good for you?'

'As soon as you can,' he returned promptly. 'Come out and have some family time – wow, how weird is it to say that? – meet with Los, spend a day or two at our offices, explore the area and meet with HR. They have a whole relocation programme and can guide you through everything you'll need to know when considering whether you want to make the step.'

Shakily, she laughed. 'Shall I hop on a plane now?'

A hesitation, then his voice softened. 'Lily, tell me if I'm out of order, but how about you do that? Janice has been talking to Carola and we know your mums and your sister aren't around this Christmas. When we last saw each other it ended badly but we'd like to make it up to you.'

'Erm,' she said again, rocked at the idea of doing something so crazy at no notice. 'But I'm supposed to make the desserts for the pub lunch on Christmas Day. And I'd never get flights or get my car booked on Eurotunnel or a ferry. Would I? I've never tried to travel at Christmas,' she finished doubtfully.

'Surely someone else can do the desserts?' Garrick sounded impatient and all-business. 'If I'm able to get you booked? My assistant's a whizz at that kind of thing.'

'Oh . . . well . . .' Lily thought about it. What she'd be missing was Christmas morning in the pub kitchen with Isaac – so near and yet so far once again – and lunch with whichever villagers had booked. Then she'd spend the rest of Christmas alone apart from working at the pub on the evening of Boxing Day. 'Yes,' she said recklessly. 'If you can do it, then do it.' With a feeling of unreality, she gave him her passport details.

In twenty minutes he called back to tell her she was booked on the 18.50 out of Birmingham airport tomorrow, Christmas Eve, and that he or Tubb would meet her at the airport. 'We'll have the key to Los's annexe but Harry and Janice say why not stay with them? They can easily put Dugal and Keir into one bedroom and you can have the other. They'd love you to share their Christmas and Los will have his own plans.'

'Really? If they're sure it won't be too much trouble,' Lily said, feeling pleased to be wanted as a houseguest. Tubb *was* family.

'We Brits will stick to exchanging our gifts on Christmas Day rather than join the Swiss doing it on the evening of *Heiligabend*, which is Christmas Eve. On Boxing Day – St Stephen's Day here – Los and Tanja have invited us all for fondue. Then you'll have your meeting with Los and other key staff on the 27th, Friday. If that goes well, the day in the office and meeting with HR will come on Monday the 30th. Then we can book you on a return flight whenever you want but you're welcome to stay longer. You might want to go hunting for somewhere to live,' he added tantalisingly.

'Phew.' Lily felt almost overwhelmed. But she needed a job, Switzerland looked a fantastic place to live, and her reasons for staying in the village were shrinking. She even had a moment to conjecture that if she left, Duncan could move into her apartment until he got himself sorted out. With a long slow breath in to steady herself she said, 'That all sounds fantastic. I can't wait.'

When the call was over she sat back, mind in a whirl. It was happening. She was going back to Switzerland to investigate a new life. After another cup of coffee and more biscuits to calm herself down she called her mums and sister to tell them where she'd be, getting quite excited as she explained. Then she raced off to brave the shops to buy small Christmas gifts that would go in her case for Tubb and Garrick and everyone because she couldn't possibly turn up empty-handed.

Once home again, she packed, deciding to slip away without fanfare because Carola and her other friends all had their own Christmas plans anyway.

But, still, her mind turned to Isaac. Should she ring him too? It seemed appallingly rude not to. But then . . . Hayley. Bad news. Back to the hospital. A call might be intrusive. Then, while she was wrestling with these thoughts, she received a text from him. *I wanted to return your call this evening but Mum and Dad have turned up. Argh! Will try later or tomorrow morning before hospital appointment. Things are a bit crazy. Hayley very emotional. xx*

She gazed at the phone, trying to imagine seeing him and explaining her decision. It seemed trivial compared to everything else and would give him an additional thing to deal with when he so obviously had enough on his plate. She texted back: *I have plans tomorrow. Don't worry about me. I know you have a lot happening with Hayley and with Christmas at the pub.* Her conscience twinged that she wouldn't be there to help him with Christmas lunch but she could make the chocolate mousses and gingerbread people tomorrow afternoon and leave them in the fridge. The Christmas puddings were bought in ready-made and would only need heating.

Rather than bother Isaac with the staff rota she texted Baz to offer him her shifts while she was away. Baz had seriously overspent and was happy to take them.

Then she returned to the half-composed text to Isaac and rounded it out: *I hope it goes well tomorrow at the hospital*, and added two kisses to match his. She didn't go back to her packing with quite the same gusto because the knowledge that she was getting further away from Isaac all the time encased her heart like ice.

Chapter Twenty-Six

Isaac drove back from the hospital while Hayley sobbed.

'Sorry,' she snivelled, blowing her nose. 'I'm such a crybaby these days but it's just the relief! I could have kissed the consultant when she said there were clear surgical margins and no sign of cancer in the lymph nodes, that I shouldn't require further treatment apart from oestrogen blockers! I didn't think I could bear it when they moved the appointment from yesterday to today and I had to wait *yet another twenty-four hours* to find out if I had a future. I even convinced myself that they'd done it because they were getting things in place to give me awful news.'

'Me, too,' Isaac admitted candidly. He'd tried to remain positive but the prospect of supporting Hayley through news of further surgery and worse had kept him awake last night. It had been great of his parents to turn up with flowers for Hayley but they'd stayed later than his dad could usually manage. The moment they'd left Hayley had collapsed, weeping that they were only being so kind to her because they thought her future bleak. They hadn't been so supportive when she'd been his girlfriend. Between patting her shoulder and Doggo's head as he circled anxiously, Isaac had run around checking deliveries and that Tina had everything in hand to open the pub. He'd never found the opportunity to talk to Lily.

Lily. Why had she called him yesterday? It was inconsistent with the distance she'd created between them. It burned that she'd reached out to him right when they were awaiting a call back from the hospital scheduling the new appointment, but missing that had been unthinkable. In the past couple of weeks he'd come to realise his mother had been right when she declared serious illness took over lives. It was appointments, appointments, appointments. Rescheduling even one of those appointments caused seismic shifts in the lives of all concerned.

Slowing the car for a junction he glanced at the clock on the dash. Tina had seemed to think she could cover for him this afternoon without asking an off-duty member of staff to give up part of their Christmas Eve, especially as so many wanted to be with their kids. If he could get Hayley settled, take Doggo for a run, get himself and Hayley a meal, shower and change he could get behind what was bound to be a crazily busy bar by six. The dining area was fully booked and Chef was prone to explosions if skilfully prepared food wasn't instantly ferried to the diner awaiting it.

As he drove into the village, home after home twinkled with lights. The winter afternoon was already darkening but he spotted Lily's purple hatchback coming towards him and slowed, flashing his lights, catching a glimpse of her waving before she swept by.

Was she off out on the town this evening? Maybe she was wearing that stunning blue dress that clung to her in all the right places. He tried to force the image from his mind because it went hand-in-hand with one of men hitting on her and fuck*sake* that knotted his guts.

After a till-bustin' Christmas Eve at The Three Fishes, Isaac began Christmas Day shattered.

However, he was conscious of a feeling of relief as he scrambled down to the kitchen to begin Christmas lunch. When Lily arrived this morning he could tell her that Hayley was on the road to recovery. His stint caring for her had a cut-off point at last. He'd be alone with Lily this morning. The stainless steel kitchen wasn't the most romantic of surroundings but he wasn't going to let that stop him telling her that he wanted to find a way to pursue what they'd begun in Switzerland.

Chef had left him turkey crowns, potatoes – already par-boiled – in the fridge, prepared veggies in bags, cold starters and a list of timings to follow. At the end of last night tables in the dining area had been pushed together to make one large one set with green crackers and red napkins, gold table confetti and white candles.

All he needed now was Lily.

But as ten o'clock passed and then ten thirty, his heart slithered slowly south.

Lily didn't show.

The turkey crowns went in.

No Lily.

He checked his phone for messages: zip. He tried to call her and found himself talking to her voicemail. Giving way to anxiety, he sent her another text. *Lily, are you OK? Please contact me when you get this message. Please call me. I don't know how to contact your mums or sister to check you're OK.*

340

He heated the fat in the roasting tins for the potatoes. Where was she?

He'd just decided to risking interrupting Carola's Christmas Day to ask if she knew when he opened the dessert fridge and there they were: trays of chocolate mousses and gingerbread people. Slowly, he closed the door and returned dismally to his duties. She'd been and gone, probably yesterday. That must have been what she'd wanted to tell him when she rang.

Crappy Christmas, Isaac. Lily has found something better to do. Maybe when he'd seen her yesterday afternoon she'd been on her way to a hot date. Could be in bed with the man now. A cold sweat beaded his skin and he wished he could call back that sappy text.

Lily had *chosen* not to be here.

Isaac produced Christmas lunch for twenty people on autopilot. When Flora arrived she helped him while their parents looked after Jeremy and Jasmine at the gaily decorated table. 'No Lily?' she asked.

'Nope,' he said moodily. Flora didn't press him for more. She simply kept smiling and ferrying plates and gravy boats.

Hayley had come down for lunch, happy and animated, beaming about the bliss of not having tubes stuck in her body putting simple things like a shower out of bounds. Isaac's parents embarked on a discourse about their bathroom set-up for the less able, Don from Acting Instrumental chimed in about how awkward personal hygiene arrangements had been when he'd had his wrist in a cast, Jeremy and Jasmine pulled every cracker on the table and Isaac went through it all in a dream. A bad one.

He barely tasted his turkey and didn't want a chocolate mousse. Sitting through the Secret Santa was a chore, though he was mildly surprised to discover he had two gifts instead of one. The first proved to be a typical Secret Santa gag gift, a pair of socks bearing reindeer with light-up noses. The second was a case for his phone bearing pictures of Schützenberg and Zürich, the Raten and St Jost, all the places he and the Middletones had gone, and a photo book of the trip. He turned the pages of images of the minibus with the Middletones lined up in front, the French countryside, the first snow, the snowball fight, Isaac laughing, Doggo bounding, Lily smiling, teenagers snowballing.

He turned it in his hands. Were these from Lily? Had she slipped them in the Secret Santa box in the same way Flora had made sure there was a DVD of princess stories for Jasmine and for Jeremy a book about the body? The children had eaten two chocolate mousses each and wore brown smears on their faces, hands and clothes. They looked as excited and overfed as every kid should at Christmas.

Then, finally, his phone beeped and there was a reply from Lily. *I'm fine, thank you. Sorry to leave with no notice but you obviously had plenty on your plate. I know you feel we have unfinished business but we ran out of time, didn't we? The pub's being sold and soon you'll be carrying out your new career plans. I'm taking time out but Tubb knows about it. Baz is taking my shifts for a bit. x*

Dazed, he stared at it. A brush-off? It was a fucking brush-off! The vision of her with another man swam once more into his mind.

Jumping to his feet he took his phone out into the kitchen and called her. She picked up almost before it rang. 'Hi.' Her voice was soft, tentative. 'Merry Christmas.'

'Not very,' he said bluntly. 'Lily, I'd thought that at the very least we'd have Christmas lunch together. We do have unfinished business. Why are you so sure we've run out of time?'

In the background several people called her name. Over them she said, 'I didn't want to put you in the position of choosing, or me in the position of waiting for something that's not going to happen. I'm in Switzerland, staying at Max and Ona's.'

'*Switzerland*?' he gasped.

She sounded sad. 'I've been invited over to talk about taking a full-time job here. You'll be off on your travels too. Look, I've got to go. I'm being called for Christmas lunch.' She hesitated and when she spoke again, her voice was husky. 'I hope everything goes brilliantly for you – you know, your plans. Your courses. I hope you travel to loads of different countries and have a wonderful life.' Then she was gone.

'Bye,' Isaac said dully, even though he'd just heard the *beep, beep, beep, silence* of an ended call. His lungs felt half their proper size. Slowly, he slid his phone into his pocket, staring unseeingly at the stainless steel of the kitchen littered with pans and splashes of gravy. He didn't have to ask her what she meant by 'choosing'. It was choosing between Hayley and Lily. So while he'd been concentrating on Hayley, Lily had slipped away.

Hayley's voice came from behind him. 'What just happened? Is Lily OK?' She looked more like the composed Hayley he'd known. She'd managed make-up today.

He hadn't known she was standing behind him but there was no point trying to disguise his feelings. She knew him too well and she'd obviously overheard enough. 'Lily's gone to Switzerland. She's been offered a job.'

Her eyes widened and what colour she'd had drained away. 'Because you've been helping me,' she whispered. 'What are you going to do?'

It almost seemed too difficult a question. 'Talk to her some more . . . when I get the opportunity. She can't talk right now.' He heard his own voice, flat, defeated, but his heart felt as if it was in a puddle of blood at his feet. Unless Nicola and/or Vicky turned up like magic Hayley still couldn't live alone for another week or two.

'Leave it with me,' said Hayley crisply, seeming more like the old Hayley every minute. 'Let me see what I can do.'

Chapter Twenty-Seven

Dugal and Keir burst into her bedroom before seven bellowing, 'Happy Merry Christmas to you! Come downstairs 'cos we're not allowed our presents till everyone's together!'

Then they screamed out of the room again leaving Lily blinking. Recalling the joy of Christmas morning when you were five or three, she clambered into jeans and a top and hurried downstairs where she could hear childish voices bellowing, 'C'mon, everybody, c'mon, come *on*!'

Present-giving was chaotic but lovely. Lily relished the fairy-tale Christmas sight of the acres of snow glittering outside and the sound of church bells drifting up from the town. Dugal and Keir tried simultaneously to rip into their presents and hand out other people's – which they offered to share if edible. 'Lego!' one would yell.

'Duplo!' squealed the other.

'Grand-Tubb, this is for you from Mummy!'

'Grandma, here's yours from us!'

Lily, laughing, let them hand out all of her gifts of

pashminas, DVDs, vouchers and everything that had been easy to grab. For Dugal and Keir she'd bought matching Minions pyjamas and was gratified when they stripped off to wriggle straight into them. Baby Ainsley lay in a Moses basket on the floor, occasionally flailing his arms and mewling then flopping back into sleep. Like his brothers, he had Max's sandy hair.

Everyone had managed a present for Lily, even at short notice: heavenly Swiss chocolate, a carved wooden box, perfume and, from Tubb and Janice, a pair of ski pants suitable for the depths of Swiss winter. 'Janice was pretty sure of your size but we can exchange them if needs be,' Tubb said gruffly. Then, looking awkward, he gave Lily a lilac envelope. Inside was a Christmas card and printed in gold foil on the front, *Merry Christmas to my sister*. Lily looked at it through a veil of tears, her chin wobbling.

'Why are you making a silly face?' demanded Keir, peering at her.

Dugal sighed at the stupidity of younger brothers. 'She's going to sneeze,' he explained loftily.

Everybody laughed and Lily gave Tubb a hug – the first ever – and let a couple of her tears soak into his dressing gown. He and Garrick had had a long talk with her last night when they'd fetched her from the airport, clearing any lingering ill feeling as they explained their shock at Marvin's past behaviour.

'You see,' Tubb had explained gently, 'he was a very good dad, the kind who always came to football matches and knew how to fix broken kites. To realise that he'd had a secret affair was painful and we stupidly lashed out at you as the living proof of it.' He cleared his throat. 'Garrick saw sense first and made me see what an

346

unreasonable shit I was being in blaming you for keeping the secret for so long, I felt terrible. You must not have known what to do.'

It had been worth a flight to Switzerland just to hear that.

Garrick, Eleanor, Myla and Xander arrived and while the small children went wild again, Eleanor took her own opportunity to clear the air with Lily. 'I'm sorry that I leapt to conclusions and was so unpleasant.'

'None of us knew what was going on with the other,' Lily had been quick to say. 'Let's put it behind us.'

If it hadn't been for thinking about Isaac she would have floated away in a bubble of happiness. But then his voice on the phone was so . . . disbelieving. Hurt. If everyone hadn't been shouting for her to come to the table she would have broken down and cried. As it was she had had to end the call or lose it completely.

For the rest of the day she pinned on a smile, helped in the kitchen, played with Dugal and Keir, held baby Ainsley with her heart melting as he stared stolidly up at her. Ona, now he was safely delivered and she was getting over the C-section, pretended to be glad to get rid of him at every opportunity while the love glowing in her eyes when she looked at any of her kids belied her joking words.

Before the daylight faded Lily went out with Max, Dugal and Keir to try out the boys' new sledges and her ski pants which, being a smoky grey, went well with the blue coat from Zinnia and George. The whole outfit proved admirably suited to flying down a slope with Keir on her lap and being dumped in the snow when they overturned, roaring with laughter.

Later, when the young kids had finally gone to bed in

their new pyjamas the adults and the older kids, Myla and Xander, settled with glasses of champagne.

Lily wondered whether to call Isaac back. Or at least text him and apologise about cutting their earlier call short. She listened as Tubb talked about putting The Three Fishes on the market and getting another relief manager until it sold. 'I would have loved Isaac to stick around to manage it but he doesn't sound prepared to stay.'

'No,' Lily agreed hoarsely.

Janice patted Tubb's arm. 'It's a wrench for you. The pub's been your life.'

Tubb laced her fingers with his. 'We all have to retire sometime.' But he looked a little misty-eyed. They began to reminisce about past Christmases at The Three Fishes and Lily's mind went back to Isaac, wondering what he was doing now. Spending Christmas evening quietly with Hayley?

She reread his text from this morning – which was a distinctly sad thing to do – smiling to herself at the casual way her referred to *your mums*. It was good when someone treated her family as if they weren't weird.

Gently, she put her phone down. She wouldn't call Isaac.

For self-preservation she couldn't let in a man who would so soon be getting out.

If anything, Lily preferred Boxing Day – or St Stephen's Day – to Christmas Day. Garrick and his family had their own plans so, with Ainsley in a papoose on Max's front, the rest of them walked down into Schützenberg and around the lake, pausing for hot chocolate or lemonade, making a snowman with Dugal and Keir, which the boys then took enormous pleasure in kicking down.

Then they struck off into a wood where the snow was less disturbed and it was still and magical, examining animal tracks in the snow and kicking it into crystal showers or trying to blow 'smoke' rings with their white breath in the frigid air. Tubb and Janice walked hand in hand – or mitten in mitten. Lily found herself watching the easy way they chatted and how often each made the other smile. In relationship terms they were still at the honeymoon stage, only having been together a year, but they might as well have been wearing badges that said 'in love'.

Funny how the cold air stung her eyes to watch them.

Finally, they tramped back up the hill to Max and Ona's house and Lily helped Janice put together 'Boxing Day Pie', which involved slicing up the leftover turkey and sausage meat, pouring gravy and wine over it in a roasting tin and mashing up leftover root vegetables for the topping, then sticking it in the oven to cook. The boys were happier with fish fingers, little jacket potatoes and peas, but the Boxing Day Pie did very nicely for the adults, washed down with beer and followed by plunging into the stash of chocolate.

Lily helped Dugal build a Lego house while Max showed Keir how to put a wooden train track together, which Keir much preferred taking apart. Then they all got ready to march further up the hill to Los's house for fondue.

'It's lovely that the children are invited, isn't it?' Lily said to Ona, who was pushing Ainsley in a buggy that seemed to be his car seat fixed to a set of wheels.

'The Swiss are very family-minded.' Ona's ski jacket was a dark gold and set off her pretty freckles as she tipped up her face to admire an especially beautiful balcony hung with swags of greenery and lights like icicles. 'It's great not to need babysitters but not so much when we want a night off on our own with a bottle of wine.'

Lily had been feeling slight butterflies, not just because approaching Los's house brought forcibly to mind the days she'd spent in the annexe with Isaac. It was meeting Los again in view of the job on the horizon – a job that seemed almost too good to be true. Los, though, was a great host. He welcomed Lily with a kiss on each cheek and a firm, 'You'll find a few people from British Country Foods amongst the company this evening but we leave business until tomorrow, yes?'

'Marvellous,' Lily agreed gladly and was able to settle down to enjoying herself without feeling she was supposed to be networking. Stephen, who she knew from her last visit, was there with his partner, but otherwise she wasn't always aware whether those she met were potential colleagues or not.

The meat fondue was delicious and she ate more than she'd thought possible after Boxing Day Pie. Dugal and Keir ate so many marshmallows dipped in chocolate that Lily thought they'd burst.

Finally the children were so tired that Ona said to Max, 'We need to get them home.'

Tubb and Janice were ready to go too, Tubb tiring easily these days, and so Lily thanked Los and Tanja and joined the procession for the short walk back. A thin veil of snow was falling, muffling the sounds around them as it drifted softly from the dark sky between star-like lights strung above. It was like an advert for a magical Christmas holiday in the mountains. Lily fell silent, admiring the even carpets of white on the chalet roofs, thinking ahead to Garrick picking her up to meet with Los tomorrow and whether the trousers and jacket she'd packed would be right for the occasion.

As they turned into the drive in front of Max and Ona's house, she heard vague exclamations and a surprised laugh, with Max saying, 'This is an unexpected pleasure. Lily, did you know we were to have an extra guest?'

'No?' She tried to see past Ona and Janice, who were both turning to grin at her. Then she caught sight of the tall man on Max's doorstep, woollen hat pulled down over his ears, standing very still and gazing at her. 'Isaac!' she gasped. 'How did you get here?'

'Plane from London City to Zürich, train to Biberbrugg and taxi here.' One corner of his mouth quirked up. 'I brought your Christmas present.' He pointed to a gift-wrapped box balanced on top of his rucksack in the porch.

'More presents!' Dugal hollered, suddenly fully awake.

Isaac crouched down to pat his head. 'Sorry, mate. There's only this one. Santa left it in England for Lily by mistake.' He shifted his gaze to Lily. 'Probably she forgot to tell him she was coming here.'

'Aw, OK,' sighed Dugal, while Lily's cheeks burned at the dig.

Lily found she was trembling as Max and Ona stamped the snow from their boots and ushered everyone into their home. Isaac gave Ona a hug and shook Max's hand. 'Don't worry that I've come expecting hospitality. I've booked a hotel room. Congratulations on becoming parents again.' He smiled at Ainsley, who was just beginning to whinge about it being his feed time.

Max and Ona took the boys upstairs but Tubb resisted as Janice tugged discreetly at his sleeve. 'So what's happening with my pub while you're out here playing Santa Claus?' he demanded.

Isaac didn't even look at him. 'It's only a friggin' pub! There are more important things.'

As Tubb gaped at this heresy, Janice linked his arm and steered him away. 'He's right. You and I have already come to the same realisation or we wouldn't be here. You left him in charge. I expect he's left Tina at the helm. It *is* only a pub.'

Tubb dug his toes in again, this time demanding of Lily, 'Are you OK with him being here?'

Dumbly, Lily nodded.

Finally, Tubb let himself be towed away. Then at last there was just Lily and Isaac in the living area, the Christmas tree lights winking merrily as the door closed. She licked her lips. 'I haven't seen you get snappy before.'

'I'm human, same as anyone. You and Tubb have made it up?' When she nodded he said, 'Good.' He came no closer but his body heat seemed to bridge the gap between them, luring her like the Sirens' song lured sailors onto rocks.

She resisted its pull. 'How's Hayley? Was her bad news very bad? Is it OK for you to have left her so you can come here?'

He frowned. 'She didn't have bad news – thankfully it was good. No sign of the cancer spreading and no further treatment. In time she'll have further surgery to complete the reconstruction but she's on her way back to normal life.'

Lily was stunned. 'But I rang your phone and she was sobbing about the histology results!'

His brows shot up. 'She hadn't *got* her results at that point. What was upsetting her was that her appointment to hear her report was postponed until the following day because the consultant was called away. The extra wait got to her. She's been super-emotional throughout her ordeal, which she can be forgiven for.'

Lily gaped at him. At the darkness of his eyes and the weariness around them. 'She's going to be OK?'

Realisation dawned in his eyes. 'That's what it was,' he said slowly. 'When you rang and she was emotional you assumed she'd had bad news. You gave up on me.'

'I—' She took a physical step back at this interpretation of events. 'I thought she needed you.' She didn't say '. . . more than I did' because it wasn't true. There was 'need' and 'need', that was all.

He thrust his fingers through his hair. 'Holy hell, I wish you and I could have just found time to *talk*.' He took a couple of deep breaths and then continued in a gentler tone. 'I had to be there for her until she had her results but she didn't get those until Christmas Eve. I saw you leaving the village late that afternoon and the evening shift was crazy. I knew – or thought I knew – I'd be alone with you on Christmas morning so I planned to talk to you then. As it was—' he threw up a hand in a hopeless gesture '—I didn't get that chance. But as soon as Hayley realised you'd left she coolly made arrangements to stay with my parents because she doesn't need the level of care she got from me now her last drain is out. She was determined to free me to come after you and Mum backed her up. Said Hayley was doing what she thought right – and her and Dad thought she was right too. They've even taken Doggo.'

'Wow.' Lily wasn't quite able to absorb it all and re-adjust her thinking. She'd been so certain that Hayley had a long, hard road ahead and would need Isaac until she could get her support elsewhere. 'So you're leaving to take your instructor courses?'

Ignoring the question, Isaac scooped up the Christmas present wrapped in blue paper sprinkled with gold stars. 'This is for you.'

Automatically, she took the box-shaped gift, fumbling when it proved unexpectedly heavy.

Hastily, he put one of his hands beneath it, brushing against her and making her jump. 'It might be better to unwrap it on the table.'

She let him place it on the polished wooden table top, then, wonderingly, she eased the paper apart at the seam. Under the paper was a plain brown box and she had to pull off the tape that secured it shut. Inside was a cloud of white tissue paper.

She pulled it aside to reveal wood and carvings.

She stared. 'It's a cuckoo clock,' she breathed. Packed snugly around the little wooden chalet with a stack of logs outside were the chains, weights and pendulum that had made the parcel so heavy.

'A Lötscher. I'm probably the only person ever to bring a cuckoo clock *into* Switzerland. I ordered it online and had it delivered to the pub.' Most of the frustration had left his voice now and uncertainty had taken its place.

With one trembling fingertip she touched the little door sheltering the cuckoo. 'It's the one I loved in the shop in Zürich. It was incredibly expensive though.' She glanced at him.

He'd jammed his hands into his back pockets and shrugged. 'It was supposed to be symbolic. I was going to explain on Christmas Day. But you'd buggered off.' His voice was flat. Tired.

Glancing around, he selected a medium-sized picture hanging on the wall and took it down. Then, carefully, he took the clock from the box and hung it on the hook, set the hands to the correct time, hung the pendulum and smoothly pulled one of the weights to wind the mechanism.

Its *TICK-tick, TICK-tick* permeated the room.

Lily gazed first at the beautiful clock and then the no less beautiful but decidedly less cheerful man before her, dark brows down over dark eyes. She had to swallow before she could coax words out of her throat. 'What's the symbolism?'

For several seconds she didn't think he was going to reply as he set the clock's hands to a few minutes to nine. Then, finally he turned towards her. 'You kept saying we had no time. The clock was meant to say I had all the time in the world for you.'

'But your courses—'

'Balls to the courses. If you'd let me talk to you, I would have explained my plans have changed.' Finally, slowly, he moved towards her, one step, two, until he stood only inches away, close enough for her to hear him breathing.

'So what are your plans now?' She spoke calmly but her pulse was thundering in her ears.

His eyes smiled. 'To discover what your plans are and try and persuade you to let me be part of them.' He took her hand and carried it to his mouth, brushing her knuckles across his lips.

'But you're on your way somewhere else,' she protested shakily.

His smile reached one corner of his mouth. 'You're currently "somewhere else". Can't that be the somewhere else I'm on my way to?' He loosed her hand and slid his arms around her, making her eyes half-close at the feel of his body against hers, a feeling she thought she'd never have again. 'I can find courses here,' he went on. 'Or if you go back to the village, I can base myself there. Doggo's pining for you,' he added. Then, more seriously, 'I'm pining for you too, continuously and painfully. My heart's spinning in my chest just to be in the same room with you again.' Behind him the clock murmured TICK-tick, TICK-tick. His Adam's apple bobbed. 'Do you have time for me, Lily?'

Joy broke over her in a hot wave. 'All the time in the world,' she breathed, giving him his own phrase back.

Beneath her hands she felt his body relax. 'A couple of weeks ago you told me not to kiss you any more. Will you unsay that, please?'

In answer, she pulled his head down to hers, pressing against his hard body as if trying to get right through his clothes.

His hands dropped to her behind, the line of his body following the curve of hers. 'I lied about the hotel room,' he groaned against her mouth. 'I just didn't want to get involved with the others feeling they had to find me somewhere to sleep.'

'That's OK.' Lily rubbed against him to make him catch his breath. 'I have the key to Los's annexe because I had the choice of staying there but preferred to be here – with my own family.' The final words came out shyly.

Behind them a tiny wooden bird shot out of the Lötscher clock. 'Cu-ckoo, cu-ckoo—'

Isaac grinned. 'That clock is so not going to hang in the bedroom unless we can find a way to shut it up.'

Lily giggled. 'We can't leave it here. It might wake the baby or Dugal and Keir could find it in the morning and take it apart.' So they took it down from the wall and found out how to disable the cuckoo mechanism before packing it back in its box.

Without telling the others, who had all discreetly stayed

upstairs, they bundled up in their coats and set off hand in hand along the snowy streets to Los's annexe, Isaac carrying the clock, letting themselves in and closing all the blinds.

Then Isaac pulled Lily back into his arms and began to steer her in the direction of the bedroom with its welcoming double bed. 'I love you, Lily. Let's begin that shared time.'

Epilogue

January, thirteen months later

Lily sat in one of the new mini-armchairs at The Three Fishes, Tubb and Janice to her left on a matching sofa, Tubb looking slightly out of place. 'Weird for us all to be on the customer side of the bar.' Lily grinned, giving her brother a nudge with her toe.

'Hmm,' he said, sipping his alcohol-free gin and slimline tonic.

'We love it,' said Janice firmly, giving Tubb's arm a squeeze. 'Retirement's wonderful, isn't it, Harrison? We can live in the village, travel whenever we feel like it and reap the benefit of all those years of hard work.'

'Hmm,' he said again.

Lily exchanged a conspiratorial look with Janice. Tubb loved being retired except when he visited the village pub that had been his life. Lily knew Isaac had never regretted leaving the trade but she wasn't so sure about her older brother.

Two new people running it now, both men: Ferdy and

Elvis. Yes, Elvis was his real name, as he told everybody as soon as he introduced himself. They'd 'done a refurb' and the red-patterned carpet was a thing of the past. Wood flooring had been laid in front of the bar, multi-coloured tiles in the dining area and grey carpet in the rest. Lily thought the carpet looked as if someone had shaded it with a pencil in a way her art teacher used to call 'hatching'. There were more gambling machines and a bigger telly. Of the bar staff Lily had worked with, only Tina, Vita and Flora remained.

Lily could hear Carola telling Elvis and Ferdy about last winter's trip to Switzerland and the Middletones. Warwick and Eddie were at uni now, Alfie working in Bristol and Franciszka, though still seeing Neil occasionally, had moved out of the village to be near her sister in Peterborough so, judging from their baffled expressions, Elvis and Ferdy weren't completely following the tale.

Owen was holding Carola's hand and listening, a role he'd settled into well. Lily knew they were incredibly happy together, especially now Duncan had found another job in London. He'd only moved into Carola's basement for nine months and now it was once again an Airbnb.

Lily let her mind return to last winter and all it had brought. Roma and Patsie's break-up, which, to Lily's immense sadness, had proved permanent.

Zinnia and George's house fire. Their baby daughter, Leonie, was now eight months old. Lily saw a lot of her and found she loved being an aunt and was a willing babysitter. Playing with her niece, bathing her and getting her ready for bed never felt like a chore. Leonie thought Doggo was the funniest thing on the planet. As Doggo had a similarly high opinion of his charms, they played together beautifully.

Hayley, currently cancer-free, had returned to heading up the casino in Peterborough, which was even more swanky than before. She turned up every week for a Doggo-date.

But by far the most important thing that had happened in Lily's life last winter had been Isaac.

She checked her phone. No messages. Peeped behind the curtains – grey linen now, not red velvet – and shaded her eyes so she could see through the glass. Snowflakes were wafting down like the fall-out from a gigantic pillow fight. Four inches of snow lay on the ground and British road and transport systems were grinding to a halt. Isaac had called hours ago to say he was stuck on the M6 with hardly any phone battery and he'd broken the lead to his in-car charger. Since then nothing, so his battery must have died.

It seemed ridiculous to worry about a fully-fledged instructor in bracing outdoorsy stuff and survival training, but Lily was anxious nonetheless.

Absently, she chatted to Tubb and Janice. Finally, her phone chirped with a text. *I'm home. Come and get me. xxxxxxxxxxxx* Her pulse jumped in several places.

'Night then. Gotta go.' Ignoring the knowing grins from Carola, Owen, Tubb and Janice as she called hurried goodnights, she dragged on her coat without finishing her drink. She skated rather than ran down Main Street to Rotten Row, slithering and sliding all the way to a brick cottage with dormer windows that had been their home for several months. Breath burning in her throat she fumbled with her key and burst in.

On the quarry-tiled floor of the tiny hall stood a rucksack and a pair of hiking boots in a puddle of melting snow. A delighted Dalmatian burst out of the sitting room shouting a welcoming, 'Hnuh, hnuh, WOAH! Hnuh, hnuh, WOAH!'

'Hey, Doggo,' Lily panted, patting his wiggling back. 'Where's your human?'

'Waiting for you.' Isaac appeared in the doorway and swept her into his arms, kissing her slowly and thoroughly, only letting her up for air when she was completely breathless. 'Do you mind that I didn't come to the pub? I just wanted to be with you.'

'Not one bit,' she assured him. 'I want to be with you too.' Then, between kisses, she added, 'Carola was telling Ferdy and Elvis about last year in Switzerland.'

His movements slowed and he pulled back to look into her face. 'Did it make you wish you'd taken that job with Los at British Country Foods?'

She nibbled his throat, tasting the salt of his skin. 'Switzerland would have been fantastic but I love my wonderful job with the hotel chain and I love Middledip.'

'And . . .?' he murmured, nestling her against him.

She grinned and planted a soft kiss on the corner of his mouth. 'I love you too.'

The light in his eyes softened. 'I love you. I love you, Middledip and the home we're making together.' His mouth slipped down to her neck, his hands roving over her body as if he had to assure himself that she hadn't moved any of the good bits around while he'd been away instructing in Wales. His voice dropped. 'I think it's bedtime.'

Raising her eyebrows, Lily glanced at the cuckoo clock that had pride of place on the sitting room wall. 'It's only twenty-five to eight.'

He picked her up and buried his face against her. 'The perfect time.'

Loved

Let it Snow?

Then why not try one of Sue's
other cosy Christmas stories
or sizzling summer reads?

The perfect way to escape
the every day.

One Christmas can
change everything . . .

Curl up with this feel-good festive romance,
perfect for fans of Carole Matthews and
Trisha Ashley.

Available in all good bookshops now.

It's time to deck
the halls . . .

Return to the little village of Middledip
with this *Sunday Times* bestselling
Christmas read . . .

Available in all good bookshops now.

*For Ava Blissham,
it's going to be a Christmas
to remember . . .*

Countdown to Christmas with your new
must-have author, as you step into the
wonderful world of Sue Moorcroft.

Available in all good bookshops now.

Come and spend summer by the sea!

Make this a summer to remember with blue skies, beachside walks and the man of your dreams . . .

Available in all good bookshops now.

What could be better than a summer spent basking in the French sunshine?

Grab your sun hat, a cool glass of wine, and escape to France with this gloriously escapist summer read!

Available in all good bookshops now.

*In a sleepy village in Italy,
Sophia is about to discover
a host of family secrets . . .*

Lose yourself in this uplifting summer
romance from the *Sunday Times* bestseller.

Available in all good bookshops now.